T0279188

CASTERS
─ AND ─
CROWNS

OTHER BOOKS BY
ELIZABETH LOWHAM

Beauty Reborn
Astra Remade

CASTERS
— AND —
CROWNS

ELIZABETH
LOWHAM

SHADOW
MOUNTAIN
PUBLISHING

To the pariahs and perfectionists—
The difficult road forward
is worth the journey

Library of Congress Cataloging-in-Publication Data
CIP on file
ISBN 978-1-63993-320-4

Printed in the United States of America
1 2 3 4 5 LBC 28 27 26 25 24

CHAPTER

1

At eight years old, Aria began recording her mistakes. She took a crisp sheet of parchment from her writing desk and dipped her quill in ink before making a slow, neat stroke to indicate each of the day's faults—one mark for raising her voice at dinner, which had earned her a glare from her father; one mark for incorrectly answering her tutor; one mark for yawning at Father's adviser, who'd told her the daughter of a king should have better manners.

Her father had said everyone should be accountable for their mistakes.

So Aria made them countable.

And after counting, she didn't like what she saw. The liquid ink looked slimy, the three black marks like worms crawling across her skin, making her squirm.

There was only one logical thing to do: Aria resolved to never make a mistake again.

The very next day, she was back at her desk, adding three new marks to the page. In *one day*, she'd already forgotten her promise, so as punishment, she had to feel the sliminess again. She would have to do better, become a perfect princess, then a perfect monarch. Just like her father.

Never did she imagine passing *one hundred* marks. The one-hundred-and-first spurred her from her chair, parchment crinkling in her sweaty fingers. She threw both parchment and quill into the fireplace, her empty hands trembling, and she sighed in relief as a crackling tongue gobbled up the evidence. Perhaps she shouldn't record her mistakes after all; what if someone found her parchment and *realized?*

Realized what a terrible crown princess she was.

The parchment blackened and smoked. The frills of the beautiful peacock quill curled up like dying spider legs.

Aria watched the fire. Then, in her mind, she picked up a new quill, an invisible one, a hidden one, and she made a stroke for burning quality writing materials, which her father would never do.

Wasteful. Mark.

For the next ten years, she mentally recorded every mistake. Then—soon after her eighteenth birthday—she made the worst mistake of all, a single mistake worth a thousand marks.

She trusted a Caster.

Aria arrived first for the meeting. She always arrived first to any council of the Upper Court because she loved the feeling of the empty throne room, so much like a chapel with its vaulted ceilings and stained-glass windows above a polished granite floor. The guards nodded to her but didn't speak, didn't break the sacred quiet, and she ascended the dais alone before settling into her throne. High-backed though it was, her seat appeared insignificant beside her father's.

After drawing in the hallowed air, she pulled a leatherbound journal from her satchel and reviewed her notes for the meeting.

As she read, other members of the Upper Court trickled in. Duke Crampton and Earl Wycliff held a hushed conversation, murmuring about trade possibilities with countries across the ocean. Both of them bowed to Aria before taking their seats in the dais wings. Marquess Haskett tried to engage her in conversation, but he wanted only to know if she had considered his eldest son as a suitor. Aria smiled thinly and promised consideration yet again. Thankfully, he was forced to move along as her father's two advisers arrived, followed by the king himself.

Aria stood and curtsied to her father. The king wore his standard white uniform with red edging at the hems, the royal crest sewn beneath his left shoulder. Though his crown was only a gold circlet, he needed nothing extra to exude authority when it was simply in the way he stood. The way he breathed. Just as no one would question if a mountain knew the clouds, no one would question if King Peregrine knew his business as king.

With a subdued smile, he tilted his head, regarding the journal in Aria's hand. "Dutiful as always, I see."

Then he took his seat, leaving Aria glowing under the praise.

Settling in her own chair again, she tilted forward. "Father, I . . . I thought I might lead the meeting today. If you'll let me."

"Today's matter is a sensitive one. I'll conduct it myself." He must have caught her disappointment in his glance because he added, "In a month, we'll hold Eliza's birthday celebration with the entire court in attendance, Upper and Lower. I trust you could act as host to such an event?"

Restraining her eagerness, Aria gave a dutiful nod.

"I'll expect it, then. Keep your welcoming speech brief, and be sure to remind the court she's now of age to entertain suitors."

As if Eliza would let anyone forget. She'd been dreaming of suitors since the moment she'd learned to dance. Aria smiled, and she made a note in her journal to host her sister's celebration. Without intending it, her penmanship grew extra loopy across the word *host*.

The final members of the council arrived—minus the queen, an absence no one mentioned—and the king called the meeting to order.

"Today's matter," he said gravely, "is once again regarding Morton."

Aria's nails pressed into the leather of her journal. The faces of the court turned grim.

Five months earlier, Charles Morton, heir to the Morton estate, had been executed for crimes against the kingdom. His mother had withdrawn from court for the traditional three-month mourning season. They were now two months past that.

The king went on, "Dowager Countess Morton has not only refused summons and rejected messengers, but as of yesterday afternoon, she has sent a declaration of aggression against the Crown."

At the king's gesture, his senior adviser stood and unfolded a sheet of parchment, the seal already broken. Lord Philip stood below average height with a rounded face that managed to look worried even when he smiled, but his voice carried strongly through the throne room as he read.

"I, Clarissa Morton, countess and Caster, hereby renounce King Peregrine II and all his house. For centuries, those of us possessing magic have bent our backs to carry peace within this kingdom, and you, in your malice, have broken them at last. To the Crown, I offer two options: His Majesty will either gift freedom of magic in Loegria, or I will buy it in blood."

Though Aria had already heard the letter's contents, she felt goose bumps anew. She'd met Dowager Countess Morton only briefly—first, at Earl Morton's funeral, then more recently at a musical recital the queen had hosted for women of the court. Despite the fearful magic the woman possessed, Clarissa Morton had seemed aloof, not bloodthirsty.

But that was before the execution of her son.

As Lord Philip sat, one of the king's generals scoffed. "Flinging stones or flinging Casts, it makes no difference. What can one woman do against the Crown? Majesty, give the command, and I'll have a squad of soldiers drag her in for trial at once."

"Trial for what? *Grief*?" Earl Wycliff shook his head. "Threatening or not, these are just words, spoken by an angry mother in rightful mourning. Give it time, and she'll see reason. There's no need to exacerbate the situation with military action."

Duke Crampton spoke with quiet thoughtfulness, as he always did. "She's been *given* time. A full mourning period. Holding off action in the face of a direct threat is asking too much."

From the opposite wing, Marchioness Elsworth nodded. "You say 'one woman,' but she's talking about all magic users. She may plan to raise a full-scale rebellion."

Arguments sprouted on either side—wait it out or treat the declaration as criminal—and no one seemed willing to explore the middle ground.

Aria bit her lip, scanning through her notes on how past court disturbances had been handled.

"I have an idea," she said.

Too hesitantly. No one heard. And in the back of her mind, a quill scratched. *Speaking without confidence. Mark.* After shrinking for a moment in her seat, she straightened and repeated her words at a louder volume.

"Yes, Aria?" Her father waved two fingers to acknowledge her.

"We could extend a compromise. A peace talk. She asks for freedom of magic, and in regards to laws governing both Stone and Fluid Casters, I think the witch's mark is the main—"

"*Compromise?*" Marquess Haskett scoffed. The man looked like a vulture, shoulders hunched around a balding head. "A threat is made against the Crown, and your suggestion is to indulge it? With respect, Highness, a worse option couldn't be found."

Heat flooded Aria's cheeks.

Suggesting the worst option. Mark.

She would have fallen silent but then Lord Philip said, "Perhaps it's worth discussing. After all, the countess did . . . lose her son. Perhaps a concession can be made in acknowledgment of that sacrifice."

Turning a page in her notes, Aria said, "I read of a past conflict with my grandmother similar to this. During Queen Theresa's reign, a young girl named Dorothy Ames was executed. Different reasons, of course—she was a shapeshifter—but my grandmother—"

"No," said her father sternly. "Lord Haskett is correct. Bending to threat is weakness, and there's no compromise I can make that the countess would accept."

"We don't know that," Aria protested, though her voice lacked strength. "Not without trying. If we sent someone to negotiate with her, we could—"

"Aria." The king held her gaze until Aria at last looked down. Then he added quietly, "Compassion is a noble thought but rarely a viable action. You must know when to abandon an idea."

"Yes, Father," she murmured.

Raising his voice, her father addressed the court once more. "Dowager Countess Morton wishes to cry injustice when no injustice was done. Her son's death, though worthy of grief, was unavoidable. The countess will either come to accept that, or she will move against the Crown and face sentencing of her own. For now, we must consider her a potential danger to the kingdom, along with any Caster she comes in contact with. If she has not rejoined court by month's end, we will revisit this matter with a squadron of soldiers."

The matter was settled. Though Aria nodded to her father, her spirit sank. She looked up at the stained-glass windows, drawing comfort from the familiar, fragmented pictures.

For a moment, she wondered about the first craftsman who attempted such a thing. When he gathered a collection of broken glass and declared he would make the shards into something more beautiful than an unbroken pane, had one of his colleagues called it the worst option possible?

She left the meeting, clutching her journal.

———❄———

"You're right and they're wrong!" Eliza declared.

Aria's heart agreed, but her mental quill had something else to say.

Arrogance. Mark.

"It's not that simple," she said with a sigh.

Aria sat at her writing desk while Eliza flopped across the bed. Though Aria was meant to be reviewing a list of potential suitors—at her father's urging—that parchment sat forgotten on the desk corner. She had instead pulled her journal out again, frowning down at the pages.

She couldn't chase Lord Philip's voice from her mind. *The countess did lose her son.*

As a Fluid Caster, the countess could have poisoned the royal water supply or performed some equally malicious magic. Instead, she'd sent the king a letter. Words instead of action. Surely that meant something. Surely it meant she wanted to *talk*.

Eliza pushed herself up from the bed. "Why isn't it that simple? *You're* right and *they're* wrong. An attempt at peace is always better than waiting for a problem to explode or exploding it yourself."

Truthfully, Aria shouldn't have relayed the meeting to her younger sister. Since she wasn't the royal heir, Eliza wasn't a member of the Upper Court. Yet Aria felt vindicated to have her support. It pushed back the scratching voice of the quill that kept Aria in check.

"I think I could do this," Aria said quietly. "I think I could mend the situation."

What would her father say if she managed to broker peace with a powerful, estranged member of court? When she'd given her input on the trade agreements with Pravusat, her father had called her insightful, and yet he was still reluctant to let her conduct meetings or run affairs of court. She was eighteen now, ready for additional responsibilities.

Perhaps she could prove she deserved them. A good ruler could resolve conflict. If Aria negotiated with Dowager Countess Morton, if she reached a successful agreement and avoided what might be a growing rebellion, her father would have to admit she could do more for the kingdom.

Just as she opened her mouth to share her reasoning, she remembered her father's voice. *You must know when to abandon an idea.*

"I'm being foolish," she whispered. Decisively, she closed her journal and pushed it aside, turning her attention to suitors, though she couldn't seem to focus on the names.

"You always do that!" Eliza huffed. She stalked over and stood directly beside Aria's chair, arms folded across her chest.

"What do you think of Lord Kendall?" Aria turned the parchment over to see if anything was written on the back, then wondered what she was looking for. It was not as if the list her father had given her came with individual sketches or information about each candidate. It included only the prestige of their lineage. Lord Kendall was the son of Duke Crampton, and Aria generally appreciated the duke's comments in court meetings.

"*Aria,*" Eliza said sternly, snatching the parchment away. "You always come up with a great idea and then talk yourself out of it."

"It's not a great idea to disobey Father."

"Did he say you couldn't speak to Dowager Countess Morton?"

"He said she would not agree—"

"*Did he say you couldn't speak to Dowager Countess Morton?*"

Aria sighed. "You're splitting hairs. Father rejected the idea of a compromise, and he made his intentions clear."

"Father hardly listens to anyone besides himself! Did he even give you a chance to explain your full idea?"

"Not the full idea, I suppose." Aria poked at her journal. "Based on what I know of Patriamere's system for registering Casters, I think we could imitate their country, making a simple adjustment that would still offer protection for non-Casters."

"See? How could he say there's no chance when he didn't even know the offer?" Eliza shook her head. "Don't talk yourself out of it just because Father moved on. You're the crown princess, and that means something."

There was danger in that line of thinking. It tempted her to believe she had real power, that she could *do* something to help her father. A crown princess could protect her kingdom.

A crown princess could prove herself.

"There's no harm in offering to meet," Aria said slowly. "Right?"

With a devious smile, Eliza slid Aria's inkwell closer on the desk.

CHAPTER

2

Baron looked up from his desk as someone tapped on the open door.

"My Lord Baron," the man said with a bow. Despite his advancing years, marked by a trimmed white beard and balding head, Martin moved with the same spry step and crisp formality he'd always possessed.

Baron tensed. After a moment, he forced himself to relax, saying quietly, "I still look for him when you say that."

For the majority of his life, Guillaume Reeves had gone by the moniker "Baron"—his father's idea. Inheriting the title had only been a matter of time, and Guillaume had always thought the burden associated with it would be the responsibilities of a landholding nobleman: caring for the estate and neighboring hamlet, managing the lemon orchard, and attending court functions.

The true burden, he now realized, was that in order to fill a space, it first had to be emptied. And twenty years was far too short a time to learn everything he needed from his father.

Martin inclined his head. "If you'd prefer, my lord, I could call you 'Gill.'"

Then Baron would be six years old again. Only Silas still called him Gill—sometimes "Gilly" to be obnoxious.

"It isn't the name, Martin. It's the absence."

When Baron gestured, his father's head of staff—*his* head of staff—entered the study, a folded parchment in his hands. "An invitation from Lady Bennett."

Silas's mother. For a moment, Baron perked up. Then Martin continued the announcement.

"Miss Margaret Bennett is turning seventeen. There is to be a celebration in her honor, held—"

"Send my polite refusal. I'll continue to refrain from social events through the full mourning season." Baron pushed aside a few sheets of parchment. The fall harvest estimates were too low. The carriage house was in need of repair, among other things, though priority . . .

Martin shifted.

Baron looked up. "What's the matter?"

"It's passed, my lord. The mourning season."

Baron blinked. Three months already? He turned his gaze to the window. Trees lined the path to the estate, their green leaves untouched by autumn, not because it hadn't arrived, but because the Reeves estate boasted a climate warm enough to support the lemon orchard. Every year, winter passed without sting, and it was easy to lose track of the seasons in such an unchanging paradise.

Except it had changed. The best part of it was gone.

"When my own father passed on . . ." Martin hesitated, rubbing the dome of his balding head. He lowered his hand with a small sigh. "It's impossible to put a time frame on grief."

Yet society had.

"No more hiding, then," Baron murmured.

He'd made a promise to his father, and at the thought of it, an invisible weight settled across his shoulders, bowing his back. It was no easy task to change an entire kingdom, but Baron had somehow felt up to the challenge when his father had stood at his side, the solid rock he could always rely upon.

Now he had to be the rock. For himself, for his two brothers, for every magic user in the kingdom.

Three months was not enough time. Twenty years was not enough time.

"Lady Bennett notes that your absence would be excused." Martin had his eyes on the parchment. "She mentions the 'ill political climate' but nothing more specific. As if everyone in the kingdom hasn't heard Morton's letter to His Majesty by now."

All the more reason to attend. Clarissa Morton had implicated all Casters in her rejection of the king, and it was Baron's responsibility to show everyone a Caster *could* be a faithful member of court. He could not do so by remaining at home.

Forcing a tight smile, he said, "Inform Lady Bennett to expect us."

———❄———

Baron adjusted his gloves again. If he kept at it, he would develop a rash.

"This is stupid," Leon announced for the third time, his voice too loud for the enclosed carriage.

"If you say it again," Corvin growled, "I'll peck your eyes out."

"A modicum of civility, please." Though Baron was no more excited than his half brothers to be approaching the Bennett estate.

The estate's rigid black gate and strict rows of trimmed hedges was a familiar sight. Everything in its place, everything devoid of frivolous color—exactly the way Lord Bennett liked it. Considering this was the home of Baron's best friend, he ought to have felt more comfortable visiting, but he and Silas had developed their friendship at Fairfax, and most of their time together had been at the school. Silas was more likely to pop up unannounced in Baron's training yard than to invite him over for tea, especially after the event two years ago.

"This is stupid," Leon repeated.

Corvin squawked, but before he could lunge at his twin, Baron raised his cane to block the way, braced against the back of the carriage seat between the boys. While many noblemen embraced a cane for fashion purposes, his had always pulled double duty as a brother barrier.

"A modicum," he repeated, holding each boy's gaze for a moment, "of civility."

Corvin deflated, and Leon sighed. At a glance, the two thirteen-year-olds did not seem to be twins, not with Corvin's angular, dark features compared against Leon's rounded face and heavyset frame. Yet given any chance to bicker, their similarities became obvious.

Gravel crunched beneath the carriage wheels as they entered the estate drive. Baron flicked the curtain aside and grimaced at the number of carriages already in line. Lord and Lady Bennett did not do things by halves; their daughter's party would be no modest affair.

Lowering his cane, he adjusted his gloves once again. Rather than the black armband the twins wore for their residual mourning, Baron had opted for full black attire—pants, gloves, tailcoat. Leon had been quick to tell him he looked like a crow, one of the boy's favorite insults.

Leon bounced his leg. "A court appearance, I get, but Baron's not looking to get married, so going to a girl's coming-of-age party is pointless."

With a scowl, Corvin grabbed his twin's knee. Leon bounced the other leg.

Baron said, "More important than the reasons for going would be the reasons for abstaining. *That's* what would be gossiped about. Though this is not a royal function, it's still attended by members of court, and support of court society is support of the king himself. If I failed to make an appearance without the excuse of mourning, everyone would connect me in their minds to Widow Morton."

Both twins fell still at that. Baron wished they didn't have to worry about such things—wished *he* didn't have to worry about such things.

"Can I trust you both to be on your best behavior?"

"Yes," said Corvin. Leon grimaced.

"If there's any concern at all—*any*—find me at once."

"If there's time for that," Leon muttered. Beside him, Corvin tensed, absently scratching the back of his wrist.

"I have full faith in you," Baron said, nudging Corvin with his cane so the boy looked up. "Remember, their focus will be on me. I wear the brand."

Things had been simpler when the boys could stay home, but after turning twelve and passing their Caster tests—proving, supposedly, that they had no magic—they were expected to enter society like anyone else from a titled family. Perhaps Baron could have come up with an excuse for their absence, but at the moment, he couldn't afford scrutiny of any kind. Greater safety lay in blending in.

"Don't worry about us." Corvin smiled, curling his hand into a fist and resting it on his knee.

After a moment of silence, the carriage pulled into place outside the manor entrance.

Before exiting, Baron said, "This is a quick social appearance, nothing more. We're to be seen by the right people, I'll give my regards to Miss Margaret, and then we return home."

Leon snorted. "It's hilarious you think it's that simple, Baron."

CHAPTER

3

The wind howled against the frosted mountainside. Aria shivered, urging her horse forward. With her free hand, she pulled her cloak more tightly around her but found the black wool lacking. At the palace, it was barely autumn, with a whisper of chill in the air painting the leaf edges gold. But up the mountain in Northglen, winter had come early, reaching fingers like icicles inside every hem of her clothing and raising goose bumps on her neck, her wrists, her ankles.

Perhaps the chill was not entirely from the wind.

She looked up at the towering structure before her, taking in its looming pillars and pointed façade. The cream stone looked pale in the frigid air, like a woman staring down a storm, her cheeks colorless in the cold.

Morton Manor, home to Dowager Countess Morton, potentially the most dangerous woman in the kingdom and one her father insisted couldn't be reasoned with.

Aria had never before hoped her father was wrong.

She swung down from the saddle, then adjusted her silk vest and thick trousers. Had the countess agreed to meet at the palace, Aria would have worn a proper gown, but she'd done the best she could with a meeting in Northglen. She'd worn a deep purple shirt that hid the grime of travel, along with a pale-yellow vest. An embroidered falcon rose across her left shoulder—an artistic representation of the royal crest. She'd secured her tiara by braiding her hair directly over it; she didn't envy her maid, Jenny, the task of untangling later.

Aria gave care of her horse to a Morton stablehand and approached the manor. A footman met her at the door, bowing low, and she heard herself announced in the echoing hallway as "Her Royal Highness, Princess Aria de Loegria."

The two burly guards behind her shifted. It must have felt strange for hired mercenaries to serve as personal guards to a princess, but she couldn't very well have brought members of the royal guard. They would have told her father what she was doing.

Willful disobedience. Mark.

That shouldn't have earned a mark; after she *succeeded*, she would prove this meeting wasn't a mistake. But the quill in Aria's mind did not obey her commands. It hadn't for a long time.

The warmth of the manor's interior made her chilled skin tingle. A servant stepped forward to take her heavy cloak, and she gave a brief nod of thanks, walking forward with purpose.

Halfway down the hall, she met her hostess.

"Your Royal Highness, you truly came."

Dowager Countess Morton stood a few inches shy of Aria's height, though her slimming black dress gave her the appearance of a taller frame. She wore her light brown hair bundled in a knot on her head, held in place by a cylindrical hat bearing a slanted black veil that shadowed her eyes without concealing them. From the moment Aria had entered the hall, those pale blue eyes had watched her like a falcon observing a field mouse, and considering the falcon's royal symbolism, Aria clearly heard the countess's silent message: *I am queen here.*

Aria shrank as a shiver ran down her spine.

Displaying intimidation. Mark.

Straightening, she held herself as a princess should. "Dowager Countess Morton, thank you for agreeing to meet with me."

"Widow Morton, I prefer. There's no need to be so formal if we are to attempt honest negotiation. May I call you Aria?"

Aria stopped herself before saying yes. She had to walk a delicate line of winning this woman over while still being a strong, commanding representative of the Crown.

"A mere 'Highness' will do," she said, much too late.

"Very well, Highness. This way."

Following Widow Morton, Aria entered a rounded sitting room, her guards taking position at the door. The windows were narrow rather than expansive, limiting cold but also limiting light, and a fire crackled low in the hearth. A small table waited in the center of the room, spread with writing materials and a tea tray.

Widow Morton took the wooden chair on one side of it, motioning Aria toward the cushioned, high-backed chair opposite—a subtle nod to their difference in station. With clear deliberateness, the widow turned her own teacup face up on the tray but touched nothing else before settling back into her seat.

"As hostess, I would offer to serve, but I imagine you'll be far more comfortable taking that role."

Aria's throat tightened. "A servant could—"

"Servants are not permitted to pour in my household. It would be like allowing a non-priest to perform funeral rites; the right and power is mine, so I will not have it sullied. I will, however, make an exception for royalty."

It was a test.

Aria's fingers twitched, and she regretted surrendering her riding gloves along with her cloak. The heavy material would have at least impeded the nervous fidget.

Royalty was not timid. Her father would have known exactly the right course of action. With a steadying breath, Aria grounded herself in the things he'd taught her and a lifetime of watching him rule.

If she chose to pour, she would be lowering herself to a servant's role. It would show weakness, remove bargaining power. On the other hand, if she drank something poured by a Fluid Caster, she may as well dig her own grave. The cardinal rule for a Stone Caster was to never touch them skin-to-skin, lest risk being turned to stone. The rule for a Fluid Caster was just as simple: *Do not drink anything they've touched.* A Fluid Caster could poison any liquid with a touch.

Aria's eyes darted to the witch's mark on the widow's throat. The pattern was simple, a gentle swoop of lines which began at a single point beneath the woman's jawline, widened across the left side of her neck, then dipped into another narrowing point above her collarbone—like an S that had been stretched taller until it retained only an impression of the former letter. Such an innocuous symbol for the hidden danger that was magic.

Widow Morton waited, hands folded primly in her lap. Had she touched the teapot ahead of time? Was it possible to lay a Cast in advance? Despite Aria's efforts at research, she hadn't found many specific details on the process of Casting, only warnings to avoid them.

Setting her jaw, Aria made her decision.

"In the spirit of our meeting here today . . ." She turned over her own teacup, then reached for the teapot. She poured a steady stream of deep amber liquid, which seemed as normal as she could imagine. Then she set the pot on the far side of the tray, nearer the widow. "A compromise. We shall each serve ourselves."

Widow Morton pursed her lips momentarily, and Aria couldn't tell if she was disappointed or impressed. Then she smiled, her eyebrows lifting, some of the severity leaving her expression. "Impressive, Highness. Perhaps there truly is a chance for us."

Aria worked to keep her face impassive despite the warm glow she felt inside.

Widow Morton poured her own cup, but unlike Aria's, the widow's tea swirled light green against the white porcelain. It did not waft steam. As the widow lifted her cup in a toast, the liquid glowed faintly before two small ice cubes took shape, gently bobbing.

Using magic seemed to cost the woman no effort at all. Not a drop of sweat, not the slight twitch of the eye. Fluid Casters could create either healing tonics or deadly poisons by the same casual wave of a hand, and Aria squirmed to witness the ability in person. Although her books agreed Casting had limitations, she couldn't imagine what they might be.

After too long staring, she finally lifted her own cup, toasted, and sipped the warm tea, letting it soothe her insides and renew her resolve.

"So." Widow Morton settled her cup on the tray. Though she hadn't taken more than a sip, it was now bone-dry. "The Crown wishes to talk peace."

Aria drew in a deep breath, catching a hint of rose hips from her tea. She rehearsed again the words she'd already rehearsed a dozen times. Reaching to set her cup on the tray, she opened her mouth to speak—

The teacup shattered in her hand.

Startled, Aria grabbed for something already gone, clenching her fingers around porcelain shards. Heat scalded her hand, dripping in tongues of flame down her sleeve, splashing onto her lap. Though she stood quickly, she felt the tea soaking down her thigh.

For one heart-stopping moment, she thought it was an attack, thought—

But Widow Morton leapt to her feet with a soft oath and called for servants.

Witnessing her clear surprise, Aria relaxed. Only an accident.

There was a flurry of movement around the princess: hands to whisk away the broken pieces, towels to sop the spilled liquid. At least one of the towels came away from Aria's hand bloodied.

Clumsiness. Mark.

Not clumsiness. She'd not dropped the cup. *Inattentiveness.*

"It must have been cracked and failed beneath the heat," Widow Morton said, giving word to Aria's thoughts. She grimaced. "I'll have someone bandage your hand while I deal with my kitchen staff."

After issuing a few more orders, she left the room, and Aria retook her seat as a woman approached to dress her wound. The woman wore a dress with a deep V-shaped collar, her neck clear of any brand. Her blonde hair—mussed where strands had come free of her bun—was the palest wheat shade Aria had ever seen, wisping around her head in a halo of light. Aria tried to focus on studying that beauty rather than on her stinging hand as the servant applied an herbal paste to numb the wound before bandaging it.

The sharp pain faded to a low throbbing. "Thank you," she managed, but the servant was already gone, ducking from the room.

Aria spent a moment reassuring her guards, who'd come to flank her at the incident, and they resumed their posts while she tried not to think about how terribly this meeting seemed to be going.

The widow returned and took her seat with a deep frown. "I'm sure you assume that was some kind of sabotage. I—"

"Accidents happen," said Aria.

Too late, she realized her father would have used the moment to his advantage, pressuring the widow's guilt for leverage.

Wasted opportunity. Mark.

After staring for a moment, Widow Morton nodded an acknowledgement. "I would hear what you have to say, Highness. What reparations are you prepared to make for my people? What is your compromise?"

"My father—"

"Not him. I would know what *you* offer."

Aria hesitated. She held no power of her own; she was only a representative. "My offer is His Majesty's."

"I see." The widow seemed disappointed, so Aria rushed into details of a compromise she thought her father would approve, if only the widow accepted it first.

"In your letter, you requested freedom of magic, yet Casters are already permitted to practice magic freely so long as they submit to registration by branding. Therefore, it must be the branding you object to. As our compromise, we could do away with the witch's mark." Briefly, she outlined a new registration system that could be maintained by palace scribes, open to the public should they wish to consult the list of Casters in the kingdom. For everyone's safety, it was still important that Casters be known entities, of course.

"Of course," the widow agreed, her expression unreadable. "Safety of the public." Her sharp eyes held Aria pinned. "And one question more—what reparations is His Majesty prepared to make for *me*?"

Without meaning to, Aria clenched her hands, sending a fresh jolt of pain through her injured finger.

"The incident with your son was most unfortunate. No one desired his death," she finally said. Her father's words.

"Surely His Majesty did, else he would have left his sword sheathed."

Flinching. Mark. "Charles Morton was a spy within the palace, infiltrating a meeting of the king's private council. His Majesty acted in accordance with the law."

Though Aria knew the words to be truth, her soul shrank. An apology parted her lips, but she clenched her teeth, closing her mouth. Apologizing would indicate wrongdoing; it was her responsibility to stand steady in her father's place, no matter how difficult the situation. *The law is the law.*

Widow Morton's cold smile rattled Aria's heart just as wind rattled the windows. In the silence, the countess angled her gaze away, considering something distant.

Aria allowed her a stretch of uninterrupted thought.

"One hundred days." The widow clicked one fingernail lightly against the table between them, a steady countdown to some unknown. *Tick, tick, tick.* "One hundred days marks the traditional mourning season. Who do you think it was, Highness, who decided the death of a child could be erased in a mere three months?"

Aria felt something slipping beyond her reach.

In desperation, she said, "Widow Morton, I wish to avoid violence. You threatened blood in your letter, but my father commands an army. Even if you hoped to gather other Casters to your cause, you would always be outnumbered, and a rebellion will not avenge your son, nor will it bring about more favorable laws for Casters."

"No," the woman said softly, her fingers falling still. "There is no easy path forward for me, and it is not my desire to spread more death."

A surge of hope rose within Aria, nearly lifting her off her chair. "Then let us reconcile! Please."

Slight though it was, the widow's shoulders slumped. "It appears I have no choice. My path forward will be through you."

4

Leon's dismal prediction about the party turned out to be right. No sooner had Baron stepped foot in the Bennett Manor ballroom than he realized it was a hive of wasps, filled with all the sharpest gossips of society. He'd denied them a good swarming for three months, and they certainly made up for lost time.

"My Lord Baron!" said one such wasp, buzzing too close and truly looking the part in her bright yellow gown tied with a black sash. "It must be so bittersweet, taking the title. On the one hand, you've lost your father, yet on the other, you may be the first Caster to hold a court seat in three generations. Morton doesn't count, of course, marrying in as she did."

Baron gave a relaxed smile over a tight jaw. "There's no 'may' about it, madam. I am Lord Baron of the Reeves estate."

"You've not yet presented yourself to the king. Inherited title or not, nothing's official until His Majesty approves it."

"Which is exactly what he'll do at the next court event. If you'll excuse me."

Rather than allowing him escape, the woman hooked her arm through his and steered him directly into a hive of her buzzing compatriots. Baron gave an inward groan. Hopefully the twins fared better. They'd joined a group of other young teenagers, and he'd lost sight of them in the crush.

"We were discussing Lord Reeves's possible seat at court!" the woman beside him announced.

All five of the gossips they'd joined were happy to swarm around that topic. From all around Baron came expressions of false concern—what a tragedy for his house if the king did not give his approval, he must prepare himself for the worst, and oh dear, what stress he must be under directly after the loss of his father.

"Listen here, Guillaume—Guillaume, isn't it? Gwee-yahm." Lord Stanley clapped Baron on the shoulder. "These Patrian pronunciations really are hopeless, Reeves. Your mother should have gone with a sensible 'William' rather than this Grillam nonsense. As if you don't have enough working against you with that witch's brand!"

His wife swatted his arm. "Dear, you'll embarrass the poor chap. It's Gillan. Not so hard at all."

It was actually *Ghee-yum,* as Leon liked to say—the boy enjoyed any reference to food—or Corvin's more correct *GEE-yohm,* but Baron did not volunteer a pronunciation. Some people speculated that he hid behind a nickname out of shame for his half-Patrian heritage, but that was not true. Baron's name was the final remnant of his birth mother, and he would never allow others to tarnish it.

Resting one hand on the dress sword at his side, Baron spoke with a tone as hardened as the steel within the sheath.

"Lord Reeves"—he held Lord Stanley's gaze until the man's eyes retreated into the depths of his wine cup—"is the correct pronunciation."

Sweeping his eyes over the group silenced the rest. Perhaps he should have remained as nonthreatening as possible, because he knew the truth: behind the mocking laughter lay fear.

One woman's eyes darted to the witch's mark on the side of his neck, and Baron clenched his jaw, feeling a phantom pain against his throat. The brand couldn't be missed, reaching as it did from beneath the left side of his jaw nearly to his collarbone. When the mark had first been given, it had nearly resembled an S, but time and growing had stretched it out of shape until it was barely more than an impression of curved wings in opposition to a central point.

No matter how it looked, the message was clear: *Beware.*

"If you'll excuse me." Baron bowed and turned away.

Dodging a few more groups, he reached Margaret Bennett at last. The girl stood with her father while her mother made rounds of conversation through the room. Since Baron had previously met Silas's sister, no formal introductions were required. He merely bowed.

"Miss Margaret, congratulations on—"

"Baron!" Margaret gave a genuine smile at his appearance, the first to do so. "Has my brother sent word from Pravusat?"

"It's 'Lord Reeves,'" her father corrected gruffly. "That distasteful nickname has always been a blight, and Marcus was a fool to encourage it."

Baron inclined his head. "Lord Bennett."

Silas's father was a stern man in all things but especially in social hierarchies. Despite being only a viscount—a single step above Baron's own position—he conducted himself with the superiority of a duke. Luckily, his children hadn't inherited the ailment.

"I'm afraid I've not heard from Silas recently," Baron said. As Margaret's face fell, he added, "His last letter indicated the university is quite spectacular. Almost another world."

It was a small deception to say "last letter" as if Silas had sent more than one. Honestly, Baron had been surprised to receive anything from him—Silas was not one for writing unless keeping research notes. In that spirit, his entire letter had been exactly three lines long, including the signature:

> *It's a different world in this country, Gilly.*
> *It's freedom.*
>
> *Silas*

"I'd hoped he might be home by now," said Baron.

Margaret's expression drooped again. "I'd hoped as well. At least by my birthday."

Though the silence tempted Baron to slip away, he hesitated. Margaret did look lovely, her pink gown a complement to her easy blush, and she was the only person who'd been welcoming all evening. Surely he could stay a little longer.

Baron smiled. "While I'm no substitute for Silas, I'd be honored to share a dance with the lady of the evening."

Her own smile blossoming, Margaret reached for his extended hand—

Only for her father to catch her wrist.

"She's not dancing with a Caster," Lord Bennett said. "Not with this Morton business. It would taint her image."

The brand on Baron's neck—hanging exposed above his collar—seemed to burn as hot as the day he'd received it. After the branding law had been implemented generations earlier, Loegria's fashion standards had changed to accommodate it; no more high necklines for either men or women. No opportunity for a Caster to hide. A witch's mark remained visible at all times, an announcement to the polite men and women of society concerning the deadly magic user in their midst.

With the brand, Baron was permitted to practice magic if it caused no harm. But *permission* was not *trust*.

One might wonder, he thought, *why I even received an invitation.*

But, of course, Lord Bennett's strict enforcement of social hierarchies would not allow him to slight a member of court by lack of invitation. Caster or not, Baron was a titled lord until the king himself said otherwise.

Which was exactly why Baron could not allow the king to say otherwise. He'd promised his father to serve as a voice in the court representing those like himself who grew more threatened and misunderstood each day.

"I see," said Baron softly.

Margaret's face flushed as she looked down, tucking her arms against her middle. She'd never possessed the fortitude to stand against her father. That was her brother's prerogative—and the reason he'd been exiled to study abroad.

"Happy birthday to you, Miss Margaret."

After a bow, Baron retreated into the crowd. At least he was not overtaken by a swarm this time. Most of the wasps had flown onto the ballroom floor or migrated to the edges of the room, burrowing into cakes and finger pastries.

Time to leave, then. Yet as he craned to look for the twins, a new figure intercepted him—Lady Bennett in all her hostess glory, layered skirts flouncing with every movement. "Lord Reeves! Enjoying the evening?"

Before he could respond, a maid rushed up.

"My lady!" The girl's wide, terrified eyes knotted Baron's insides, reminding him of another servant and the wrenching words, *Your father's collapsed. Come quickly!*

"It's your grandmother's vase," the maid cried. "It's been shattered!"

That distressed him for a different reason. If something had been broken, he was certain he knew the culprit.

Two culprits, to be precise. Both surnamed Reeves.

—·❄·—

The twins had gotten into a fight, lost track of their surroundings, and knocked the family heirloom from its shelf. Though they'd wandered from the main party into the annex, there were still plenty of people gathered to witness the drama.

Lady Bennett wailed, clutching her heart like it had shattered along with the vase. Between her sobs came the story of how the vase had been a wedding gift to her grandmother from Duke Something himself, one of a kind, irreplaceable, invaluable, imported, a piece of history, her most prized possession.

Baron wanted to melt into the floor. As a Fluid Caster, he might have been capable. Just drip through the floorboards and never be seen again. Tempting.

Instead, he stepped in front of Leon and Corvin, offering profuse apologies on their behalf.

"This behavior reflects on you, Reeves!" Lady Bennett wailed. "I raised two children in this house, and they never so much as cracked a saucer!"

Leon bristled. "Hey, Baron isn't—!"

Baron shot the boy a look that silenced him on the spot.

"Of course, Lady Bennett," he said. "I take full responsibility. I'm truly sorry I can do nothing to restore the vase."

Amid a buzz of whispers from the other guests, he ushered the twins to the waiting carriage, holding tense until they'd passed beyond the gate. Then he released a sigh.

"It was an accident, Baron," Corvin whispered. The boy had pressed himself all the way to the far end of the carriage bench, his eyes on the floor.

"Accident or on purpose," Leon muttered from the other end, "it was *us*. She shouldn't have screamed at you."

Sitting across from them, Baron took a steadying breath, holding his tongue as every possibility passed over it.

Can't you stop fighting?

What if one of you had transformed?

I already have so much—

"You're not hurt?" he finally managed. When both twins shook their heads, he said, "Good."

"We're sorry." Corvin shrank in his seat, the posture he always assumed before a lecture. Had Father been alive, he would have received one, at twice the volume of Lady Bennett's. Worry always brought out the worst of Father's temper.

But Baron wasn't their father. He never could be.

"It's been hard for all of us," he said.

Both boys relaxed.

After a few moments of calming silence, Corvin muttered, "I bet Silas broke at least ten saucers growing up. She just never found the pieces."

Even Leon smiled at that.

CHAPTER

5

Aria returned to the palace with a smile on her face despite the late hour. She'd paid and dismissed her guards, and she tended to her own horse to avoid waking a stablehand. Then she snuck into the castle through the servants' entrance in the kitchen.

Cook had dozed off on a bench. The woman spent far too many late nights and early mornings tending to Aria's family and the frequent palace guests. Aria fetched a blanket from the linens closet beside the laundry room, then returned to tuck it around the woman's shoulders. Cook shifted in her sleep, turning her head, but did not wake.

Aria continued creeping through hallways, holding tightly to a letter bearing Widow Morton's seal that outlined the points of their discussion. The king's seal would finalize the agreement. Simply holding it, Aria felt as if she held a cloud. She floated toward her room.

Though she convinced herself not to wake her father until morning—already imagining his pride, his deep voice saying, *Well done, Aria*—she couldn't manage the same restraint with her sister. She ducked through the door between their adjoining bedchambers, tiptoeing up to Eliza's four-poster bed, where the younger princess's silhouette could be seen beneath the rise and fall of a thick comforter.

"Eliza!" Aria hissed. Playfully, she slapped the covers a few times. "Eliza, wake up, I'm back! I did it!"

But Eliza slept on. Aria frowned; her sister was not a deep sleeper. The girl insisted servants put thicker coverings on her windows because even a small amount of light disturbed her rest.

Aria lit a lamp.

Eliza slept on.

No matter how Aria shook her sister or shouted, she would not wake. Finally, in a rush of terror, Aria fled to her father's bedchamber, Widow Morton's letter falling from her hands.

"Father, something's happened to Eliza!"

But the king would not wake either.

At last, Aria realized what she should have noticed immediately. No one had come running when she shouted. Not a single guard stood awake at post. Instead, they snoozed against doors, slumped like Cook on her bench.

The entire castle had fallen under a sleeping Cast.

With numb steps, Aria returned to the hallway and picked up the widow's letter. She pried the seal free and read the interior, but it was only their peace agreement, every word exactly as she'd witnessed the widow inscribe it.

As she watched, the ink began to run. It trickled in tiny liquid rivers down the page, dripping from the bottom edge but vanishing before it hit the floor.

"Confused, Highness?"

Aria stiffened at the voice. It brought a winter chill, reminiscent of a frosted mountainside. Slowly, she turned. The shadowed hallway stretched before her, moonlight spilling through arched windows.

A thin sheen of water slid along one wall, drawing closer until it came to rest before Aria like a full-length mirror. Except it was not her own reflection looking back at her. It was a woman in a black-lace dress.

Widow Morton stood as stoic and pale-faced as her manor house. "I apologize for my deception. Though I prefer a straightforward approach, strategy must be adjusted to match an opponent."

"What's happening?" Aria rasped, reaching a trembling hand for the wall behind her.

Displaying fear. Mark.

"His Majesty claims my son's death was an unfortunate necessity. I wonder how he reached that conclusion so easily; it was not easy for me. What's happening now is also an *unfortunate necessity*. One hundred days, Highness. Over the next one hundred days, His Majesty's line will die—beginning with you."

"We talked peace! You signed—"

"There can be no peace between tyrant and oppressed. I did not begin this war; it began three centuries ago with a brand. As you seared your contempt into us, we at last sear our response into you: *No more*."

Aria's trembling stilled. The water mirror rippled at the edges, droplets bursting free to splatter stone.

"You claim to prefer honesty," Aria said. "Then be honest. This can't be about the brand, since our peace agreement would have removed it."

The widow ignored her. "You have always demeaned magic, and those of us possessing it have kept our heads down out of a desire to live peaceably. Now King Peregrine has removed the option for peaceable living."

"This is about your son. You bear a personal grudge, but you are dragging an entire kingdom into it with you!"

Lifting her chin, the widow stared Aria down from within the rippling dark. "You are a naïve child, displayed in the very way you speak to me. If you comprehended the smallest droplet of my power, you would flee."

"Power to make iced tea, you mean?"

Loss of temper. Mark. Aria flinched at her own words. This was the woman she'd meant to make peace with. Instead, she was provoking her further.

Widow Morton smirked. "Tell me, Highness, what is tea?"

When Aria didn't respond, she went on, "Fluid Caster, I have been called—a frivolous title, as if I perform party tricks, turning wine to water for the enjoyment of others. But I'll invite you to listen to your *heart*. Listen as it *pumps*, as it picks up speed within your chest, as the thundering truth rushes through your mind. What is it pumping? What sustains your *life*, Highness?"

Aria followed the widow's gaze down to her bandaged finger. In the chaos of other events, she'd forgotten about the broken teacup, about her injury. At the reminder, she heard the rush of blood in her ears, just as the widow predicted.

"Blood is only fluid," Widow Morton said, "and a princess is only blood."

When Aria looked up, she saw that the woman held a small white towel, stained red down the center. One of her servants must have delivered it to her after tending Aria's injury. Too late, the princess realized her mistake, the worst she'd ever made.

Her father had been right. This woman had never been interested in compromise or reconciliation. She had called for blood, and Aria had delivered it right to her door.

"In the morning," Widow Morton said, "the castle will wake as usual. But each night, they will slumber, and you will not. As the king is determined to see us divided between Casters and non-Casters, so shall you, Highness, be divided as well. By day, you will feel your exhaustion, an impulse as natural as magic, but if you succumb, you will be punished. By night, you will have your strength but no one to share it with. You will be left to wander alone, isolated. Perhaps you might use the time to ponder the isolation of magic users, alone in a world that ought to be home. Perhaps you might use the time to finally accomplish something good.

"Regardless, as the curse draws strength from you, it will grow and spread to your sister, Eliza. When this is finished, I will see His Majesty's family destroyed as mine has been." The widow's smile was cold. "One hundred days, Highness. Start counting."

CHAPTER 6

Baron knelt beside a lemon tree, pulled his gloves off, and reached through a patch of clover to the soil beneath. Was it drier than usual? He wished his magic could give him an impression beyond his physical senses, as it did when he touched liquid, but he was not a Stone Caster, so the ground did not yield to him.

"My predictions could be off," said Walter nervously from above him. Though the groundskeeper was younger than Martin by a few decades, he stood with a permanent stoop, likely from too many hours atop an orchard ladder.

"Even if they are . . ." Baron stood, brushing the dirt from his fingers and replacing his gloves. "The harvests have been declining. That much is undeniable."

He inspected a few leaves but found no discoloration or holes. The orchard was well-tended and healthy, but a surprise cold snap two winters previous had cost them a line of trees at the edge of the estate, and the remaining trees had produced less in subsequent harvests. The loss hadn't yet spelled disaster for the estate, but it would if Baron did nothing to fix it.

"Try the new fertilizer," he ordered. "In the meantime, I'll reach out to a friend to see if she can assist."

"Yes, my lord." Walter bowed, then hurried off.

The orchard carried a dim glow in the remnants of morning

fog, each yellowing lemon peeking like a candle through dense green leaves. As Baron made his way up the rows of trees, he paused beside a stone bench, the only one in the orchard. It was not crafted of polished stone, but rather was the dull gray of natural rock. *Natural* had been his father's preferred decorating aesthetic.

How many times had Baron sat beside his father on this bench, surveying the orchard and discussing harvests? Now, after more than three months, he'd still not touched it. Just looking at it brought to memory a chaos of panicked voices.

Baron closed his eyes, surrounded by ghosts in the morning fog.

My lord, your father's collapsed!

The physician's on his way.

Baron, what do we do?

Lord Reeves, can you hear me? He's taken on fever.

He's convulsing! Hurry—

Exhaling slowly, Baron stepped forward, forcing the ghosts back as he refocused his attention on the orchard. The Reeves estate lay directly on the border between the southern and northern regions of Loegria. To the north, places like Sutton—the capital, where the palace was—would soon be seeing frost as autumn advanced and then regular snowfall in winter. To the south, places like Port Tynemon experienced thick humidity year-round with a particularly miserable heat in the summer. The lands between danced the climates, and Baron's land in particular was an oddity—warmer than its closest southern neighbors and possessing a perfect humidity. A few dozen acres that seemed handcrafted for growing lemons.

Baron's father had thought that to be exactly the case; he suspected one of his ancestors had hired a few Stone Casters to work in tandem and cultivate the land. If so, it would have been before the law requiring Caster registration, as the event had never been recorded.

It would explain why winter temperatures at the estate had been creeping steadily colder the last few years, why lemon production was dropping. A Cast, once placed, was generally considered to be permanent, but nature could erode even the most permanent of things, and it seemed the natural Loegrian climate was reclaiming the Reeves estate at last.

One more worry for Baron to juggle.

As he approached the manor house, he heard the loud squawk of an antagonized bird. A flurry of black feathers erupted on the far side of the mansion, presumably from Baron's bedroom window. With a few more furious *ca-caws*, the black crow disappeared into the clouds.

Baron's breath quickened. He glanced around, but though servants bustled through the yard and estate buildings, none of them paid the sky any mind. Even if they had, they were familiar with the crow, at least by reputation. Supposedly, it was Baron's easily flustered messenger bird.

In truth, it was his easily flustered half brother Corvin.

The messenger-bird lie had been an accident. Mr. Shaw, one of the residents of the nearby hamlet, worked as a falcon trainer for the nobility, and he'd been first to notice the black crow that frequented the skies around the Reeves estate. While Baron had assisted his father in the hamlet one afternoon, Mr. Shaw questioned the lord baron directly about the bird's strange behavior.

"He don't fly like a crow," the man said, squinting with suspicion. "And he's young-size, but I never seen his murder or his roost mates."

Baron's father told the man he was imagining things, yet Mr. Shaw would not be dissuaded.

"He's mine," Baron said, speaking without thought. He swallowed. "He's my . . . messenger bird."

"Oh?" Mr. Shaw's squint grew more suspicious. "Crows are crafty beasts. How'd you ever get one tamed?"

Seeing no other option, Baron gave a partial truth. "My brother Corvin has an affinity for birds. He managed it."

Mr. Shaw's face lit up with glee, shining around a toothy grin. He wagged a finger first at Baron, then up at the sky, as he said, "You send that crow with a message for me. I want to see it. And then you send that brother of yours to my door. I won't let a talent like that go to waste—I aim to see what he can do with a falcon."

For the last four years, Corvin had apprenticed as a falcon trainer to Mr. Shaw, and the boy had never been happier. With a proper outlet for his talent, he managed to transform with more control, which meant a better guarded secret. Baron's father had opposed the arrangement for a few weeks until Corvin's newfound joy won him over, but he never stopped worrying.

Baron worried as well, yet as much as his father wished to keep the boy contained at home, Baron knew a truth only another magic user could understand—Corvin's gift was half his identity. Rather than keeping his brother caged, Baron wanted to offer him an excuse to be in the sky when he desperately needed it.

Even so, it froze him in place whenever his brother transformed. Just the chance of discovery . . .

With quick steps, Baron resumed his path. He swung by the stables first to request that his horse be saddled and ready in an hour, and then he circled the house, seeking the back entrance to the kitchen.

In order to reach it, he had to wade through a small herd of stray cats first. At least a dozen of them, with patterns of gray, black, and orange splashed across white, all mewled as if they'd never been fed a day in their lives despite the fact that Leon and Helen both stood at the kitchen door, actively tossing scraps of food to the insatiable horde.

Leon met Baron's eyes and looked away, like a criminal caught. He hadn't turned into a cat, which meant whatever war the twins had waged, Corvin carried more emotional stake in it than Leon.

Though Baron had intended to confront his brother, Helen's presence gave him pause. His hesitation allowed one of the smaller black felines to climb the leg of his pants. He glared down. The cat yowled up.

"Ooh." Helen laughed, the lines of her face crinkling with

grandmotherly enjoyment. "Come to feeding day without food. That's your fault, my lord."

Carefully, Baron pried the cat free. "Helen, I wonder if you might send a tea tray to my study. I'll be visiting Stonewall shortly, but I have business to attend first, and I'd welcome the refreshment."

"Certainly, milord." She tossed her final handful of scraps to the cat army. "I always hope to see my favorite on feeding day, but she's rarely here. That big white one with the sleek coat and those adorable peach-colored tufts on her ears."

Beside her, Leon blanched. "That's a boy! He's a boy."

"Nonsense! You should see the way all the other ones crowd around her, trying to impress the pretty girl."

"He's the king," Leon said hotly. "That's why they crowd around. He's in charge."

Baron cleared his throat. "The tray?"

Helen retreated into the kitchen, and Baron stepped forward to pull the door closed. He sighed.

"What did you say to Corvin?" he asked quietly.

Leon scowled, picking at the bone scraps in his hands, flinging bits of fish meat to his noisy subjects below.

"I told him I'm not going to school," the boy grumbled at last.

That hadn't made the list of expected answers. Baron raised an eyebrow.

"Birdbrain's all set on going to Fairfax next year, like you did, and *fine,* he can go if he wants, but *I'm* not going. That's all."

"All right . . ." Baron considered his words. "I enjoyed my time at Fairfax, but that doesn't mean it's suited to everyone."

"Exactly. School's for people like you and beak-face."

"People like . . . ?"

"People with brains." Leon hucked the remainder of the fish carcass across the yard, sending the cats dashing after it. "People with manners. People with sense."

Baron smiled gently. "If you're interested in a formal education,

I don't doubt your capability for a moment. Besides that, manners can be taught and sense can be practiced."

"You forgot brains."

"It's a misconception that anyone can operate without one, so I think you'll find yourself already properly equipped for that requirement."

Leon picked at a spot on his apron, avoiding Baron's eyes. "Dad wasn't going to let either of us go."

Baron swallowed. "He said that?"

When Leon looked up, the boy's eyes had shifted, his pupils narrowing to those of a cat. It was a swift change, there and gone in a blink, but it betrayed the emotion churning inside. Just because Leon hadn't fully transformed didn't mean he wasn't bothered.

The great secret of the Reeves estate was that all three of Marcus Reeves's sons had been cursed with magic. Despite the scorn and fear directed at Baron, he was still the safest of the group. His twin brothers were Animal Affiliates. Shapeshifters.

The last time an Affiliate—Dorothy Ames, a little girl of ten— had been discovered in the kingdom, she'd been executed. There was no registration law, no branded witch's mark that could protect the twins. The official folklore of Loegria said only one shapeshifter was born to each century, a savage animal that consumed a human child and took its place. Once the demon was rooted out, supposedly, the country would be safe for another hundred years.

Ironic, then, that Baron knew three Affiliates, none of them particularly savage, though Leon put in a good effort with some insults.

"Father didn't understand," Baron said softly, "what it's like to live with . . . this. But he tried. More than anything, he wanted to protect you and Corvin."

Leon didn't respond other than to slide his hands into his pockets.

"I have an errand in Stonewall. If you'd care to accompany me, we can stop by that bakery you like, and you can interrogate them for the secret of their blueberry scones."

"Sure." Leon looked away. "The crow will want a few biscuits too."

"I'm sure that can be arranged."

They reached Stonewall just before noon. True to its name, the city stood encircled by a wall with four gates, one oriented in each major direction. As a central market of the kingdom, it was always bustling, shepherds grazing their flocks outside the wall, traders on every street calling greetings through open windows.

Despite Leon's grumbles at being forced to dress nicely and ride a "smelly horse," he cracked a smile at a few of the sights. Once he focused on the bakery, though, his expression turned feral.

"Practice those manners," Baron reminded him sternly, "even if they refuse to hand over an ingredient list."

Which was exactly what they did. Leon and the head baker exchanged heated words over the priceless nature of baking secrets, and Baron bought a dozen scones and half as many biscuits to smooth over the encounter.

"A real cook would teach me," Leon complained as they exited. "I could do an apprenticeship like feather-head."

Baron was inclined to agree, but he only shrugged—and secretly hoped the boy hadn't been turned away because he stood with a Caster. Baron hadn't missed the baker stealing glances at his brand, just as everyone did.

Seeing to his errand at last, Baron visited Edith alone. Leon chose to wait outside, dissecting a scone as if its layers could be read like pages in a book.

The Stone Caster took several minutes to answer her door, and her scowl softened into a smile upon recognizing Baron.

"You too?" she asked, beckoning him inside with a nod.

Baron blinked. "Me what?"

As he stepped inside, he saw her home had been completely emptied of furnishings. All that remained were a few personal trunks and a table of odds and ends.

"You're . . . moving?"

"Abandoning a sinking ship is what I would call it," Edith said, shaking her head. "Didn't you get a letter from Morton?"

Clearly seeing his bafflement, she brought him a letter written in a tall, slanted script. An invitation from Clarissa Morton for any willing Caster to join the woman at her estate in Northglen.

Baron's blood ran cold.

"Don't look at me like that," Edith snapped. "Weston Knowles might be going to Northglen, but I'm not. I'm leaving this whole sinking country. Been considering it for years, honestly; this is just the final push. I've been branded and berated, and once Morton gets on with whatever *this* is—some hopeless rebellion against a king— even the freedoms I have left will be taken. So I'm taking my leave."

She tossed a few items into the uppermost trunk and closed it with a decisive *click*.

"I hadn't imagined . . ." Baron trailed off as he stared at the letter in his hand.

When he looked up, Edith's expression had softened once again. "What did you need from me, Baron?"

"My father's orchard. He thought it was cultivated by Stone Casters years ago, and I hoped you might renew the Cast."

Before he finished, she was already shaking her head. "Marcus visited me about this in the spring, a few days before he passed. I told him it's possible in *theory*, but it's far beyond my Casting capacity. Common folk hire me for house repairs and to craft statuary—though honestly, I've stopped taking orders larger than busts because anything else leaves me laid up in bed for days with my head pounding like death itself. So to imagine putting my hands on *acres* of land and ordering it to obey? I can already hear the soil laughing."

Baron knew well the feeling of inadequacy in magic. He forced back the memory of his father's death and said, "Perhaps working together with other Stone Casters, then."

Edith raised an eyebrow. "Marcus suggested that as well. Did he get the idea from you? I've never heard of a combined Casting. We're all solitary creatures, I thought."

"The idea came from Patriamere." That was an oversimplification, but Baron didn't feel the need to explain his inheritance. His mother had come from a bloodline of magic users in the neighboring country, and though there hadn't been a Caster in her direct line for several generations, her family had nevertheless passed down a set of priceless books containing information about magic.

The books were gone now. Just like his mother.

His stepmother was still alive, still out there somewhere. Baron had tried to find her after his father's death and accomplished nothing.

"You have family in Patriamere," Edith said with a nod. "That's where I'm headed. My advice? Do the same. Leave now, while you can."

Baron gave his thanks for her consideration, then helped her carry the trunks to a waiting carriage.

But he didn't leave. He couldn't. Not with his father's last wish repeating constantly in his mind. Baron had a duty in Loegria.

Once he and Leon returned to the manor, Martin met them at the door, delivering a folded parchment with a wax seal. This one was twice the thickness of a regular party invitation and as smooth as a sheet of ice. Even before registering the falcon stamped in wax, Baron knew it had come from the palace.

Idly, he rubbed the brand on his neck, feeling the indentations of an old wound long since healed. Then he broke the royal seal to read the invitation, though the details didn't matter—whatever the event, he would be required to present himself for approval to a court seat.

A ball. Princess Eliza's seventeenth birthday.

"We'll attend," Baron said. Somehow the words emerged in a normal tone despite the tightness of his throat.

Martin nodded.

Leon pursed his lips toward the parchment. "How many heirloom vases do you think a palace has?"

His brother's words seemed the perfect summation of Baron's dread.

CHAPTER

7

Aria was late to the meeting.

She rushed into the throne room at least ten minutes after everyone else had arrived, interrupting her father mid-sentence. He paused only a moment, casting her a glance, but Aria could tell by his deep frown that her efforts to compose her disheveled appearance hadn't entirely succeeded. The fact that he chose not to comment on her arrival boded worse than his frown.

This was her third tardy attendance; he now expected it.

Though she wished to turn and run, Aria instead slunk up the dais and into her seat. Only then did she realize she'd forgotten her journal.

Disorganized. Mark.

It was worse than that. Without something to keep her hands busy, she would inevitably fall asleep.

Not now. Please, no.

"You're certain of it?" her father asked Marquess Haskett, though Aria couldn't remember what the man had said to begin the exchange.

"Undoubtedly, Your Majesty. Our border guards report an increase in travel to Patriamere. Most noteworthy is how many of those traveling are branded Casters with a large number of possessions. It seems to be an exodus. I would be interested to hear from the southern ports."

Whispered conversations spread through the wings.

Aria resisted the urge to flex her hands. Instead, she wiggled her toes within her shoes as much as she could without displaying movement. The action barely dispelled her weariness, and worse still, though she stifled her yawn by clenching her teeth, she couldn't prevent her eyes from watering.

Every morning for the last two weeks, she used a stash of her mother's best powders and concealers to paint the skin around her eyes, hiding the puffy bags. The purple of her tired skin nearly matched that of her amethyst pendant and gown.

Every night for the last two weeks, the entire castle fell under Widow Morton's thrall. Except for Aria. She remained awake, desperately combing the library for knowledge of magic, of Casters, of curses—anything to combat her situation.

Her search had proved futile so far, and her one comfort had come in reading of the ancient Vallan invasion, when the palace had been besieged for six months. She, too, faced an enemy waiting out of reach, hoping she would starve. And if that enemy was to be believed, Aria's resources would last only one hundred days.

Eighty-six now.

At least no one in her family seemed to be suffering besides herself. Yet. She glanced at her father and saw no sign of tiredness in his rigid posture and attention.

What was being discussed again?

Aria stifled a groan. She felt her mind determined to float away, and she continuously tethered it in place only to find it free again, leaving her to wonder if she'd not tied it well enough or if she'd never tied it at all and only imagined the effort.

At night, she felt no tiredness at all. Instead, restless energy burned in every limb and would not abate unless she *moved*. She even had to pace while reading.

Yet during the day, every weariness imaginable suffused her bones, dragging her into sleep at the worst possible moments.

If she could have slept the days away to make up for the nights, she would have gratefully given into the temptation, but it was not that simple. Even alone in a quiet, dark room, she could catch no more than half an hour of sleep before her body awoke on its own, heart racing as if she ran with hounds at her heels, an unexplained terror squeezing her chest. It seemed worse to sleep than to resist, though she often couldn't help it.

After resisting for a week, trying and failing to solve things on her own, she'd at last decided to tell her father about the curse, no matter how shameful she felt about having walked herself into this trap. But when she'd tried to speak of it, her jaw clenched shut. Just as the curse forbade sleep, it forbade discussion.

And so, day and night, the madness persisted.

"What do you think, Aria?"

At the sound of her father's voice, Aria sat up with a jolt. She didn't know how long her cheek had been slumped against the side of her high-backed throne, but the eyes of the Upper Court rested on her, awaiting an answer she didn't know how to give.

"I agree," she said with feigned confidence.

Her father's lips tightened to a line. His brow furrowed.

Wrong answer. Mark.

"We'll table this matter for now," said the king. "Reconvene tomorrow morning. In the meantime, I have family matters to deal with."

There could be no mistaking his implication, and as Aria caught the members of court offering her father pitying glances, her skin chilled, and she shivered. A manifestation of the curse. Along with her other gifts, Widow Morton had sent Aria home with the frost of Northglen coating her bones, and every so often, the cold rose to the surface. As if she didn't have enough reminders of her terrible mistake.

Once they were alone, her father's posture softened at the edges, allowing his shoulders a curve as he sat at a slight angle in his throne. He studied her without speaking. Aria hated that more than a lecture.

"I won't be late again," she promised.

False promises. Mark.

He raised an eyebrow. "How am I to believe that, after three meetings in a row?"

Aria licked her lips but couldn't think of a response. Her mind seemed like molasses when called upon, slow to deliver anything beyond the constant muted cry for *sleeeep*.

"You are excused from Upper Court meetings," her father said. "At least for the time being."

Aria bolted upright in her chair. "Father, no! I wish to be here. I—"

He held up a hand.

"*If*"—his fierce gaze bored into hers—"you can attend a separate duty with diligence, I will allow you back to the meetings. A fair trial."

It *was* fair. If only Aria had the motivation to tend to *any* duties. All she wanted was to yank the nearest tapestry off the wall, curl up in it, and disappear into a blissful oblivion.

"Yes, Father," she forced herself to say. "Name it."

"You have entertained a few suitors at this point, but none for more than a single meeting. You are eighteen now, Aria, and cannot continue putting this off. Find a young man to court, show me you take the future of our kingdom seriously, and I will welcome the return of my dutiful daughter."

Of course, that was the problem—Aria hadn't been dutiful at all. She'd been rebellious and foolish. She'd thought herself wiser than her father, who had led his kingdom through a recovery from famine, then through decades of peace.

If she could go back and never speak to Widow Morton, she would.

Instead, she bowed her head and said, "I'll do it, Father."

She ought to have been dutiful from the start, but the least she could do was never disobey again.

——— ❄ ———

The day of Eliza's ball, Aria was asleep at her writing desk when her sister burst into the room, shrieking exuberantly.

"It's here, it's here, it's *here*!"

Aria sprang to her feet, eyes bleary but the rest of her awake with panic. She looked frantically over her shoulder for an enemy that didn't exist.

No, her enemy *did* exist; it just couldn't be seen.

Eliza deflated. "You haven't even laid out a gown. Aren't we readying together?"

"Yes, of course." Aria turned away, fumbling scraps of parchment into her journal, blinking hard. "I got caught up in . . . finalizing my welcome speech."

By that, she meant she'd lifted her quill and remembered nothing after. Her first time hosting a court event, and she was going to make a fool of herself. Worse, she was going to embarrass her sister.

Eliza seemed to take the excuse at face value, just as she'd readily accepted the lie Aria had given about her visit to Northglen. *Morton turned me away at the door*, Aria had said. *I guess she changed her mind.* Eliza had huffed and puffed about the woman's selfishness and foolishness, leaving Aria with a churning stomach and a secret she couldn't speak, not even to the one person she would have told *anything* to.

The sister she would lose if she couldn't find a way out of this curse.

Aria forced a smile, gesturing to her wardrobe. "Help me choose a gown?"

Eliza could have complained that Aria hadn't commissioned one for the event—as she'd intended to—but the birthday girl threw open the wardrobe without hesitation.

Alternating the leg she stood on and rotating the opposite ankle,

Aria managed to keep herself awake somehow. "Come on, let's hear them."

"Hear what?" Eliza called innocently.

"The young men of court you'll be seeking out tonight."

Peeking out of the wardrobe, arms draped in fabric, Eliza gave a devious smile. "Lord Alexander, I think. Did you know he saved his sister from *drowning* last winter? He's a hero!"

Aria made a face. "That's Marquess Haskett's heir. Even if his son *is* a hero, you don't want a vulture for a father-in-law."

"Psh!" Eliza waddled over to the bed and dumped her chosen garments with a grand flourish. "Obstacles are expected on the road to true love! And I am such a gem, I could win the esteem of the crustiest of vultures."

Aria laughed. Her sister scurried over, hooked her arm, and dragged her to survey the gowns. For a few precious moments, Aria managed to push down her fatigue in earnest—not *banishing* it, but at least shrinking it, hushing it—enough to soak in the bright, energizing sunlight that was Eliza.

"This one!" Eliza declared after an extended debate. The winner was a cream-colored gown with black-vine accents, which she deemed "the most elegant dress ever made." It was one of Aria's favorites, and she tried not to think of how it would sag on her rapidly thinning frame.

At least the ball wouldn't last all night. In Patriamcre, royal parties began in the late evening and lasted until dawn, something Aria's father called a "useless indulgence." He rejected any tradition aligning with his wife's birth country, so Loegrian parties were afternoon affairs, finished by early evening so the entire castle could adhere to the king's strict schedule of retiring early.

Good news for Aria, since she'd not yet heard panicked questions about the unexplained sleeping Cast which set in every night at midnight and lasted until dawn. Surely the night watchmen had noticed, but if they'd brought their concerns to the king, he'd not brought the matter to the court's attention.

Eliza suddenly seized her hands, and Aria blinked herself to attention. "This ball is for you, Aria," she said with an unusual level of seriousness.

Aria smiled wryly. "I believe it is, in the most literal sense, for *you*."

"The cake is for me, and I'll be eating plenty, thank you." Eliza squeezed her hands. "But don't you see? Today is your chance to find your *own* suitor. I know Father's been pressuring you about it—Jenny said all the servants are gossiping—but don't you dare let him choose for you!"

Right. *That.* Aria had tried to revisit her list of potentials, but after a few names, she always dropped to sleep.

Neglecting duty. Mark.

"Eliza, I—"

"I have a feeling about this, I mean it! This afternoon, you're going to find the most perfect man of court, one who really lets you be yourself. You'll dance and fall madly in love, have seven children—"

Partly to interrupt that thought, Aria pulled Eliza into a hug, breathing in the lavender scent of her sister.

"I promise I'll remedy my situation," she whispered. Though it was not suitors she spoke of.

With a squeal, Eliza hugged her back, gushing about how the most romantic gestures always happened at a ball and the vast multitude of men there would be available to choose from.

Aria had only one man in mind, and he was not at all a candidate for suitor. After twenty days of siege, she had grown desperate enough to try an unthinkable tactic. Since books had failed her, she began seeking information on Casting from its source, only to find the two Casters in Sutton Town had abandoned their homes, perhaps warned by Widow Morton of the princess who might come seeking aid.

However, there would be one Caster attending Eliza's ball.

Guillaume Reeves, son of Marcus Reeves. The late baron had passed away, leaving a Caster to inherit his title, and Eliza's ball was the first court function after his mourning season. He would have to present himself to the king.

Though Aria's knees trembled at the thought of seeking out another Caster, she squeezed her sister tightly and reminded herself why she had to.

This time, she would not fall for a trap.

She would set one.

CHAPTER

8

"Whoa." Corvin craned his neck back, looking at the painted ceiling patterned with arches. "Royals go all out. I wonder what it would feel like to climb—"

"Absolutely not," Baron said.

"I wasn't going to! It's not like Leon hasn't thought about slinking off to the kitchen at least three times now."

Leon said nothing, too busy sniffing the apple pastry in his hand. He sampled a corner, then muttered something about freshness and spices. All along the refreshments table, nobility milled in small groups, conversations held at a low volume that didn't carry to the vaulted ceiling. Social functions at country estates were lively affairs, but everything at Castle de Loegria felt subdued, as if even the air in the room had to rationed.

"Lord Reeves," a voice said from behind him.

Baron turned to find a silver-haired man in a crisp red suit. Though he'd tensed on instinct, his shoulders relaxed at the familiar face, and he shook the earl's hand with eagerness. "Lord Wycliff, a pleasure to see you."

The earl raised an eyebrow. "Don't be pleased, lad. I'm quite cross with you. Hugh's been practicing his swordsmanship, you know, and I intended to see him best you at Jasper's melee. It'll be months before I can hold an event of my own."

"Ah, then I won't apologize for the disappointment. Had I participated, you would have experienced the same."

The earl chuckled into his wine glass. He nodded toward the twins. "Finally old enough to participate in these events, I see. If you're looking for company, my youngest is down at the other end of the table."

To Baron's surprise, Corvin shook his head. "I'd rather stay. As soon as the king arrives, Baron has to present himself."

Baron's chest warmed at the unfailing loyalty. "Go on," he said gently, nodding down the table.

After another few moments of hesitation, Corvin moved off, dragging Leon with him, the blond boy still transfixed by pastries.

"It's for the best." Earl Wycliff grimaced. "There's nothing they can do, and perhaps Osric can distract them from making a scene. There's nothing I can do either, for that matter, and I am sorry, Gill."

Baron frowned. "What are you implying?"

The man paused, cup raised. "His Majesty won't appoint you. Surely you know that."

"Dowager Countess Morton already—"

"Married into it and never actually sat at court."

Baron's neck itched. He resisted touching his brand.

"Besides, I wouldn't use Morton as a defense of anything at the moment. She's made your situation infinitely worse. You're a good lad, Gill. One of the finest. But that doesn't change the kingdom."

After a long pause staring into his own glass, Baron admitted, "I intend to. Change the kingdom. My father raised me to have a voice in court, and I won't surrender it."

Lord Wycliff sighed. He stepped forward to grip Baron's shoulder. "Marcus was . . . optimistic."

"You don't think I'm dangerous, do you?"

"Of course I do." The earl's grip tightened, then released. "Every sword ever forged is dangerous. It's a matter of who's wielding it, and

I trust you to wield, but that doesn't mean I'm against the restrictions on Casters. I'm sorry."

At least he was honest.

Just then, the palace guards snapped to attention, calling the announcement for His Majesty. Lords and ladies alike turned from conversation, sinking into respectful bows and curtsies as the royal family passed in procession. Once the four figures settled on the dais, the room seemed to exhale, though personal conversations did not resume.

Baron handed his wine glass to a servant, noting the way the boy handled it like a loaded crossbow, tiptoeing to ensure the deadly weapon didn't impale him.

King Peregrine and Queen Marian did not sit together on the dais. Instead, the king's throne occupied the center spot, and his eldest daughter, the crown princess, sat immediately to his right. The queen and youngest daughter sat in a removed position to the left, as if meant to be mere audience to the true monarchs. An odd arrangement for a family.

To Baron's surprise, it was not the king who stood to address the crowd, but rather the crown princess. She wore an elegant gown in muted colors—black and cream—rather than the flamboyant purple dressing her sister. Judging by her solemn expression next to her sister's beaming smile, their fashion preferences reflected their disparate personalities.

All the same, Princess Aria spoke with a warm voice as she welcomed everyone.

"Eliza de Loegria," she said, glancing over her shoulder with a widening smile, "is now seventeen. The Crown presents her to the court as a young woman of eligible age, accepting suitors."

Princess Eliza stood and swept a graceful curtsy. Then she *winked.*

A few chuckles rippled through the crowd. The king gave a stern frown but said nothing. Though Baron had expected the crown princess to continue with a welcoming address, she floundered for a moment, as if forgetting her words. Then she jumped to the next matter of business.

Baron would have liked it much better if that next matter was not himself.

"The Crown has another presentation to make as well," she said, nodding to her father. She took her seat with cheeks that had gone slightly pink.

If the king thought her abruptness strange, he didn't comment. He stood and crooked the fingers of one hand. "Guillaume Reeves, approach."

All eyes turned to Baron. He fought to keep his expression impassive, but it felt like one eye was twitching. He strode forward, careful to keep his hand off the hilt of his dress sword; comfort though it would have been, he would not give anyone reason to call him threatening.

At the foot of the dais, Baron made a formal bow, arms folded over his stomach, head dipping low. Then he straightened. And waited.

The king's voice boomed over the silent gathering. "Lord Baron Marcus Reeves, may he rest, was an honorable man, a credit to his noble title. Guillaume Reeves, you are his firstborn heir?"

Swallowing past a tight throat, Baron managed a "Yes, Your Majesty."

He'd witnessed other presentations. They ended here. The king pronounced his approval, welcomed the newcomer to court, and the celebration began in earnest.

But instead, the king said, "You bear the witch's mark?"

As if it wasn't burned into his skin for all to see. As if people hadn't been stealing glances at it since he'd arrived.

As if the crown princess wasn't gawking at it now.

"Yes, Your Majesty."

"The Crown cannot, in good conscience, give seat to a Caster."

Quiet murmurs rippled through the crowd like wind rustling

leaves. There it was, in the open. One small part of Baron had always been convinced it wouldn't happen, that his dread of this day was only born of fearful imagining, that after all his efforts to follow the rules with exactness, he would be afforded the base rights of society after all. Casters were not lesser citizens, the law insisted. The witch's mark was merely a precaution to keep all people safe, including magic users themselves.

He wore the brand for *them*. But their *good conscience* could not afford him a seat to his own *birthright*.

Calm down, he ordered himself. Ever since the event invitation had arrived, he'd braced for conflict, carefully piecing together arguments he could use to defend himself when inevitably challenged.

And he'd also considered the alternative.

If the Reeves title was stripped and given to another family, it would be a humiliation, a blight to his father's legacy. A landholding title had never been revoked in Loegria except for criminal offenses. However, it would also mean less scrutiny on the twins. As long as Baron drew attention, he drew it to the whole family. If he were an ordinary citizen—not a lord—he could offer his brothers greater safety, farther from the Crown's attention.

Yet both Baron and his father had agreed the only true hope for the twins was change in the kingdom. Otherwise, the best he could offer was a lifetime of hiding, a life of fear. The twins deserved better.

Baron wanted to give them better. Wanted it so fiercely his knees trembled.

Breaking the silence of the room, the king grunted in what seemed to be approval. "The Reeves title—"

"Is mine," Baron said. "By rights."

The crowd's murmuring doubled, shaking not only imaginary leaves but the trees themselves. The entire room seemed to vibrate with an excited terror. Perhaps the court wondered how a Caster dared interrupt a king. Perhaps they thought him a fool.

Perhaps he was.

Baron lifted his head. "Your Majesty, the law of title inheritance does not exclude Casters. I intend to uphold every rule of court. I ask only for my legal birthright, as any other person in my position would receive."

He stumbled a bit, voice shaking, and he forgot most of the points he'd intended to make. All he could do was stand firm and wait.

The king spoke coldly. "You imply the kingdom has an imperfect law?"

Baron knew better than to answer that. His palms grew sweaty.

"I've done nothing wrong," he finally said.

King Peregrine's brows drew down, like clouds lowering to deliver a storm. Baron's heartbeat provided the thunder, rumbling with fear in his chest. By antagonizing the king, would he advance the oppression of magic users? Had he made everything worse?

Then the crown princess stood.

"You are the firstborn heir," she said. "But not the only?"

For a moment, all Baron could do was blink before his senses caught up enough that he could nod.

As if she'd been part of proceedings from the beginning, Princess Aria said, "Esteemed members of court, we have suffered a recent wound. A threat of aggression. Scarcely can the Morton name be spoken without remembering it."

Baron tensed. For a moment, he'd dared to hope she would, in some way, defend him. But she'd returned the topic to the untrustworthiness of Casters.

"We would be ill-advised to ignore the threat at hand. However, we would be just as ill-advised to ignore other considerations, such as the benefit of trust within this court, built over generations of strong, dutiful families. The Reeves family is part of that legacy. A strong kingdom is built on the foundation of a strong court. We have such a thing here, built by all in attendance, and Loegria is better for it."

With all the charm a creature might possess, she smiled out at the ballroom, earning a few smiles in return.

Baron didn't smile. He watched the king.

The man's eyes still threatened storms, but the wind had turned from Baron's direction, focusing instead on the girl poised to inherit the kingdom.

When His Majesty at last spoke, he said, "The Reeves title will pass to the second-born heir, Corvin Reeves. Seeing as the boy is not yet of age, the court will appoint a steward to manage the estate and title, as well as to oversee his preparation for future duties. Though he has passed his twelve-year Casting test, one more will be administered at age seventeen. He must pass to inherit. This matter is settled. Begin the ball."

The king waved his hand, and the galley orchestra struck up a loud melody.

Baron whirled, searching the crowd for his brothers. Corvin stood at the far end of the long table, his jaw slack, his dark eyes wide with fear.

Baron's heart sank from his chest. The hollow it left behind was carved with a new title to replace the one he'd lost: *Fool*.

CHAPTER

9

80 DAYS LEFT

Aria's first attempt at hosting had been a disaster. She'd bungled her welcome speech—skipped it, more accurately—and managed to embarrass her father all in one fell swoop. Even the quill in her mind could not list all the day's flaws. Perhaps she'd failed so spectacularly, it was worth praise rather than a mark. Surely no one could outdo it.

When her father extended his arm to invite her to dance, she took it with a forced smile, a display for the watching members of court. She wore that smile through the first bars of music until the rhythm of the steps was established and her father relaxed his own court mask.

"I'm sorry," she said preemptively.

"Regret does not erase foolishness, Aria."

She felt his frustration in the tenseness of his dance posture, saw it in his scowl.

Even though she'd apologized, even though she'd promised herself never to act against her father again, she found her voice clawing its way into justifications. "I thought it an elegant solution. By passing the title to the second son, the problem of a Caster in court is avoided, but so, too, is the problem of offending a loyal family or of making others in court fear losing titles without crime."

"Yet you maintained a bloodline of magic in a titled position. If the second-born heir bears a Caster of his own, what then? Did you preserve them only to disown them at a later generation?" Her father

59

sighed. "You undermined my position by interruption. Then, by referencing the court itself, you placed the power of decision-making outside the Crown. The court is *only* auxiliary to the Crown."

"Auxiliary, perhaps, but still foundational," she protested. "Loegria was founded upon the idea that the Crown should not hold *absolute* power. What of the law where even a monarch can stand trial by Upper Court?"

"That law is ancient and has never been practiced."

"So it's a mistake?"

"It's simply an unnecessary precaution, and it isn't the topic at hand. You presented a weak front when, always, the Crown must be strong. Far better for one family to lose a title, even undeserving of the loss, than to introduce weakness to the Head of State."

He was right, of course. Aria had spoken without thinking the entire matter through, and she couldn't blame her thoughtlessness on her curse. It was the same failing that had pushed her to attempt peace with Widow Morton against all sound advice.

Recklessness. Mark.

It had felt so unjust—watching Lord Reeves make such a heartfelt plea that no one seemed to hear. His words still echoed in her mind: *I've done nothing wrong.* Personally, Aria could never imagine making that claim with confidence, yet his bright eyes had been genuine, his stance firm. Facing ruin for his entire family, he'd been composed rather than angry, firm rather than belligerent, and . . .

And here she was, defending a Caster. Again.

"It seems I cannot get anything right," she whispered. "No matter how I try."

As the music ended, her father gave another sigh, this one softer. "I never doubt your earnestness, Aria, but unbridled emotion serves no one. Remember that. In the future, you may bring concerns to me beforehand, but you will not challenge me before the court."

"Yes, Father."

They parted, and the king led Eliza to the dance floor next. Eliza practically bounced beside him, light on her toes, expression eager. The queen had already vacated her throne; no doubt she'd gone to join the orchestra. Aria couldn't remember the last time she'd seen her parents dance.

Lord Christopher, a potential suitor, sidled up to introduce himself. He invited Aria to dance, and numbly, she agreed, though her legs already ached. By a stroke of luck, he was happy to hold the conversation without a partner.

By the time the music broke, so did her ability to smile, and her head had taken on a pounding ache.

"I'm terribly sorry." She mustered a shallow curtsy. "I must step out for a moment."

Exhaustion made her teeter as she walked. She caught a glimpse of Eliza surrounded by a group of friends. Her sister's beaming smile faltered, meaning Aria's breezy expression was not as convincing as she'd hoped. Aria looked away, unable to stop the wretchedly ungrateful thought that, right now, her sister was simply one more person to disappoint.

The hallway leading toward the kitchen was empty, and Aria didn't make it far before her legs gave out. She staggered into a pillar, then sank down, tucking herself as close to the wall as possible.

She'd come to the ball armed with a plan—win the favor of Lord Reeves, subtly interview him about the abilities of Casters, probing for ways to undo a curse—and she'd failed spectacularly. It was how things always happened.

For a few moments, the burning in her eyes kept her awake. Then she blinked the tears away, and exhaustion dragged her into sleep.

Aria woke as arguing voices approached from down the hall.

" . . . expect nothing less from a birdbrain like you!" an angry young voice shouted.

"You're jealous my birds are smarter than you," another voice snapped in return. "There's nothing you can do that a falcon can't do better except irritate me!"

Face flushed, Aria dragged herself up on shaky legs, trying not to tumble out of hiding. With every second, the voices drew closer.

"I'd like to see a falcon bake a pie. On second thought, I'd throw in the whole bird!"

"Take it back, Leon."

"Make me, beak-nose!"

Aria braced herself to be discovered—her mind still humiliatingly blank of excuses for her position—when she realized the arguing parties had no interest in her. The two teenage boys who came into view elbowed and jostled and grabbed until one finally seized the other and rammed him into the wall.

Aria gasped, but before she could step in, a familiar man caught up, separating the boys with the help of his cane.

Guillaume Reeves. Dressed in his black mourning attire and more handsome than any Caster had a right to be, due mostly to the ripples in his tawny hair and the single dimple in his right cheek.

Though it might also have been his green eyes, bright as spring, warm as summer.

The green eyes staring right into hers.

Of all the people to find her . . .

While Aria gaped, Lord Reeves recovered.

"Your Royal Highness." He made a proper bow, just as he'd done to her father.

Behind him, the two boys—who Aria now realized were twins—stared at her. They each wore cornflower-blue suits and black armbands, but one was thin as a twig, with long, sharp features and dark hair. The other was rounded in every sense of the word, with wheat-blond hair and what seemed to be a permanent frown. They were the exact same height with the exact same brown eyes.

"Boys." Lord Reeves tapped his cane sternly against the floor.

"Y—Your Highness," stammered out the dark-haired boy. After a half second, he seemed to remember the bow, tacking one on.

"Hi," said the other, narrowing his eyes without even a semblance of a nod.

The abrupt lack of formality startled a nervous laugh out of Aria. She tried to smooth her hair and sleep-skewed dress.

Slovenly. Mark.

"That's not how you greet royalty," the dark-haired boy hissed.

The blond boy clenched a fist. "I'll greet how I please, you skinny chicken!"

Lord Reeves stepped smoothly in front of the twins, blocking them from view as they continued their hushed argument.

"My deepest apologies, Your Highness. We were just on our way out."

"Don't go," Aria said in a rush, transparent in her desperation. She'd meant to be more composed than this.

Her initial plan, formed before the party began, had been to ask Lord Reeves to dance immediately after his presentation. Foolish of her not to think it through. Of course her father wouldn't want a Caster in court, not after Widow Morton, and she couldn't blame him. It was unsafe for the kingdom.

Lord Reeves stared, as if waiting to hear a single reason she wanted him to stay. Even his brothers had stopped arguing to watch.

"Truthfully, I'd hoped to ask you to dance."

The blond boy snorted. Though his twin shot him a warning look, Lord Reeves kept his attention on Aria, his brow creasing in a frown. Clearly, she'd done something to earn a mark, but she was too frazzled to pinpoint it.

"I'm afraid I don't . . . know your names." She smiled weakly at the twins, shifting on her feet as they protested standing in one place. Though she wasn't certain how long she'd slept, the nap had done nothing to refresh her, and with the embarrassment thus far, all she wanted was to slink away to the kitchen and disappear.

But she thought of Eliza, and she stayed.

The twins introduced themselves as Corvin and Leon before Leon promptly asked, "You're not even at the dance, so how could you want to dance with Baron?"

Aria blinked. "Baron?"

Lord Reeves cleared his throat. "Another time, Your Highness. Please accept my apologies."

She couldn't very well bludgeon him into staying, and her mind grew dizzy as it spun through possible excuses, rejecting each one in turn. Her etiquette, finally, managed something. "Please accept mine as well. I was sorry to hear of your father's passing, and I did not have a chance to pay my respects at the funeral."

She'd been confined to her room with a fever. Strange how that now seemed a happy memory, full of blissfully uninterrupted sleep.

"Thank you, Highness," Lord Reeves said softly, his voice hoarse. Clearly the passing of his father was still fresh, and Aria felt a pang of guilt realizing that her only thought toward him this evening had been to set a trap.

"I'm on my way to the kitchen," she said, leaving it open in invitation, then realizing how foolish she was. She had to be the only member of court to ever waste time in a servant area.

Undignified. Mark.

Leon surged past his brothers to stand directly in front of her. "Can you take me? I want to investigate the pastries!"

Aria took a step back, offering a startled laugh before she relaxed. As his eldest brother moved to intercept, she waved him off. "Yes, of course. Though I never thought them suspicious until now."

Corvin rolled his eyes. "He just wants to complain about spices and order people around."

"This is a palace kitchen, you flightless ostrich! They'll have a real cook!"

"All ostriches are flightless, and all cooks are real, so you're—"

"It's this way," Aria said, gesturing quickly. As she took the lead, her knees wobbled, and she stumbled.

Lord Reeves stepped up beside her, offering his arm, though he did so stiffly.

"Thank you, Lord Reeves," she managed, biting her lip. "I'm afraid I'm a bit clumsy these days."

"Not at all, Your Highness." He gestured over his shoulder. "With these two knocking down walls every hour, I can hardly ever catch my own bearings."

From behind them, Corvin snickered to his twin. "Baron said you're so clumsy, you knock down walls."

"When we get to the kitchen," Leon shot back, "I'm gonna shove a pack of herbs down your throat and cook you like a turkey."

"The one we should cook is you. You could feed a whole hamlet. I'm not even food enough for a cat."

He paused as if realizing what he'd said, and Leon hooted with laughter.

Aria smiled, though she should not have; indulging fights between siblings was surely unmannered behavior.

"This is a generous offer," said Lord Reeves, "but I hesitate to keep you from your other guests."

"They're Eliza's guests, truly." Aria had already mismanaged her job as hostess, and she couldn't imagine making it better by standing around, nodding off during conversation. Better to let her father smooth out the event with no further interference from her. "It's no trouble, Lord Reeves."

"It's no longer 'Lord Reeves,'" he said, a bit of an edge to his voice.

Surely it must sting to have the title taken from him, but without Aria's intervention, it would have been taken from his family completely. Could she not earn a moment's gratitude?

Bitterness. Mark.

"Lord Guillaume, then." He was still part of a titled family, after all.

ELIZABETH LOWHAM

"You didn't have to ask Baron how to say it?" Leon piped up, suddenly right on their heels.

Aria frowned. "Of course not."

"But it's a weird name no one uses."

For that, he earned another sharp elbow from his twin.

Aria was left with only the former Lord Reeves to address her remarks to, so with a side glance, she said, "It's a Patrian name, isn't it? Like my mother's. It's lovely, if a bit uncommon."

"No one aside from my own mother has ever found my name lovely."

No matter how she tried, she could not get a thing right. How was she meant to slyly interrogate a Caster for information on curses when she couldn't even manage a regular conversation with one? She could hardly manage anything given the steady pounding in her head and the increasing heaviness of her eyelids.

Lord Guillaume said, "I forget the queen is Patrian."

Aria startled upright, blinking hard. "Most of court does, encouraged by both my parents. It was a necessary political union, not a pleasant one." She rubbed her forehead. "Forgive me. I'm not myself."

"So you've said." He studied her, green eyes much too piercing.

Realizing her makeup would be more obvious up close, Aria quickly looked away. She spoke for a moment about the tapestries they passed and the historic scenes they depicted. Something she said made the twins bicker again, and she winced, though Lord Reeves hardly even glanced back. As long as their arguments remained verbal, he did not seem inclined to intervene.

"Your Highness is fond of history," he said.

"Very much so." She meant to expound, but the walk to the kitchen was a short one, with its necessary proximity to the ballroom. So as it turned out, Aria had seized an opportunity, then accomplished nothing with it. Per usual.

"Here we are," she said, somehow managing to hold back her grimace at such an inane comment as she swung open the kitchen door.

66

CHAPTER

10

Leon burst eagerly through the door, Corvin only a step behind. Baron winced inwardly, trying to maintain an outward confidence that his family was completely normal and not the least bit ill-mannered in royal company.

Oddly enough, he seemed to care far more than the royal herself.

Princess Aria slipped her arm from his and greeted the kitchen staff like old friends, asking briefly after families and well-being. Just as Leon seemed about to burst with questions, the princess made proper introductions between the boys and "Cook."

"Don't you have a name?" Leon demanded.

The stern, graying woman regarded him severely, one hand on her hip, the other in possession of a long wooden spoon which seemed to be her staff of office. Her presence loomed large, due in no small part to her height, which must have been more than six feet. The princess was not a short woman, standing practically at Baron's own height, yet Cook rose another half-head above them both.

"If you're here to chatter, boy, you can march right back to the other mouths in the ballroom. It's hands I need in my kitchen."

Leon made a show of clamping his mouth shut, then lifted both hands, palms out.

Baron smiled—as did the princess, he noticed.

Cook grunted. "Let's see how fast you ruin bread."

"Hey!" Corvin barked. "Leon's bread is the best! Probably in the whole kingdom."

Baron tried to remember the last time he'd heard either twin compliment the other.

"Then prove it." Cook shoved a large bowl into Leon's hands. "I need a batch of dough for six loaves. You'll be at this station with me." With the tip of her spoon, she pushed Corvin toward a kitchen hand. "You'll gather ingredients."

Then she turned on Baron, wooden spoon held like an unsheathed knife. He tensed.

"No Casters in my kitchen."

Both twins bristled. Leon set down his bowl, opening his mouth to speak.

Princess Aria beat him to it.

"Lord Guillaume is my personal guest, and I'm sure he'll keep his hands to himself."

Cook grumbled a bit, then dismissed the whole matter with a wave.

The princess took one limping step toward the wall, then sank down onto a wooden bench as if she could no longer stand. She pushed a stack of spare aprons to the side to give herself space.

After a moment's hesitation, Baron sat beside her.

"Thank you," he said quietly.

The crown princess was not what he'd expected. In the ballroom, she'd seemed every bit the royal heir—speaking commandingly before court, gliding on the dance floor, giving aloof nods in interaction.

Outside the ballroom, she was a different person entirely. Her shoulders bore a tired slump, and her conversation staggered between frazzled and curt. Yet she seemed earnest. Not once had she censured the twins for their improprieties; a few times, Baron had even caught her smiling at one of their comments. The twins were both quite witty when they wanted to be. It was a shame that wit displayed itself most in argument.

"I always like it here." Princess Aria offered a faint smile. "Cook finds a place for anyone. It's like a big family."

"You come here often?" Baron raised his eyebrows.

"I know. How very un-princessly of me."

Her smile vanished. Despite his best efforts to be polite and courteous, he seemed to have a negative effect on her. The same was true with most people—the curse of being a Caster.

"It smells nice," Baron managed, then wished he hadn't spoken at all.

The princess gave a single laugh, just a small burst of air. "That too."

Foremost was the heavy smell of yeast and fresh bread, deep and warm. Behind that came a sweet tangle of smoke and spices. Movement bustled in every direction, servants calling out jovially, Cook barking orders. Leon had fallen right into the rhythm, soaking in every command with eagerness. Corvin carried more hesitation but the same wide-eyed wonder, and the tension had finally drained from his shoulders as if, for the first time since the king's declaration, the boy was not thinking about the Reeves title.

Unfortunately, Baron couldn't say the same for himself.

"Leon enjoys cooking?" The princess leaned her head back against the wall, eyelids drooping as if simply watching the frantic motion of the kitchen made her weary.

"Yes, he's an excellent chef. He spends most of his days in the kitchen at home while Corvin uses his time to train messenger falcons. They're both remarkably diligent in the things they enjoy."

"And you're remarkably proud of them." She smiled as she said it, glancing at him.

Baron stiffened, though the comment was friendly. Why did he take every interaction as an attack? He realized he'd raised an idle hand to his witch's mark, so he lowered it, interlacing his fingers across his lap.

While attending other events, the twins were either regarded with concern, ignored, or, at best, begrudgingly accepted. No one else bothered to learn their names. No one else smiled when they fought.

Baron surveyed the kitchen, though he was truly watching the girl in the corner of his eye.

"No one calls me Guillaume." He said it too abruptly, like an attack of his own.

If she heard it that way, she did not return the hostility. Rather, her voice seemed as soft as her eyelids. "Yes, I noticed even your brothers do not."

"Friends and family call me Baron. It's unorthodox, I'm aware. Especially now. But . . . you're welcome to use it if you like."

He was on a foolish streak. As if royalty would ever indulge what Lord Bennett repeatedly called a disgraceful nickname. At best, it was improper, and at worst, she would remark on some insult to the court, some degradation of titles, especially now that he no longer possessed one.

"If I do," she said, "does it make us friends?"

The words were like lightning down his spine. He sat more rigidly, but when he looked at her, he realized in the scarce moment after speaking, she'd nodded off. Her eyes had slipped closed, and her breathing had evened, though her fingers twitched restlessly in her lap.

Baron frowned.

The princess looked exhausted. Her black hair—while styled to perfection, pinned up and fastened with a net of tiny citrine gems—carried a dull, unhealthy look, and once she relaxed in sleep, there was an obvious sallowness to her cheeks. The skin beneath her eyes appeared puffy, and the few times she'd met his gaze, he'd noticed the red strain around her brown irises.

Baron had far too many problems of his own to wonder what might plague a princess. Nevertheless, as she continued twitching in her sleep, he found himself debating the most foolish action possible.

Given the day's events, one more madness seemed only natural.

"Corvin," Baron called out softly as the boy passed. When his brother looked up, Baron nodded to the bowl of water he carried. "Ladle some of that into a cup, would you?"

Corvin's eyebrows shot up into his dark fringe, but he nodded. A few moments later, he scrambled back with a wooden cup, careful not to tip it. The moment it passed into Baron's hands, he felt Cook's eyes on him, but she made no comment. Clearly she respected the princess's word as binding.

Even through the dense barrier of the cup, Baron felt the liquid humming within, the silent music that sang to whatever power rested inside him. With reverence, he gently traced his fingertip around the cup's smooth rim. The liquid briefly turned gold, glowing like captured sunlight. A few servants paused to watch, wide-eyed, but for once, the stares didn't bother Baron. Nothing could bother him in the moment he held magic, the moment when his lungs breathed deeper and his vision sharpened, opening within him a connection to all the unseen parts of the world at once.

Then it passed. The light in the cup faded, leaving behind not water, but an amber-tinted liquid, gently steaming.

Cook barked a command, and everything that had paused in the kitchen snapped back into action.

Baron felt the twins shooting him glances, asking silent questions. It wasn't too late to change his mind. He could make the liquid vanish entirely. Forget the whole notion.

Instead, he reached out and gave the princess the barest of nudges on the shoulder.

It had hardly been more than a feather's touch, but she sat upright at once, drawing in a deep, desperate breath. For an instant, her brown eyes shone with raw fear. Then she blinked, and it vanished, in the same way as Baron's magic.

"Forgive me." She cleared her throat. "The hour must be growing late, I . . . I should return to the ball."

"Of course." Baron extended the cup. "Something to ease your tiredness. If you'd like."

Princess Aria stared at the cup of tea. A hint of that raw fear flashed through her eyes again, replaced by hardness.

Baron noted the unsteadiness of his hand, and he tightened his hold. Since he wore the brand, it was no crime for him to do magic, but offering it to royalty was another thing. Perhaps she would take it as an insult, an attack. Perhaps—

Just as he began to withdraw his hand, she took the cup.

The entire kitchen, Baron included, held its breath.

After her first hesitant sip, her eyes widened, and she drained the entire cup.

Baron winced; the tea would have been hot. "I tried to make it invigorating." He could think of nothing better to say.

Slowly, she lowered the cup, pressing her fingers to her lips. Her brown eyes brightened with alertness, then with a sheen of tears. One drop slipped onto her cheek, and Baron's heart lurched. He reached for her face, stopping himself just in time. One gloved thumb barely grazed her skin.

"I'm terribly sorry, Your Highness. I didn't mean . . . to . . ."

She laughed with a bright, delighted sound that somehow gave Baron no choice but to smile along. Ducking her head, she wiped her eyes. "I'm not sad. Quite the opposite."

Cook called out to ask if she was all right, and the princess waved off the concern. Kitchen activity resumed once more, allowing Baron to breathe.

"I've never moved someone to tears with a cup of tea," he admitted.

Of course, he offered magic only to his family and Silas. Being the sole Caster born into nobility, he was privileged to have that option. Those born to average families, like Edith, had to make a living for themselves, and when regular professions wouldn't accept them, they sold what magic could offer, though it required enduring though it required enduring scorn and suspicion.

Princess Aria stared down into her empty cup with enough mourning that Baron almost offered her another. She said, "It was like . . . flowers in bloom under light rain. How is that possible? Even my *soul* seemed to taste it."

Heat crept through Baron's neck. When was the last time someone had spoken positively of his magic?

All at once, the princess leaned closer, reaching her free hand to grasp his. "Thank you, Baron."

The heat increased. He barely managed a nod, distracted by the way his fingers tingled even inside his glove.

"Highness!" A young maid with black hair burst through the door. She was perhaps the age of the twins. "Terribly sorry, Your Highness, but His Majesty searches for you."

Princess Aria's fingers tightened on the cup as she rose. After a brief exchange with the servant girl, she grew tense, and Baron found himself strangely regretful at the clear ending to the evening. By the time she made a quick curtsy and hurried off—though not without giving personal goodbyes to the twins—he felt he'd given away something very terrible indeed. Something more than magic.

Something personal.

CHAPTER

11

Aria rushed back to her father's side, still reeling from the events in the kitchen. Her steps felt light; her thoughts raced with clearness through a fogless mind. The moment she'd sipped Baron's tea, it had washed away every ounce of exhaustion and left her feeling like *Aria* again. She couldn't believe it.

Had he known she was cursed? Was it something another Caster could see or feel? Had breaking her curse been his thanks for something as simple as showing his brothers a *kitchen*?

Aria felt as if her history professor had handed her a new textbook on a time period she'd never studied, full of unknown writings waiting to inspire her with truth. There was more to magic than she'd ever dreamed. The people of her kingdom coexisted with it and knew *nothing* of its processes. *She'd* known nothing. Not for eighteen years.

"Ah, there you are." The king nodded as she reached him beside the refreshments table. He gestured to the woman beside him. "Duchess Newburn has a son who would like to present himself as a possible suitor. I told her this matter has your utmost attention."

"It does," Aria said, her voice strong, "and I would be delighted to consider your son, Your Grace. If you'll direct him to me, we can share a dance before the evening is out and spend some time evaluating if we might be compatible partners."

She didn't have to drag the words one by one into sense; they flowed almost without effort. Had conversation been this easy before the curse?

As the duchess curtsied and excused herself to find her son, Aria's father raised an eyebrow.

"Well handled," he remarked. "Though I cannot excuse this event's hostess disappearing for the past hour."

"It was for a good purpose. I was with a member of court, and I found him most . . . enlightening."

The king raised his eyebrows, taking a sip of wine. "*Enlightening*. Is that what they're calling trysts these days?"

Aria gasped, fighting her blush. "*Father*. It was *not* like that."

"If he's your decided-upon courtship, I won't complain."

For a moment, she thought of Baron's vibrant green eyes, the tawny shades to his hair, which gave its thick waves a captivating depth. She thought of the way he'd looked at her when she'd touched his hand. Vulnerable, perhaps, though she couldn't imagine why— not when he held a power that made others uncomfortable with its very existence.

"Who was it, then?" her father asked. "Lord Alexander? Lord Christopher? I noticed you two seemed to connect when the evening began."

"No one of consequence," she said, then hated herself for the words.

Ingratitude. Mark.

If Baron Reeves had freed her from a curse, she should be rushing to reward him. Instead, she found herself slightly wary, the way she'd felt a moment before drinking his tea. She'd decided to take that risk because her overwhelming exhaustion meant she could not turn away even the *possibility* of assistance, and she was gambling he wouldn't offer poison in clear view of a room full of people.

Surely the results spoke for themselves, didn't they?

"Father, I . . ." Aria hesitated, then set her shoulders. "I was c—"

Her jaw clamped shut. She couldn't speak.

Which meant the curse was still in effect. The blow of that nearly staggered her.

"Yes?" said her father.

Not now, Aria. Indulge in self-pity later if you must, but not now. After weeks struggling through fog, she couldn't waste a moment of clear thinking. Whether by accident or intention, Baron had given her a reprieve. She would seize it.

"I was curious," she said, "about the state of affairs regarding Northglen."

Her father nodded. "You wish to rejoin Upper Court meetings. This evening doesn't entirely fill me with confidence, though you *are* taking the suitor business seriously."

"I hoped we might discuss a few things now, just the two of us."

With his wine glass, he gestured at the packed room. "Just the two of us?"

Aria grimaced. As if invited by her careless comment, a group of court members approached her father. Not a moment later, Aria was pulled away by a well-intentioned Eliza, and she couldn't deny her sister.

One hour, she promised. One hour to give Eliza the celebration she deserved, and then Aria could slip away to a washroom—not to sleep, but to plan. With a clear mind, she would lay out her battle tactics for the next eighty days of siege.

And she would figure out where Baron fit into those tactics.

Aria danced like she'd never danced before—without an ounce of exhaustion, with anyone available and willing, with joy in every step. She held conversations with a dozen potential suitors, and she made at least half of them laugh, though she couldn't remember a word they said. If her mind went anywhere, it went to a single cup of tea in a kitchen, pondering furiously at the motives driving the man who'd made it.

For the third time, she searched Eliza out of the crowd, pulling her sister away from a gawky young boy who clearly breathed a sigh of relief at no longer needing to impress a princess. Her sister's irritation melted into a laugh as Aria linked arms with her and spun them both.

"Aria!" Eliza giggled, then hushed her voice. "*Aria.* You have been *wild* all evening."

"There are worse things than wildness." *Exhaustion, for one.* "Look there, Eliza, but subtly." Aria nodded toward the corner of the room, where a young man had been watching her sister for the better part of twenty minutes, smiling to himself whenever he heard the princess laugh.

Eliza, of course, was not subtle, blushing openly when their eyes met. She rippled her fingers in the young man's direction as if playing the notes of a scale on the harpsichord. Taking the invitation, he approached.

"I believe he is one of Earl Wycliff's sons," Aria said. "I can't be certain which one, though I've heard no poor reputations about any."

The younger girl leaned in, touching her forehead to Aria's.

"He's *gorgeous*," Eliza whispered fiercely. "True-love material for certain."

"I suggest you begin with single-dance material," Aria whispered back, "and worry about true love *after* a formal courtship."

But she grinned at her sister and stepped away, allowing the two to meet. Since her father had retired to his throne, she took a break from dancing to join him, bringing them each a pastry from the table.

"You're certainly enjoying yourself." The king smiled.

"I find myself with a great appreciation for life today."

Her hour was nearly up, but before leaving the joyful event, she had one last thread of curiosity to chase.

"Father, what do you remember of the late baron? Marcus Reeves."

The man hadn't been a member of the Upper Court, and it was clear her father had to think a moment before responding. "Marcus was well-mannered, though he showed a certain disdain for fashion norms. Questionable taste in his personal life, considering he married, first, a foreign woman of Caster bloodline and, second, a woman who later left him. But he managed his estate well. He never caused headaches in court. Not a scheming type, nor overly prideful. Noble, as I said."

Though her meeting with Baron had been brief, Aria thought he echoed some attributes of his father.

"I think perhaps we should reevaluate the Reeves title," she said. "I've given it thought, and while a Caster at court presents dangers, it presents opportunities as well. Casters occupy a minority in Loegria's citizenship, but they're still a presence. And one with no representation at court. Is it not better to understand *all* the peoples of our kingdom? If we'd had a voice for Casters available, perhaps Widow Morton would not have felt so isolated. Perhaps she might have even been reasoned with before things escalated."

To her surprise, her father nodded. "These are valid points, certainly."

Encouraged, she added, "Guillaume Reeves seems to conduct himself with grace, and he was raised by a man you've described as noble. If anyone deserves the chance, I'd posit he does."

Still nodding, her father said, "And when does Lord Guillaume present at court?"

Aria frowned. "He . . . he presented today."

"Correct. Past tense." Her father shook his head. "The time for deciding this matter is already gone, Aria, yet still you churn it in your mind. This is one of your weaknesses. A monarch cannot second-guess every decision, cannot waste time *reevaluating* when the path moves ever forward. Tell me—what is a mistake, by definition?"

It took Aria a moment to answer, since her ears still rang with that word: *weakness.*

"Something . . . wrong," she managed at last.

"What defines 'wrong'?"

"The law, I suppose."

"Would it have been wrong of me, then, to appoint Guillaume Reeves a seat at court? He himself called upon the law to justify it."

Aria hesitated, then shook her head.

"And would it have been wrong of me to strip the Reeves title and appoint it to another worthy family? There's no law against it. See, Aria. You are dissecting situations as if you will find a clear distinction between the *right* path and the *wrong* one, but ruling a country is not so simple. There will always be many paths. A few wrong. Many not wrong. Only one right."

Aria frowned at the seeming contradiction. "Only one? You said . . ."

"Right is the path adhered to. It is your consistency as a ruler that forges *right*. Consistency is the only foundation stable enough to carry a kingdom."

Not for the first time, Aria felt a debate with her father was like being dropped into a lake having never learned to swim. The sheer pressure of it overwhelmed her. His arguments seemed so *logical*, so *precise*. He spoke with confidence and a depth of experience Aria couldn't hope to match.

She nodded and told herself to accept what he said, because he said it with such authority. Meanwhile, a tiny piece of herself shifted in discomfort, squeaking with an almost inaudible voice that she didn't agree, though it could not put words to the disagreement. It was merely a feeling. A feeling about *wrong*. A feeling that remembered Baron standing strong before a king, then walking away untitled.

But the rest of her remembered his witch's mark and thought of Widow Morton. The rest of her did not know the right path either, but it knew the last time she'd tried to find it on her own, she'd climbed a frozen mountain and returned home cursed. *All* of her knew her father never would have fallen into such a fate.

The only right path she could worry about at the moment was the one that led out of the pit she'd dug for her family.

12

T*ruthfully, I'd hoped to ask you to dance.*

Of everything the princess had said, why did *that* keep echoing in his mind?

"My lord?"

Baron shook himself. "Sorry, Martin. Say again?"

"I said you should leave things to a carpenter. A servant, at the very least."

With a smile, Baron tightened the final screw. "I'm perfectly capable of fastening a hinge."

He finished his work, wiped his hands, and tested the door to the loose box. It swung freely and silently. If only the stable roof were such an easy fix. Luckily, the leak was over an empty stall, but it would still need to be repaired before the damage increased.

Martin gave an exasperated sigh. "It isn't about 'capable.' It's about what others think seeing a titled lord repairing his own fences and doors."

"How fortunate, then, that I am no titled lord."

The air turned frosty, and Baron forced himself to relax, if only to set Martin at ease.

"My lord," the man said after a moment, "you'll always be our baron."

Baron swallowed hard. "Thank you, Martin."

Shortly after the ball, he'd received word that a steward had been appointed, as promised, and would arrive within the week. He'd thought the worst outcome of his presentation would be losing the Reeves title. He'd never thought to imagine a nightmare where a member of the king's staff came to live at his estate.

For the next four years.

What chance did he have of keeping the twins undiscovered for *years* from a spy within his own household?

Corvin had grown so stressed, he'd begun scratching red trails across the backs of both wrists, a nervous habit he adopted whenever resisting his magic. Baron hadn't seen him transform once in the week since the ball, as if he were practicing for what he anticipated to be the rest of his life.

That morning, Baron had asked for the boy's help with the stables, hoping it might be a worthy distraction, which was why Corvin currently stood in the rafters above the newly repaired loose box.

"How does our roof look?" Baron called out.

Corvin strode along a beam, crouched slightly to avoid brushing his head on the ceiling. He never glanced at his feet, never faltered. "That storm really took its toll. I found another three leaks."

Baron grimaced. "Very well. Come down, if you please. At least until we've done the repairs. For all I know, the rafters have taken damage as well."

Corvin stepped off the beam, catching its edge with his fingers before swinging down to the divider between two stalls, then to the floor. Baron's gray stallion snorted, unimpressed, though Martin paled as he always did witnessing the boy's acrobatics. Corvin was in the air more than he was ever on the ground.

"Thank you for the help," said Baron. "Tell Mr. Shaw I'm sorry to have kept you."

Corvin rolled his shoulders like a bird settling its wings after flight. "We finished training Ash, so Mr. Shaw's delivering him to the earl. No work for the next two days."

The three of them exited the stables into fresh air that was crisp but not cold, the sun shining brightly overhead.

I'd hoped to ask you to dance.

Even the *sunlight* somehow reminded him of her.

"Has Mrs. Caldwell been by?" Baron asked.

"Yes, my lord. I was trying to tell you earlier. She delivered a hamlet report, as requested. My written transcription is on the desk in your study."

"Excellent. Thank you, Martin."

With a bow, Martin excused himself to confer with Walter about the orchard's progress.

A small hamlet bordered the western edge of the estate, and Baron's father had always cared for the people there like his own family. He'd balanced his books well, kept estate staff to a minimum, and performed as many tasks as he could do himself, all in the interest of devoting the reserved funds and resources to the support of others. Baron intended to keep the tradition alive, even if he had to strong-arm a palace steward into doing so until Corvin could assume the title.

As if he'd summoned bad luck by the very thought, a bird warbled somewhere on the estate grounds, and Corvin paled.

"Carriage approaching," the boy rasped.

That would be the steward. Baron took a deep breath and gripped his brother's shoulder.

"If you need to fly," he said, "do it now."

He'd already discussed additional precautions with the twins in private, though there wasn't much they could do that wasn't already being practiced. They only ever transformed in Baron's room, which he kept locked and forbidden to all staff, even Martin. No one was surprised to see a Caster keeping secrets or maintaining his own space.

The biggest danger remained, as always, in loss of control. If Baron grew too scared, frantic, or angry, his magic closed off to him. For Affiliates, the effect was inverted—a flood of emotion caused their magic to ignite, and they transformed. The twins had never suffered a full loss of control in public, but there had been many close calls through the years.

"I should be there with you," Corvin said, though his eyes had gone wide. "To greet him. It's my . . . my responsibility now."

"Can you do that without transforming?" Pointedly, Baron looked down at Corvin's arm, where the boy's nails had dug into the line of red scabs.

Without another word, Corvin took off running toward the manor.

Baron followed at a slower pace, and by the time he reached his room, a black crow sat on his windowsill, pacing with jagged energy. Baron gave his brother an encouraging smile, and the boy took flight at last.

Baron quickly washed his face and changed his shirt, and by the time the carriage pulled up to the house, he stood on the front step to greet it, gloved hands resting on his cane.

The man who descended from the carriage used his own cane for support more than fashion, stooping to the left. It must have been injury rather than age, because his dark hair bore only a touch of gray at the temples. He introduced himself as Auden Huxley.

"You must be William Reeves," he said, consulting a folded parchment in his hand. "Former lord of this estate?"

Baron kept his smile pleasant. "Guillaume Reeves, Mr. Huxley."

"Give us a tour then, William. I'll need to examine the condition of the manor house promptly." Mr. Huxley gestured to his manservant, who unloaded a trunk from the carriage.

Even having expected it, Baron found the blatant disregard irksome. But he'd dealt with irksome all his life.

Calmly, he said, "Mr. Huxley, we are going to be in one another's close company for a number of years. It's best we start things on a respectful foundation. I'd be happy to give you a tour of the house, but not until you address me properly. A simple 'my lord' will do. I am, after all, still a member of the Reeves household."

The man sized him up and read correctly whatever he saw. "Lead on, my lord."

With a nod, Baron opened his home to a court-appointed stranger.

— ❋ —

Acquainting Mr. Huxley with the house took the rest of the day. The man was alarmingly thorough, prodding at every portrait and cabinet, kneeling to examine floorboards, pausing to write a greater number of notes than Baron thought necessary. The house was old but in good repair.

In Baron's bedroom, the man even found the hidden compartment in the floor.

"What's this for?" he grunted, sweeping one hand through the hollow space, as if more suspicious to find it empty than filled with contraband.

"Whatever I wish to keep secret."

"Got no secrets?" The man huffed in disbelief.

"Not at the moment, it seems."

Baron tried not to think of the books that used to reside there—his one inheritance from his birth mother, destroyed by his stepmother.

At long last, the dinner bell rang. Mr. Huxley's trunk had been moved into a guest suite by his manservant, so he excused himself to ready for supper. Baron took the opportunity to duck into the kitchen. The boys had been briefly introduced to the steward, but he'd made it clear he expected more thorough introductions over dinner.

"Leon, you'll have to dine with us."

The blond boy angled his shoulder toward Baron, turning pointedly away as he bent over a pot of lentils.

Baron waited.

"He only needs birdbrain," Leon said at last.

"Well, your birdbrain twin needs you. Let's go. Apron off, vest on."

Leon hissed over his shoulder, showing pointed canines. He snapped his jaw closed, lips moving like he'd run his tongue over his teeth.

"It goes without saying"—Baron smirked to soften the words—"but don't hiss at dinner."

The boy grumbled, but he did it as himself, leaving Baron to search out Corvin and give him a few words of encouragement.

Then it was time for dinner.

Despite Baron's protest, Huxley insisted on taking the seat at the head of the table. The man gave a curt reminder that Baron was no longer head of the estate and holdings, and the sooner he accepted such facts, the better.

It wasn't that Baron had meant to claim the seat himself.

It was that no one had sat in it for months.

With both twins looking at him, Baron forced his expression to remain impassive as he took his seat, forcing back a rush of memories with his father. He could not afford distraction.

Amelia brought plates first, then drinks.

"No," said Huxley sharply as the maid moved to pour him wine. He covered his goblet with one hand. "I'll prepare and serve all my own drinks while I reside here. It's the only way to be safe."

Amelia glanced at Baron, and at his nod, she retreated, having already filled everyone else's cups.

Huxley cut into his roasted squash, chewing with vigor, as if the awkward atmosphere didn't bother him. Perhaps he thrived upon it.

Corvin shifted food around his plate, and even Leon seemed hard-pressed to find his appetite.

"Leon Reeves first, then." Huxley swallowed. "Tell me about yourself, boy."

"So you can criticize it all?" Leon snorted. "No thanks."

"I'd heard things about your dismal social manners. Seems it's all true."

"You're no peach either, Huxley."

Baron cleared his throat.

"Right," said Leon. "You're no peach either, *Mr.* Huxley. Better?"

It was going to be a long night.

"You enjoy common chores, it seems, including cooking. An activity far beneath the son of a lord."

"If it's so common, how come everyone can't do it? And you seem to be enjoying my squash just fine."

Mr. Huxley shifted focus to the other side of his plate, taking a spoonful of spiced lentils.

Leon smirked. "Made those too," the boy muttered.

"Corvin Reeves," Huxley said, speaking over Leon. "I hope you are more impressive than your twin."

Baron could see Corvin tempted toward sarcasm, but he generally had better control of his tongue than Leon, or at least more inclination to *try* controlling it. In the end, he listed a few hobbies—falconry, reading.

"Baron's teaching me dueling," he said.

"There's no need for that. We'll find a proper sword master to teach you."

Corvin frowned. "Baron's the best swordsman at court. He's won every melee he's ever participated in."

"I have never seen him compete."

"Well, not everyone invites him, but that's not—"

"A proper sword master, then. I'll find one at once. You'll also need to be proficient in jousting and other sports. Hunting, of course. Have you ever been pheasant hunting, future lord baron?"

Corvin's face paled. He almost dropped his knife.

"I don't kill birds," he choked out.

"You'll have to. A proper lord of court must be able to hunt with the king whenever His Majesty invites."

Baron said, "If Corvin has no interest in hunting for sport, he's free to abstain. Last I checked, there was no list of hobbies required to hold a title."

"You would know so very much," Huxley said scathingly, "having lost your title before you even held it."

Baron smiled. "And how many titles have you held, Mr. Huxley?"

Leon snickered into his squash.

Huxley fell quiet for a time, but he soon recovered and continued interrogating Corvin. The boy never ate, only fidgeting in his chair and answering a barrage of pointless questions. Baron called for dessert early and, after that, a swift end to dinner, but even so, it was a torturous hour. When Huxley retired at last, it was to everyone's relief.

The three Reeves boys collapsed in the sitting room, Baron in his favorite chair and the twins on the sofa.

"Well," he said, pulling his gloves free and tucking them in his pocket, "we survived the evening. Only a few thousand left to go."

"*Four years.*" Corvin groaned. Pulling one of the sofa pillows from its corner, he pressed his face to it and groaned louder. When Leon brought out a full tray of cucumber sandwiches he'd apparently stashed, the future lord baron inhaled three.

Around his own mouthful of sandwich, Leon said, "Baron, you should write Lady Her Highness and tell her to pick a better steward. Preferably one named 'Guillaume Reeves.'"

Baron smiled faintly. "I doubt Her Royal Highness concerns herself with decisions of this nature."

"It's her fault we got stuck with one at all, so she owes us."

Corvin tossed the pillow at him. Leon batted it away.

After swallowing, Corvin said, "Honestly, though, are you going to write her? Not about the steward. Just about . . . things."

Baron raised an eyebrow. "Why would I presume to do that?"

Never mind that his encounter with the princess kept sneaking back into his mind. She was a *princess*. Even aspiring to be a full member of court, Baron had never pretended he would be on close terms with the royal house itself. It would have been enough simply to be an influence for good. Now . . .

He bit into his own sandwich to avoid further thinking down that line.

The twins exchanged a look before Leon said, "Because she's the only person you've Cast for since Dad died."

Baron felt a shock. It hadn't been that long since he'd used his magic, had it? He soothed the boys when they were sick. He made calming drinks for himself.

Though perhaps not in recent memory.

"I should see to the hamlet report," he said at last. "With Huxley's arrival, it's been neglected."

Leon shrugged, darting his hand out faster than Corvin's to snatch the last sandwich. "Just thought you wanted a voice at court. It'll be years before the skinny chicken has his, but everyone sure listened when Lady Highness spoke. Even the king."

Corvin blinked like he'd not thought of that.

Baron shook his head. "You are far too conniving for your own good, Leon. The sandwiches were delicious."

"Of course they were. I made them."

"Good night, boys."

Baron ducked away and climbed the stairs to his study.

It didn't take long to lose himself in work. A few men of the hamlet needed supplementary income; Baron could hire them during the upcoming autumn harvest. One family had lost their plough horse to disease and lacked the funds to replace it—a more difficult

ELIZABETH LOWHAM

challenge to tackle. Baron could secure a new horse, but his father had always been careful in his assistance.

"The goal is to help," he'd said, "but to do so without creating a dependence."

Perhaps he could secure a discount for the family. He made a note to look into it.

As his quill scratched, his traitorous mind wondered what Princess Aria would think if he *did* send a letter. Would she be pleased to hear from him?

History did not incline him toward that option.

He rubbed his witch's mark and shook his head, forcing his attention back to the matters at home.

CHAPTER

13

72 DAYS LEFT

Aria split her life into days and nights. By night, she tested the limits of her curse. Could she sleep if she left the castle grounds? Could she speak of the curse at night? Could she recreate a tea with an effect like Baron's but using herbs instead of magic? The result of every test was disappointing.

Since Widow Morton had used Aria's blood for the curse, the princess had even tried an administration of leeches on her arm, hoping they might suck out whatever had been applied. Bloodletting was an outdated medical practice, rarely used by reasonable physicians, but she hoped perhaps Casters had discouraged the practice for their own secret purposes.

Like all the others, that experiment failed, leaving her with nothing but a sore arm and three fat, happy leeches.

Still, she persisted. Somewhere, new information would lead her to an answer, a weakness in the curse that would allow her to crack it open.

By day, she made certain not to repeat her worst mistake and obeyed her father with exactness.

Which meant she chose a suitor.

"He's perfect for you!" Eliza squealed.

Aria smiled, a more subdued response. As her sister skipped around the room, she held still, allowing Jenny, her lady's maid, to dress her in a fashionable but impractical gown with buttons Aria couldn't reach.

"Eliza," Aria said, "you've not even met Lord Kendall."

"No, but Ryelle Mormont claims he possesses the *dreamiest* eyes. 'When he holds a maiden's gaze,' she says, 'he captures their very soul.'"

"A man with a jar of souls beneath his bed. Every girl's dream."

Silently, Aria willed Jenny to hurry. As if sensing it, the maid finished buttoning Aria's bodice in record time and reached in to fasten her necklace. As she did so, their gazes met, and the younger girl paused, frowning.

"You look tired, Your Highness," she whispered.

When Jenny had first come to the castle—almost a year earlier—as a starving, barefoot girl of twelve, she'd refused to speak beyond single-word answers. Now she could be prompted into conversation, usually by Eliza, and though still thin, Jenny at least filled out her maid's shirt and trousers. She remained formal at all times and performed her duties diligently.

Aria found it easy to befriend any member of the castle's staff. So why did her voice sometimes die in her throat when addressing Jenny?

She knew the truth.

A truth her father forbade her to speak of.

Even Eliza did not know—because Eliza, along with the queen, had been on a visit to Patriamere when Jenny had first arrived at the castle, when the starving girl had looked into the eyes of a king and pled for mercy from a man she called "*Father*."

Jenny was more than a maid. She was Aria's half sister.

"I'm fine," Aria whispered back.

Lying. Mark. A chill touched her skin, and she clenched her jaw to keep it from chattering until the invisible frost retreated.

"Back me up, Jenny," said Eliza.

Clearly she'd made some argument about true love that Aria

had missed. Rather than repeating it, Jenny simply murmured that it wasn't her place, to which Eliza gave a good-natured harrumph. Then she ducked into her adjoining room, returning with a bundle of fabric weighing down her arms.

Technically, Aria didn't require a chaperone to meet with a suitor—it was an outdated requirement, as were arranged marriages or year-long engagements—but she was counting on Eliza to carry most of the conversation because her own attention would be focused solely on lasting *at least* half an hour without sleeping in front of her new suitor.

After completing the final touches on Aria's ensemble, Jenny transitioned to readying Eliza, and Aria sat at her writing desk, her mind wandering where it always did these days.

To a certain green-eyed former baron.

Guillaume Reeves had made no attempt to contact her since their single encounter at Eliza's ball. That night, she'd spent her waking hours prowling the empty halls, dreading the moment when a trap would be sprung on her just as it had been the night she'd returned from Morton Manor.

But nothing happened. Baron's single cup of miracle tea truly seemed to come with no strings attached: no surprise curse, no attempt at blackmail, no ill side effects—at least none beyond the unfortunate fact that it did not last forever.

What was she to make of that?

"Aria?"

Aria shot to her feet, banging her hip painfully into the corner of her desk. She pressed one hand to it, grimacing. Eliza and Jenny both stared.

"Daydreaming about my dreamy-eyed suitor. Are you ready at last, Eliza? It won't do to keep Lord Kendall waiting."

"Yes, yes, I'm ready. Although, the periwinkle dress may have—"

Aria strode toward the door, and Eliza scrambled to catch up.

Together, the two of them went to meet the man Aria was determined to court.

Lord Kendall waited in the music room. He had presented himself to the king that morning, so Aria's father was nowhere to be seen, although her mother sat at the harp and urged them to "pay her no mind." As if a queen could be so easily ignored.

Queen Marian practically lived in the music room; the only thing missing was her wardrobe. She'd already had the servants bring her a couch for relaxing and a writing desk for composing. There was even a small table to use when taking her meals. She didn't go about in her dressing gown, thankfully, but she wore a casual set of trousers beneath a ruffled shirt without even a vest over the top.

Lord Kendall stole enough furrowed-brow glances at Her Majesty to make his discomfort at the situation clear.

One of the attendant guards made the formal announcement: Kendall Crampton, second son of Duke Robert Crampton, with hope to court Her Royal Highness, Crown Princess Aria de Loegria, daughter of His Royal Majesty . . .

The long introduction gave Aria the opportunity to study her chosen suitor. She'd surely crossed paths with him at court functions before; there was a familiarity to his lanky build and awkward elbows, which extended like the wings of a flustered chicken.

Unflattering comparisons. Mark.

"Your Royal Highness!" Despite his chicken elbows, Lord Kendall swept an elegant bow, turning to offer the same gesture to Eliza, which she answered with an equally elegant curtsy.

Aria—her legs aching and her fatigue bordering on comatose—gave a dip well beneath the dignity of any crown princess.

She saw her mother frown from the corner.

Eliza spoke at once, gushing about how wonderful it was to host

Lord Kendall and how he would not be disappointed by Aria. Aria gave an inward wince at the implications there, but at least Eliza dominated the conversation as she'd hoped. It was a good five minutes before Kendall snuck in a word to Aria.

"Might I serenade you, Your Highness?" he gestured to the nearby harpsichord. "My musicality is quite boasted of across our estate."

"*Ooh.*" Eliza beamed. "A *musician.* It's said only the tenderest of hearts can speak music."

Said only by their mother, who smiled as Eliza spoke.

The queen offered to accompany Lord Kendall, which set the room in motion as servants arranged chairs and instruments so the queen and lord could take their respective places.

Aria couldn't think of an appropriate protest.

I don't wish to hear you play. That would be beyond rude.

I would prefer an activity in the fresh air. Selfish.

I am under a curse and would trade this entire castle for a single night's sleep.

Well, she could not say *that.*

Finally, Aria took her place as an audience member beside an enthusiastic Eliza, who leaned close to bump their arms together.

"How do you find his eyes?" Aria whispered.

Eliza closed her own eyes, fanning herself with one hand.

Perhaps in addition to stealing her sleep, Aria's curse had also rendered her blind to dreaminess. In her estimation, Kendall's eyes seemed an ordinary hazel, not unflattering, but simply . . . murky.

In comparison, Aria's mind offered her a memory of striking green eyes. Tawny hair. An extended cup of tea, and a hesitant, gentle voice. *Something to ease your tiredness.*

Had he known of her curse or was he only observant? Was it all somehow a trap?

Or was it simply . . . kindness from a Caster?

Lord Kendall's performance began, a soothing, syrupy melody that could only be meant for hushing colicky babies. The queen's harp crooned along in alluring harmony, never a sour note to jar the performance.

Aria stood no chance.

Eliza poked her in the side, and Aria woke, sitting rigid as sweat broke out across her skin.

"What is wrong with you?" her sister demanded in a whisper. At least the performers didn't seem to have noticed.

"It's a *lullaby*," Aria protested weakly.

"Do you also drop into slumber in the mere presence of a pillow?"

Heat spread not only through Aria's cheeks but through her ears and neck, hardly the demure blush of a princess. How long before everyone thought her incompetent, unable to perform the simplest of duties? How long before she truly *would* be unable to perform the simplest of duties? She'd chosen a suitor, but if she returned to Upper Court meetings only to sleep through them . . .

Kendall smiled as he continued to play his never-ending lullaby, gently caressing the harpsichord keys with long, thin fingers. Aria had the very unkind thought to break them off one by one, for which she gave herself *two* marks.

She swirled her ankles, hidden beneath the length of her gown. She dug her thumbnail into her opposite palm with such force she felt the bone beneath. She imagined a full retinue of tiny sailors perched on her head, harpooning her eyelids and dragging back with all their might to hold them open, shouting encouragements to the entire crew. *Come on, lads, just a little longer! Hold!*

Kendall finished with a lingering three-note rise, and before the final note faded, Aria lurched to her feet, applauding with force not because he deserved it but because *she* did.

He grinned, clearly pleased with her reaction. "Your Highness, I'm fla—"

"A marvelous gift!" she declared over the top of him. "Simply stunning. Lord Kendall, I cannot wait to see your further talents in action. Let us make our courtship official."

His chicken elbows flapped around in shock, and she took that as agreement.

"Wonderful! You can discuss it with my mother." How kind of the queen to be so helpfully available. "I am overwhelmed by the performance. I shall return."

She fled the room, not caring how it might look. It would look worse to simply collapse across the floor.

Which was exactly what she did upon reaching the washroom. The instant she bolted the door, Aria slumped to the ground. The fur rug beneath her seemed to be the softest bed invented.

Failure. Mark.

It was not precisely a mistake, more a state of being, one she had been unable to escape for nearly a month. What would her father have said, witnessing the heir to his kingdom abandoning her duty and succumbing to such a little obstacle as *fatigue*?

Through his political union with Queen Marian, her father had secured resources from Patriamere and revitalized all of Loegria after famine. By contrast, after finding decisions too difficult, Aria had chosen an eligible name at random and landed herself with Lord Kendall.

While she had always tried so hard to mirror her father's effectiveness, she found herself instead modeling her mother's laxness. In the same way her mother chased music with single-minded devotion, even to the point of ignoring her family, Aria now abandoned everything in pursuit of rest.

Perhaps it was better she not take the throne; she would only fall asleep on it.

Somewhere near the half hour mark, Aria's senses betrayed her, screaming danger where there was none, shoving her to her feet and leaving her disoriented. When she exited the washroom, she plowed right into Jenny.

"Oh!" the smaller girl squeaked. Recovering, she hurriedly gave a formal bow. "Your Highness, I'll be off now. With permission."

Aria had angled herself away in embarrassment. "Of course. You . . ." She hesitated. Struggling to focus, she took in Jenny's clothes—not her usual maid's uniform. Sturdier. For travel. "You're going somewhere?"

"We discussed . . ." Jenny's voice faded, as did some of the color in her face.

"It's not a problem." Aria tried for a reassuring smile, though it was surely half grimace. She willed her senses to function. "I've simply been busy. Tell me again?"

"Harper's Glade. My mother . . ."

Her mother's grave. It was the anniversary, wasn't it?

At once, Aria felt like a heel. "Oh, Jenny. I'm sorry. I meant to arrange a carriage for you. And travel supplies. Do you have money for an inn? I can provide an advance payment on your wages—"

She was rambling, but the corner of Jenny's lips twitched upward, and that was an encouraging response.

"It's only past Stonewall," was all the girl said. She bowed again. "Your Highness."

"Wait." Aria's mind raced for a different reason. "Stonewall, that's . . . near the Reeves estate, isn't it?"

Jenny blinked. The girl couldn't be expected to know where every lord and lady in the kingdom held their estate. But Aria knew. If only her foggy mind would tell her what it expected her to do with that knowledge.

"Jenny, would you . . ." Aria swallowed, considered, then dedicated herself. "Would you be open to a traveling companion?"

CHAPTER

14

After several days of cataloguing the manor house and surrounding buildings in excruciating detail, Huxley finally moved his attention to the grounds, specifically the orchard, once again demanding Baron accompany him. The official reason he cited was that, as former heir, Baron had crucial information about the estate.

They both knew the real reason: Huxley feared letting Baron out of his sight. A Caster might get up to any number of devious misdeeds if left unwatched.

Baron didn't care. As long as Huxley's attention was on him, it was not on Corvin.

"What's this?" Standing in the orchard shed, Huxley used his cane to poke at a few stacked bags in the corner.

"Fertilizer, sir!" said Walter. The head groundskeeper had answered every question like a soldier suddenly called to war. Every so often, when Huxley wasn't watching, Walter dabbed at his face with a handkerchief, scowling at the steward's back.

Huxley squinted at Baron. "Already had fertilizer over there. This kind's different. What's the business of having two?"

Nefarious Caster matters, thought Baron. *What else?*

He cleared his throat. With every added day of Huxley's presence, he found his natural responses needing to be restrained more and more.

"This new blend should better insulate the soil, since we've had a few dangerous cold spells in recent winters. The details are all in my orchard report, Mr. Huxley."

With a grunt, the man poked his cane into the bags a few more times, then handed it off to his manservant, who, in turn, placed a stool on the ground. Huxley sat and took notes, his favorite pastime. Surely he must have filled an entire journal on the Reeves estate already, and Baron couldn't help imagining most of the lines contained variations of *What is that Caster up to?*

The door to the shed banged open, startling them all. Huxley nearly toppled off his stool.

"Baron!" Corvin stood in the doorway, pointing behind himself. "There's a royal carriage coming!"

Baron glanced at Huxley, but the man seemed equally surprised by the news. While the steward struggled to gather his things, Baron hurried to the door, catching a moment's privacy with Corvin.

"See anything else?" he whispered.

Corvin's dark eyes shone with excitement, and he grinned. "Sure did—it's *her.*"

It was not excitement that gripped Baron, but fear. The crown princess turning up unexpectedly at his estate could not be for any good reason, considering the state of the kingdom and the history of his luck. All the same, he kept his expression neutral.

Huxley caught up to them and grabbed Corvin by the shoulder, turning him one way, then the other. The boy tensed.

"I'd hoped to get you a proper suit before you had to greet anyone of import." The steward gave a pitiful moan, then shook his head. "Stand up straight, boy. Half the title is bearing."

"Wait, I'm—*I'm* greeting?" Corvin looked at Baron.

"Of course!" Huxley snapped. "You're the future lord baron. Now hold yourself like it. Haven't you got a pair of gloves at least?"

Corvin looked down at his bare hands.

"Hopeless," Huxley murmured. With a firm push, he directed

Corvin down the path, dismissing Walter before following close behind. When Baron moved to walk beside his brother, Huxley's cane rapped against his shinbone, and the steward nodded up the path toward the manor house.

"Considering your last experience at court, my lord, surely you'd be more comfortable waiting inside. At least until we know the purpose of this unexpected visit."

Baron gave a thin smile. "Thank you for your concern, Mr. Huxley, but I feel no need to hide."

Thankfully, the steward didn't press the matter. As they reached the gravel drive, the estate gates opened to admit a sleek black carriage trimmed in red accents, with the royal crest wrought in painted metal on either door. The carriage driver and footman sat tall in the red-and-white livery of the palace. Slowly, the carriage crunched its way up the drive.

"I thought it would have arrived already." Mr. Huxley frowned. "How did you know it was even coming?"

Corvin blanched. "I saw it from—I was on the—sitting on the roof."

"*Again.*" The steward scowled. "We'll discuss your improper climbing behaviors later. For now, remember to bow with both hands on your stomach, and use the most formal address possible for whoever this messenger is."

The carriage pulled to a halt. Mr. Huxley positioned Corvin next to himself—both of them a step in front of Baron and Huxley's manservant.

Baron adjusted his gloves once, then forced himself to be still, waiting as the footman leapt forward to open the door.

The girl who stepped out of the carriage was not Princess Aria, but rather the dark-haired servant who'd come to fetch the princess from the kitchen. Corvin didn't seem to realize that, because he gave a proper, formal bow, squeaking out, "Welcome, Your Royal Highness."

Huxley drained of color and possibly life itself.

Baron swallowed a laugh.

The servant girl blinked, glancing down at her plain brown attire and touching her hair, which was bound in two simple braids and tied with a handkerchief. Apparently not knowing how else to respond, she gave a deep curtsy.

Once she'd stepped out of the way, the footman handed down the true crown princess, and Corvin straightened just in time to give a little squawk.

Princess Aria smiled brightly as if the boy's response was perfectly normal. "Thank you, future lord baron. It's a warm welcome indeed."

Had she been this lovely the night of the ball? Perhaps it was a trick of the autumn sunlight, gleaming down on her unfastened black hair, imbuing it with a rich glow beneath her tiara. Perhaps it was her travelling attire—a dark blue shirt and pale green vest, the combination more vibrant than her ball gown. Perhaps it was simply her smile, which found Baron and, for some unfathomable reason, lingered, her dark brown eyes touched with a slight ring of gold in the light.

"Lord Guillaume," she said, "you look well."

"As do you, Highness. Welcome to the Reeves estate."

The steward stepped forward—leaning heavily on his cane—and swept a deep bow, free hand pressed to his stomach. "Your Royal Highness, I am Auden Huxley, steward of this estate. We are honored beyond measure by your presence, though I must say the visit is unexpected."

"I apologize for the abruptness, steward, and I don't intend to put you out. Truthfully, we're only passing through on our way farther south."

Somehow Huxley's bobbing nod conveyed both relief *and* disappointment.

"Since we were in the area," the princess continued, "I only wondered if I might have a few moments of Lord Guillaume's time."

Both Huxley and his manservant turned stunned expressions on Baron. Corvin looked smug. Baron felt a strange thrill dart up his spine, pulling his shoulder blades back, leaving him standing tall.

Until she said—

"I could use the opinion of a Caster on an important matter."

Not *him*. Simply the brand.

Baron resisted the urge to touch his witch's mark.

Huxley frowned in disapproval, as if he thought royalty would be sullied by mere association with magic.

"Of course, Your Highness." Baron bowed stiffly. "Whatever you need."

"Excellent. Then let's find a private place to speak. This won't take long."

—❄—

Since he was going to be uncomfortable no matter where they went, Baron took Princess Aria to the lemon orchard, where at least the scent of citrus in the air might brighten his damp mood.

She looked up at the trees in wonder, reaching to gently brush a ripening lemon with her fingertips.

"You manage *all this*?" The princess craned her neck, peering at the long row of trees that stretched ahead of them.

"It's a moderate size only," he said.

"It's breathtaking!"

Despite himself, Baron's lips twitched. As a keeper of lemons, he really ought to be better at remaining sour.

"You needed a Caster," he prodded.

"Right. Of course." She shook her head, then reached into her side satchel and withdrew a leatherbound journal. "I have notes here from my personal study on Casting. I wondered if you might read through them and correct the errors."

He blinked. Somehow, she managed to dodge every expectation. Out of curiosity more than anything, Baron accepted the journal, scanning the open pages.

They were a mess.

The princess had a loopy penmanship style, one that did not remain terribly consistent across the page, the loops shrinking on some notes and expanding on others. Hasty black boxes isolated some sections while curving arrows highlighted others. Curiously, her neatest marks were those crossing out words or lines—just a single, straight line through. Thin. As if she simultaneously wanted the information removed but also needed to clearly see what the mistake had been.

Baron tried to piece the scattered fragments.

> Magic inherited. Strict bloodline, either Fluid or Stone. Skips generations.
> Must choose to be Caster? Dugal writes, "The Caster is activated of effort." Dugal is confusing.
> Ability can appear as early as twelve years old.
> Physical pain causes magic response, therefore the Casting test. Casting also causes physical pain? Dugal writes, "Like the man lifting a weight too great collapses, so, too, the Cast too great collapses Caster." Really need to find a better source than Dugal.
> Casting is permanent once made. No exceptions??

She had sections on the page for both Fluid and Stone Casters specifically, with arrows drawn to group information to its respective category.

Baron's curiosity naturally led him to his own Casting type first, where she'd noted, incorrectly, that Fluid Casters needed direct contact with liquid, that they could change physical attributes—flavor, composition—and also change the effect of a liquid for someone drinking it. Along the margin, she'd written *tea cures tired*, her lines particularly loopy across each word.

Most interestingly, she'd crossed out a single line related to Fluid Casters:

~~Safe if you don't drink.~~

And beneath it, she'd written a very small word in rigid letters without loops.

Blood.

"Well?" the princess asked.

Baron looked up, realizing she'd stepped right next to him, looking down over his arm at her own journal. Her cheeks burned slightly pink.

"These are quite . . . extensive." Baron hesitated, then handed the journal back to her. "If I may, Highness, why the interest?"

Surely it concerned the matter in Northglen. Princess Aria was the royal heir, after all. No doubt she intended to gain an edge over Widow Morton, to find some weakness in Casters that could be exploited against Morton's growing faction.

The princess opened her mouth, then clamped it shut again. She grimaced, as if finding the topic painful. Up close, Baron could see the same evidences of strain he'd seen the night of the ball—the redness in her eyes, the way her clothing hung slightly loose, as if she'd lost weight since it had been tailored. Something clearly troubled her deeply. She even swayed on her feet.

With a glance and a moment of decision, Baron guided her onto his father's stone bench. He sat gingerly beside her, breathing through the memories.

Aria breathed deeply as well, as if sorting her own internal pain. Her eyes slipped closed.

"It's warm here," she whispered. Opening her eyes, she sighed.

"I'm not sure I could explain anything to satisfaction. I only thought . . . The night of Eliza's ball, you seemed to want to help me, and if I may be honest for a moment, I desperately need help."

Her brown eyes carried the red touch of exhaustion but also that lighter golden ring, as if danger and hope clashed in the same arena.

Baron nodded slowly. "This has to do with Northglen, doesn't it?"

"It does."

"Then a question of my own. This all began with the execution of Charles Morton, but I've heard multiple accounts of what happened. If you could correct my knowledge of that event, I may, in turn, correct the errors in your notes."

The princess studied him for a moment, then spoke.

"My mother was hosting a series of musical events, so we had several families of court staying at the castle. One evening, Father was in private council with his advisers when he discovered Charles Morton concealed in the room. Spying. Because the discussion had been of sensitive matters of State, Father enforced the law against espionage himself, rather than awaiting a trial. If he'd waited, the information Morton had overheard could have been spread any time between arrest and sentencing."

It matched at least one version of events Baron had been given. There were members of court who speculated the late Earl Morton had been tangled in treason, and that after his death, his son was the final loose end to be tied. Others thought the king must be hiding something.

Casters whispered something different. They wondered if a prejudice against magic had influenced Charlie's death, if the son of a Caster suffered for something his mother had done.

"How could His Majesty be certain it was a malicious act rather than a mistake?" Baron asked. "This was the son of an *earl*. Was there no consideration for his family, not even for a proper goodbye?"

Aria winced, and so Baron softened his voice.

"He was fifteen," he said quietly. Though he spoke of Charlie, a youth he'd only met briefly, his mind was on two boys just up the hill from the orchard.

"My father would not have done it if it wasn't necessary."

"You're implying the king is infallible?"

"I'm *implying* he doesn't execute his friends' children for *enjoyment*. Jonathan Morton was the man my father invited to hunts most frequently, the member of Upper Court he sought out for counsel more than any other. Even though they weren't family, my father wore black after the earl's death." She looked away. "I have no doubt finding Charles as a spy was the worst day of my father's life. His eyes grow haunted whenever the topic arises."

As silence fell between them, the princess rubbed her eyes, clearly struggling to keep them open.

"I must leave," she said quietly. "Jenny has important business in Harper's Glade, and I wouldn't keep her from it."

"Wait." Baron held his hand out for the journal. "I'll write on a fresh page, if you don't mind."

CHAPTER

15

Long after midnight, Aria reviewed Baron's notes. Though her trip with Jenny could have been done in a day, she'd arranged to split it over two as part of her experiment to discover the limits of her curse. They'd paid for a night at the Stonewall inn, and Jenny slept soundly in a narrow bed along the far wall while Aria paced beside a small table, her journal tilted to catch the lamplight.

Unlike her own chaotic handwriting, Baron's flowed smoothly across the page, neat and orderly.

> *Magic is inherited through bloodline, but the inheritance is not strict. Stone and Fluid may arise in the same family. Casting is a dormant ability at first, and must be awoken by effort on the Caster's part.*
>
> *Age plays no part in activation. Though testing begins at twelve years old, I received my witch's mark at six.*

Of all his corrections, that haunted her most. She pressed one hand to her mouth as she paced, her eyes fixed on that number. *Six.* Her soul ached to think of a small child awaiting the blistering touch of heated iron.

As soon as she returned to the palace, she would review her great-grandmother's branding law. If it forbade early branding, as she imagined it must, she would hunt down the officials who'd registered Baron and see discipline administered. After that, she would speak to her father, and . . .

And what? Persuade him to change the law?

She heard his voice in memory, giving the answer already: *A monarch cannot waste time reevaluating when the path moves ever forward.*

Aria clenched her jaw. She lowered her journal, staring around at a room silent beyond Jenny's breathing. The nervous energy inside pulsed, urging her to pace again, to move, to dance, to accomplish great things! All she wanted was a moment of peace to think.

Unable to focus, she tossed her journal on the bed and proceeded with the second task of the night—testing her curse.

Tonight's experiment was easy; no leeches required. Aria crossed the room and shook Jenny. The girl continued to sleep as Aria expected.

She ducked out of the room and knocked sharply on the next door over, where her footman, driver, and two guards slept. The guards and the driver had been in her family's service for years, but the footman was new, hired *after* Aria visited Widow Morton.

Aria knocked again, with more insistence.

After another moment, the door swung open, and a bleary-eyed footman peeked out at her, his shirt haphazardly buttoned, one section of hair sticking out above his ear. He gave a hasty bow.

"Highness?" he croaked. "What's wrong? I'll wake the—"

"Shh." Aria pressed a finger to her lips. Inside, she bounced with the joy of discovery, and she strained to hold back her smile. "I don't need the guards. It's no pressing matter. I seem to have misplaced my journal. Do you remember seeing it in the carriage?"

"No, I—I'll go search at once—"

"Never mind. It can wait until morning. Forgive me, I have lost track of the lateness of the hour."

The poor man didn't scowl at her as she deserved but merely nodded in confusion, gave another bow, and returned to bed.

After the door closed, Aria rubbed her hands quickly with all the nervous energy inside. This was something new! By leaving the castle at night to enter Sutton town and other areas, she'd already discovered the sleeping Cast did not follow her like a storm cloud, dropping anyone within its radius. It remained over the castle, even if she was not present.

But that was not quite accurate. The Cast captured people *of* the castle, no matter where they were. Jenny, the guards, the driver—they all slept, even hours from the palace.

But the newly hired footman could be woken.

Aria jogged down the stairs of the slumbering inn. She stepped out onto a deserted street, looking up at a canopy of stars. Even in the middle of the night, the autumn air barely held a chill, and it wrapped her in a calming cool.

Until a deeper chill emerged from within.

If the sleeping Cast was not a storm cloud hovering above Aria but rather an individual thing, did that mean Widow Morton had somehow cursed each member of the castle staff individually? *How?*

Spinning, Aria raced back up the stairs and into her room, the door banging against the wall with a loud thud that did nothing to wake Jenny. She snatched her journal and reread Baron's notes.

He had very little to say about Stone Casters—presumably because he himself was Fluid—but his few sentences stood out.

Aria's initial note had read, *Stone Casters control stone. Straightforward.*

Baron had clarified, *Stone Casters can affect both surroundings and people as readily as Fluid Casters can. However, the influence of Stone Casters on others manifests in physical restraint or limitation, such as holding someone in place or putting them to sleep.*

Widow Morton's curse grew more tangled the more Aria learned of magic. Did the sleeping effect mean the widow was secretly a Stone Caster? Why claim to be a different Caster type?

Aria remembered how Widow Morton had displayed her powers

with tea, changing the temperature, vanishing the liquid. A Fluid Caster, then. What of the rest? Was it possible to be *both* Stone and Fluid Caster?

She could not hope to unravel this on her own.

She looked down at Baron's neat, orderly writing. She'd asked for help, and he'd given it. She'd even tasted his magic and not regretted it.

To overcome one Caster, it seemed clear she needed another.

But despite the determination surging in her chest, the chill returned. She thought of another moment when she'd written to a Caster. She remembered a peace agreement in her hands turning to liquid and dripping right off the page.

No matter how noble one might seem, a Caster couldn't be trusted. Aria couldn't afford to repeat the same mistake. Not when she was still paying the cost from the first time.

She closed her journal once more.

The morning after her return home, Aria's father summoned her to the throne room. With nothing but lessons to occupy her for the day, Aria wore trousers and a vest, enjoying the freedom of a day without formal attire. She had enough dragging her toward sleep without the added weight of trailing skirts.

"You wished to see me, Father?" Aria stopped at the bottom of the dais.

Barely glancing away from conversation with his advisers, her father gestured for her to take the seat next to him. She climbed the stairs as slowly as possible, trying *not* to appear like a ninety-year-old woman ready to rest after a single step.

Luckily, the three men quickly finished their conversation about exports, and by the time Aria settled in her throne, Philip and Emmett had taken their leave.

Her father angled to face her, expressionless.

In the silence, Aria's heart beat faster as she considered every mistake she'd made that morning and the day previous. And the day before that.

Did he know of her visit to Baron? If he asked why she sought out a Caster, what could she say?

"So." Her father raised an eyebrow at last. "Crampton's son. Of all the options."

Aria released her breath in a rush. Of course—she'd not had a chance to speak to her father since making her courtship with Lord Kendall official.

"I distinctly remember pointing him out to you at the falconry event this spring, and you said the boy had the bearing of a plucked rooster."

If only that impression had stayed with Aria as a warning. Alas. The mere thought of choosing someone else was too exhausting, so she would make do with Lord Kendall. Besides, how large a flaw were chicken wings, really?

"There are more considerations to be made than *looks*," Aria said, settling more comfortably into her throne.

"Yes, but looks must be braved first."

Aria released a puff of laughter.

Then her traitorous mind dangled before her the thought of the most handsome man she'd seen recently—her first view of Baron as she left the carriage, his tawny hair tangled in sunlight, his green eyes bright as the orchard leaves behind him. The faint smile crossing his face as they locked eyes.

Her father squinted, and Aria suddenly feared he'd been speaking while her mind wandered. Thankfully, if he had, he didn't wait for a response before continuing.

"Very well, then." The king waved a hand, dangling casually from the arm of his throne. "If looks have been ignored, tell me his other virtues."

A most refreshing cup of tea. Manners in excess. Enough diligence to maintain a stunning orchard.

It took Aria's foggy mind far too long to focus on the *right* young man.

"Lord Kendall is skilled at . . ." She couldn't mention the music. It would only remind her father of the queen. "At bowing."

Inwardly, Aria groaned as her day-brain failed her again. *Speaking nonsense. Mark.*

Her father's pointed stare questioned her capability, so Aria rushed to add, "Many women of court find his eyes quite dreamy."

Other women? Wake up, Aria!

"I see." The king nodded slowly, his good humor fading into the familiar mask he wore whenever conducting difficult royal business. "Aria, speak honestly. Did you choose your suitor on a whim?"

"Perhaps I was not as careful in my consideration as I might have been. However—"

Her father cut her off with a sharp sigh. He straightened on his throne, looking out at the room's towering stained-glass windows.

"A royal," he said with slow deliberateness, "can never be reckless. Action by whim, without consideration, leads to mistakes. If the Crown is seen to make mistakes, all authority is lost. Do you understand?"

Aria heard those mistakes in her mind, tallied by a quill that slept as infrequently as she did.

"Yes, Father," she said quietly.

He allowed the silence to lengthen before he said, "Your visit to Northglen. Was it considered, or was it by whim?"

All at once, Aria returned to that mountainside, the frigid wind bearing down on her neck, spreading goose bumps. As if her tongue had fallen asleep, she struggled to manage a single word. "What?"

"Hiring a mercenary guard, paying them from the royal treasury—did you think I would never discover? Do you think me *daft,*

Aria? I've been waiting for you to admit the matter yourself, but it seems you foolishly thought you could keep the secret forever."

The king's dark eyes pierced her, and she shrank against her throne.

"Father, I . . ."

What could she say? Her own body refused to allow her to speak of her curse.

"Once I'd tracked them down, your guards had quite a story about peace negotiations, which they swear ended favorably with a signed, sealed letter, yet I've seen no hint of it."

Aria had burned it, the way she'd once burned a quill and parchment, hoping fire could erase her mistakes. Widow Morton gave her signature to peace with one hand yet wielded an assassin's knife with the other.

"I did go to discuss peace." Aria sagged in relief as her voice came free. As long as she avoided addressing the curse, it seemed she could still speak of that night. "I sought to mend the relationship between our families, to avoid a possible rebellion, and Widow Morton assured me—"

Her father swore, leaning away. "Aria, that woman declared open hostilities against the Crown. You entered her *home*, alone, unaided—"

"I had guards."

"Paid mercenaries who could just as easily have been paid by her!" The king's voice rose. "In eighteen years of tutoring, have you learned nothing? You could have been killed! You could have been retained as a hostage against me. Did you not *think*?"

Aria's heart thudded with extra weight in her chest.

"No," she whispered. "I didn't think. I only hoped."

Mark.

She'd hoped to prove to her father she could do something right for the kingdom. Instead, she'd drawn his ire more than ever, and rightfully so.

She *was* a hostage, marching toward death. All his worst fears were confirmed.

"I'm sorry, Father."

He sighed, raking one hand through his black hair. They sat in cold silence, alone in a stone room too big to be a prison cell but with the feeling of one all the same.

At last, he said, "What of the letter?"

Aria swallowed. "It was a lie."

CHAPTER 16

Baron tried to keep Huxley separated from Corvin as much as possible, but considering the purpose of his stewardship, it had been a doomed endeavor from the start. After finishing his examination of the estate buildings and grounds, Huxley turned his full attention to preparing its new titled lord.

"Stand up straight," he barked. "Like a lord ought."

Corvin snapped to attention. He was being fitted for a suit, since Huxley refused to repeat the embarrassment of greeting a royal visitor "in shambles." The tailor was one Huxley had summoned, and, unsurprisingly to Baron, the man carried the face of a sour lemon with a personality to match.

"You pricked me," Corvin said, the reason for his earlier flinch.

The tailor merely rolled his eyes and stabbed another pin through the jacket cuff.

"Rather than making excuses," Huxley said, "hold still."

Baron clenched his jaw. He stood at the far side of the room, arms folded over his chest, cane hooked at his elbow. If he stood like a bodyguard, it was purposeful.

"Hold this." The tailor slapped a piece of chalk into Corvin's palm, then continued pinning the cuff. After the second pin, Corvin gave another wince.

Even through gloves, Baron's nails pressed into his arms. "Corvin's thirteen. He's already been tested."

Corvin dropped the chalk as if it were a snake.

The traditional Caster test was done with a cup of water in one hand and a polished stone in the other. The king's tester made a small cut on the person's arm, because pain prompted reflexive magic. A Stone Caster would make the stone glow, and a Fluid Caster would do the same with the water.

Affiliate magic didn't trigger either response; there was only the danger of the Affiliate's panic triggering an uncontrolled transformation. Baron's father had coached both of the twins before their tests, ensuring they'd pass.

But Huxley was a new type of stress.

"I'm aware," said Huxley, shrugging the matter off as if he'd never conducted underhanded tests.

The rest of the fitting continued in tense silence, but at least Corvin was spared further jabs. He was not, however, spared further tests. After the fitting came a handwriting test, a reading test, and a quiz of his knowledge of court procedure. Baron watched with concern as his brother grew more frazzled.

"You have a rash, boy?" Huxley demanded.

Corvin stopped scratching his wrist. Though he sat straight as a rod at the study desk, his eyes darted with growing frequency toward the window.

"Corvin," Baron said softly.

Those brown eyes had never looked so tormented.

"That's enough for today. Mr. Shaw will be expecting you; don't be late."

The boy bolted for the door, gone before Huxley could voice his stunned protest. Then the man's brows pulled down, his expression pinching to reflect the same sourness as his tailor.

"In the future," he said, "I'll thank you not to interfere in his schedule."

"Corvin still has a duty to his apprenticeship. Surely you don't want a future lord baron neglecting duties. It sets a bad precedent."

"A future lord baron has no need of a common apprenticeship." Huxley stood from behind the desk—Baron's desk—and retrieved the estate ledger, leaning heavily into his cane. He opened the thick volume. "Actually, I'm glad we have this opportunity to speak in private, my lord. It seems your stint as estate manager, however limited, created an alarming number of concerns."

Baron's fingers dug into his arm again, but he said nothing.

"Increase in orchard spending—that would be the unnecessary second fertilizer." Huxley looked up; Baron remained silent. The man returned to the page, running his finger down the side. "Various expenses regarding the nearby hamlet, all extraneous. It seems you *twice* paid for a physician's visit. Such expenses aren't the duty of the estate lord."

"It seems our definitions of duty are in conflict," Baron said.

While he carefully considered how much to help in most financial matters, Baron couldn't restrain himself regarding illness. Health was not a plough horse; he would always bear the cost if those he cared for could not.

The memory of his father as the one in bed was still too fresh.

"Here's a perplexing one: You hired an investigator mid-summer. To investigate what, might I ask?"

His stepmother. After Sarah's abrupt departure four years earlier, Baron's father had closed off, refusing to speak about her though it strained his relationship with the twins. Baron couldn't bring their father back, but he felt the pain of being an orphan acutely enough; he would spare the twins if possible.

Unfortunately, the venture had been a dead end. Sarah hadn't been found. She'd hopped between relatives immediately after leaving her husband, but none professed any idea of her whereabouts within the last year.

There was nothing to be done for it. She'd given no indication she was leaving at all, and when she left, she'd given no indication where she might go.

Baron had been the first to see the smoke, to find his stepmother in the yard beside the smoldering spines of former books, their pages crumbled to ash, her eyes alive with the fire that had already burned out at her feet. It hadn't taken Baron's father more than a minute to catch up, and then there had been arguing, desperate pleas and struggles to understand met with a wall of refusal. The twins had arrived just as their mother swung into Ruby's saddle. Baron would always wish they hadn't heard her parting words: "This family is damned, and I will not stand idly to witness it."

The books she'd burned hadn't been from the shelves of the study but from the cubby beneath the floorboards of Baron's room.

Books on Casting, on Affiliation. On every known kind of magic. Books left to Baron by his real mother. Destroyed by his stepmother.

And no investigator could tell him why.

Huxley closed the ledger. "After careful review of the finances, I see a change must be made. Namely you, my lord. Rather than living off your brother's estate, I think it's time you find a sustainable living of your own. Perhaps, with your unique *talents*, you could desalinate water for farmers in Port Tynemon."

"A tempting offer, Mr. Huxley, but I think there's a more pressing calling for me closer to home."

"Surely you don't think the estate should pay you to hover around, hindering your brother's progress?"

Slowly, Baron lowered his cane to the ground, stacking his hands atop it. "The estate will pay me to lead the autumn harvest."

"We don't need—"

"Unless"—Baron raised his voice slightly—"you can find someone else in the next few days with the required knowledge and experience of how to handle the orchard. Harvesting is a delicate process, I'm sure you understand, and any loss of crops is a loss of revenue for the estate. I suppose you could oversee the process yourself, steward, but I wouldn't want to burden you with lemons and ladders."

With a pointed look at the man's weak leg, Baron gave a shallow nod and excused himself from the study. He found himself trembling as he walked.

It was a temporary solution. By the time spring harvest came, Huxley would realize Walter could lead. Losing Baron would mean hiring an extra worker or two, but *cost* was not Huxley's true motivation. Clearly, he wanted to push Baron out of the estate.

What do I do?

Baron wished he had someone to direct the question to.

After checking on Leon in the kitchen, more for his own peace of mind than anything, he made his way to the edge of the estate's land, just north of where it met the hamlet. There a small corner had been dedicated as a cemetery, since there was no churchyard until Stonewall. The Reeves family tomb stood in a copse of trees that had never been cleared, the stone structure pierced by sunlight only through the small windows in front and back.

His father's casket was there, encased in stone and marked by a plaque on the wall. So was his birth mother's, marked not only by plaque but also by a small statue of an angel mother with wings curled to protect her baby. Baron gently traced the feathers of one wing.

With a sigh, he leaned against the wall and spoke to parents who could no longer hear him.

"Huxley is worse than I'd feared."

The man had grown bolder faster than Baron had anticipated, and Baron couldn't see a clear path to spring harvest, much less to Corvin's seventeenth birthday. Perhaps the steward truly thought he was benefitting Corvin by distancing the estate from its Caster connection. Perhaps he simply feared for his own safety.

Something tapped at the window, startling Baron, and he heard a sharp *caw* just before a crow swooped into the narrow tomb enclosure. In a burst of black mist, the crow turned into a gangly boy. The transformation took barely a moment, and the mist dissipated at once, fading to imitate a puff of dust in the sunlight.

Baron forced himself to relax. This place was likely safer than his bedroom.

"You abandoned Mr. Shaw," he said disapprovingly.

"He's in Stonewall today, but I wasn't about to tell Huxley."

Corvin rested his hand on their father's plaque, shoulders drooping. Then he moved beside Baron, leaning his back against the stone wall, eyes on the floor.

"It's hopeless, isn't it?" he whispered at last.

Though Baron had been thinking along much the same lines, he wrapped an arm around Corvin's shoulders. "We won't let it be," he said.

Corvin smiled. From somewhere distant, a bird screeched, and the boy perked up.

"Another carriage?" It was foolish how quickly Baron spoke, more foolish still how that was his first hope.

"No, it's—hang on." Corvin weaseled out from under his arm, turning with a clever gleam in his eye. "Do you *want* it to be?"

"I want only to be prepared for any unexpected visitors. The last caught us all off guard." Baron pushed away from the wall and ducked into the fresh air.

Corvin scrambled to catch up. "Did she say she'd come back?"

"She said no such thing."

"Oh." The boy's steps slowed, then increased again. "Maybe we could go to the castle. Or to Sutton, at least. I'd like to talk to Jenny again. She hardly said anything with Huxley hovering, but I think she grew up near here."

Baron relaxed, coming to a stop beneath a tree, dappled with the shadow of leaves. "I suppose a trip to Sutton could be arranged."

Though Huxley would no doubt find an excuse to deny it.

Corvin nodded. "Great. Then you could talk to Aria, like you're dying to."

A leveled stare did nothing to wilt the boy's devious grin.

"What I said about Jenny's true. And what I said about Aria's true too."

"*Princess* Aria, and you're far ahead of yourself, Corvin."

"You could send her a letter, you know. You don't even have to leave for that. I happen to know the *best* delivery crow in the entire kingdom, one you never use for anything. Mr. Shaw told me he's worried you don't appreciate what an incredible rarity that trained crow is."

Baron snorted. "I appreciate that crow plenty, even if he sometimes pokes his beak where it doesn't belong." He sobered. "It isn't . . . simple, Corvin. Not as simple as I might hope."

The boy's expression fell. "What do you mean?"

The matter was tangled up in words like *royalty* and *Caster* and *Northglen*. If that weren't enough, there was *steward, harvest, twins.* Baron could not risk dividing his attention. The cost for a failure at home was far too great.

Even if he thought of the princess's strange journal and remembered Leon's words about her voice at court. Even if he could not remove the memory of Aria in the orchard, looking up at the trees with the sun shining against her dark hair, reaching for a lemon and saying, *It's breathtaking.*

"Come on." Baron nodded toward the path to the hamlet. "If Mr. Shaw is gone, that means you're my assistant for the day, and last I heard, there was a concern about the central well."

Hopefully he could find a way to solve the problem without access to estate funds or resources.

CHAPTER

17

60 DAYS LEFT

Something's wrong with you," Eliza said.

Aria tensed, throwing Jenny off as the younger girl pinned Aria's hair.

"That's rude," Aria said. *Inaccurate as well. There are many things wrong with me.* She had a mental tally at the ready, should Eliza require specifics.

Her sister squinted. "Well, someone has to say it." Eliza huffed. "You're courting Lord Kendall, but you don't even *like* him."

"On the contrary. He has dreamy eyes. When he holds a maiden's gaze, he captures her soul." *Dreamy.* Now *there* was something she'd like to court. A long, uninterrupted dream.

Using mockery in place of honest conversation. Making light of duty. Double mark.

Since confronting her about Northglen, her father did not look at her the same. Though he'd invited her to the most recent Upper Court meeting, he'd not once given her opportunity to speak while the court had discussed Widow Morton's latest offenses—namely, conspiring against the Crown by actively gathering a force of dangerous individuals. One of her father's advisers had presented an intercepted letter from Widow Morton to a prominent Stone Caster, Richard Langley, inviting him to join her resistance in Northglen.

The response was unanimous: Widow Morton would be stripped

of her title as countess, and a squadron of soldiers would be sent to arrest her.

And Aria's father did not seem to notice or care that he'd never called for her vote.

Self-pity. Mark.

Inability to stop marking. Mark.

Preferring marking flaws to fixing them.

Mark. Mark. Mark.

"Aria." Eliza spoke softly this time. "Are you . . ."

Aria smiled. "I nearly forgot to ask—how is Henry?"

It was a dirty trick to prey on her sister's weakness for romance, but it worked. Eliza performed a full swoon, sagging against the wall as she recited a sonnet from her favorite poet, something about an everlasting spring and drinking deep but never quenched. Aria nodded along, but she might also have nodded off.

"A lovesickness," said Jenny quietly.

Aria straightened, blood pumping, skin cold. The maid had finished Aria's hair and stepped away. Whatever else she'd said to Eliza hadn't registered. Aria blinked hard.

"Oh, hush, you!" Eliza giggled. "Without courting, there can be no lovesickness. I'm simply . . ."

"Enamored?" Aria supplied.

"Smitten?" Jenny offered.

Eliza gave a dramatic gasp. "Beset by pests! Two of them. Jenny, how are you so tall already, and why am I cursed to be in need of risers in all my shoes?"

Because you take after Mother, Aria wanted to say. Eliza and the queen shared the same golden-brown hair, the same straight nose, and the same diminutive stature. To say nothing of their shared love of music. Aria's face carried the angles of her father, and she stood a good half-head taller than her sister. She'd also inherited her father's black hair, dark as a night without stars.

Jenny carried that same shade, though the girl kept her hair tied beneath a white kerchief as she worked.

"Henry is short as well," Aria said, forcing a smile. "It's a perfect match."

Henry Wycliff, second-youngest son of Earl Wycliff, had been the young man watching Eliza at her birthday ball, and Eliza had taken it as a sign of romantic fate that they shared the final dance of the evening—though it didn't hurt that the boy made a return trip to the palace soon after, supposedly to claim a lost coat but also bringing Eliza a handful of white snowdrops. Eliza had carefully pressed the blossoms into her personal journal, then walked around with the whole thing clutched to her heart.

Eliza raised an eyebrow. "Don't think you can distract me. Especially when I know Lord Kendall's not giving you flowers."

"I have no need of flowers," Aria said honestly.

She had need of cures. Perhaps when her father's soldiers brought Widow Morton to the palace, Aria could find some leverage against the woman, force her to revoke the curse in exchange for her freedom.

Unrealistic expectations. Mark. Planning the release of a dangerous criminal. Mark.

"I'm leaving," Aria said, striding for the door before she could be lulled into sleep by idleness.

Eliza gave a squeak of protest, but it was Jenny who truly halted the princess.

"Highness," the girl said softly, then licked her lips and spoke with real concern. "I fear you've taken ill. Not lovesickness. True sickness."

Jenny was not only too observant but too kind. Aria still hadn't found a way to apologize for forcing her way into Jenny's trip, especially when the girl had asked if Aria would walk with her to her mother's grave and she had instead waited in the carriage like a coward.

For the sake of the sister she didn't know how to embrace, Aria smiled and said, "Thank you for the concern. I'm a little tired, that's all. Too much excitement of late. I'll retire early tonight."

She tried not to think of how quickly she approached the fifty-day mark. Half her time spent with nothing gained.

At least she'd not lost her mind to the curse yet. All things considered, it held stable, an ongoing torture but not an increasing one. If only that could have comforted her. Instead, Aria felt tension in every bone, anticipation pulling her skeleton tight. Surely Widow Morton had something else planned, another strike against the king. But expecting an ambush didn't mean she could spot it among the shadows.

Jenny nodded, and Aria exited at last.

Lord Kendall surprised Aria by suggesting they go out riding together. Apparently, he wanted to prove he had a range of interests beyond lullabies.

Eliza caught up with them at the stables, puffing from her hurried dressing and pursuit. While the stablehands saddled horses, she and Lord Kendall held a conversation Aria lost track of immediately. She leaned against the corral fence, begging herself not to be so obvious as to rest her head on her arm.

She woke to a crow swooping out of the sky, diving so close that its feathers brushed Lord Kendall's ear. Eliza shrieked, stumbling backward, and Aria's suitor dove heroically to the ground. Perhaps it was the exhaustion slowing her reflexes, but Aria only blinked.

The bird landed on the fence, directly beside her. He opened his beak and gave a loud *caw*.

"Well, aren't you a friendly one." Her lips twitched.

"Guards!" Lord Kendall cried, scooting away from the fence. "Rid us of this demon bird!"

"No need." Aria pointed to the tube fastened on the crow's back, between its wings. "He's a messenger bird."

Eliza eyed the bird. "I thought only falcons were smart enough to carry messages."

With another *caw*, the crow ruffled his feathers as though he'd taken the insult to heart.

Aria had no avian experience, but *someone* clearly trusted the crow. As she unfastened the tube's lid, she pitched her voice low to impart a secret. "I think you make a fine messenger bird."

The crow twitched his beak up and down as if in agreement. She stroked his feathered head gently with her thumb, then, with a rush of wind against her face, he took flight, disappearing into the sky.

"This can only be for you," Aria said, extending the rolled parchment to Eliza. "Your Henry is certainly an interesting one."

Her sister took it with shaky fingers, a smile budding on her face.

Lord Kendall pointedly changed the topic, determined to act as if nothing had happened even though his face still burned red and his pants carried a streak of dirt. He leapt into the saddle at the first available moment.

Once riding, Aria didn't have to keep up with conversation, and she found a truly enjoyable trait in her suitor—*competitiveness*. Lord Kendall goaded his mount faster, which Aria matched in kind, until they were both galloping, the wind billowing her riding coat and twisting strands of her hair free from its pearl net. She grinned, and she even heard Kendall laugh.

Perhaps there was hope to this relationship after all. Perhaps . . .

A cursed girl pretending at a future. Mark.

Eliza called from behind, but Aria did not slow. She leaned in, pushing hard until she rode ahead of Kendall. He shouted something she didn't hear. The trees passed in a golden blur streaked with orange, and the drumming hooves kept a steady rhythm that soothed her heart.

Soothed her mind.

Soothed her soul.

Aria didn't realize her eyes were drooping until the world disappeared in a blink, and she felt herself falling, sliding into a waiting blackness pierced by pain.

Aria dozed. A fitful sleep, interrupted by the voices of her father and the physician, Eliza and Jenny. Everyone seemed concerned about her.

She wished they would let her *sleep*.

"She hasn't been herself."

"Falling asleep in random places—"

"Why did no one inform me?"

"Aria always denied it, Father! I thought—"

"She needs rest, Your Majesty."

Shh, Aria wanted to say, but she couldn't manage words. She couldn't manage dreams. She could only reach desperately for a thing just out of grasp, her fingers grazing its surface, her soul weeping at the loss.

Aria sat upright in bed, her fitful sleep stripped away by the onset of night. The familiar restless energy pooled in her belly, demanding that she move. She groaned at the sharp pains that surrounded her, taking inventory of her bandage-wrapped elbow, shoulder, and head. Everything throbbed, and when she moved her left arm, she hissed in agony. At least the physician had not affixed a splint or tied her arm against her body, so she assumed no broken bones. By the feel of it, he'd reset her shoulder back into its socket.

Her father slept in an armchair beside her bed, snoring intermittently.

Aria reached out to squeeze his warm hand, though it remained slack at her touch.

As she pulled back the covers, a rolled parchment fell to the ground.

Frowning, Aria crouched to retrieve it, recognizing it as the letter the crow had brought. Had Eliza left it behind in the chaos of Aria's accident?

Then she noticed *Princess Aria* scrawled across the side of the roll; she hadn't bothered to look when she'd first taken it. Aria blinked. Anyone seeking her simply came to the palace; they didn't send a letter. And who would use a crow?

She thought of green eyes, beautifully out of place in the rest of court.

Barely able to breathe, she untied the parchment and rolled it open.

> *To Lady Your Highness* Her Royal Highness, Crown Princess Aria

The first half was written in one style of handwriting and the second in another, which sprawled halfway on top of the first.

She clamped a hand over her mouth, but it didn't hold the laughter. All at once, the world felt lighter, and the pounding in her head became a bit euphoric. Crossing the room, she lit the oil lamp on her dresser and tried to parse a message between the two handwritings fighting for dominance.

> Thanks for showing us the kitchen. Your cook is top cut. I make great bread, just so you know. I make even better cake.
>
> Our brother is an idiot. Much like a certain bread-obsessed person I won't name.
>
> Our brother really likes you. We told him he should tell you himself, but he is an idiot.
>
> Baron says it isn't simple. That's because he's too noble and nobles make everything hard

because nobles are stupid. Things don't have to be hard. You know that. Otherwise you wouldn't have visited a kitchen during a ball.

What we mean is you should write to Baron. If you want. He's really great.

> Sincerely, etc., Corvin Reeves
> and Leon

Aria read the letter through five times, smiling all the while. The paranoid part of her brain still fretted about mistakes and Casters and traps while the logical side held a curled letter to the lamplight and reasoned that if *this* was a trap, she could not be blamed for falling for it.

She thought of Baron, standing tall before a king, asking for the same rights anyone else in his position would receive. Too late, she admitted something to herself with honesty.

If she removed the witch's mark from the picture, she would have trusted him. She would have sought to get to know him better. Perhaps she even would have chosen someone other than Lord Kendall for a potential courtship.

There was no need to go *that* far, but while holding the petition of his brothers to see him in an honest light, Aria found it impossible to deny. *He's really great.* The simplest recommendation imaginable.

In that moment, she chose to believe it.

Leaning over her desk, she penned a letter.

To Lord Guillaume Reeves,
Baron,

Permit me to speak frankly. Brief though our meetings have been, I find conversation with you to be easier and more genuine than any I have found before or since. Your brothers are charming and good-hearted, and I suspect both traits originated in or were at least encouraged by you.

At your estate, I requested the aid of a Caster, something I admit I still require. What I now realize is that I failed to say other things. I failed to request your aid—the man behind the mark. I failed to thank you again for a timely cup of tea which gave relief when needed. I failed to mention the beauty of Reeves Manor, painted in warm yellow tones and surrounded by creeping ivies. Was the house decorated to match the orchard or do you favor yellow?

I should like to know your thoughts, Baron. On estate colors, on Casting abilities, and on a great deal of other topics. If you'll count me worthy of them.

With hope,
Her Royal Highness, Aria

P.S. I should also like to know if Leon is properly aerating his dough. While I have no notion what such a thing means, Cook was most upset I did not inquire when I had the chance.

She creased the parchment and rolled it tightly, then tied it with a thin string. As she did, she glanced at her father, the lamplight reflecting softly against his gold circlet, which he still wore even in sleep.

Something inside told Aria the letter she held was as dangerous as a weapon. In sending it, something would break. Her curse, perhaps.

Perhaps something deeper.

Aria sent the letter anyway.

CHAPTER

18

It was early morning when the falcon tapped at his bedroom window. Baron had never seen the bird before, but Corvin trained dozens under Mr. Shaw, and he always tested them first with deliveries to the Reeves estate, though he usually sent them to badger Leon.

When Baron opened the window, the falcon walked gracefully inside, turning to present her message canister. She was a sleek thing, certainly expensive. Corvin must be training her for a duke's household. Baron expected a scrap of parchment at most, marked with a few words on how next to guide her. But it was a fully bound message.

One addressed to *Guillaume Reeves.*

He stood there for a full minute, frowning, before he shook himself. He fastened the canister's top before touching the falcon's head. She took the signal for flight. Fully trained, then. A real message, not practice.

It wasn't from Sarah. He'd not forgotten her handwriting. An invitation from Widow Morton? He should have considered ahead of time how to diplomatically reject that inevitable message.

He tugged the string loose, carefully unrolling the tight bundle.

And his heart began to pound.

He read the letter. Twice. He stared at the princess's name on the parchment for a long time, and then, realizing it was not going to disappear, he tucked it in a pocket and carefully readied for the day. After reviewing the hiring list for the harvest—and reluctantly surrendering it to Huxley—Baron read the letter again. He fidgeted with his gloves.

He went to the kitchen to make tea. As soon as he settled a kettle over the fire, Leon eyed him.

"Brewing it long-hand? What's wrong?"

The boy was the only one in the kitchen. Helen had left to visit her daughter and grandchild, a luxury she could often afford since Leon ran the kitchen anyway.

"Trouble in the hamlet," Baron said. The kettle's whistle screamed at his deflection; he removed it from the heat. "Widow Fletcher's taken ill."

Leon wiped his floured hands across his apron. "I'll make leek soup."

Baron touched his pocket, ensuring the letter was still real. He checked the cupboards and pantry for tea bundles.

"What are you doing, idiot? You won't find anything better than what you can make."

I should like to know your thoughts, she'd written. To what end? And why him? She could write to anyone in the kingdom, so why *him*?

Baron finally set a bundle of tea leaves to steep with vanilla bean. Leon re-sorted the cupboards to his liking—glaring at Baron as he did so—then returned to chopping leeks and gathering ingredients in a soup pot.

Once the tea had steeped, Baron poured himself a cup, not bothering to ask if Leon wanted any since the boy always preferred straight milk. Baron stirred in a generous helping of lemon and cream.

I requested the aid of a Caster, something I admit I still require.

Matters in Northglen had grown worse. The king had dispatched soldiers, though no one had yet heard confirmation of arrest. Baron imagined how *he* would react if soldiers arrived at his door, and he did not find the options pleasant. Widow Morton could do great damage—not only to the military force, but to every Caster left to face the king's wrath in the aftermath.

Perhaps the princess could mitigate that. Perhaps it was treason for him to even consider leveraging a correspondence with her to his own personal benefit. Then again, she asked for help. Could they help each other? Could a relationship between a royal and a Caster ever be that innocent?

"You'll wear grooves in the cup," Leon said.

Baron realized he was still stirring. He set the spoon aside. The tea did little to ease his thoughts; after all, it was only leaf and lemon.

Leon crushed garlic and stripped herbs. He kneaded pasta dough.

The princess had said other things. Things like *charming and good-hearted*. Like *the man behind the mark*. Things that stirred Baron's mind the way he'd stirred tea and left it a hopeless whirlpool of thoughts chasing feelings.

She'd written his name correctly first, then added *Baron*. Proper, then personal. He'd never imagined a princess would call him Baron.

He'd never imagined a princess would write. He was a Caster. A magic user. A thing not to be trusted.

Both traits originated in you. Charming and good-hearted.

Baron laughed to himself; she didn't even know him.

"You're being creepy, Baron," grumbled Leon. Tasting his soup, he threw in another clove of garlic.

"Are you properly aerating your dough?" Baron asked.

Leon stiffened. Then he narrowed his eyes as if sizing up a mouse. "It's aerating flour, and why?"

"The palace cook wants to know."

At once, the boy brightened. "Yes! Tell her to teach me more secrets."

"You're not at all concerned I'm in correspondence with the palace kitchen?"

"While you're at it, get me one of their weekly menus in writing. I want to see what they serve in that place, and I mean when the whole court isn't there."

Shaking his head, Baron lifted his teacup only to find it had gone cold.

Amelia tapped at the door to inform him Mr. Huxley required a tour of the hamlet, so with reluctance, Baron prepared himself for another day of entertaining the court jester. Leon made him wait fifteen minutes for the soup to be ready.

"It's not like Mr. Peachy can get any crankier with a bit of a wait," the boy said.

Baron wasn't so sure.

As soon as Baron explained the purpose of bringing soup along on a hamlet tour, Huxley disparaged the notion.

"More coddling," he said. "There will be no estate funds spent on this widow, I hope you're aware."

"In turn," Baron said, "I hope you're aware a nobleman who does not care for those on his lands cannot call himself noble at all."

Even now, he could hear his father's voice clearly, as if the man sat beside him in the carriage. *In court, we represent not just the interests of our own house but of every person we oversee, every individual given to our care. We are a collection of voices that represent an entire kingdom.*

He'd wanted Baron to be the voice for magic. Baron touched his pocket, feeling a concealed letter, a silent offer.

Huxley sniffed but otherwise fell silent. Though Baron usually walked the short distance, the steward insisted on taking a carriage, since his weak leg favored neither walking nor riding. At least that made transporting the soup easy.

The hamlet had a simple layout, just a collection of houses around a central well. The largest house belonged to Mrs. Caldwell, a would-be leader in the community who took it upon herself to care for her neighbors. Baron introduced Huxley to her, then excused himself to see to Widow Fletcher, ignoring Huxley's scowl.

Widow Fletcher kept a small, well-tended house at the hamlet's edge. After Baron knocked and admitted himself, she stood to greet him, but she trembled in every limb, so Baron ordered her to bed and ladled soup, waving off her protests.

"I've sent for a physician from Stonewall," he said. "He'll arrive this evening."

She insisted there was no need for a physician, but the hacking cough betrayed her. No doubt she was concerned with cost.

"The cost is covered, widow. Worry only about your health."

If Baron had to pay from his own pocket, so be it. In the back of his mind, he heard voices: *Your father's collapsed!*

Baron forced the dark memories away.

"I've heard the steward . . . he doesn't approve . . ." The widow fell to a coughing fit, and when she spoke again, her voice could barely be heard. "Surely milord can . . . can just sort me right."

Widow Fletcher managed a weak smile, her eyes glassy with fever.

Baron stopped himself from rubbing his witch's mark. Listening to her struggle for breath, he said, "I'll see what I can do."

The widow's small house held an even smaller kitchen. She was almost out of fresh water; he would draw more for her after Mrs. Caldwell arrived. He filled a wooden cup and gently traced his fingertip around the smooth edge, like coaxing crystal to sing. He heard that song in his mind, but it wavered. Fractured.

He saw his father thrashing in bed.

Heard the physician. *There's nothing I can do—*

Nothing I can do.

Baron blinked, looking down at the cup now filled with sour milk. Useless. He opened the window and emptied the cup, slopping milk curdles across a bed of dried brown leaves. Though his head pounded with an ache, he filled the cup for another attempt. Usually, magic was an instinctive thing, and he could perform a Cast with hardly a thought, but when he overexerted himself or tried to force it, his own mind retaliated with spikes of pain.

After two additional attempts, he finally silenced the memories enough to make a honeyed tea, though it was far from his best work.

After drinking it, Widow Fletcher dozed fitfully, her cough eased but her sickness lingering. Baron couldn't cure her, just as he'd been unable to cure his father. He could only ease the symptoms.

Baron's fingers trembled. He interlaced and clenched them.

Mrs. Caldwell arrived after the widow finally slipped into a deep, restful sleep. Once he'd finished informing her of the remaining soup and coming physician, the matron stopped Baron at the door.

"You do this hamlet good, my lord," Mrs. Caldwell said quietly. "The former baron, rest his soul, he would be fiercely proud."

Baron nodded his thanks, but he did not tell her how much better he could do if he were worth his salt as a Caster. The books Sarah had burned had contained incredible stories of Stone Casters who constructed castles, of Fluid Casters who redirected blood flow in the human body. Even purified it.

A Caster like that could have cleansed his father's infection. Could have saved his life.

Before he left, Baron remembered to draw water. It was the only thing he could do.

— ❄ —

When he returned to the manor, he sat in his armchair by the fireplace and read Princess Aria's letter once more. Of all the remarkable details in it—one after another—perhaps the most remarkable was the closing signature.

With hope.

What, exactly, was she hoping for?

And more important still—

If Baron sent a response, what was *he* hoping for?

She'd seen joy in his magic, that was something. But Sarah had also seemed accepting at first. His father had trusted her, loved her, and lost her. Baron had no intention of loving a princess, but he did not know if he could even take the first step to trusting one.

And yet . . .

Promise me, son.

Even had he obtained his seat at court, he would have been one voice in a sea of dissention. There had always been slim chance of him affecting real change; he had simply agreed with his father that any chance was worth the effort.

Princess Aria was not one voice in a sea. Hers was the voice of the future monarch, the woman who would, in a matter of years, lead the entire kingdom. If there was *any* chance, no matter how slim, that Baron could convince her that Casters deserved an equal place within that kingdom, it was certainly worth the effort.

If he failed . . .

Well, at least Leon could get his palace menu.

59 DAYS LEFT

While the physician evaluated Aria and cleaned and reban-daged her wounds, her father received a report from a guard. Though they stood in the hallway, her father kept one foot in her room, the door propped open against him, and their voices were just loud enough that she heard the news.

The soldiers sent to Northglen had not reached Morton Manor. They'd been met with a rockslide, forced to retreat. Several wounded. The widow had employed a Stone Caster, and she'd made her first open strike against the Crown.

They had no idea it wasn't the first.

Once the physician gave his unintentionally ironic parting words—*plenty of rest, Highness*—Aria waited for her father to speak.

He did so quietly, retaking his seat. "The physician could find no diagnosis—no seizures, no injury—that would cause you to fall from your horse. Kendall is quite certain the animal did not trip or otherwise throw you. You simply . . . collapsed."

Aria's fingers tightened in the blanket, her left arm throbbing. She looked down. "I've been clumsy of late. It's not—"

"Eliza says you've been falling asleep. That you sometimes escape to the washroom or abandon your studies."

Cold settled across Aria as surely as the covers, biting through the thick material and leaving her shivering. She wriggled deeper into the bed, hiding from both the cold and her father's stricken gaze. Finally, she gave a slow nod.

"Aria." Her father's voice cracked. "Tell me."

She wanted to so badly her heart lurched forward in her chest, reaching for him with every straining beat.

I'm cursed! she screamed internally, but instead she whispered, "I'm so tired, Father."

He leaned forward onto the bed, resting his forearm parallel with her legs. "Have you not been sleeping nights?"

"I find myself unable."

"Unable? What does that mean?"

"I . . . I mean . . ." Her throat tightened. As she drew in a shuddering breath, a single tear dripped down her cheek.

Her father's expression pinched in a frown. "This is my doing. I've put too much pressure on you."

"No!" she gasped. "This isn't you. It's—" *Magic.* "It's a—" *Caster.* "It's—"

Gently, he patted her knee. His face said it all.

"This is a small concern," Aria tried desperately. "I'm feeling rested already."

The king shook his head. "I have been blind to an ongoing problem, but no longer."

"Father, I—"

"When I noticed your attention drifting in meetings, I thought it only a teenage rebellion, a manifestation of how our wills seem to be growing at odds. I thought to point you more diligently toward your duty. Now, I . . ." He sighed. "You fell from your horse, Aria. You could have been trampled. What kind of father would I be to ignore such a concern?" He clenched his jaw, looking away. "What kind of king?"

While Aria floundered, he stood, his bearing regal. Even with his white uniform rumpled from a worried night, he was every inch the king who'd rejuvenated a kingdom.

"Rest, Aria," he ordered. "I will determine the solution to this matter. In the meantime, you are relieved of all duties."

Relieved of all duties. Mark. She knew he meant it as a boon, knew he wanted to help, but she also knew he could not.

Rest, said the physician. *Rest,* said her father. She wanted to cry. She wanted to scream.

Aria let her head fall against the pillow, pulled by exhaustion, and she watched her father leave through dimming eyes and lowered lashes. She slept.

But half an hour later, she was awake again. Heart pounding. Counting the days.

When the crow arrived, Aria was pacing her room. Despite the chill of autumn, she'd left her shutters open, welcoming the fresh air. Her mind felt like a maze of insanity, one where she grew more lost with each passing moment, trapped in the fog of unremembered nightmares of being chased by death itself. Fresh air at least made breathing easier. Small comforts.

The *caw* that echoed in the sky was a much larger one.

The crow swooped gracefully onto her windowsill, catching a perch with his talons. Then he peered in, as if evaluating her living conditions.

"Those aren't mine," Aria said as he looked to Eliza's discarded books on her bed, though she had no reason to think a crow cared if she read poetry.

The crow lifted his beak and gave a clicking rattle sound, like staccato laughter. In the slanted afternoon light, his black feathers bore a sheen of blue, and his dark eyes reflected a spark of undeniable intelligence. He pecked once at the sill, then turned to proudly present his message canister.

Aria smiled when she recognized the elegant, orderly script addressed to *Princess Aria*.

"Baron certainly didn't delay," she said. "I sent my message just this morning."

True, it was nearing sundown, but still. He'd not waited a full day.

The crow *cawed* his agreement. She thanked him for the delivery and gave him a gentle pat on the head.

The bird ruffled his feathers, stepped side to side, but didn't take flight. Trained messenger falcons always departed after a message had been delivered, but perhaps Baron's crow was more wild-minded.

Since he wasn't harming anything, she left him alone and opened the letter.

> *Your Royal Highness, Aria,*
>
> *I was pleased to receive your message. Leon would assure you he is aerating his flour—and he was quick to correct me that it was flour; for my part, I possessed as much understanding as you—and he also humbly requests a copy of a palace menu, should that be possible.*
>
> *If frankness may be allowed on my part as well, I hoped our discussion in the orchard would not be our last. Also, take care how much charm you assign to the boys. Just this afternoon, Corvin stole Leon's favorite set of tongs and hid them on the roof. I have not heard the end of it.*

Aria bit her lip, holding back a smile and savoring every line.

> *Thank you for your distinction between Caster and individual. Although I am proud to be both, one certainly overshadows the other within society. On the topic of things not said, I don't believe I explained my hesitation to speak of magic. It's not that I wish to be secretive, only that I have never before been asked for honest details. Many*

people are content to acknowledge that magic exists when it might benefit them or when it might be blamed for their misfortune. Nothing else.

I am grateful you asked, grateful you count me a worthy source of information. I'll do the best I can to provide it.

No, I don't favor yellow.

Sincerely, etc., Baron Reeves

The abrupt ending drew a laugh from Aria. A smear of ink marked the valediction, as if Baron had hesitated, considered adding more, then simply ended it. She'd had the impression when they first met, but now she felt certain—he was not a conversationalist. He spoke haltingly, at times even awkwardly, and yet he became all the more intriguing for it, as if stripping away the easy pleasantries Aria was accustomed to left only the simple truth behind.

I was pleased to receive your message, he'd written.

How she hoped that was true.

It was *possible* Baron and his brothers were just as they seemed. It was possible there was no underlying plot, no pitfall waiting to snare her. It was possible at least one Caster in the kingdom possessed a kind heart and upright motivations.

Wasn't it?

Glancing up, she saw the crow still perched at her window, pecking curiously at the stone frame.

"Did he instruct you to wait for a response?" she asked.

The bird squawked, as if she'd startled him, but he didn't take flight.

With a smile, she said, "I'll write quickly."

Aria sat impatiently through breakfast the next morning. It was unrealistic to expect every message to arrive with the swiftness of the first, yet she found herself watching windows just the same, hoping to see a crow tap upon the glass.

"You seem in brighter spirits, dear," said her mother from across the table. "A day in bed must have been just what you needed."

Aria glanced at her father, sitting at the head of the table. It was the first time they'd all sat at a meal together in weeks; if her mother didn't take meals in the music room, her father took them in his council chambers. Now the four of them sat together at a long dining table, indulging in heavy food and even heavier atmosphere.

"It was. Thank you, Mother." For a moment, Aria's hand forgot how to conduct a meal, reaching for her glass only to stop short and hover above her fork. In the end, she grabbed her napkin and dabbed at her mouth, though she'd spilled nothing.

Growing flustered. Mark.

Eliza leaned forward in her seat. "Father, I wonder if you might invite Earl Wycliff and his family to court."

The king regarded her for a moment, taking a sip of wine. "What prompts this request?"

"I desire a view of his second-youngest son. The most handsome of the bunch." Eliza didn't bother to conceal her grin.

As their father chuckled, so did Aria.

"Henry, isn't it? He's made no formal request to court you."

"Then give him an opportunity! Something where he may display heroic attributes and I may praise all of them." Eliza interlaced her fingers, pleading. "Please, Father. You keep the earl so busy, he rarely hosts events of his own. I'll never see Henry at this rate."

"Perhaps a sporting competition," Aria suggested, not at all because she was thinking of a certain green-eyed gentleman and the dress sword he carried.

"Yes, that's perfect! Henry is an accomplished jouster!" When their father raised an eyebrow, Eliza amended, "Lord Henry. It's not as though I've seen his skill in action, only heard it spoken of."

The king grunted. "I suppose Kendall claims some jousting skill as well. The two of you could fawn over suitors together."

Aria filled her mouth with eggs to avoid reply.

"It's growing cold for a joust," said the queen. "If it's court events we desire, a musical exhibition would be more appropriate."

The king kept his eyes on his plate. "No, we shall hold a joust. We'll do it quickly, while the weather permits. The matter is decided."

"The matter is always decided with only your voice."

"Perhaps because I tire of hearing yours, echoing at every hour in the music room."

Aria's hand tightened on her fork. Eliza nudged bits of parsley to the edge of her plate with the concentration of a surgeon.

The queen maintained a pleasant expression, pushing her plate away with her fingertips. "I find myself without appetite. Not a problem you've ever experienced."

She left.

Aria's mouth had gone dry around her quail eggs, and she struggled to swallow. She had raised her glass to drink when her father spoke.

"Aria."

She fought to maintain her focus. "Yes, Father?"

"I've considered your situation."

Eliza perked up but remained silent.

"Eliza, leave us."

"Father—"

At his look, she gathered her plate and moved into the smaller, adjoining dining hall. Once the door closed behind her, the king returned his gaze to Aria.

"When did this tiredness first afflict you?"

"I—a few weeks ago, Father."

"After your visit to Northglen."

Goose bumps lifted on Aria's neck, but she didn't deny it.

"Did you drink anything she gave you?"

Aria stiffened. "I know better than that."

Her true mistake had been assuming she would be safe if she *didn't* drink. Assuming she knew anything about magic at all.

"Widow Morton has my—" Her voice halted abruptly before she could mention the broken teacup. She grunted in frustration. "I mean she had my . . . She had me fooled, but not that much."

With a flinch, she retreated to her wine glass, hoping it would hide the burn in her face. *Unintelligible speech. Mark.*

"You're certain she did nothing to you?"

Aria swallowed. "She . . . she lied."

"I'm speaking in terms of magic, obviously."

The frustration in her father's expression could not compare to what she felt straining within her own chest.

"She . . . I watched her . . . after I returned . . ."

"A straight answer, Aria, honestly. It's not a difficult question."

She gave a helpless shrug, tears burning in her eyes.

Her father's expression hardened. "You'll resume your studies today. See that you take *them* seriously."

Though he'd not finished breakfast, he pushed his plate away just as the queen had, leaving Aria alone at the table.

CHAPTER

20

Baron played a dangerous game. What began as a single letter quickly tumbled into something more, like pulling one lemon off a branch only to have all the others cascade at the rebound. The rational side of his mind questioned the end of this path; the emotional side had already been captured in the journey.

Her Highness's second letter arrived while Baron was visiting his parents. Corvin found him at the tomb enclosure, handed off the letter with a grin, then dashed to find Huxley. The boy had been gone longer than he should have, and Huxley would no doubt lecture him on the strict punctuality of a proper lord. Baron should have gone with his brother, but he lingered, opening Princess Aria's letter right there in the graveyard.

Baron,

Thank you for regarding my correspondence as a pleasure rather than a nuisance. Leon's menu will arrive by courier, along with a few specialty ingredients and recipes Cook thinks will test his skills. I hope he has by now recovered his tongs.

In reviewing your notes on Casting, I cannot overcome the detail of your witch's mark. It breaks my heart. How could you have been branded at six? I've never heard of anyone tested before twelve.

If it is too painful a memory to revisit, please disregard my inquiry.

You noted Stone Casters could cause sleep. Could one put an entire crowd to sleep at once? How would such a thing be achieved and what might be the purpose? Also, is it possible for one person to wield both Stone and Fluid magic, causing, for example, both sleep and healing? One final question regarding Casting: I've read the most powerful Casts must be anchored to an object, called an Artifact. If the Artifact were discovered and broken, would the Cast end?

I apologize for the bombardment of questions, but I'm afraid I have more. I'm familiar with Leon's interests, less so with Corvin's. At the ball, you mentioned he trains falcons. I've heard that's a process of incredible difficulty! How did he adopt such an interest?

I would also be curious to hear of your own interests. Your formal attire included a dress sword. Is it only for show or do you engage in dueling? What of jousting?

Enough of my questions. I'm afraid I find myself in need of good conversation, and you are the person unfortunate enough to cross paths with me in these dire straits, so I'll thank you for your indulgence once again.

Yours,
Crown Princess Aria

Baron took the letter inside the tomb and read it aloud. After finishing, he tilted his head toward his father's plaque. "I wish you were here."

If Baron were any real use as a Caster, he would be.

Shaking off the dark thoughts, Baron returned his eyes to the parchment. Her Highness confused him more than Huxley did. The steward was a villain, but of the type Baron was accustomed to dealing with; he'd simply never had one living in his home, wielding power over him daily.

Aria was a mystery, the likes of which he'd never encountered before.

Why did a princess apologize as if her very existence was a bother to him? He would have been more comfortable had she demanded information rather than requesting it politely. And she remembered the names of his brothers, asked after them with pursued interest. If she'd desired only to be polite, she would have asked after their well-beings, not their hobbies.

I find myself in need of good conversation.

How could a crown princess be lacking in anything, the least of which conversation? Yet Baron felt an echo of the sentiment in his own soul. And something else . . .

It breaks my heart, she wrote.

It was not the first time Baron had mentioned his early age of branding to someone, but it was the first time he'd been answered with compassion. *It breaks my heart.*

He was rubbing his witch's mark. He curled his fingers in, then folded the letter. With quick strides, he returned to the manor, joining Corvin and looming over Huxley to remind the man he'd not been forced out yet. The minutes seemed a continuous torture until, at last, night fell, duties ended, and he could craft a reply.

> *Your Highness, Aria,*
>
> *To your questions—*
>
> *Managing an entire crowd would be unreasonable for a single Stone Caster. In theory, it's possible, but the Caster would need skin-to-skin contact with each person in order*

to lay the Cast. They could delay the activation to trigger sleep for all at once, but the mental strain for the Caster would be immense, likely rendering them unconscious. It may even fracture the Caster's mind.

Such a thing might be possible with an Artifact—which you asked after. Many Casters like the idea of Artifacts, because if a Cast is anchored to one, it removes the burden from the Caster and greatly increases the strength of the Cast, creating feats otherwise impossible.

Truth, but misleading.

First, because the process of creating an Artifact is complex. You cannot take an item at random; the object must be tied to the emotions and purpose of the Cast.

Second, because not just any Cast may be anchored. The process of anchoring expands potential power but also introduces limits. Every anchored Cast must be constrained within a time period that, like the Artifact itself, is relevant to the Caster's purpose.

Third, because of the inherent danger. Destroying an Artifact doesn't destroy the anchored Cast, but rather the opposite—while the Artifact exists, the Cast is easy to remove, but once destroyed, the magic grows wild, spiking in unintended ways and becoming stronger, often rebounding on the one who Cast it.

I have experimented with Artifacts and found them disappointing. Perhaps it's the swordsman in me, but I prefer to lean on my own strength to accomplish things. Discipline and practice make for better aids than any exterior crutch.

Big words for the failed Caster. Not that an Artifact could have saved his father, but Baron's supposed strength had done no better. He shook his head, then returned to writing.

Corvin has always been interested in birds. Father nearly had a heart attack the first time we found the boy in the rafters of the stable—a toddler perched among the larks. Even now, I can't prevent Corvin from climbing rafters and rooftops. Leon tried once to follow but grew paralyzed by the height. I count myself lucky for that—I can only imagine the chaos if they were to hold their arguments in tree branches.

And finally, my witch's mark.

It's a rather long story. I wonder if I might tell it in person sometime?

Sincerely, etc., Baron

P.S. Without fail, I would be embarrassingly unseated in the first pass of any joust.

The following morning, Corvin delivered the letter and returned with a new one in hand.

Thus began the tumbling slope.

Dinner at the Reeves estate had quickly grown to be the most stressful event of the day. Keeping Leon from claws was difficult enough, but Huxley had claws of his own.

It was at dinner that the steward announced, "It's time to discuss schooling. Most children of court start attending at fourteen, and the process isn't a quick one, so we're behind in preparation."

Leon stiffened in his chair, eyes fixed on his plate. Baron clenched his jaw but said nothing, waiting to hear the direction Huxley intended to take.

But it was Corvin who spoke.

"I'm going to Fairfax."

Though the boy often shrank in Huxley's presence, this he said with conviction. The corner of Baron's lips tugged upward, and when Corvin caught his eyes, he gave a nod.

Huxley frowned. "Fairfax? Prestigious, to be sure, but expensive. Since you're not the son of an Upper Court seat, there's no need to overreach with accolades. It's enough to be schooled at a reputable institution. You may choose between Luton or Burnley."

"Baron went to Fairfax."

"A waste of estate funds, how unsurprising. We won't make the same mistake."

Leon gave Huxley the side-eye. "Falcon-head said he's going to Fairfax."

"Ah." Huxley dabbed his mouth with his napkin. "We'll need to address your schooling as well. While I doubt either Luton or Burnley are equipped with a strict enough etiquette program to save you, we will nevertheless make the effort. Whichever school your brother turns down is the one you may attend."

Silence reigned at the table, broken only by the scrape of Huxley's fork as he continued eating.

"You'll split us up?" Corvin's voice had gone small.

Huxley chewed, swallowed, then took a drink from the hip flask he always kept on his person, out of Baron's reach.

"It must be done," the steward said. "We can't afford broken vases or other accidents to reflect on the barony. Now, with regard to the estate finances, there's simply no allotment for six years of schooling, so the expected three will be given to Corvin, as future lord baron. Leon will attend a single year. It's not ideal, but twins aren't ideal for financial budgets."

Leon looked away from the steward—which was good, because his pupils had narrowed to vertical slits. Corvin seemed not to have absorbed the situation enough, sitting paralyzed, and Baron didn't dare wait for the boy's emotions to fully catch up.

"*Enough*," Baron said. "Boys, leave us, please."

Leon's chair tipped backward as he stood, and the twins slipped away in a rush.

Huxley returned to his food. With a tone of forced calm, he said, "I'll remind you I'm in the direct employ of the king. He'll be informed of any threats you make."

"Threats are not my intention, Mr. Huxley. No matter what you believe, I am not out to curse you the moment your back is turned. I do not spend my waking hours plotting how I might transform your drinks to poisons. I have better things to do with my time and attention—like care for the safety of my brothers."

Huxley opened his mouth.

"I'm not finished," said Baron. "You *will not* separate them, for school or any other reason. You *will not* imply they are a burden, financially or otherwise. They did not arrange to be born twins, nor did they arrange to be orphaned at such a young age. They do not need more grief in their life. They need safety, and they need each other.

"Additionally, I realize your attention as steward is focused on Corvin, but your position gives you no right nor excuse to belittle Leon. You cannot demand respect and proper manners without displaying any yourself."

Huxley wouldn't meet Baron's eyes. He took another sip from his flask. "You play the part well, my lord."

"The part of a concerned brother?"

"The part of a baron." Huxley's eyes flickered toward Baron's throat. "Then again, perhaps the confidence and authority come from something *other* than the family title." He stood. "I'll consider your suggestions, my lord, but in the end, I will do what my stewardship requires."

It was always the same.

CHAPTER

21

50 DAYS LEFT

Aria's mental quill had never been so active, constantly marking her growing list of faults. It was all the secrets; they consumed her.

Baron told her of magic, and with each explanation, she felt a renewed surge of hope that her curse *could* be defeated. He told her of Artifacts, and she made a list of items Widow Morton may have used to anchor her curse: the broken teacup, the towel with Aria's blood, the false peace agreement.

She hoped it was not that last option, because she'd thrown it in a fire.

Foolish. Mark.

The other items could be recovered from Widow Morton, if Aria only had a way. In the daytime, she forced herself to walk upright with her journal, murmuring plans aloud to keep the exhaustion at bay. Ironic how fighting exhaustion created more of it, like battling a hydra with continuous heads.

She also wrote to Baron.

Questions upon questions. She asked what he loved about swordplay, asked about the greatest difficulty in tending an orchard, asked if the twins' arguments ever dragged him in or if he possessed a superhuman ability to remain peacekeeper. Remembering that their dialogue was a *conversation* rather than an interrogation, she also volunteered information about herself. She told him of Eliza, her optimistic sister who saw romance bloom in every flower and sunlight break through every storm. She told him of Jenny, though she couldn't mention the sisterhood there, and that she was a kinder companion than anyone deserved, certainly Aria.

She did not write of her parents. Any attempt left her with halting words and smears of ink blotting the page, forcing her to crumple it and begin anew. Secretly, Aria had always wondered what people in court thought of her parents' relationship. No one said anything was wrong, but everyone could *see*. When Baron saw her parents sitting apart at court events, never dancing, never speaking, what did he think?

She wanted to know.

She could not ask.

Coward. Mark.

Nor did she ask about his steward. Their brief meeting had been too little to judge the man by, but Aria had later looked into Auden Huxley's service to her father, then shied away. Not because the history was bad—the opposite. The man was devoted to the royal house and the ideals of Loegria. Upright in service. It should have been a good thing.

But did Mr. Huxley take her father's discredit of Baron to heart, or did he simply tend his duties without adding unnecessary judgments?

She wanted to know.

She could not ask.

I can't help but worry that you'll think me very flawed, the more you get to know me.

Even admitting that felt like a weakness, and a crown princess could not be weak. *Mark.*

Yet Baron's response was overwhelmingly gracious.

*In my estimation, the goodness I have seen so far ex-
cuses a great deal of failings that may be revealed.*

It was only after doing a full circuit of her room with his latest
letter pressed to her heart that Aria realized she looked like Eliza.
She blushed, then began working on a reply. Baron's crow waited for
replies if she asked him to, though he'd taken to fluttering off while
she wrote, then returning to collect the letter. Perhaps he enjoyed
investigating the perches of the castle or had made friends with another crow nearby.

When duties delayed her response and Aria had to use her own
falcon, Eliza caught her sneaking into the mews.

"What are you up to?"

Aria whirled around, tucking the letter behind her back. Around
her in the dim light, the falcons stirred gently, letting out little gur-
gles of sound. Her own falcon, Dawn, perked up, wriggling out of
her personal nook to stand at the ready on a post.

"You're sending a letter." Eliza lifted her eyebrows. "Why? To
whom?"

"Kendall." In Aria's panic, she named the first non-green-eyed
man to come to mind.

Then she flinched.

Dishonesty. Concealment. Lies. All marks.

Running out of words to properly convey this failing. Mark.

"No, you're not. Jenny told me you asked him to visit the castle
again today, so he has to be on his way right now. Why didn't you
invite me? Just because I was cranky about his last visit? I still want
to *support* you—that's exactly why I think you should court someone
you actually like—but if you want me to be silent on the matter, I'll
. . . No, that's impossible. I can't be silent on the matter."

Despite herself, Aria cracked a smile. Then she sighed, her arm
falling slack at her side, revealing the letter. "I invited Kendall to visit
because I'm ending the courtship."

It had been unfair to him from the beginning. He was a gentleman, with qualities to admire, and he deserved someone who could admire them properly. Someone who would appreciate his musicality or the fact that he thought a flute to be the most appropriate "sorry you fell from your horse" gift. Aria had given it to her mother.

Kendall deserved better. Perhaps Aria did too.

Her mind tingled with the wild possibilities of what *better* might be.

"Aria!" Eliza gasped, snatching the parchment and rotating it until she found the name. "*Baron*? Which baron? Baron Atherton? No, he remarried. Baron . . ."

She looked up, noted Aria's grin, and *harrumphed*.

"You must tell me *something* about him," Eliza demanded, "or I will hug you and not release. Not even for dinner."

"He has two brothers," Aria said, taking back her letter. She gestured for Dawn, and the falcon stepped forward, holding still to have her message canister affixed.

"Something *unique*. Almost every man of court has a sibling!"

"Very well. He also has a crow."

Crooning softly, Aria carried her falcon outside, then tossed her arm for Dawn to take flight.

"The messenger crow!" Eliza blurted from behind her.

Laughing, Aria dodged the rest of her sister's questions and returned to the castle with a light step. A little joy did wonders for her curse, shrinking the ever-present fatigue to a heavy shadow, pushed behind her as she faced the sun.

Aria's journal filled with more notes each day. Things from Baron—*While I must have contact with fluid to Cast, it can be indirect, such as through a cup or bottle, though indirectness can hamper effect*—as well as things from her own reading—*Most sources agree there*

is a third type of Caster, arguably gone extinct, and all *insist shapeshifters do not fall into this category but are a far darker kind of magic.*

Reading through the journal, she realized she'd gone off track somewhere. Rather than pursuing only questions related to her curse, she'd begun studying magic in earnest, soaking details in eagerly even if they had nothing to do with her specific circumstances. In the past, only a study of history had been of this much interest to her.

Perhaps it was because this *was* her history, being created in the very moment. At least, it *would* be her history, if she could manage to survive it.

Sitting in an Upper Court meeting, fiercely scribbling in her journal to keep herself awake while everyone discussed the problem of Widow Morton, she spoke up.

"A suggestion." Aria forced her voice to remain strong even as her eyes drooped.

After a moment's hesitation, her father gestured for her to continue.

"Rather than a direct assault, perhaps we might consider the option of stealth."

The debate took up immediately, led by her father's generals and others possessing military knowledge outside Aria's understanding. She'd not realized the difficulty involved with trying to infiltrate *up* a mountain. Pressed between the mountain face and a cliff's edge, Morton Manor had only two approach points—the first being the road itself, which would offer no cover, and the second being the sheer cliff, difficult for obvious reasons.

"Perhaps a Stone Caster could be of service." Aria spoke without thinking. "They could create steps within the cliff."

Everyone stared.

"Forgive me, Highness," Lord Emmett said, "but you mean of service *to us*? You suggest employing the very people we're against?"

Aria's face heated. "We're not against all Casters, Lord Emmett. Widow Morton is the danger, along with anyone joined to her, but there are others in the kingdom who are lawfully branded and practicing. Upright citizens."

"No Caster is *upright*," Marquess Haskett interjected. "No one's said it yet, but I can't be the only one thinking it's good they're all either showing their true colors with Morton or leaving the country."

"These are Loegrian citizens!" Aria protested. "It isn't fair—"

"Enough." Her father waved a hand. "We've diverged from the topic. Lord Crampton, you had another suggestion regarding stealth."

Shrinking in her seat, Aria returned to her journal and wrote a question for Baron, which she later transcribed to a letter.

> *How do you face it? When people take one look at your mark and think they know you, how do you face it?*

In his next letter, he responded.

> *Practice—I've had a lifetime of it now. Controlled temper—no one has ever changed their opinion of me because I bested them in a shouting match. Comfort food—Leon makes a lemon tart that, in his own words, "makes anyone forget about the idiots."*
>
> *Most importantly, I stand tall, because even if they don't know who I am, I do.*

He was so dignified. Confident. If Aria possessed a tenth of his composure, perhaps she could make herself heard in meetings.

Perhaps her father would *listen* when she explained why she broke off a courtship.

She told him directly, because after Northglen, she hoped to never again keep a secret from him—except the curse, which she did not keep by choice. They sat together by the fireplace in his sitting room, playing his favorite strategy game, which involved marbles of four colors spread across a board and far too many move options for Aria's tired brain.

"I am no longer courting Kendall," she said.

Her father looked up sharply.

"You were right to criticize my choosing of him," Aria said. "I made the decision recklessly, and it was a mistake. We've talked, and while he isn't *happy*, I think we parted amiably. I have no intention of abandoning my duty, so I intend to find another suitor. After proper consideration this time, I've decided to look for someone attractive to me in appearance and personality but who also balances my weaknesses." She ducked her head. "I suppose that means finding someone who can temper my recklessness."

Someone she could truly talk to. Someone who would let her speak ideas in their entirety and help her examine alternate options. Help her find the best path forward. Someone who would listen.

Someone like . . .

"No intention of abandoning your duty?" Her father scoffed. "What of the duty to follow through with your decision?"

"You yourself said it was a mistake, Father. Besides, I was not *married* to Lord Kendall, nor even engaged. Courtship always has the option of ending."

"So you committed to this *intending* to break it." He shook his head. "I don't know why I'm surprised, considering your other decisions of late."

The words stung. She heard the meaning woven within: *I expect you to fail. It's what you've proven you do.*

"As a queen," he said, "do you expect you can change decrees on a whim? Revoke laws once passed? Will you condemn an entire kingdom while you flit from impulse to impulse? You cannot put the cracks in the foundation yourself, then expect your kingdom to stand without falling."

Two impulses battled within her—the first to shrink, to apologize, to tally her mistakes. The second, to rage at the unfairness. She clenched her jaw.

She thought of Baron's words. *Patience. Controlled temper. Stand tall.* If he could do that under worse circumstances, she could at least try.

"I understand, Father," she said slowly. "And I'm not trying to be impulsive. I'm just . . . I . . ." She mouthed wordlessly before looking away. "I have this . . . quill in my mind, marking every mistake I make. I'm just trying to make it mark less."

Her father was silent. The firelight cast gray shadows across his white uniform as he moved a marble on the board, then gestured for her to do the same.

Aria looked down, blinked, and realized she'd lost track of whatever strategy she'd been attempting. Anything she tried to hold in her mind slipped away, like a book falling from tired fingers.

She nudged a blue marble diagonally into the next notch, and her father captured it with a marble she'd looked right past.

Dismal grasp of strategy. Mark.

"Just do your duty," her father said at last. "Stop looking back."

He made it sound so simple. *Just get it right the first time, Aria.*

When she'd started marking mistakes, that had been the idea—get it right the first time. How was she so bad at that as to keep running in circles *ten years later?*

— ❄ —

That night, alone and isolated, she wrote to Baron.

> *I've never told anyone this, but when I was eight, I started tracking my mistakes. I thought it would help me learn from them. Instead, I'm more aware of them, more trapped by them. Sometimes I believe they're all I'm capable of.*
>
> *I want to be capable of more.*
>
> *What if I don't ever get the chance?*

She didn't give that letter to Dawn. She burned it in the fireplace, like her quill from long ago, like Widow Morton's melted promises. Then she waited for morning's light to break the gloom.

But the morning brought a new horror. Aria should have seen it coming—after all, she'd reached the halfway point of her curse, and Widow Morton apparently wished to commemorate the occasion.

Someone had infiltrated the castle overnight. While Aria had been in her room, pacing, feeling sorry for herself, someone left a message for the king, stabbed through with a dagger right into his throne.

Aria heard him read it out loud, and it spread goose bumps on her skin.

"When you are vulnerable, Your Majesty, when you are exposed, tell me—would you have me extend mercy or a sword?" He crumpled the parchment in hand. "Morton."

With a growl, he spun to face the north wall. Outside the stained-glass windows, the nearby mountain loomed, home to Northglen, and Aria could picture Widow Morton looking down at the valley below, as stoic and steady as her granite-pillared home. Perhaps she exhaled in satisfaction, manifesting it in the throne room as a chill breeze through the open doors.

CHAPTER

22

When Baron first heard the news, he thought the castle had been attacked. Mrs. Caldwell assured him it wasn't that serious, though everyone remained on edge—a break-in at night, somehow passing every guard without opposition. A threatening message.

He wrote to Aria immediately, asking if she was all right. Receiving her next letter allowed him to breathe again.

The event itself isn't nearly so frightening as the implications. Rebellions, riots, wars—these things are a monarch's worst nightmare. Worse still is seeing the conflict approaching while being powerless to stop it.
May we speak of brighter topics? I am a coward.

Baron couldn't blame her. His own mind grew restless whenever he considered Northglen, and while it was not his responsibility to resolve the matter, he would certainly bear the consequences of it.

For both their sakes, he distracted her with a story from his school years, and he answered her latest question about Casting—*Is it possible for a Cast to change over time?*—before falling, as usual, into news of the boys. She never chided him for how much of his letters were about his brothers.

They're lucky to have you. A caring, trustworthy

sibling makes all the difference when facing the difficulties of life. I would know; I have Eliza.

How often she did that—soothed fears he'd not even meant to express. He hadn't told her of his deep worry that he was failing the twins, that his presence caused them more harm than good.

At times, you seem to read my mind. Are you certain you're not the magic user?

Only after sending the letter did he realize he'd never joked with a non-magic-user about magic. The topic had always been too full of teeth.

But Aria's response didn't bite.

Ah, the mythological third type of Caster—apparently a mind reader. If the ability allowed me to anticipate the needs and wants of others, I would get a great deal more things right in life. Mind Caster Aria. I am envious of the mythological me.

The crown princess envied a version of herself with magic. Baron never could have imagined the day—never could have imagined his part in it. Had he known changing the kingdom would be this enjoyable, he could have spared himself a lot of worry.

After one message handoff, Corvin joked, "You could at least tell me what the princess says, since I'm the best brother and never peek."

She said a great deal of things, and far too many of them stirred Baron's emotions in ways he didn't expect.

All he said was, "She warns you not to climb the palace roof."

After his stories of Corvin's climbing, she'd shared one of her own.

It is best that Corvin made no attempt to climb the palace roof while here, an activity which brings immediate wrath from the guards and many lectures to follow—he may take eight-year-old Aria's word for it.

Corvin's cheeks flushed red. "I don't!" Then, under scrutiny, he admitted, "I may have been tempted by a tower. Once. I may have perched—I have no need to explain myself."

Baron's stomach tightened. Leon still had a good sense of fear in him while transformed—a cautious cat—but Corvin seemed to find as much freedom in transformation as he found in flight itself. He went places he shouldn't. He lost track of time, of watching eyes.

And the most difficult line Baron walked was encouraging his brothers to hide without instilling in them a sense of shame. If they could not announce their nature to the world, he at least wanted them to stand proudly before a mirror.

"Don't be seen," he said, softening the words by ruffling the boy's hair.

Corvin smiled. "Don't worry about me."

Ironic, since Baron did little else. Especially as Huxley's sourness increased. When Corvin spent time under Huxley's tutelage, he left with scratched wrists and desperate eyes, often transforming immediately after. If Baron distracted him with letter deliveries, the boy remained upbeat, but Huxley grew more temperamental. For now, the steward directed his sourness at Baron, assuming Corvin's elusiveness was a direct result of Baron's interference. In part, the man was right, and since Baron could handle the hostility, he continued his path, each new letter renewing his own mood.

In addition to writing to Aria, something else kept him optimistic. For the first time in Baron's life, he was looking forward to a court event.

When he'd asked to speak in person, Princess Aria had responded with an invitation to an upcoming court joust.

Your brother will no doubt receive an official

invitation soon, but what it won't include is this: Come to the kitchen an hour early. I'll bombard you with the usual number of questions, and if you're willing, you could make tea. I've not forgotten the incredible effect of the last cup.

As the joust approached, Baron made drinks for his brothers without thinking.

"Glad to see you're back in the practice," Leon said, purring happily. "You must have lemons on your mind, because you made buttermilk, but I'll accept it."

For Corvin's part, he seemed to stand a little taller and more confidently in Mr. Huxley's presence, so Baron resolved to offer him morning tea more regularly.

Leon was correct—besides magic and letters, Baron did have lemons on his mind.

Autumn harvest had arrived.

—·❄·—

"My lord, you've no need to overburden yourself," Walter scolded.

"I'm far from overburdened," Baron said. "You needn't worry."

He loaded another bushel of lemons into the wagon, expertly dodging the set of hands that attempted to take it from him. Most of the orchard workers were quietly accepting of Baron's leadership, but Walter seemed to find it necessary to voice his protests in light of that fact, as if speaking for all of them.

"But, my lord, you've gathered more than any of us!"

"Indeed, I have!" Baron gave a roguish grin. "One can't expect to earn a title of such significance as 'Grand Gatherer' without a little sweat and work."

"That's not official!" Corvin shouted from atop a nearby ladder. "I'm still in the running."

"I'm three bushels ahead of you, Corvin."

"For now!"

The boy attacked the branches with ferocity, dropping lemons to the waiting hands below. Baron chuckled, along with a few of the workers. Walter gave a long-suffering sigh. Secretly, it pleased Baron to hear the man's protests each day.

After all, the same protests had been given to his father.

Through the nearby trees, Baron could see his father's bench. He'd expected to grow melancholy, working in this part of the orchard, yet he found himself surrounded by the best memories of harvests with his father. He also remembered a princess in the orchard.

She was right. It was breathtaking.

The cheerful atmosphere dimmed as Mr. Huxley limped into the workers' circle, accompanied by his ever-present manservant. He took an accounting of the two wagons so far.

With a sniff in Baron's direction, Huxley said, "Not as productive as yesterday."

Walter stiffened as if both his parents had been insulted at once. Some of the other workers exchanged nervous looks. Baron only pushed his hair back to wipe his forehead with a handkerchief.

"Nothing to say, my lord? You are responsible for this harvest, after all."

"Variety is standard," said Baron. "What matters is the accounting of one full harvest compared to another."

"And that is on a downward trend. It seems your expensive fertilizer was a waste, as I said."

Huxley looked up at Corvin. Though he gave no order, his disapproving gaze wilted the boy right down the ladder to the ground.

"Carry on," Huxley said to the rest of them, motioning for Corvin to follow.

Corvin walked with shuffling steps and head down, his enthusiasm drained.

Baron's fingers itched to throw a lemon at the back of Huxley's head, but with great discipline—and his father's imagined disapproval—he resisted.

More than once, Baron had considered writing to Aria about the steward, then retreated from the idea. So far, he had been honest with her as much as he could, only concealing the true nature of the twins. What could he honestly say about Huxley without betraying Corvin's secret?

Nothing, he decided. Though he may have lost responsibility for his title, he'd not lost it for his family. This was his problem to solve.

As the light faded, the fully loaded wagons returned to the manor. A few bushels were reserved for hamlet workers and their families, and a few more were labeled for the manor's personal use. The remainder would be taken to markets in Stonewall and Harper's Glade. The rest of the harvest thus far had already been collected by Mr. Pembroke, who sold to the navy in Port Tynemon, since lemons popularly warded scurvy at sea.

Baron had missed dinner due to a small accident in the orchard. No permanent injury, though they were now short one ladder. He hurried into the kitchen to find Leon studying recipes from the palace cook as if they were the most sacred of religious texts.

"You're late," the boy grumbled without looking up.

"Corvin?"

"Crow-lips is fine. We all survived."

Baron quickly found himself seated at the cramped kitchen table with a warmed bowl of stew and a slice of lemon pie. Leon returned to his recipes.

The kitchen door swung open, allowing Corvin to slip in, his expression creased in a frown.

Baron swallowed. "I'm sorry I missed—"

"We need to talk about Aria."

Leon's eyes flicked up, then returned to his study, though he tilted his head in a clear display of listening.

Raising his eyebrows, Baron said, "*Princess* Aria. What's the concern?"

"I think she's in trouble, Baron. She always looks so tired. Like she did during the ball, except now it's worse. And I've heard things, hovering around the castle, like how the guards can't stay awake during night watch. They think it's some kind of fatigue illness passing through the castle and that Aria has it. They said she fell from her horse."

Baron's breathing hitched. "Is she injured?"

"Just minor injuries. They said she was lucky. But there's something else—I was listening at the laundry window, because laundry workers always talk the most, and—"

Baron winced. "Corvin, you shouldn't—"

"Yeah, I know. *Listen.* Aria went to Northglen."

Leon's head shot up at that, recipes abandoned.

"Weeks ago," Corvin said. "Before we met her. Apparently, she didn't tell anyone, not even the king, and she hired her own guard and went to meet Widow Morton *alone*."

Leon snorted. "No idiot would do that."

"She's not a—never mind. The king tracked down the guards and brought them in to be questioned and got the whole story. Apparently Widow Morton made a peace agreement, except no one's seen it."

With great calm, Baron set his spoon down. "What are you saying, Corvin?"

"I think something happened!"

Leon rolled his eyes. "Obviously something *happened*. You can't even speculate right."

"All right, what do *you* think, since you know everything?"

As the twins fell into bickering, Baron's mind raced. All of Aria's questions about Casting, her interest in magic, in *him*—what did it mean? Did Aria want a better understanding of Casters because she had to decide upon Widow Morton's offer of peace?

She always looks so tired.

Baron had wondered, of course, the night of the ball—the way the princess stumbled out from behind a pillar, disheveled and bleary-eyed, the way she nodded off in the kitchen. Even the way she responded to his tea. It wasn't normal. Days later, she'd carried that same weariness in his orchard, like a cloud was raining above only her.

Dread constricted his breathing. Had she run afoul of a Caster?

The twins had fallen silent. With a blink, Baron came back to himself.

"Spit it out," Leon said. "You've got a face like the stew's sour, and I know it's not."

"Corvin, run up to my desk and bring the princess's letters, please."

Before Baron even finished the request, the door was swinging closed on Corvin's heel. Baron ate a few more bites of stew, then pushed his slice of pie toward Leon, who'd been eyeing it. By the time Corvin returned, he'd cleared space on the table.

One by one, Baron sorted letters, seeing them in a new light. There were enough now that they crowded the small table, overlapping corners and edges. He'd hoped to send her a response that day, but the harvest had gotten away from him, so he would manage only one more before the joust in two days.

Slowly, with the words on the table, he pieced a narrative.

"No . . ." he whispered.

During the first moments of his study, Corvin had politely averted his eyes, though he clearly fidgeted with curiosity. Leon showed no such self-restraint, craning over the table to read upside-down, and after some glaring at his twin, Corvin's defenses crumbled to join.

"She really did warn me not to climb the castle, even though *she* climbed the—Baron, how did you not ask for more details on that?"

"I am *not* afraid of heights," Leon said. "I'm just not stupid. Why is so much of this about us, anyway?"

"She's under a curse," Baron said softly. "She's hoping I'll break it."

"I don't see that anywhere," said Leon.

Baron ran his finger across a few of the details he'd picked out. "In her very first letter, she says she requires the aid of a Caster. Here, she asks about Artifacts, specifically wanting to know if destroying one will break a Cast. She asks about length of Casts, permanence, application. . . . She even mentions how she's studying the account of the last member of court known to be cursed. Here, she asks if one Caster can interfere with another, and then, here, about my strength as a Caster."

Leon nodded, then reached over to slap Baron's shoulder. "You're right. Good luck."

"Very funny. You remember you're the one who first encouraged me to speak to her."

"I said 'get a voice at court.' How was I supposed to know this voice runs around drinking everything Casters hand out? I thought she swallowed your tea too quick."

"Aria's just kind," said Corvin.

"Kindness is 'let me show you the kitchen,' not, 'let me drink something that might turn me blind.'"

Baron gave him a flat stare, and Leon held his hands up. "*I* know you wouldn't, but she didn't even know you. All anybody sees is the brand."

Baron's eyes lingered on the words of her very first letter: *The man behind the mark.* He'd really believed she saw him that way—as Guillaume Reeves, son, brother, lemon keeper. The individual, not just the Caster. In the same way, he'd felt he had started to see her as the woman behind the crown. He'd grown comfortable referring to her, at least in his mind, as simply *Aria*.

Though they'd discussed magic in every message, they'd also discussed siblings and interests, the way she looked forward to daffodils blooming in spring, the way he wasn't certain he made the best decisions for the hamlet.

It's a hard thing to bear direct responsibility for others, she'd written. *In truth, I worry every day that I'll fail as queen, but I can't seem to stop trying anyway. You care for those people, Baron. That means something.*

He'd told her about his first spectacular fails in swordplay, about how he loved reading the legends of Einar. She'd related some of her favorite historical accounts, including the story of a woman named Leah, who stood before an angry mob and prevented them from burning a town.

If I could be half the woman she was, she'd written. *Brave, resolute, caring.*

And Baron had been bold enough to say, *It seems to me you already are.*

Now he realized she'd been using him all along. Even her favorable view of his magic made sense if he could do for her what no one else could.

In his very first letter, he'd told her, *People are content to acknowledge that magic exists when it might benefit them. Nothing else.* Somehow, he'd forgotten his own words. Gotten carried away in the dream of something different and forgotten one thing:

When it came to how people viewed Casters, it was always the same.

"Baron?" said Corvin. "Do you think you can break the curse?"

Leon said, "Imagine what kind of reward you can ask for saving a princess. They'd give you the title back for sure."

Corvin's face brightened, and Baron took a deep breath. Leon was closer to the truth than he knew. Baron was an opportunity for the princess, but she was one for him as well. Nothing more.

"We'll find out at the joust," he said.

Either way, their relationship—whatever it was—would end there.

CHAPTER

23

30 DAYS LEFT

I t's today!" Eliza squealed. "It's today! It's today!"

She danced around the room in a way that made Aria's tired legs twinge even while standing still. But inside, she was dancing too.

Because today, she would see him again.

She glanced out the window; it was still morning. Never had a day crept slower.

Jenny finished lacing Aria's sleeves and began fastening sections of her hair. The princess's mint-green gown, commissioned especially for the tournament, bore the styles of summer, with sleeves that draped at her elbows and a skirt split at the front across a white underskirt. Her wide neckline traced a line beneath her collarbone and didn't close until just before the points of her shoulders. Her mother had warned that, without gloves, full sleeves, or even a shawl, Aria would freeze in the wind. Perhaps she would, but she hadn't been able to resist a last breath of fresh air before the heavy winter descended. Besides, the curse froze her often enough no matter what she was wearing; winter had become her companion long before the season arrived.

A better reason for the dress was that the green reminded her of Baron's eyes, and the style was more flattering on her than any of her other gowns.

Now I sound like one of those damsels from Eliza's poetry, she thought.

"Aria!" Eliza gasped, hands pressed to her mouth. "You're *gorgeous*!"

Too generous a description—Aria's eyes were sunken, revealing her for the tired skeleton she was—but if she was merely bones dressed for viewing, at least the viewing was elegant.

"Have you prepared yourself, Eliza?" Aria glanced coyly over her shoulder.

Eliza spun once more and leaned, dizzy, against a bedpost. "For what?"

"For when Henry wins the joust and declares to the entire court his intention to be your suitor."

Eliza turned as red as crushed tomatoes. Jenny's composure cracked into a smile.

"He has promised no such thing," Eliza said demurely. "Though when I see him before the joust, I shall be sure to remind him the most romantic acts are performed by a hero before a crowd." She raised an eyebrow. "And what of your mystery baron? Will you finally reveal him to me today?"

"Perhaps."

"Perhaps *I* shall just look for the man with two brothers and a crow."

"His brothers he may bring to court, but I doubt the bird will attend."

Jenny laughed, fumbling a pin. She righted it in the next moment, then stepped away. As requested, she'd left most of Aria's hair flowing down her back, taking only sections from each side to braid with ribbons and pin at the center. It was not as formal a style as Aria usually wore to court, but she remembered the way Baron stared at her when she'd visited his estate—and that day, she'd worn her hair down.

"Why have you kept him secret all this time?" Eliza whined. "Is it Christopher Hatcher? It's Lord Christopher, I'm certain. He hasn't quite inherited yet, but he *will* be a baron."

Secret. The word pierced Aria's ribs, and she shifted beneath the blow. There was no reason to keep her correspondence with Baron a secret; they were both unattached, eligible members of court.

Though one of them had been removed from title because he bore a witch's mark.

Hypocrite, her quill accused. The stroke it made seemed bolder than others, a thick, dark line marring the parchment of her imagination.

She was not ashamed of Baron. Not ashamed to be friends with a Caster.

Hypocrite.

Jenny helped Eliza dress, and they spoke of suitors and love, Eliza pestering the maid about her own romantic interests but earning no information beyond a mischievous smile. Jenny always seemed relaxed around Eliza while remaining formal around Aria.

Aria nearly joined the conversation, then stopped. She couldn't think of anything to say.

Once Eliza was ready at last, she and Aria left together, though Aria made her way to the kitchen alone. Eliza had her own secret rendezvous with Henry—earlier than Aria's meeting with Baron, since Henry was a tournament participant and Baron was not.

The kitchen buzzed with chatter, active as a hive. Everyone looked forward to a joust, including servants, who were relieved from duties during the event and allowed to stand behind the banisters at the edge of the field. Cook wouldn't attend—she carried no love for sporting events—but she would keep her staff busy so their few hours of absence wouldn't matter. Aria didn't want to be underfoot in the chaos, so she ducked into one of the nearby servants' quarters to wait.

To stave off exhaustion, she paced with purpose. She thought if she refused to sit, no matter how her body begged, she would be fine.

She didn't remember sitting.

She didn't remember closing her eyes.

But she woke sprawled against a servant's bed, with a curious maid hesitantly prodding her awake. Heart thundering, Aria sat up, feeling a wave of nausea.

She couldn't have.

Not the *one day*—

"Highness," the maid said urgently. "Are you all right? Are you ill?"

"The joust?" Aria's voice rasped. Inwardly, she prayed for a way to turn back the time.

The poor girl was baffled. "Less than an hour off, Highness. If you need—"

Aria thanked the girl, already dashing through the door and around the corner. She practically flung herself into the kitchen.

And she ran directly into Baron.

He grunted at their collision, barely catching himself with one hand on a rack of pots that clanged and rattled. His other arm darted around Aria's waist, keeping her from tumbling to the floor.

Leon's cackle echoed through the kitchen. "And you say *we're* clumsy."

A dull *whack* likely signaled Cook's wooden spoon against Leon's shoulder. Aria didn't check because she was busy looking up into Baron's eyes, as striking as she remembered—though much closer than she remembered—a lovely green speckled with faint hints of gold, like the first touch of autumn on a late summer day. A section of tawny hair had fallen across his forehead, and Aria felt the urge to reach for it.

She'd grabbed his arm by reflex, and she felt the corded muscles beneath his suit jacket, evidence of the swordsman beneath the noble.

She was staring. And blushing.

Baron's lips quirked into a wry smile.

Aria cleared her throat and stepped back. "There you are. Not that you were meant to be anywhere else. I'm sorry—I was in a rush because I didn't want to keep you waiting. I'd *already* kept you waiting, I mean, and I . . ."

Causing physical endangerment. Mark. Babbling. Mark.

"Think nothing of it. Better you bumped into me than into that." Baron nodded meaningfully toward the far wall, which held a display of hanging knives.

Aria pressed her hands to her cheeks, fingers cool against the heated skin. She drew in a deep breath before lowering them, composing herself.

"Thank you," she said. "For your good humor and for waiting. I'm afraid I . . . fell asleep."

At her words, his smile fled, leaving him with a grim expression as if he'd remembered an unpleasant duty. He ran one hand through his hair, pushing the unruly section back into place among the rest of the thick waves. He tugged at his gloves.

With a glance at a passing kitchen worker, he said, "Perhaps we could speak in the hallway."

"Yes, of course." Aria hesitated, then said, "Or, I thought we could visit the observatory tower, if you're interested. It's secluded and has a lovely view. I thought Corvin might enjoy it more than the kitchen."

Corvin perked up from where he'd been cracking walnuts. "Oh, I've seen it. I—" His face blanched. "I mean, I snuck up there the—the night of the ball."

Aria smiled. "It's lovely, isn't it?"

"Yes, it—fantastic view. I'm good. I'll stay here."

Baron had paled as well. No doubt he'd warned the boy not to go sneaking in the castle. For his sake, Aria restrained her smile.

"The hallway is fine," Baron said. "This won't take long."

One hand braced on the hilt of his dress sword, he disappeared through the door, and after a moment of confusion, she followed.

The empty hallway felt strange after the bustling kitchen, like they'd stepped into the night air away from a fire. Aria pointed down the hallway at a bench, and Baron strode to it alone, without offering his arm for her. It wasn't like she *needed* an escort for a twenty-foot walk, so Aria shook off her momentary disappointment and sat beside him.

He held himself stiffly, looking forward. "I apologize for Corvin. He has a bad habit of . . . going places he shouldn't."

"Curiosity's not a crime. Besides, it's not as though he . . ." Her voice trailed as she thought uncomfortably of Widow Morton's son, then finished softly, "Spied."

Her posture stiffened to match his. They sat in silence.

All these days, Aria had looked forward to seeing him again. How could an in-person conversation be more difficult than words on paper?

"I know—" he started.

"You promised—" she started.

They looked at one another. Aria coughed a small laugh.

"You first, Highness."

Highness. She'd hoped he would call her *Aria*, but she wasn't about to suggest it. Though it felt a silly distinction, she wanted him to choose informality without any influence from her.

"You promised me a story." She reached up and lightly touched the top of his witch's mark with her fingertip, just beneath his chin. "About how you got this."

At her touch, a line of goose bumps dotted his neck, and she felt a flash of guilt. She'd not considered her fingers might be cold. His skin was certainly warm, with the faint prickle of stubble, and though it seemed a shame to lower her arm, she did, rubbing her hands in her lap to warm them.

For a moment, Baron didn't speak. He cleared his throat, leaning back against the wall as if away from Aria's touch.

At last, he said, "You're aware Casting ability is woken by an effort on the Caster's part."

She nodded.

"Most often it's in response to their physical environment. I'm told Richard Langley, at ten years old, cleared rubble to save his friend. Dowager Countess Morton reportedly grew frustrated with cold bathwater and warmed it herself. She was seven."

Aria's eyebrows shot up. "Such a trivial thing?"

"To change an entire life, yes. It most often happens in childhood because children want things desperately without regard to consequence."

And we brand them for it. Aria squirmed beneath the thought.

"By the time un-activated Casters reach adulthood, they've learned to tamp down the call of magic, reaching for other solutions in its place. Eventually, the spark vanishes altogether. There's a reason the law doesn't bother testing after seventeen."

"And yourself?"

"I'm something of a . . . unique case. I've been activated as long as I've been alive."

Aria frowned but didn't challenge him. His green eyes flickered in her direction, then away.

"At my birth, there were complications. My mother bled far too much. Father says when he first held me, I cried, but I also faintly glowed with a Casting. He thinks I activated my abilities in an attempt to save my mother."

"As an *infant*?" Aria's eyes widened. "How . . . ?"

"A great deal of magic is instinct rather than thought." He lifted one shoulder, though the careless gesture didn't match the strained lines of his jaw. "Regardless, whatever attempt I made failed, and my mother died. My father was left with arguably the world's fussiest child, one who soured milk without meaning to, or vanished bathwater in a tantrum. Many of the servants refused to work with me, and it was nigh impossible to keep a nursemaid. I scared them."

His bittersweet smile at his description of vanishing bathwater faded, leaving Aria with an ache. She'd never seen this side of magic.

She'd never seen this side of Baron.

"Father was never afraid. He could have kept his distance for safety's sake, but while I was small, he carried me almost constantly. After that, he led me around by the hand. He never even wore gloves."

"You could have affected his blood," Aria said, realizing. *Blood is only fluid.*

Baron gave a curt nod. After a pause, he said, "I wanted to be just like him. He was . . . everything." He blinked a few times. "On to the witch's mark. There was no chance for me to be a well-kept secret, not with the constant cycling of nursemaids. Father received pressure early on to have me branded, and by the time I turned six, it was no longer a request."

"But twelve is—"

"The age for testing unknowns," Baron said, "but once a Caster is identified, branding happens quickly. I believe Widow Morton was eight for hers."

"I didn't know," Aria said softly.

She'd read her great-grandmother's branding law, but the official documentation covered only the age of testing and subsequent branding after a failed test. The policy for how to handle a Caster discovered outside of testing must have been documented during her grandmother's reign, though Aria hadn't yet found it.

Baron rubbed his witch's mark with his thumb, following the curves of the misshapen *S.*

Aria stared at the warped skin, imagining him as a little boy, imagining how much it must have hurt.

"Were you scared?" she whispered.

He cast her a rueful half smile, lowering his hand. "Obviously."

Her cheeks burned. *Asking insensitive questions. Mark.* But before she could apologize, he pressed on.

"Ironically, the day I gained my mark was also the day I gained my name. The man wielding the iron tried to console my father—not about his child being in pain, but about losing his heir. A Caster couldn't sit at court, after all. Among some other choice words, my father told the man I *would* be baron, and that's exactly what he called me from that day forward."

With a soft smile, Aria said, "I think I would have liked your father."

Baron hunched forward at that, bracing his elbows on his knees, staring down at his loosely knit fingers.

"It doesn't matter now," he said. "None of it matters. He's gone." He clenched his fists. "At least he doesn't have to see he was wrong."

In the silence, Aria's quill trembled, then dipped.

Mark.

She didn't know what it was for. There were no words for what she felt, but she *had* to have made a mistake somewhere, because only that could explain the sharp twist inside, the pinched pressure that made it hard to breathe.

Maybe it wasn't *her* mistake, but she was tangled in it. Her great-grandmother had written a hurtful law. Rather than correcting the policies, her grandmother had expanded them. Her father had been the iron voice that solidified the doubt cast on Baron all those years ago: *A Caster cannot sit at court.*

Aria had to *do* something. Something to mend it. *Something.*

Because it wasn't right.

Gently, she rested her hand on Baron's back, between his shoulder blades, and began rubbing circles with her fingers. She felt his muscles shift, but he didn't sit up or pull away. He looked up at her, a question in his bright eyes.

"I intend to abolish the branding law," she said. It wouldn't fix everything, but it was a place to start.

He frowned, as if he didn't quite believe it.

"I . . ." All at once, she found herself admitting things she shouldn't. "Truthfully, I met with Widow Morton once, and we discussed changes to the laws regarding Casters. She was not impressed with my offers, I'm afraid, but still, I—"

"Do you mean it?" Baron asked.

She met his piercing eyes. There was a vulnerability in his expression. He held his lips slightly parted, as if he considered speaking more but couldn't find the words.

"Yes," Aria said.

She didn't know whether to give that a mark or not. If she did, it wouldn't be for lying.

CHAPTER

24

Baron had come to the castle so sure of how he felt. Betrayed. Used. Resigned to a world that did not intend to give him anything he hoped for but still dangled the chance before withdrawing it.

Then Aria came barreling in—quite literally—to confuse it all again.

She moved her hand down his back a few inches, still massaging, and brushed his spine in such a way that he gave an involuntary shiver, forcing him to sit up at last. She pulled her hand away. That was for the best. Otherwise, he might have stayed like that forever, enjoying comfort from a girl he'd come to care about but wasn't sure he could trust.

If what she said about the branding law was true . . .

With their closeness in height, he could not avoid her eyes, deep brown and earnest. Touched with a tired red. Even if she meant it *now*, circumstances could change. There was an entire Upper Court advising the king, all of whom would surely be eager to explain to the princess why freeing Casters in any way would only damage the kingdom.

At least there was one thing Baron could be certain of.

"You sought me out," he said, "because you're trying to break a curse."

Her eyes widened, but she said nothing.

"After enough time, your specific inquiries concerning magic painted a picture. I'll warn you now, there's no guarantee I can reverse it, but if you tell me the details, I'll do what I can."

In the back of his mind, he tried to push away the memory of his father thrashing in bed, the frantic servants, the physician's voice—

"I can't," Aria whispered. At Baron's frown, she mouthed soundlessly before looking away.

"Physically can't," he said. Not a question.

Her gaze returned with hope.

Well, that excused some of her subterfuge. Baron grimaced.

"Any physical restraint is a Stone Caster's work. Did Widow Morton have someone else with her? Richard Langley, perhaps? Did he touch you?"

The Cast restricting communication wouldn't harm her, and it wouldn't be particularly strong, but it would act as a blanket over Widow Morton's work. Her fluid Cast, the real curse, would be harder to find beneath the Stone Caster's cover.

Aria frowned. "Only a . . . servant woman. She had the palest blonde hair I've ever seen, almost white. But she had no witch's mark."

For a moment, Baron started at the description, thinking of his stepmother, Sarah. As if no one else in the world were blonde.

"Perhaps Widow Morton allied with an unbranded Caster from Patriamere," he suggested. "For the curse itself, what did the widow give you to drink?"

Her frustrated expression spoke volumes.

"All right." He raised a hand. "It's a blood curse, then."

Remembering the curious notes from her journal, the warning not to drink crossed out and replaced by *blood*, he'd guessed the truth, but it had been worth hoping otherwise. Any number of curses could be Cast in freely spilt blood, as long as there was enough hatred behind the intent. Considering the death of her son,

Baron imagined Widow Morton had been able to manage a great deal of hatred.

Curses. The worst side of magic, the side fed by rage, discontent, fear. Baron had Cast only one in his life, shortly after his branding. He remembered the hot tears, the raging fury inside, the desire to *break something.* He'd poured all of that into one of the orchard trees, superheating the water in every branch and leaf. The tree had exploded, as if by lightning strike, and Baron had been lucky to escape with his life, though a surgeon had spent the rest of the day pulling splinters from his skin and stitching him closed. He still had scars across his chest.

Curses were like that. The Caster always paid a cost.

"Do you need my blood?" Aria's voice trembled.

Considering the last time she'd bled in the presence of a Caster, the fact that she offered spoke to a wealth of bravery. Baron realized he'd not given her enough credit for that day in the kitchen. *Anyone* would have been afraid to take the cup he offered, but she had reason beyond most to refuse. Instead, she'd given him a chance.

"No," said Baron softly, "just your hands."

She wore no gloves, and he removed his, extending his hands. She slid her fingers into his. Soft. Warm. Nearly flawless.

"What's this?" He brushed his thumb over a long, thin scar on her pointer finger.

Aria winced, squinting through one eye. "My first foray into the kitchen. That wall you pointed out has been off-limits to me ever since, and on that subject, thank you again for saving me earlier."

"I haven't saved you yet."

He closed his eyes, focusing on the steady point of contact between their hands, pushing away the distraction of her lilac perfume. For a moment, there was only darkness—then, pulsing faintly at the edge of his senses, he found the song of her blood. It rose to envelop him. The Cast already in place revealed itself in the rhythm of her heartbeat, like a sharp note in every third chord of a melody. If it were a beast in a lair, it rumbled with the contentment of a king resting on a throne of skeletons, a beast which would not be removed except on condition of its own death.

It was worse than Baron had imagined.

"This is fatal." He opened his eyes, grasping her hands with more force than intended. "She means to *kill* you."

Aria's expression did not reflect the same shock, only a resignation.

All at once, Baron's memories crashed in—

Your father's collapsed! Come quickly!

Do something, Baron!

Sitting on the bed beside his father, everything shaking, clinging to the man's clammy hand, calling on all the power within himself, reaching desperately for a miracle.

Coming up short.

"I can't," he whispered, feeling sweat break across his forehead. "I can't combat this. I'm not strong enough."

Aria looked down. Her fingers slipped from his.

Baron swallowed. He opened his mouth to speak again—

From somewhere in the castle, a brass horn sounded. Aria leapt to her feet as if the bench had burned her. "The joust!"

25

Aria ran to the courtyard where her family waited in an open carriage, ready to head to the lists.

The queen sat peacefully in a deep red gown, her bundled hair woven with strands of tiny white roses, her expression breezy as she hummed a tune to herself. By contrast, the king was a red-and-white thundercloud beside her. The moment Aria sat next to Eliza, he waved for the carriage to move.

Causing delay. Mark.

"I'm sorry, Father. I . . . fell asleep."

"I am not surprised," he said, and his tone added a wealth of extra, silent words. After a quick glance in her direction, he added, "Don't mistake me, Aria. My anger is not directed at you. Not completely."

She shared a look with Eliza. The younger princess shrugged.

"Have the latest soldiers returned from Northglen?" Aria asked.

After the break-in at the castle, her father had ordered another strike against Northglen, though Aria didn't know the full details. Despite her best efforts, she'd nodded off in the meeting. She had, however, managed to speak to the captain in charge, briefly explaining Artifacts and asking him to bring back any suspicious items Widow Morton might have used to anchor her power. It was the best she could do.

Her father's expression darkened at the mention of soldiers, so Aria didn't press.

If Northglen became a true battlefield—if Casters became the *enemy*—what would happen to Baron?

Aria twined her fingers in her lap, missing the warmth of his hands around hers and trying not to think of his words. *She means to kill you. I can't combat this.*

Despite the chill breeze and overcast sky, the stands hummed with excitement. All of court was in attendance, with the rest of the seats given to castle staff and people from Sutton—one of the benefits of living near the castle. The contestants rode on prancing horses through the lists, giving parade to the audience, basking in cheers and, occasionally, catching a tossed handkerchief or flower.

Biting her lip, Eliza pointed out Henry, the contestant bearing a blue siren on his coat of arms. The sisters shared a smile.

The contestants took up their line, and the king stood to begin the formal welcome.

To Aria's surprise, he gestured for her to join him.

Brushing her skirt quickly, she strode to the front of the royal box, looking out over the canopied stands. Too many faces to find Baron, but he would see her, and she smiled at the thought.

"Esteemed members of court and people of Loegria," the king boomed, silencing the crowd. "Welcome to the Crown's joust. If only it could be a welcome beneath fairer circumstances. Instead, our kingdom is in dire times. Beset by wicked magic."

Aria's smile faltered. She glanced at her father, but he stared resolutely across the lists.

"The Morton family, once beloved in our court, has committed treason." Raising a hand, the king brandished a sheet of parchment, torn in the center by a dagger. "First, Clarissa Morton, once-countess and Caster, denounced the authority of the Crown. Next, she invaded the royal castle. Warned to desist, she persisted. Stripped of title, she persisted. Now, she has delivered a blow to the heart of the kingdom—she has cursed my daughter and heir!"

Widow Morton wasn't the only one delivering a blow. Aria's father had finally realized the truth, but rather than speak to her in private, he announced it to the kingdom. Aria felt as exposed as if he'd passed her journal out for everyone to read. Shouts rose in the audience, and conversations grew, like the first rumblings of a rockslide.

She wished she could find Baron's face in the crowd.

The king spoke louder still. "Thankfully, my valiant soldiers have managed to recover the malicious Artifact used in this curse."

At a gesture from the king, a servant came forward, carrying a thin display cushion with something atop it. Aria lurched forward, then stopped herself. It was not a broken teacup or bloody towel the servant carried. It was a strange bronze box, small enough Aria could have lifted it with one hand.

What is happening?

Her father continued without falter. "As a result of these events, I make two proclamations. First, all Casters within the kingdom are confined to their homes until this matter is resolved. Any found to be sympathetic to Morton will be arrested."

Illness swayed Aria on the spot. She remembered Baron standing before her father, speaking truth: *I've done nothing wrong.* Condemned for it anyway. He was out there right now, hearing this, bearing it like the burn of a fresh brand.

But the madness only grew.

"Second, any eligible man within court may take the Crown's challenge—to destroy this Artifact, thereby rescuing my daughter. The man successful in this endeavor will be awarded Crown Princess Aria's hand in marriage."

"*Father*," Aria hissed.

He didn't look at her.

"Be warned—those who fail this challenge will receive punishment in accordance with failing their kingdom. I seek only the most inexorable among you, those with the power and determination to protect this kingdom, now and forever.

"We will prevent our kingdom's fall from peace. We will stand strong, as Loegria has always done. In the face of threat, we will be noble, fearless, and undaunted!"

A cheer went up from the stands, shaking Aria's world like an earthquake.

"Let the tournament begin!"

CHAPTER

 26

The flags fell. Jousters galloped forward, colliding in storms of splinters. The crowd roared. By the end of the first round of eliminations, a contestant had already been carried prone from the field. Senseless competition with deadly consequences.

"I'm surprised you're still here," Huxley called to Baron, craning his neck above the twins sitting between them. "You did hear the king, did you not, my lord?"

Corvin inched away from Huxley on the bench, nearly climbing into Leon's lap, but for once, his twin didn't protest. Leon sat like a statue, fingertips digging into his knees, no doubt resisting all the emotion boiling within.

For their sake, Baron adopted his signature calm. "Seeing as we share a carriage, Mr. Huxley, I thought you would appreciate the postponement of my house arrest until you could enjoy the tournament's conclusion. If you'd prefer, we can leave now, and you'll forfeit the bets placed on Lord Nicholas to win."

Huxley returned his attention to the field, retaining a hint of satisfaction in his expression. As the next contestant was unseated, he cheered with the crowd.

The twins didn't cheer or shout insults. At the last joust they'd attended, before Father's death, Leon had been so eager to bellow abuses at a fallen jouster that he'd overbalanced on the stands and fallen himself, bruising his tailbone. Corvin would never have let him live down such an event, but he hadn't seen it because he'd been trying to climb Baron's shoulders to cry foul play at the other contestant.

Now they watched in silence.

Baron glanced toward the royal box where Aria sat in the canopy's shadow. He could no longer see her face, but from her shocked expression earlier, her father's declarations had been as unexpected to her as to the rest of court. Baron took a small bit of comfort in that.

Any amount of comfort was welcome—better than the veiled glares he received from all directions in the stands.

At last, the final clash roared from the lists and stands in crashing metal and screaming cheers. Henry Wycliff stood victorious over every participant.

Baron managed a hint of a smile. Earl Wycliff had seven sons, and there wasn't a bad one in the bunch—not even Hugh, who had declared himself Baron's official rival in swordsmanship years ago. Henry was second-youngest, barely eighteen, yet Baron wasn't surprised to see a Wycliff distinguishing himself yet again.

From the field, Henry bowed to the royal box, helmet lodged under one arm, dripping sweat yet beaming all the same.

The king stood. "Your inexorable champion!"

The field thundered with applause as already-hoarse voices cheered once more. One of the field attendants hurried forward to present Henry with a golden trophy, which he raised high.

But the king wasn't done. "A trophy is not all you have earned today, Henry, son of Earl Wycliff."

Henry turned back, grinning.

Somehow, Baron knew what was coming. *Inexorable.*

"You shall also be the first to take the Crown's challenge and compete for my daughter's hand!"

Like a man suddenly Cast to stone, Henry's smile froze, arm still hoisting a trophy that seemed to have dulled in the light.

Aria's expression couldn't be seen.

Baron applauded with the rest of court because people watched him from all sides, and he refused to meet Corvin's gaze no matter how the boy tilted on the bench.

As the royal family descended from the stands, Baron stood with the rest of the audience.

"Time to go home," he said.

Where he would then have to remain. Imprisoned for the actions of another.

He'd been wrong not to leave the country when he'd had the chance. He ought to have packed up his brothers and taken them to his mother's sister in Patriamere. She was a kind woman; she still sent him letters every few years. There were also lands across the sea, like Pravusat, where Silas attended university. It was a country boiling with war but welcoming of magic.

Edith had warned him to run. Most of the Casters he knew personally had already fled.

But every time Baron had considered it, he'd remembered his father's hopes, remembered that his parents were buried on Reeves soil. This warm land with its lemon trees was all Baron had ever known.

He'd sacrificed his life for lemons.

27

While the rest of court applauded Henry's victory and her father's declaration, Aria watched her sister, who sat hunched, never lifting her eyes from her lap.

As the king moved to exit the royal box, Aria caught the sleeve of his red coat.

She found she couldn't speak, yet whatever burned in her eyes was flame enough to make her father lean away from the heat of it.

"I did not decide the tournament champion, and selecting another for the challenge would have been a slight to young Wycliff's victory." His eyes moved briefly toward Eliza before he shook his head. "The matter at hand takes precedent over preference, and Eliza's romantic whims are such that she'll find a new boy within the week."

"You didn't have to do this," Aria whispered. "You didn't have to do any of this."

"You did not have to visit Northglen all those weeks ago. *I* did not begin this, Aria, but I will see it sorted right before the end."

He exited the box onto the field, moving to speak with Henry and Earl Wycliff.

Aria set her jaw.

Quickly, she crouched before Eliza, grasping her sister's hands. "I'll fix it. All of it. Trust me."

Her sister barely had time to blink before Aria was off again. As she left, the queen said something she didn't catch and didn't stop to hear repeated.

"Sir!" Aria barked at a royal guard. He snapped to attention. "Run ahead and find the carriage belonging to the Reeves family. They're not permitted to leave until I give word."

With a salute, the man rushed off. Her usual guards noticed Aria's departure and stepped forward to escort her, keeping the crowd at bay as she passed—though no one was in a rush to speak with her. They only stared, their bows and curtsies delayed, their minds no doubt full of the king's revelation of her curse.

Two proclamations her father had made. Two insane, terrible proclamations. Aria's mind reached frantically for a solution to each, and with every thud of her steps on the brown grass, she used the drumming to press away an ever-constant thought.

She had *asked* for an Artifact. Clearly this was some trap from Widow Morton, and once again, Aria had walked right into it.

— ❄ —

The guard Aria had sent ahead was not the only one waiting at the Reeves carriage. A squad of Loegrian soldiers waited as well, crisp in their red uniforms, with horses at the ready. Their presence had drawn attention, and every nearby carriage lingered, the owners keeping pretense of friendly socializing while the frequent glances toward the Reeves boys exposed their conversation for the gossip it was.

The sight stoked the earlier fire in Aria's chest. As she marched forward, she received bows and salutes from everyone present, but her attention did not waver from Baron and the twins.

"You're all right?" she asked without preamble or formality.

Baron gave the faintest of nods, easing her heart. The twins had been quietly arguing when she'd approached, but they both looked to her now, unable to mask their fear.

"Corvin!" Aria reached forward to catch the boy's hand, lifting his arm. He'd scratched himself raw at the wrist, even to the point of blood.

"Oh, nothing—it's nothing." Corvin pulled away, ears blazing red.

"It most certainly is not. Wait here a moment."

She moved toward the soldiers only to find her path blocked by a thin man with a pinched face, leaning heavily on a cane. The steward, Mr. Huxley.

"Your Royal Highness, may I—"

"I'll speak with you in a moment, steward."

Curtness. Mark.

She didn't care.

She turned to the officer in charge and gestured at the full squad. "What is the meaning of this?"

The officer stepped forward. "Per the king's proclamation regarding Casters, my squad was given orders to escort Guillaume Reeves home after the tournament."

As if he were a *prisoner*!

Aria breathed slowly, willing herself to consider the full situation, to weigh the responsibility of her kingdom against her personal feelings. Yet she found herself unable. Everything she had done in recent months, she had done for her kingdom, yet she'd gotten it all wrong. Widow Morton thought her an opportunity. Her father thought her a liability. She had tried desperately to be a worthy princess and wound up as nothing more than a scared girl, destined to either be auctioned off in competition or to be killed in it.

Perhaps it was time to do something simply because she *wanted* to.

Raising her voice to be heard by everyone nearby, Aria said, "Lord Guillaume is perfectly capable of finding his own way home. I imagine he knows the route better than you, officer. Your squad is dismissed."

The officer started. "Highness, I—"

"Was it my father who gave your orders?"

"No, Highness. Lord Philip—"

"I outrank an adviser to the king. For the second and final time, soldier, your squad is dismissed."

Though clearly still baffled, he saluted the order, and the soldiers peeled away.

"Boy, you told them." Leon grinned.

Baron gave a slight cough, though it did nothing to cow the boy's open enthusiasm.

"Your Highness." The steward was back, sweating along his brow line. "If I may, *I* would feel much more at ease with an escort of soldiers. You see, during my time at the Reeves estate, I have found the Caster to be belligerent at best, and at times even—"

"You may not," Aria said flatly.

He blinked. "Highness?"

"You said 'if I may,' Mr. Huxley, and based on the implications that followed, I have given my response: You may not."

When Baron had first presented himself to the king, she'd missed the opportunity to fight for him. When she could have told Eliza of the man who'd begun worming his way into her heart, she'd kept him secret.

I'm sorry, she thought. She couldn't fix it all, but she could fix *this*.

"Your Highness . . ." The steward gave an uncomfortable chuckle, glancing at the crowd blatantly eavesdropping on their confrontation. He was right; she couldn't forget the crowd. Everything she said and did in this moment would determine their opinion of Baron.

So be it. She would give them something to consider.

Aria made a little shooing motion, and after a moment's hesitation, the steward shuffled away, leaving Aria with the people she actually wanted to speak to.

"Corvin." Her voice softened. "You're certain you're all right? I could send for a physician's ointment."

"I'll be fine." The boy smiled, and he seemed to mean it.

"Very well. Leon?"

Leon's grin said it all.

Aria looked, at last, to Baron. His tawny hair caught the afternoon light in a lovely way, turning strands of it nearly orange, a striking combination with his green eyes. She wished they could have another hour of privacy, though it would still not have been long enough to discuss everything she wanted to. Of everyone in the kingdom, he was the only one whose opinion she cared to hear.

Raising her voice again, Aria said, "Concerning our earlier conversation, Lord Guillaume, I would be delighted to accept your invitation."

Baron raised his eyebrows, but he waited without speaking.

"I will indeed be the guest of honor at your upcoming celebration. Feel free to invite only those you hold in the highest esteem. I imagine this will be quite the exclusive party."

Whispers erupted from the crowd, and what had been shrouded glares became quick smiles with a desire to impress.

"Highness!" The steward sputtered. "He's under house arrest!"

"How very convenient, then, that the party shall be held at his house." She leaned in slightly. "Leon, I expect spectacular food."

"You got it!" the boy declared.

"Excellent. It's settled, then. Two weeks from today, was it?"

The good thing about a curse with a deadline was that it made scheduling easy. She would outlive Baron's party by another two weeks.

Her skin pebbled with goose bumps, and she swallowed hard to be so casually counting the rest of her life in mere weeks.

Then she focused on Baron, awaiting his response. Though he kept his expression mostly impassive, he stepped closer and spoke with a voice low enough not to be overheard.

"Highness, I told you I can't . . . help. I'm afraid it would be a waste of your time to—"

"Baron." She touched his arm, her heart twisting. "Did you think I cared *only* if you could help?"

Perhaps at first, but they were many letters past that.

After a moment, his expression melted into the most breathtaking smile she'd ever witnessed, twisting her heart in quite a different way. Her hand tingled where it remained on his arm, and she lifted it self-consciously.

"Two weeks, then!" Her voice came out too high. She cleared her throat. "I look forward to it."

"As do I," he said softly.

How she wished there wasn't a crowd present. Her eyes traced the lines of his face, lingering on his lips, still in a soft curve from his smile. She glanced back up at his green eyes. Watching her. Did he wonder, as she did, how it would feel to close the distance between them? She remembered the feeling of his strong arm around her waist, saving her from a fall. If she kissed him, *really* kissed him, the way she suddenly wanted to, would he feel any strength in her? His letters seemed to outline a version of Aria that she couldn't see, but one she wanted to become. Someone strong enough to find the right path, a path that helped others, like she was trying to do right now.

She saw the best version of herself reflected in Baron's eyes.

Finally, she tore her gaze away.

"Steward." She gestured Mr. Huxley forward again. The man no longer seemed eager to address her, focused on mopping his forehead instead, at least until she said, "I have a most serious charge for you."

Then she had his full attention.

"These three men"—she gestured to Baron and his brothers—"are very dear to me. You are to care for their well-being even before matters of the Reeves estate, do you understand?"

Deflating, he nodded.

"Tell him not to split us up," Leon interjected.

Aria looked sharply back to the steward. "I hope that was never a consideration."

"No, Highness! No, I . . . wouldn't dream of it."

"Good." And since it was proper, she added, "Thank you for your service. I'm sure you take your duties very seriously." She glanced once more at Corvin. "Sutton Town has an excellent physician. I suggest you visit on your way home so she may tend to the future lord baron's wrist."

"It was to be my first priority," the steward said.

She didn't call him out on the lie, instead offering a small smile of approval. With any luck, he would take her opinion to heart, and the Reeves boys would have a more comfortable time of things at home.

If only she could say the same for herself.

CHAPTER

28

At the king's invitation, several tournament participants remained at the palace for the evening feast, including the Wycliff family. Eliza was noticeably absent. The queen spoke exclusively with Lady Wycliff as if the rest of the table had faded from existence. Aria ate with her head down, not speaking unless spoken to—and no one was eager to speak to her now that they knew she was cursed. She heard one girl's whispered comment that the curse would be the death of the princess and *look,* didn't she appear dreadfully like a ghost already!

After dinner, she had no chance to speak with Henry, since everyone wanted to congratulate him on his excellent showing in the tournament and the possibility of his engagement to the princess.

Just before Aria left the room to turn in for the night, he caught her eyes. He was, admittedly, handsome. He wore his dark brown hair with a bit of length, and though it carried no waves, it flipped in adventurous little curls as it hit his ears and shoulders. Though dressed in formal attire—no doubt on loan from a royal closet, since his own clothes would have been sweat-soaked from jousting—he wore it casually, with his collar loosened and his shirt untucked beneath the blue vest. Eliza called him "heart melting." Aria appreciated that he didn't present as pompous.

But she could not banish from her mind a pair of green eyes.

Especially not when a maid stopped her outside her room and delivered a small package.

"It came by way of a courier from Sutton Town," the maid said, curtsying and hurrying off.

Aria unwrapped the bundle to find a glass vial and a scrap of parchment. She read the note first.

I'm sorry it isn't more, but know you have my thanks.
For everything.—Baron

The vial held a teaspoon's worth of clear liquid. Aria held it up, watching the yellow lamplight flash across the angles of the vial, watching the liquid roll smoothly as she turned it.

And she thought about magic.

In mythology, like *The Epic of Einar*, magic was always used to trick and deceive, whether employed by villains or heroes. It was a thing to be distrusted. In modern scholarly texts, magic was dissected and categorized by its relative danger—abide a Caster with caution, flee a shapeshifter with horror. It was a thing to be dreaded. In Aria's personal experience, magic was a confusion. Because the same power that cursed her had also brought her Baron.

She drank the vial's liquid in one swallow, and it tasted crisp as a mountain spring with just a hint of lemon. She smiled, thinking of green eyes and yellow orchards. Though it didn't carry the same strength as his tea, her aches eased, and her exhaustion faded to a dull weariness.

During her correspondence with Baron, Aria had reached out to one other Fluid Caster. It had been hard to find one still at home, but the elderly woman was likely too stubborn to leave her roots. Using a servant, Aria had disguised her purpose, pretending the request came from a merchant who hoped to ease the lingering tiredness of a long voyage. For a steep payment, the Fluid Caster had provided a single flask of "something healing."

Even with all the precautions, it had taken Aria a full, torturous day to work up her courage. The next morning, she'd tested the Caster's work and found it lacking poison, but also lacking luster. It barely eased her weariness, and the effects faded within the hour.

In her next letter, she'd asked Baron about his strength as a Caster.

Is your magic perhaps stronger than that of other Fluid Casters?

He'd responded.

There is variable strength in magic, but to my knowledge, it has less to do with the Caster themselves and more to do with their state of mind when Casting. For example, if Leon first puts me in a sour mood and then demands a correction to the level of salt in his broth, he deserves the resulting inedibility.

Aria smiled to herself, rolling the empty vial between her fingers, but her humor faded. Strangely, she felt a little like the vial—emptied of something powerful. She'd waited with such anticipation to see Baron again only to have the precious moments flee like a messenger bird vanishing into clouds.

Her night would be filled with letter writing, that was certain. But for the moment, with the newfound energy given by Baron, she snuck through the castle to have a closer look at Widow Morton's mysterious Artifact.

Although Widow Morton hadn't made an appearance since Aria's curse first settled, the princess knew as certainly as gray clouds would bring a storm that she would appear that night.

And because Aria could also employ theatrics, she waited for Widow Morton in the throne room, pacing around and between the four thrones on the dais. Aria had lit enough lamps to see by but not enough to fully banish the gloom, so her long, dark shadow played across the stone each time she turned directions.

"You seem anxious, Highness."

The cold voice came from behind, and Aria turned to find that the widow had spread her water mirror upward, rippling across the centermost of the stained-glass windows. The projection seemed thinner than before. Aria could see the iron framework of the window *through* Widow Morton, as if viewing cracks in the woman's soul. The widow still wore her black attire, but something about her looked different. A too-wide stretch to her eyes, perhaps.

Aria had asked Baron about projecting an image through water, and he'd said he'd never heard of such long-distance communication made easy and couldn't manage it after experimenting on his own.

"How do you perform a Cast like this?" Aria asked.

Widow Morton lifted her chin, as if getting a better look at Aria from beneath her slanted veil. "Curiosity about magic, Highness? I would not have guessed. Perhaps you hope the answer will give you some insight to your curse." When Aria didn't respond, the woman said, "Very well. An answer for an answer. This Cast is made possible through combination with another Caster. Now, Highness, tell me how *you* manage to resist my curse."

Resist. The woman had a sense of humor, it seemed. "I wouldn't be awake right now if I had power to resist."

"Correction, Highness. You would be comatose right now if you did *not* have power to resist. How long do you expect a person to last with mere minutes of sleep each day? At the very least, your mind should have fractured beneath the stress, yet I find you here, pacing, scowling, asking reasonable questions."

Aria blinked. She'd wondered why the curse had not grown worse over time but never thought to imagine the stability was not part of Widow Morton's plan. "I thought your magic did that. Extending the . . . torture."

"To an extent. The curse has a timeline, after all, but it is a time-line involving the others of your blood. I did not expect *you* to last this long."

That should have terrified Aria; instead, it made her smile.

"Then I question your skill in Casting, because not only am I alive, but the rest of my family doesn't suffer."

In the first days of her curse, she'd dreaded watching the effect spread. After so many days suffering alone, she'd taken for granted, without even realizing, that Widow Morton's most morbid predic-tion hadn't come to pass. Eliza was safe.

"Bridle that smile, Highness. You have surprised me, but you have not escaped me."

"Why did you give the soldiers that Artifact?"

Her father's soldiers had been forced back from Northglen, but not before capturing the suspicious Artifact, which they'd claimed had been encased in glass and surrounded by painted symbols of "suspicious warlockry."

"Perhaps I want to watch His Majesty dance."

The woman's image rippled against the wall, as if in silent laugh-ter.

"Is all of this what your husband would have wanted?"

As Aria had hoped, the question caught the widow off guard.

"My husband," Widow Morton said at last, "may have argued for your peace. But he was not a Caster, and he did not speak for me."

"Why continue pretending this is about Caster rights? Your son was not killed for magic; he didn't even possess any. He passed his test at twelve."

A shadow flashed across the widow's face, a moment of flared nostrils and hot anger. Though she returned quickly to her cold mask, Aria could not unsee it, and while her mind churned slowly over the meaning, she heard a noise behind her.

Turning, she saw a shadowed figure slowly dragging open the

throne room door. Her breathing quickened, imagining another intruder breaking into the castle, but the figure who stepped into the lamplight was a familiar one.

"Aria?" Eliza squinted, glancing around. "I thought I heard you."

As Aria gaped, her heart plummeting right off the dais, Widow Morton said her final word.

"You should not have questioned my skill. Thirty days left, Highness."

The woman vanished, and a curtain of water fell to splash across the stone.

"I couldn't sleep," Eliza said, looking around as if dazed, as if she hadn't heard the widow. "Really *couldn't* sleep, and I kept feeling more restless the more I tried. So I went to your room, but you weren't there. What is this?"

Aria stared at the puddle of water seeping into cracks in the floor.

Finally, she rasped, "It's Widow Morton's . . . gift."

At first, Eliza didn't believe it. She rushed into the hallways, ignoring Aria's calls behind her and growing more frantic with each guard she found asleep at his post. She fled to their mother's room and shook her shoulder, shouting for her to wake. But the queen did not rouse.

"It will be all right," Aria assured her.

It was a lie, and Eliza was too upset to hear it anyway. In the end, Aria gave her space. They would have plenty of time to talk. Thirty days of it. Unless one of them fell comatose or into a fractured state of mind first.

She returned to her room and stood beside her fireplace, kindling the logs and wishing the crackling little flames could sink warmth deeper than her skin. At her core, there was a chill that never left. A chill she'd gained in Northglen.

Eliza was why the widow had surrendered an Artifact. Once Eliza also suffered exhaustion, the king would have quickly realized the existence of a curse, regardless of Aria's forced silence on the matter. He would have taken bold action against Northglen. So Widow Morton had arranged proof of curse but also given him something to occupy his time. He thought, as most people did, that breaking an Artifact ended things. But the king did not even have the right Artifact.

And Morton only had to keep him occupied one month before it was too late.

If this was a siege, Aria couldn't help feeling the castle had already fallen.

CHAPTER

29

Having been directly confronted by the princess, Huxley had yet to regain his blustering confidence. Instead, he slunk around the manor, giving more suggestions than orders, making no comment when Corvin disappeared for long stretches. At times, Baron caught the man squinting at him, as if trying to reason through exactly how a Caster had won the favor of a princess.

Baron wasn't certain himself, but he found Aria was all he could think about. He remembered the panic on her face as she crashed through the kitchen door, remembered it melting into relief as he held her, and even as he logically knew the relief came from *not falling*, the most fanciful part of himself held it as something else. Relief at being in his arms. For a moment after the joust—after she'd saved *him*, repaying the kitchen and then some—he'd thought perhaps she'd glanced at his lips, held his gaze with longing.

She sent a new letter the night of the joust, and Baron woke at dawn to receive her falcon because he heard it the instant it tapped at the window. Sometimes he heard that tapping in his dreams.

It was the shortest letter she'd ever sent, speaking about nothing in particular, and at the end, her valediction both lifted and pierced his heart.

I miss you,

Aria

In his mind, Baron returned to the palace hallway, sitting beside her, feeling the softness of her fingers wrapped in his. Hearing something in her blood roar. It began to live in his memory beside the image of his father thrashing in bed. The last time he'd needed his Casting to save someone, he'd failed.

Was he going to fail again?

"Do you *have* to practice in my kitchen?" Leon whined.

Baron ignored him, waiting for the pot above the flames to boil.

"Go to the lake or something. Stop hogging my fireplace."

"I need moving water," said Baron. One of the difficulties in working with blood was the constantly changing nature of it, the combined tangle of motion and life not present in any other liquid. The living aspect he couldn't replicate, but movement he could. He had to begin somewhere.

"Then find a nice river!"

"Oh, we have one lurking in the house I was unaware of?"

Leon hissed, then turned to quiet grumbling, apparently remembering Baron's traveling restrictions.

The water began to tremble and shake, bubbles rising with the haste of drowning sailors to reach the surface. Baron dipped his fingers in. The water couldn't burn him—though the pot could if he brushed it by accident—but neither did it calm at his touch. He closed his eyes and breathed. The song of the water was not a smooth melody but an agitated staccato of notes, hard to grasp, harder to predict, but he caught it at last.

He opened his eyes to a pot holding a soft golden glow, smooth as a waiting canvas.

"Congratulations," said Leon. "Now make it boil again because I need it. And it better not taste like your fingers."

Unfortunately, it was not nearly as easy to strain out a curse as it was to filter a temperature.

"Do you ever practice your Artifacts?" Baron asked absently, heating the water as requested.

Leon's stare gave the impression of a cat flattening its ears. "What's the point of making little night-vision trinkets? Who's gonna use them? Waste of cooking time. If you're looking for help with some other weird training exercise, bird-boy is the one you want."

Artifacts worked quite differently for Affiliates than for Casters. Perhaps *Artifact* wasn't even the proper term. Without the ability to practice openly and confer with others sharing their talents, the boys had discovered the possibilities of their magic through accident more than anything. Corvin had been the one to discover they could imbue certain objects with attributes from their Affiliated animal. He was still hoping he could create an Artifact that gave the power of flight. Baron hoped he didn't accomplish it, because Corvin would undoubtedly use it to launch Leon into the sky to see if he landed on his feet.

"I was only curious." Baron stepped away from the fire. "The persistence of a cat would benefit me at the moment."

"I've seen you swing a sword for hours without even fighting a real person; you've got persistence enough. All a cat-ribute would give you is the overwhelming urge to nap in a puddle of sunlight."

He made a good point. After pulling his gloves back on, Baron headed for the training yard.

Baron's ears rang with the echo of every connection between his practice blade and the dummy's battered armor. At least temporarily, the rigorous activity banished his fears.

Something darted through the grass. Baron spun on instinct, already swinging. The long, gray snake dodged his wooden sword point with unnatural swiftness, and in the next moment, the adder vanished in a swirling column of gray mist, transforming into his best friend. Silas stood with vest unbuttoned and hands in his pockets, smirking as if he'd never left. As if it hadn't been *two years*.

"Silas!" Baron dropped his sword. His ears rang as much with the sudden silence as they had with his strikes. "I could have killed you!"

"Not with this tree branch, you couldn't." Silas wiggled the toe of his boot beneath the practice sword and kicked it up, stumbling to catch it. He gave the blunt weapon a few dramatic swings with terrible form. Though he stood tall and broad-shouldered, Silas was an academic, not an athlete. He probably had a small book or at least a collection of folded notes squirreled away in each of his pockets.

"How was the university?"

"I told you in my letter."

Baron snorted. "Your letter had barely a dozen words in it."

"You imply a dozen words can't speak the truth?"

He must have driven his instructors to madness with similar debates. Baron found himself smiling. "It's good to have you back."

Silas laughed, turning the sword so Baron could take its handle. "You are the *only* person in the entire kingdom who would say that. Even Maggie only gave me an earful for missing her birthday."

"I believe she was expecting a dance from her brother. You can make up for it next week by bringing her to the event I'm hosting."

"Since when do you host *anything*? That's one of the reasons I come here: the seclusion. Don't tell me you've been consumed by society in my absence." His dark eyes widened. "Don't tell me you've *married*."

"I haven't." To his surprise, Baron's chest pinched as he said it. He'd never looked forward to marriage, knowing well its pitfalls— after all, he'd witnessed his father's second marriage from hopeful start to devastating finish. Yet he found himself considering things he never had before.

"Come inside." Baron nodded toward the manor house, hidden

by trees and the long weapons shed. "I'll try to keep the truth to a dozen words, but no guarantee."

Leon nearly burst a vein at another intrusion in his kitchen, at least until Silas produced a leather pouch of some spice unique to Pravusat—then the boy happily accepted the bribe. Baron could have spoken to Silas in the parlor, but there was always the chance Huxley would happen in; the man never came to the kitchen or other servant areas.

They discussed the removal of Baron's title, the unrest in Northglen, and finally, Aria.

"Morton's right," Silas said.

Baron raised an eyebrow, surprised not to find a sympathetic friend in Silas. "Did you miss her attack on Aria?"

"Did you miss her son's brutal murder? Gilly, look." Silas leaned forward in his chair, resting one elbow on the table. "Revolution is ugly, and it comes with blood, but that doesn't mean it's wrong. For centuries now, Loegria has clung to prejudiced tradition rather than progress. That prejudice branded you, and it nearly killed me."

He was referring to the event that had sent him abroad. While arguing with his father, Silas had lost his temper and transformed, revealing his nature as an Affiliate. Without a moment's hesitation, Lord Bennett had tried to kill his own son.

Luckily, Baron and his father had been present, and while his father restrained the man, Baron broke the law by forcing Lord Bennett to drink a Cast. The action still shadowed his memory, but he would rather break any number of laws than see his friend dead. Baron hadn't been able to make the man forget everything—otherwise, he risked Lord Bennett's mind breaking the Cast—so he'd confused the viscount into thinking the reason for his rage was that

Silas had struck him. Silas had been banished abroad for two years, wounded but alive.

He bore the scar on his neck—not a brand like Baron's, but a thin slash beneath his jaw from his own father's sword. Had Baron's father moved any slower, the matter would have been decided in that single blow.

"Aria isn't like your father," Baron said.

"No one's like my father, Gill. The man's a dragon parading human skin. That's not the point. I'm sure your princess is darling as a hummingbird, but she's royalty, and when royalty won't bend, some Morton rises up to break it." Silas shook his head, black hair swishing against his forehead. "I witnessed *two* revolutions in Pravusat. That country is like a plate that keeps getting thrown to the floor and scraped back together into a new shape. Loegria will survive this, and the new shape might be better for everyone."

"Not for Aria."

"That's a cost, but is it too high? Not in my estimation. Pravusat and Cronith and a dozen countries I barely have a concept of—all just one ocean away. If you could *see* it. Their *architecture* when they let Stone Casters freely build. Their *medicine,* Gilly, when they let Fluid Casters do the healing. They're developing new germ theories around the understanding of blood—their research papers would amaze you—and they're even restarting failed hearts. They're saving more mothers in childbirth, and . . ."

He closed his mouth into a grimace. Silas often got carried away in excitement, but he knew Baron better than anyone.

Softly, Baron said, "Good for them."

"I'm sorry." Silas shook his head. "That's the thing, though. Imagine what you could do in a society that *encouraged* you, that trained you properly."

"Society didn't prevent me from saving my parents. The failing is entirely my own."

Silas heaved a sigh. "What's so enticing about her anyway? Your princess."

Baron thought of Aria asking after the well-being of kitchen servants, offering ointment for Corvin's wrist, barking a sharp dismissal to soldiers on his behalf. Most of all, he remembered her sitting in the silence with him, rubbing his back, offering support when he didn't even know he needed it. For a moment, his voice deserted him.

He'd never known the claws of longing could sink so deep.

At last, he said, "She cares."

The message buried in a thousand words across a dozen letters, in her questions about his interests, in her sympathy about his missing stepmother. Aria cared about him in a way he'd never imagined any girl would.

"If she cares enough to change an entire kingdom for you, then take my blessing. It's just an awfully big gamble to make, Gilly."

"She's already promised to eradicate the branding law."

"That's a start." Silas raised an eyebrow. "And how does she feel about your resident cat-and-crow?"

Baron's eyes darted toward Leon at the other end of the kitchen. The boy gave no indication he was listening, but he had sharp ears.

Silas nodded. He let the silence say it all.

Then he pushed back his chair. "Before I leave, I'll pay my respects to your father. Maybe see if I can summon an angel. Broker a deal to switch my father's life for your father's, because whoever's running life and death in the world really, *really* made a mistake." He gave another small grimace. "I'm sorry I wasn't here."

"There wasn't anything you could have done." Baron forced back the memory of the physician, the haunting voice always one step from his awareness—*There's nothing I can do*—and cleared his throat. "You won't stay for dinner?"

"Maggie would have my head if I abandoned her for the evening, but I'll make sure she knows about your *party*." He made a show of rolling his eyes. "At least that will satisfy my mother that I'm socializing again. She and Father both intend to see me married off yesterday, never mind I'm still two months from twenty, but at least she pretends it's about happiness instead of hierarchy."

He paused on his way out to talk to Leon about Pravish cuisine, and then he was gone.

Leaving Baron alone with nothing but questions and memories.

CHAPTER

30

28 DAYS LEFT

The Crown's challenge was straightforward: Any man undertaking it would stay in the castle three days, during which time he would have full access to the cursed Artifact—under guard, of course—and the freedom to destroy it through any method.

After being given two days to prepare, Henry returned to the castle, and Aria had an opportunity to speak with him at last. She met him in the display room where the Artifact was housed. Two guards stood at the door, failing to conceal their curious glances.

"Your Highness." Henry performed a deep bow, then tossed his head to move his hair from his face.

Aria didn't wear a gown as she would have for a suitor. Instead, she met Henry in a silk shirt and vest, armed to help. With a grunt, she dumped a stack of books into a chair at one edge of the room, huffing a winded breath after.

At Henry's wide-eyed blink, she patted the stack. "Any information on Casters from our library, along with my own personal notes. I should inform you—I've been warned by a trustworthy Caster that breaking an Artifact may have unpredictable effect on its magic."

Even so, she could not request he fail the challenge. Not with his own fate on the line. Besides, she couldn't see a better path forward, not when Widow Morton wanted to keep her father distracted. Baron had said breaking an Artifact sometimes rebounded the effect on the Caster, so Aria was going to break the infernal box and hope Morton hadn't anticipated the success.

She'd tried telling her father the Artifact was a trap, but he'd claimed she was under Widow Morton's thrall and would not listen to a word.

Aria gritted her teeth and grabbed her journal.

"This is not . . . what I expected." Hesitantly, Henry smiled. "I'm Henry. We haven't even really met."

"Lord Henry—"

"No 'lord,' please. I've always hated that. Six brothers and my father, and we're all 'lord.' I'd like to be just Henry."

"Very well, Henry. Let's break a box."

They spent all morning at it. By the time the call for lunch came, Aria's arms ached, either from holding books or making attempts to smash, pry, or otherwise conquer the Artifact. She'd nodded off once, and Henry had continued working without her, drawing no attention to her embarrassment afterward.

They took lunch together in the smallest dining hall. The king was in council with his advisers; the queen was in her music room.

Eliza made an appearance just as the servants brought out plates. She looked pale, her expression clearly composed with great effort, but she asked quietly to join.

Henry lurched to his feet, ready to pull out her chair, but she'd already slipped into the one beside Aria.

Awkward silence reigned. Aria picked at the bones of her chicken.

"I take it you haven't succeeded yet," Eliza said at last.

"It withstands attacks better than any knight's armor." Henry kept his eyes on his plate as he spoke, though he stole one glance across the table at Eliza, barely a heartbeat long. "To be honest, perhaps I'm blunting some of my efforts."

Aria had suspected as much, but she couldn't blame him.

"This is madness," she whispered.

At least they all agreed.

Eliza set her jaw. "You have to give it your best effort, because my father doesn't hold back on punishments."

Ingrained instinct urged Aria to defend her father's sense of mercy, but she only swallowed.

"If I do succeed," Henry said, "would any of us be happy? I mean no offense, Aria, truly."

"Oh, Aria has her own striking hero she's longing to be with," Eliza said before Aria could respond. "Father's taking that from her too. That's what he does best. Take away what everyone else cares about and replace it with what *he* wants."

"He's only . . ." Aria couldn't finish. With a sigh, she reached for her cup.

"Is it Baron?" Henry asked.

Aria nearly spit her wine across the table. Despite the gloom of the situation, Eliza gave a gasp of utter betrayal, her eyes darting between Henry and Aria, jaw gaping.

"*Baron?*" Eliza demanded of Henry. "Baron *who?*"

"Baron Reeves. That's his nickname, but I always liked it. I think his real name is something hard to pronounce." Watching Aria swipe her napkin across her wine-splattered chin, Henry chuckled. "I just wondered. There was some gossip about you two after the joust, and you mentioned a trustworthy Caster earlier. I'm not judging—I like the whole Reeves family. The twins are hysterical, and Baron always puts my brother Hugh in his place when they duel, which is great, because Hugh is insufferable."

Aria felt Eliza's pointed gaze, felt the betrayal sinking deeper, becoming real. She should have told her sister the truth from the start.

The least she could do was tell it now.

"He's the one Father removed a title from," Eliza said. "Isn't he? The Caster."

"Yes," said Aria softly. "But he's much more than that."

"Obviously, or you wouldn't like him." Eliza sighed. "You could have told me. I know Father would draw swords over the Casting and everything else, but *I'm* smart enough to know that after Widow Morton, you wouldn't be ten feet from a Caster unless he was the most spectacular man who ever lived. So he must be."

"Sorry, Henry," Aria said wryly.

Henry smiled, tossing his hair. "I'll settle for second place in this tournament."

"You're first place in mine," Eliza whispered, her gaze falling to her plate.

The earlier gloom, banished for a few precious minutes, returned, and they finished the meal in silence. Aria wanted to thank Eliza but couldn't find the words. She reached out and squeezed her sister's hand instead.

She spent so much of her life worrying about mistakes—dreading the making, obsessing once made—yet that very obsession seemed to drive her to make some of her worst decisions, like keeping secrets from her sister. She should have *known* Eliza wouldn't criticize her relationship with Baron, should have known Eliza would see the truth even before Aria did.

Baron wasn't a mistake.

In reconsidering her sister's opinion, she began to reconsider someone else's.

—— ❄ ——

After lunch, Henry and Eliza headed to the castle armorer for additional tools, and Aria sought out her mother.

The queen was in the music room, of course, and she smiled brightly at Aria's appearance, gesturing her over to the harpsichord.

Though Aria was in no mood for music, she plunked a few keys while her mother sang. After only a handful of measures, the queen laughed.

"Simply dreadful, darling. You may as well play a funeral march."

"It would be appropriate," Aria muttered.

Her mother's fingers took over the keys, light and nimble, chirping a melody like birds in spring.

"Mother . . . even if this succeeds, I can't marry Henry."

The queen kept her eyes on the instrument. The notes increased in volume.

"You heard Eliza's interest in him—it was the very reason for the joust! How can Father . . . How could he?"

At that, the queen faltered. She heaved a sigh, and the melody quieted into something gentler, like a half-remembered lullaby. Aria blinked hard, forcing herself to sit stiff and upright, defying a widow who couldn't be seen.

"You are a royal, Aria," the queen said.

"A royal in love with someone else." Aria's voice caught, snagging on the hook of tawny waves. She flushed at her own brazenness. Were a handful of interactions and a series of letters really enough to determine love? Such a thing seemed too bold.

Then again, if she had less than a month to live, shouldn't she live boldly?

"I was too."

For a moment, Aria thought she'd misheard.

"I was your age." The queen smiled at something distant. "Wild. Carefree. He was the son of a duke, with a voice to move mountains. It doesn't matter now. Someday, yours will be a forgotten memory just the same."

It didn't sound forgotten. It sounded discordant and sharp against the melody.

"You've never told me that."

"You and I hardly talk, darling. Certainly not about matters of the heart. You've always tried so hard to be your father's child that you don't allow yourself to speak."

Aria sputtered. She struggled to rise, finally untangling herself from the bench. "I don't know what—"

"You know exactly what I mean." Her mother halted the music, gaze intense. "You're no longer a child, and if you're going to be any sort of ruler at all, you'll have to accept that your father will disapprove of the things you do. That does not make them wrong."

"Just because he disapproves of you," Aria said heatedly.

Cruel speech. Mark.

She looked at her shoes. After a few moments, the queen resumed her lullaby.

Is it because you loved someone else? Aria wanted to ask. *Is that why he loved someone else?*

But her voice lodged in her throat.

Finally, she swallowed. "What do I do, Mother?"

"Whatever is right."

But Aria didn't know what was right.

She knew only one thing—the happiest she'd ever been was on a winding path of letters, bleeding honesty through parchment.

CHAPTER

31

25 DAYS LEFT

After three days, Aria, Eliza, and Henry had attempted everything they could think of.

Nothing worked.

Eliza had locked herself in her room, unable to bear the moment of judgment. Aria stood with Henry outside the throne room, waiting to be announced, and though Henry wore a brave face, he fidgeted.

"What do you think the punishment will be?"

"He may remove your knighthood." Aria's throat burned to even speak it, and Henry paled.

The doors swung open, silent and indifferent to what was about to transpire, as stoic as the king who commanded them.

Aria refused to take her place on the dais, staying with Henry. The king seemed to take that as a good sign, smiling as he asked for Henry's report.

Henry stood straight, hands clasped behind his back, fingers trembling. "Your Majesty," he said in a firm voice that betrayed nothing of the weakness, "I regret to report I was unable to pass the challenge. The Artifact is undamaged."

Slowly, the king nodded. Then he sighed. "I regret to hear it."

"Father—" Aria took a step forward.

His sharp look silenced her.

"Law is the strength of a kingdom." His Majesty stood, his golden crown catching stained-glass light in a bloodred flash. "Therefore, in accordance with our proclamation, Henry Wycliff bears the punishment of failure. Lord Henry, as of this moment, you are banished from Loegrian soil."

"Father, no!" Aria shouted.

Henry's face drained of color, his hands falling limp at his sides.

"This brings me no joy, Aria." Her father's stern eyes carried warning. He gestured to the waiting guards, who stepped forward.

"Then what is the purpose of doing it? Stop! You won't take him." Aria threw herself between the guards and Henry, one hand outstretched to hold them back. "Father, this is madness!"

"Stand aside, Aria."

"I won't! In what world do you reward a tournament champion, a knight of court and son of your *friend*, with *banishment*?"

But as she said it, she remembered what he'd done to the son of another friend. Everything inside her chilled as she felt the remembered wind of Northglen.

"A world in which he has failed his kingdom," her father said, each word clipped, "and therefore no longer holds a place in it. The challenge was clear from the start."

A challenge Henry had been *forced* to participate in. Her father may as well have escorted Henry onto gallows and called it reasonable to hang.

While she mouthed wordlessly, two guards pulled her away while another pair escorted Henry from the room. She saw the unshed terror in his eyes, but he said nothing. He walked with his head up, like a champion.

Aria wrenched free of the guards. They allowed it, no doubt afraid to injure their princess. Their powerless princess.

"You are dismissed," her father said, returning to his throne.

"I'm not going anywhere."

"Do not think you are above the need to obey me, Aria. A king's authority—"

"Is absolute. And his judgment is flawless. And he's perfect in every measure, every single measure, never a *mark*."

"No doubt this curse weighs heavily on your emotions. Take another day of rest. I'll inform your tutors. In the meantime, Lord Kendall will be summoned, having expressed his interest at the tournament should Lord Henry fail. He wishes a chance to regain—"

"*Listen to me!*" Months of sleepless nights and a mountain of worry combined within Aria, sparks building to lightning. "Please, Father. *Please*. I don't want this. The Artifact is a trick. Everything has been a trick. You can't punish Henry for the impossible. Please."

"Then perhaps you'll provide a truth I can trust. Simply tell me what happened when you, against my express *warnings*, visited Morton." He barely waited. "No? I thought not. I'll remind you that you do not govern this kingdom, Aria. Not yet."

"Not ever, you mean. That's what you *really* want. This whole challenge is your excuse to dig through the toy box of nobility, tossing men aside like wooden soldiers—"

"Aria," her father said sharply.

"—searching for a *real* heir."

"If you were competent, I wouldn't need to!" he roared.

Aria's jaw trembled. She clenched it. The high-ceilinged throne room echoed her father's voice back to her, repeating the condemnation. It rang in her ears.

Incompetent. Mark.

She crushed the quill in her mind, tossed it in fire and watched it sizzle.

But it returned.

It always did.

Incompetent.

"Regardless of your feelings toward me . . ." Aria's voice shook.

One tear escaped her tight hold, sliding down her cheek. "Don't punish Henry."

"Law is the strength of a kingdom," her father repeated. "And my word is law."

With brisk steps, he exited the throne room, leaving Aria alone.

Aria walked to her bedchamber in silence, closing the doors behind her delicately, like handling a teacup already cracked and breaking. She opened her window to the cold air. The trees had dropped their leaves, littering the castle grounds, bare patches attesting to where the servants had already raked. She couldn't tell if the skeletal trees looked relieved of a burden or robbed of their identities, but looking at them, a sudden intensity seized her chest.

She marched to the bottom of her bed, where a small but ornately carved trunk waited. Each side bore a masterpiece collection of scenes from history, beginning with Loegria's founding and touching on its proudest moments. Aria knew every story by heart. It had been her father's gift to her for her eighteenth birthday, mere months ago, and she'd been so captured by the trunk's elegance, she hadn't even convinced herself to fill it yet. Nothing seemed worthy to go inside.

Now she hefted the box from the floor, her aching legs staggering beneath its weight, and carried it to the window. The beautifully stained wood scraped across her window ledge with a horrible screech as she pushed it out, out, *out*, until she expelled it from her room, watching it plummet two stories to shatter against the ground, spilling fragments onto the leaf-covered grass like a stomach emptied of its contents.

While Aria clutched the windowsill, gasping for air, a sharp *caw* came from overhead.

She turned away as the familiar bird glided into her room,

landing on a bedpost knob. Though she rubbed the tears from her face, her hiccupping breaths betrayed her. The crow gave a soft, muted version of his call, so soft it almost sounded like a concerned word, like a voice saying—

"Aria?"

A talking animal. Panic flared in her mind, overturning the grief. She remembered every moment of intelligence the crow had displayed—every responsive nod and almost-laugh. Intelligence too sharp for an animal.

With wide eyes, Aria whirled to face the crow.

The bird squawked and dove for the window, but she was faster, pulling the shutters closed with a *snap*. The crow swerved away, flapping at the corners of her room, but every exit was barred.

Aria snatched up the fireplace poker, holding it like a sword. Her voice trembled. "Reveal yourself, shapeshifter."

Always, she was the fool. If Widow Morton had a squad of Casters at her command, why not a shapeshifter? How long since the woman had replaced Baron's crow?

Aria thought of Henry, collateral damage in the war between her father and Widow Morton. As much as her heart ached to know he'd fallen victim, it was nothing compared to the wrenching pain of imagining Baron in his place.

"Now, demon!" she shouted.

With a final pitiful *caw*, the crow dropped to the floor, shedding black mist from its feathers. The magic curled like smoke in the air, swirling around a rising form.

Aria clutched her makeshift weapon, preparing to swing—

Only to stop cold.

Because she recognized the terrified brown eyes that took shape, and the boy they belonged to.

"Corvin?" she whispered in horror.

From behind her, someone screamed.

Aria turned. Jenny stood in the open doorway, one hand

clutching the doorknob, the other pressed to her mouth. Before Aria could say a word, the girl ran, shrieking for the guards.

Corvin ducked against the wall, quivering like a frightened animal.

Was he an animal?

She heard the heavy steps of oncoming guards.

"Into the wardrobe," she said, grabbing Corvin, herding him roughly. "Be silent. Don't move."

She fastened the doors behind him—banging one of his elbows in the process—just before three royal guards spilled into her bedchamber.

"Your Highness!" The first guard reached her. "Are you hurt? Where's the intruder?"

"It was a mistake," she said. She struggled for calm, but her voice sounded manic to her ears. The towering presence of the wardrobe behind her felt too obvious, as if it strained for attention merely by existing.

"Your lady's maid said—"

"It was terrible of me. I . . . I played a joke on her. I leapt out from hiding when she entered. She must have thought me an intruder. Really, I'm—there's no need for concern, sir. I'm sorry for the inconvenience."

The guards exchanged a baffled look, but since there was no obvious danger, they took her at her word, no doubt wondering if her curse affected her sanity.

She followed them to the door, then told them to send Jenny back so she could apologize—in truth, she wanted to make sure the girl didn't spread word of Corvin.

As soon as she had the door latched, the boy spilled out of the wardrobe.

"Please, Highness, hear me out—"

Aria pulled him into a hug.

Corvin stiffened at first, then melted, gasping in shuddering breaths against her chest. She waited until his fear calmed before she stepped back, gripping his arms.

"I thought you were a spy for Widow Morton!" Even with the guards gone, she didn't dare raise her voice above a whisper. "The crow, I mean. I . . . never imagined it was you."

He laughed, though it might have been a dry sob. "You don't hate me?"

"As if I ever could."

She caught sight of her own arm, prickled with goose bumps. While Casters held a documented presence in the kingdom, restricted but accepted, shapeshifters were more myth than reality. They were the stories told beneath the moon while imagining that every nighttime rustling held an animal with too much intelligence, stalking ever closer. Casters may have been strange—deadly, even—but they were human. What could a creature be called that walked the line between human and animal?

Apparently, it could be called Corvin.

"I would never hurt you." Corvin swallowed. "Promise."

"I believe you. Now I need you to fly home"—she nearly choked on the word *fly*—"before Jenny returns or anyone else comes to investigate. I'll swear her to silence, but we can't risk anyone else seeing you."

She could only imagine what her father would do to a shapeshifter discovered within the castle. Her ears rang with funeral bells at the thought.

How could Corvin even exist? The last shapeshifter had been executed during the reign of Aria's grandmother, some forty years earlier, and they were born only once every hundred years.

But Aria's understanding of magic had been terribly wrong before. She could not be surprised to discover it again.

Corvin turned toward the window, then hesitated. "You're not scared of me? Truly?"

"I believe Leon would be appalled," she said, "if I fainted at the sight of a skinny chicken."

He grinned in earnest, lighting his dark eyes and splitting Aria's heart. An expression like that couldn't be anything *but* human.

"Baron wants to save you."

She blinked at the unexpected topic. Her lips parted, but the words were still catching up.

"He keeps practicing his Casting in the kitchen, which drives Leon crazy. He's spent enough time in the training field, he broke a dummy, and he's up every morning pacing. He's trying to figure out how to save you."

Aria's tears threatened another surge, this time from joy.

"I wanted you to know, because . . . Baron's stood up for me my whole life, and I've never done anything for him. So I can at least tell you—don't marry whatever challenger the king has lined up. Because Baron wants to save you."

The boy gave another grin, and then he opened the window. A rush of cold air washed across Aria's skin. Black mist wafted from Corvin's outline, and seeing it a second time, Aria thought there was something beautiful in the patterned swirls, like smoke messages re-writing his form before her eyes.

Then the mist vanished, and he was a crow again, stepping lightly on the sill. He dove off the edge, paralyzing Aria with fear until he flapped and rose into the sky, as able as any other crow. She watched until he disappeared around the edge of the palace.

After he was gone, she found his forgotten message canister, Baron's latest letter tucked inside. It began with *Dearest Aria*, any reference to her title abandoned at last, and it took no more than that to make everything right in the world again.

CHAPTER

32

As Baron practiced in the yard, a crow landed on the fence beside his current dummy.

"Broken a second one yet?" the crow asked. It was Corvin's voice, no mistake, though edged with the cackling sound of a crow.

Baron gave him a sharp look, glancing around to be sure they were alone as the boy transformed with a quick puff of mist that left swirling trails in the air. He was grinning from ear to ear.

Recognizing a look of mischief, Baron asked, "What have you done?"

The boy's smile turned nervous. "First of all, it was an accident."

Baron leaned his practice sword against the fence and devoted his full attention to the matter at hand. No doubt he would soon have to make peace with a snarling cat.

"I . . . well, I went to deliver your letter, as usual."

Baron tilted his head, noting that the canister was noticeably absent. "You lost it along the way?"

"No, I—oh, I guess I must have . . . dropped the container. In Aria's room."

"You went *in* Aria's room?" Baron felt the beginnings of a headache.

"I wasn't being nosy! Well, maybe I guess I was because when I first arrived, I saw her shove this box out a window, then I saw she was *crying*—"

Baron ached to hear of Aria's tears, but the greater feeling was his dread at the undercurrent he sensed beneath Corvin's words. The boy danced around something serious.

"What happened?"

Corvin licked his lips. He leapt from one foot to the other, like a bird preparing for flight. Baron waited.

"I . . . spoke . . . to her."

"You—" All of Baron's worst fears came true at once, strangling his voice.

Corvin rushed to say, "It's fine! It was an accident, I swear, and I only said her name, but she's smart, and she slammed the window closed and demanded I reveal myself as a shapeshifter, and then I did—"

Baron groaned, closing his eyes and pressing the heels of his palms to his forehead, though it did nothing to contain the growing ache. Corvin's voice kept right on going.

"—*and she's fine with it.*"

Breathing deeply, Baron struggled to regain his voice while his imagination conjured soldiers marching on the Reeves estate.

"What exactly," he managed, "did she say?"

Corvin related how Aria had hidden him from the guards, how she teased him with one of Leon's favorite insults. It was like something out of a dream, though Baron had experienced very few dreams that did not quickly reveal their true nature as nightmares. Had it been an act—a way to remove Corvin from the palace while she decided in earnest how to respond?

"Corvin, you could have been *killed.*"

"I know." Usually when confronted by his own mistakes, Corvin shrank, but now he stood tall, relaxing against the fence. "I know that's why you never told her, why you never *would* tell her, but it worked out."

"Even if that's true"—and Baron could not escape his doubt—"a lucky result doesn't justify a life-and-death gamble."

"That's not what Father taught me."

Baron frowned.

Corvin turned, bracing his hands on the wooden fence before hopping up to perch on the top railing. The late-autumn breeze rustled his dark hair, and even Baron relaxed as it passed over his sweat-soaked neck.

"When Father took me and Leon to Port Tynemon for our birthday last year, Leon wouldn't go out on the water, but Father hired a fisherman to take me out for a few hours. I think Leon might have started digging my grave right there on the beach; he was so certain I would drown."

Though Leon kept a stricter bathing schedule than anyone else in the house, he avoided open water as if it carried plague. His very first transformation had come when Corvin pushed him in a lake.

"Father said it was true," Corvin went on, "that I might drown. But he said people have to face decisions every day, and they have to know consequences come, death included. He said, 'A tree puts down roots and hopes they hold against the storm. But either way, the growing is worth the risk.'"

It was exactly the sort of thing their father would have said, and Baron's heart ached hearing it.

Corvin smiled into the breeze. "When I came back to shore un-drowned and wanting to sail the whole world, he said, 'I guess it must have been worth the risk.'"

Baron had a sudden fear that Corvin was taller than he'd ever been before, closer to grown than he'd ever imagined.

And the boy certainly wasn't wrong.

After a sigh, Baron climbed the fence one post over, and they sat together in companionable silence.

"I've been looking for Sarah," he finally admitted.

Corvin's eyes went wide. "Mom? Did you find her? Is she . . ."

"I think I did." Baron tensed, gripping the post beside him. "I think she's in Northglen."

The one place he never would have looked, if not for Aria's mention of a pale blonde Stone Caster, if not for the way he couldn't force the description from his mind no matter how he tried.

"Why would she . . ." Corvin's voice trailed off. Then it grew small. "Mom doesn't have magic."

None that she'd ever revealed. But Baron remembered one time, shortly after his father and Sarah married, when a stomach sickness had passed through the household. Though his father quickly recovered, Baron deteriorated. The physician despaired of his recovery because nothing could cut the pain. In the end, Sarah, his new stepmother but still a stranger to him in many ways, had gathered Baron into her arms like a real mother and sang a melody he'd never heard, soft as wool, gentle as a breeze. He'd slept the next day straight.

"I sometimes wondered," Baron said quietly. "At the beginning."

He'd written it off as wishful thinking. After all, Sarah had no witch's mark.

"Great." Corvin scoffed, a sound so raw it hurt Baron's throat just to hear it. "Great. She says *we're* damned. Look at her."

"She may have a good reason for—"

"Don't defend her," he snapped. "Leon always defends her."

Baron sighed. "I think Sarah may have been the Stone Caster working with Morton on Aria's curse. Though I can't imagine how she would have escaped a brand."

Corvin scratched his wrist, then curled his fingers. "So if the king ever breaks Northglen . . ."

"I fear the worst. On the other hand, if she is there, perhaps I could reason with Sarah on Aria's behalf. I planned to send a letter to Northglen today."

Corvin hopped down from the fence. "If she's really there, if she really did it . . . tell her to stay. I don't want her to come home."

Tightness gripped Baron's chest. "I began looking for her because I thought you and Leon would be better off with at least one parent at home. On my own, I've failed you at every turn, first by trapping you with the title, then by involving myself with a royal. You and Leon are in more danger of discovery than ever—you *have* been discovered—thanks to me."

Corvin frowned. He reached up with one hand, pinching all his fingertips close together, and then used it like a beak to peck Baron on the head.

Baron squinted, rubbing away the faint throb.

"That's what I think of that." Corvin smirked as if he'd been wickedly clever.

Baron resisted an eye roll. At least it was comforting to see the boy shed some of that disconcerting maturity.

CHAPTER

33

Following Henry's banishment, Eliza kept her door locked tight for three days. Jenny brought her meals; Aria spoke to silence through the door. The two of them fretted together.

"I wish I knew the right words," Aria whispered, sitting with Jenny, both of their backs pressed against the door connecting the two rooms.

Sighing, Aria pulled the tiara from her hair, tossing it to the floor. She dropped her head in her hands, fingers buried in her black hair. Exhaustion dragged on every bone, trying to suck her down to meld with the floor, urging her to stop trying to do hard things when she could just let go and sink.

"I care," said Jenny softly. When Aria looked up, the girl wet her lips, then repeated, "I care. I'm right here. I'll stay—I think those are the words that matter during grief."

"No one said them to you." Shame rose within Aria, coloring her face. "After your mother's death. I wouldn't even visit the grave when you asked."

Looking away, Jenny said, "I know it's . . . uncomfortable. She's my mother. For you, she's . . ."

"It doesn't matter what she is." Aria groaned inwardly at the sound of that, but she pushed forward. "I mean what matters is *you.* I care about you. I don't know if I've ever said that. I know I've been awkward and distant and . . . Eliza is much better at treating you like a sister. Like you deserve."

Jenny blushed. She pulled her knees up beneath her chin.

Haltingly, she said, "When Father . . . the king . . . wanted me to go . . . you gave me a place."

Aria winced. "As a servant."

Aria had never seen her father as terrified as he'd been the morning Jenny came to the castle, like he was staring at his own ghost come to greet him rather than at a starving, helpless girl. It had been the first time Aria had ever defied him, because when he'd ordered Jenny to leave, she couldn't bear the thought of the frail girl orphaned on the streets. It wasn't fair for Aria and Eliza to have a castle while Jenny had no home at all. It wasn't fair for *Jenny* to be punished.

She'd begged for Jenny to stay. Her tears had accomplished nothing until she'd thought of one offer. *She'll be my maid. I'm allowed to choose my servants, and she'll just be an orphan I took pity on. No one will think twice.*

Though his face still bore a deathly cast, the king relented, but only after ordering them both to tell no one the truth and never speak of the matter again.

"I like my place here," Jenny whispered. "I like being with Eliza. And you."

The evening deepened into night, and though Aria tried again to call through the door, Eliza gave no answer. At last, she stood, meaning to escort Jenny back to the servants' quarters so the girl wouldn't fall asleep against a door when the Cast came on. It was creeping earlier with time—while the guards used to fall asleep at midnight, it now happened mere hours after sunset.

Then something lurched inside, like a tablecloth pulled free with all its weight of dishes, revealing a strong, sturdy table beneath; Aria's weight of tiredness evaporated, leaving behind a frenzied energy.

"Your Highness?" Jenny asked.

"No," Aria whispered, staring at Jenny. "No, no, no."

She leapt toward her own door and threw it open. Looking down the hall, she saw slumped figures.

"No," Aria moaned, looking back at Jenny. "Not you too."

Jenny blinked with wide eyes.

All three sisters. The king's descendants, all claimed now. Did Eliza not answer because she was grieving Henry or had she fallen comatose already, as the widow had said would happen?

"Wait here," Aria told Jenny. She would explain things to the girl in a minute.

With the energy of her dark wakefulness, Aria searched out a key to Eliza's room, then barged in, expecting to find her sister collapsed on the floor or worse.

Instead, she found the bedroom deserted, the wardrobe in disarray.

And a letter on the pillow.

> *Aria,*
>
> *I love you. I don't blame you for anything that happened to Henry. What I'm about to do will contradict both ideas, but you must trust me, as you asked me to trust you. I know you're the heir, but it isn't your responsibility to fix everything Father breaks.*
>
> *I'm sorry we couldn't speak in person. I knew you would talk me out of it. I knew if I hugged you, I would never, ever leave.*
>
> *But I love him, and if exile is to be his sentence, I choose to bear it as well.*
>
> *Please find happiness, Aria, and tell Mother I'm sorry.*
>
> *Eliza*

Cold dread settled across Aria like winter. She rushed from the room, shouting her sister's name, but if Eliza heard, she gave no answer. How long ago had she left the note? Perhaps she was already in a port, already on a ship, already—

"*Eliza!*"

Aria burst from the castle into a courtyard, sliding on stones slick with frost. Her breath puffed in the air, and the only witness to her despair was a net of curious stars caught around a silent moon. There was no movement at the palace gate, no sign of Eliza's passing.

Only a horse missing from the stables.

When the first wisp of dawn's pink touched the horizon, Aria was already standing beside her father's bed. He blinked groggily awake as she dropped Eliza's letter on his face.

"You did this," she whispered harshly. Her unnatural energy from the night had bled into her familiar daytime exhaustion, nearly collapsing her where she stood, but she gripped a bedpost to remain upright.

It took her father a few moments to read, to wake, to grasp. Then he shouted for guards, sent runners after his missing daughter, demanded a closure and search of every nearby port.

"What if they don't find her?" Aria asked.

Her father raked his fingers through his hair. He'd thrown on a red silk housecoat and his gold circlet, and while Aria stood still, he paced the room, murmuring curses to himself and a repeated oath all its own: "Ridiculous girl. Ridiculous, lovesick girl."

"What if they don't—"

"They'll find her!" he snapped.

"And what if they do?"

He stopped pacing.

Aria gripped the bedpost tighter, using the solid oak as much for emotional support as physical. "Will you repeal Henry's punishment? Will you allow them to be together? Or will you drag Eliza home just to leave her miserable?"

"Running away is the action of a child, and I will not indulge her ridiculous, naïve heart."

"Eliza isn't ridiculous! She's—"

"She has no grasp of what she's doing!" He shook the letter in Aria's face. "Throwing her entire life away for a boy she's glimpsed at a few parties! She's always taken after her mother, with a head full of clouds and not a raindrop of sense."

"My mother."

He frowned. "What?"

"*My* mother. She's *my* mother, too, and she would never call my sister ridiculous."

"Because she shares the same deficiencies."

The early morning light cast the king's face in harsh shadows, and Aria realized it was the worst light she'd ever seen him in. It revealed things she'd never seen before.

"You talk about Mother's deficiencies often enough yet never mention your own."

He dropped Eliza's letter, dismissing her in the same annoyed gesture.

Aria's knees shivered, begging her to relax into a seat, to let everything go. It was too much effort to argue. But she thought of Eliza, and she held her ground, finally asking the one question she'd been afraid to ask for months.

"What happened with Charles Morton?"

Her father had turned away from her, so she couldn't see his expression, but she saw his shoulders tense.

"That matter was resolved months ago," he said. "I executed a spy within my court."

"He was your friend's son. *Henry* was your friend's son. Does loyalty mean so little to you?"

"I did what was required for the safety of my kingdom. I always do."

"I don't think it was required."

Silence cut the room but carried an emotional rumble, like a fault line dividing the ground between them under the first stirrings of an earthquake. Cold air seeped from the window.

"I think"—Aria's voice trembled—"you made a mistake. And I think it's been slowly killing you since."

Her father angled at last, allowing her a view of his profile, rigid as stone. He kept his eyes fixed straight ahead as he said, "A king cannot make mistakes."

Aria nodded slowly. A wall inside her was cracking, and the rest of her mind clawed to keep the stones together, to hold back the truth pounding like a battering ram.

Don't say it. Hold your tongue.

Everything will change if you say it.

Aria said, "What about Jenny? You made her."

Mark.

Mark, mark, maaark.

Her father turned fully, and they stared at one another. Aria could not guess at what showed on her face, nor could she read the strange expression on her father's.

"Why?" she whispered. "Why kill Charles?"

When he finally spoke, his voice was hoarse. "I had to, Aria. *I had to.*"

"*Why?*"

The king turned away once more, expression and posture closed off. "This rebellious mindset is an effect of Casting, and until the matter with Northglen is resolved, you're not to leave the castle for any reason."

Aria ought to have been upset, but she felt only weary. "Then I'm under house arrest along with every Caster. Ironic, Father."

"You are under Widow Morton's thrall; you practically are of their ranks. I ought to have treated it as such sooner." He drew in a deep breath, nodding. "That's the truth of Eliza's matter as well. She's being driven by this curse laid against my house. When my guards see her safely returned home, they will ensure you both remain here."

"Then I shall make myself comfortable. If you'll excuse me, Father."

She caught his quick glance, saw the frown. He'd clearly expected pushback, but there was no reason to waste her effort here. She would not convince her father of anything—that had become apparent—and amazingly, there was something freeing in the admittance.

If no words could persuade him, if no actions could please him, then every path opened to her. Rather than seeking the elusive, painfully narrow path of "the right thing" as defined by her father's approval, she could run with full purpose down a wider, sunlit road.

She could follow what *she felt* was right.

CHAPTER

34

Aria requested a meeting in the records room, and when her father's head adviser arrived, he clutched a sheaf of parchment to his chest as if to shield himself from the cursed princess.

For her part, Aria felt the same trepidation but for a different reason. She'd sent her most important letter ever to Baron, and she desperately needed a distraction from how he might respond. Or, more likely, might not.

So she'd applied herself once more to curse-breaking.

"Lord Philip, thank you for meeting me." Aria smiled, gesturing for him to join her beside the directory. Under her tired eyes, the lines had blurred into one tangle of black thread on the page. "I hope you might help me locate what I'm searching for."

The man bowed deeply, posture relaxing. "Yes, of course, Your Highness. What is it you hope to find?"

"Any and all information on Clarissa Morton, if you please."

Perhaps she should have started there all those days ago, but she'd seen Widow Morton only as a Caster, so she'd sought information on magic and Casters and curses, all while neglecting the woman behind the mark.

Philip tensed again as if she'd splashed him with cold water. "Surely Your Highness would prefer a study of more pleasant topics. What's truly fascinating in these records—"

"If you're worried I might somehow obtain untoward information, surely my father would prefer you supervise me than leave me alone with all these *fascinating* records, wouldn't you agree?"

He shuffled over at last. After scanning his finger across the page, turning it, and scanning again, he came to a tapping stop. He glanced up as if she might have changed her mind.

Aria maintained her smile.

With a pained expression, the man settled his parchment on the table and fetched the ladder, climbing to the proper cabinet in order to extract a stack of documents tied within a leather casing. Then he returned.

"Let's see . . . ah, yes." He thumbed the corners of pages, flipping through each one quickly, as if they were of no interest. "Family lineage, record of birth, Caster branding, marriage into court, bestowal of the title 'countess,' certificate of widowhood, *removal* of the title 'countess.' That's all, Your Highness. As you see, nothing—"

"What of Charles Morton? His birth record."

Beads of sweat appeared on Philip's forehead. "That would, of course, be filed with the late earl, Jonathan Morton, since Charles was firstborn and heir. It's only the daughter recorded with Clarissa."

Aria blinked. "Daughter?"

Before he could protest, she snatched the pages from him. She found the birth record, marked by an unfamiliar name: *Leticia Morton.*

"Widow Morton has a *daughter?*" Aria gaped.

"Er, yes, Highness. Two children were born to the Morton family. To my understanding, the girl is unnoteworthy."

His understanding was wrong. *Her* understanding had been wrong, so very wrong, all this time. Aria's pulse raced, pounding with newly discovered truth.

"No, Lord Philip," she said softly. "She means everything."

According to the date on the birth record, the girl would now be twelve years old.

"Get me Charles's record. The whole family, actually. Now, please!"

Philip scurried back up the ladder to obey. Aria skimmed every document. Along with Charles's birth and death certificates and his acknowledgement as heir to Lord Morton's title and estate, there was one other record. His Casting test, which he'd passed with no evidence of magic.

Leticia had no such record. Her twelfth birthday had arrived only after Widow Morton removed herself into isolation.

"This is it," Aria whispered. Just as quickly, though, she doubted herself. If the widow's true motivation was to keep her daughter from being branded a Caster, why hadn't she agreed to peace when Aria offered a compromise that removed branding?

"If I may, Highness . . . what?"

Aria sighed. "Nothing, apparently. A false hope."

She stacked the parchments neatly in order, allowing Philip to return them to the proper shelves. As she watched the man, her mind continued to churn.

"You were with my father when he killed Charles."

Philip flinched. He closed the cabinet and dusted his gloves before descending the ladder carefully.

"Executed," he said with the same amount of care. "Yes, I was in private council with the king on that . . . unfortunate day."

His extra emphasis on *private* did not go unnoticed.

Aria moved to speak again, then paused. Though not as stubborn as her father, Philip was loyal to him. She would have to tread cautiously.

The quill in her mind raised, anticipating any number of mistakes.

She clenched her jaw.

"Tell me of your family, Lord Philip," she said, as if seizing the reins of a carriage and driving it into the weeds. She winced.

Unable to employ subtle strategy. Mark.

Driving in weeds. Mark.

She sighed. Lord Philip didn't seem to notice; if anything, he seized the change of topic with vigor. He boasted about his father's service to the late queen and his grandfather's service before that. Aria began nodding off but roused herself to ask if he had a wife, and his face softened. He described a girl too obsessed with daisies, a girl he teased in early years only to see her bloom in later ones. They had a son half Aria's age.

"A good lad," Philip said, glowing more than any lamp in the records room. "A credit to us both."

Aria smiled, tired though it was. "And a lucky one, to have a father so proud."

Her shoulders drooped. The ache in her joints increased. Just as she was about to excuse herself to some couch, Philip spoke.

"What was your hope in this, Highness?" He gestured to the records, his face creased in a perplexed frown.

As always, her tongue forbade talk of curses. She worked her jaw for a moment, then said, "Loegria is blessed to be a kingdom at peace, yet we have created a war within our own borders. A conflict born of misunderstanding rather than justice. My *hope* is to end it peaceably."

Though that hope grew harder to grasp with each day closer to one hundred.

Philip's frown deepened. "Widow Morton is the only source of this conflict. She withdrew from court with aggression. She has antagonized the Crown."

"I . . ." Aria faltered, glancing down at her shoes. "Are you skilled in embroidery?"

"I—no, I, er, it's not a skill I . . ."

Oh, well done, Aria. She'd twisted him in knots, but she'd already started.

"Perhaps your wife is?"

245

Clearly confused why they were discussing needlecraft, he nodded.

"If I asked you to instruct me in a featherstitch, would you be
able?"

"No, Your Highness."

"But your wife would."

He nodded once more.

"Lord Philip, instruction is best given from understanding. So,
too, are laws. I fear the Crown has made too many decrees without
understanding. I fear, if you will, that the kingdom is being taught
featherstitches by a hand that has never held an embroidery needle,
that finds the very idea of a needle fearful. How can such a hand
create reliable stitches?"

It was the best she could do, the best substitute she could manage in place of *My father isn't cursed. I am. He doesn't understand it. I
do. He hasn't spent time around magic. I have.*

Sometimes magic had a name like Baron or Corvin. And sometimes it had a name like Widow Morton. Without understanding
such complex differences, how could anyone make laws to govern
power with any measure of justice?

"This is my kingdom," she said with certainty, "and I will save it
with a featherstitch."

Philip did not seem to understand her point. Instead, he gave
her a look of mourning, like a physician come to announce a fatal
diagnosis.

"Highness," he said gently. "Charles Morton was a threat to the
safety of this kingdom, I can say that with certainty, and His Majesty's
hand has indeed held a needle."

With a bow, he offered to escort her from the room. Aria felt the
sting of his words long after leaving, the correction inherent within
them. His words said she'd made a mistake. Again.

And soon after leaving, she received news from her father of another lord stepping up to take the Crown's challenge. Another man

to see banished on her behalf. Lord Kendall had flown his chicken elbows back to the palace, squawking about how Aria's abandonment of him at last made sense, since it was performed under influence of magic. He proclaimed his intention to save her, and just like her father, he would not hear a word she said to the contrary.

Over the next three days, Aria watched him realize his mistake, watched her curse swallow another person in the wide swath of chaos as it crept ever closer to consuming Aria. Yet after two banishments, after clear futility in the challenge, her father was not satisfied.

The third challenger had already been arranged.

CHAPTER

 35

Baron hadn't heard from Aria after Corvin's transformation, but when a letter finally arrived, he left the poor falcon sitting on his window ledge far too long while he stood paralyzed, imagining every possibility contained in the parchment. Perhaps she would try to persuade him of Corvin's dangerousness, perhaps she would express her regrets at what had to be done according to the law, perhaps she would keep the boy's secret but no longer associate with such a family.

Or perhaps the dream would continue. He felt a fool to even hope it, but it gripped him in every limb, moving him forward to claim the letter at last. The falcon glided smoothly away.

Corvin looked at him from the desk with a nervous excitement.

"Another acceptance to your party, no doubt," Huxley grumbled.

"Actually, this is from Her Highness, and she's already made her acceptance." Baron enjoyed the moment of stiff panic on Huxley's face. But as soon as he exited the room, his heart clenched in his chest just as his hand clenched around the letter.

Closing himself in his bedroom, he sat in a chair and unrolled the parchment with more fear than hope.

My Dear Baron, it started, and his spirit managed to both leap and shrink in the same instant.

A hundred thoughts I wish I could pen. I would tell you all you've done for me, all you mean to me. But I could write a dozen letters and never say the half of it, so know at least these three things:

I will never do anything to put your brothers in danger.

I will repeal the laws against magic or perish in the attempt.

I love you.

Baron's breath caught. For several moments, his eyes couldn't make it past that one line, written with all of Aria's charming loops, written without pause or the faintest smudge of ink, written with confidence. The words echoed in his soul. The longer he stared, the more they carved themselves into memory, they more they replaced the fear.

Of all the things he'd expected, it hadn't been that.

Finally, he forced himself to read the end:

I wanted you to have no doubt, to have it from my hand. I admit that my first interest in you was of a self-ish nature, yet before our first meeting ended, you had impressed me with your own selflessness. You impress me still. With you, I can be myself. No, it is more than that—with you, I see the self I want to be. I have written too many "selfs" now. Forgive me.

A smile grew on his face. He felt the ridiculous urge to curl around the letter, to protect it—and the girl behind it—from the world.

My hope in telling you is not for a matched re-sponse or to inspire a sense of obligation. I only feel that you have always been truthful with me, and you deserve truth in return. Here is the whole of it:

If I could have my choice, that future day when I rule would be one with you at my side.

If I could have my choice, you would be at my side forever.

But it's not my choice; it's yours, too. If your answer is no, I respect and understand completely. Regardless of answer, please don't give it until my . . . situation is resolved. Much as I wish otherwise, my promises are empty until then.

With all my heart,
Aria

For a long while, Baron stared at the parchment, tracing and retracing the words in his mind. She'd spared him the need for an immediate response, and he urged himself to consider the situation in its entirety.

Regardless of his feelings, he couldn't break her curse. Even she admitted there was no point to any of it without that.

Baron passed the next few days in a haze, his mind tangled in a curse, his heart tangled in a letter. At times, he made progress with his Casting, the magic coming as easily as it had in the days before his father's death. At times, it eluded him, leaving him staring at a useless cup of water until he left the kitchen.

And every day, he reread Aria's letter, trying to understand how to navigate something that was both dream and nightmare combined.

— ❄ —

A knock came at Baron's bedroom door, startling him upright in his chair. He hastily rolled Aria's letter, sliding it into his vest pocket beside his heart, where he'd kept it since its arrival.

"My lord," said Martin with a bow. "Corvin is readying for Lord Bennett's dinner party."

Baron thanked the man, then slipped down the hallway to Corvin's room. The upcoming dinner was a simple affair meant to welcome home Silas, though his parents had certainly dragged their feet in acknowledging he even was home.

Normally, Baron would have been the only one invited, but he was now an untitled Caster under house arrest, and no matter his personal connection to Silas, the invitation went, as socially proper, to the future lord baron. Huxley had snuck it right past Baron, accepting on Corvin's behalf when Baron would have rejected. Now the boy would have to go alone to a party hosted by a man who'd tried to kill the last Affiliate he'd discovered in his home.

So it made sense Corvin was struggling with the buttons of his jacket.

"Lord Bennett hates the new trade agreements with Pravusat," Baron said. "If you get cornered, simply mention them, and he'll do all the talking. He might even forget you're there."

"As long as I don't sprout feathers," Corvin muttered. "That's hard to forget."

"If the worst really happens, Silas will have a window open for you. Just get out, and we'll make our decisions from there."

Corvin fumbled the last button, then finally forced it in place. "You talked to him about tonight?"

"He came by the training yard again yesterday."

"I thought he didn't even like me. He never talks to me when he's here."

"I believe he's scared of you."

"What, really?" Corvin looked up, eyes wide.

Baron shrugged. "Not really, but the idea that birds eat snakes has been mentioned a few times."

"Heh. I don't think even Leon could make Silas taste good."

The joke had helped the boy relax, allowing him to pull on his gloves easily. He turned, craning his neck to survey himself in his new suit, which, despite being tailored, looked constricting.

"Looks better on you," Corvin said quietly.

"You're going to be fine," Baron said, resting a hand on Corvin's shoulder. "Not just tonight. Through all of it."

Whether he believed it or not, Corvin nodded. Baron walked him to the carriage, lingered as long as he possibly could, and then paced all night, unable to focus on anything else. Leon brought him a cheese tart and told him to stop wearing grooves in the floor.

Finally, after dark, the carriage returned. Mr. Huxley hobbled through the door first, and his satisfied expression was not that of a steward discovering a shapeshifter in his charge. Corvin followed a step behind, unharmed and in one piece, allowing Baron to truly breathe.

At least until Corvin met his eyes.

"What happened?" Baron asked.

The boy's expression fell. "Silas wasn't there."

Huxley took over, describing a perfect dinner event and praising Lord Bennett as the sort of nobleman every lord should aspire to be.

"If I had one criticism," he said, "it would be the bait and switch of it all. The invitation claimed to be a welcoming party for the heir's return, but Lord Bennett announced that his son is at the palace, challenging for the hand of the crown princess."

Baron suddenly understood Corvin's expression, and his stomach sank.

Silas had been convinced his father would try to marry him off immediately, and Baron should have realized the man would take the most prestigious option available. In three days, Silas would be gone again, after he'd barely been home a week.

And this time, he would be exiled forever.

CHAPTER

36

The third challenger requested to meet Aria in the library; that was new. When she arrived, she found the man already settled, perched on the window seat with one foot crossed over his opposite knee, thumbing the pages of a book with the light of enjoyment in his dark eyes.

"Hummingbird princess." He looked up with a raised eyebrow. "Heard things about you. Sit."

She couldn't have been more baffled if he'd carried a falcon perched on his head for ornamentation.

"Lord Silas," she said hesitantly. "It's a . . . pleasure."

After eyeing her for a moment, he clucked his tongue. "I guess Gilly never mentioned me, though he had plenty to say about you."

Gilly. Aria frowned. "Who?"

"Guillaume Reeves."

Her eyes widened. "You're his friend! The one studying abroad."

An echo of a smile appeared then vanished. He set his book aside and reached for a tray of apple tarts. When had he sent for those?

"You've made yourself at home, I see." She smiled, but the back of her mind screamed that she was going to get Baron's friend banished.

"It will be my home," he said matter-of-factly. "That's the challenge, isn't it? Solve the puzzle, win the princess." He brushed his fingers together, dusting crumbs back onto the serving tray.

"You intend to pass the challenge?" she managed at last.

"I'm undecided."

As if he could resolve the matter so easily after two men had failed. He was baffling.

"What has Baron said about me?"

He smirked. "Wouldn't you like to know?" He settled back into the window seat, propped both heels on a footstool, and wiggled himself into a comfortable nest. With clear purpose, he returned to his book.

"My lord."

He gave no response.

"Silas," Aria tried.

He turned a page.

Aria wished she would have asked Baron *far* more details about his strange friend. But she sensed that from the moment she'd entered the room, he'd been testing her, prodding to see her responses.

Whatever the test was, Aria resolved to pass it.

Straightening her spine, she turned away to peruse the bookshelves. After considering a few volumes, she chose *The Epic of Einar* and joined Silas in the window seat, claiming her own apple tart along the way.

From the corner of her eye, she saw him tilt his head to check the title of her book.

Then he snorted.

"Not in support of mythology, my lord?"

"Not in support of pretenders. That's Gilly's favorite book. You won't fool me with such an obvious show."

Obviousness. Mark.

Aria felt heat in her ears. Nevertheless, she spoke calmly. "Baron's favorite story is the conquering of the chimera. Mine is the Illusion Isles."

"No one enjoys the Illusion Isles," he challenged. "It's the most foolish part of the entire epic."

"Correction. It's where the most foolishness transpires, but had Einar not made his mistakes in the isles, he couldn't have learned the strengths that carried him through the three heavenly realms."

"She's a literary expert now." Silas snapped his book closed, then plucked hers from her hands. "So this is the trick. A little feigned interest in hobbies, a touch of seduction, perhaps, and you have the kingdom's strongest Caster wrapped around your finger."

Aria's tired mind scrambled to follow. "Widow Morton? I have no—"

"Guillaume Reeves is the strongest Caster this, or any, kingdom has ever had. The best another could do is match him, not surpass him."

Aria frowned. He'd told her himself that he wasn't strong enough to break her curse.

"Two years in university study, Highness—can you guess my research field? It isn't offered here." Silas closed the epic in his hands, then popped it back open to a specific page, as if he had the entire thing memorized. "Warlockry."

He displayed the illustration of Einar battling the three tempest warlocks. The warlocks had horrid faces of protruding eyes and jagged teeth, together bearing down with beams of light against the hero's fracturing shield.

"They let you study magic at university?" She ought to have been attending classes in Pravusat the last eighty-three days.

He ignored her question. "Magic is dependent on instinct, and instinct is unlearned by experience, maturity, and reasoning. Therefore, the younger a magic user's age when activated, the stronger those powers can manifest. Simple math. Which is why Gilly Reeves is the strongest Caster ever known."

Aria stared with wide eyes. She'd realized Baron's activation of his power at birth was unheard of, but Silas applied a greater meaning to it than she'd imagined. "I had no idea."

"Doubtful, but irrelevant. For several months now, Crown

Princess Aria has been presented with the best suitors Loegria has to offer. Men of rank, handsome features, and societal favor, yet she has turned her attention to a man whose rank was stripped, whose features aren't, shall we say, commonly handsome, thanks to a mixed heritage, and who not only lacks society's favor but actively attracts its scorn." He raised both eyebrows. "There's a gap in the logic, princess."

Aria bristled. "Perhaps because love does not bow to logic."

"*Love*"—the wrinkle of Silas's nose couldn't be clearer—"is an excuse people give to justify their actions. Gilly's actions and excuses, I understand. Yours remain to be seen. You want to break a curse, I've been told. Perhaps. But I find it interesting that no one has considered the obvious alternative."

"And what is that, Lord Silas?"

"That there is no curse, only a conspiracy. That the crown princess is in league with rebel Casters to overthrow the king. When the strongest Caster continued to resist the movement, you reverted to more subtle methods of recruitment."

The accusation swept back Aria's fatigue in a cold wash of shock. She leapt to her feet, gaping at him. "I—you—I am *already* the heir. What could I gain by your imagined plot?"

"Waiting heirs are often perpetrators of revolution, especially because they easily rally followers. Perhaps you lack patience to await your father's death or abdication, or perhaps you seek to avoid a disinheriting."

Aria had been under siege already, but now the assault had moved within her own walls. She felt defenses rising within her, the heat begging to be released in darts of insult against this enemy who had dared present as a friend.

But she pressed her tongue between her teeth.

Baron trusts him.

Aria had made countless mistakes in her life, and she was beginning to realize such a thing was unavoidable. Perhaps she should have spent more energy ensuring that if she was going to make mistakes, she did not make them in the areas that mattered most.

On the Illusion Isles, Einar believed the illusion which showed his wife's betrayal, and based on that belief, he made the worst mistake of his life by killing her. A mistake he journeyed through three heavenly realms to undo.

Aria sat beside Silas and looked him in the eyes.

"I wish to protect Baron because I love him. That might not mean anything to you, but it does to me, and I think you want to protect him too."

She held his gaze.

And waited.

In the end, his response was an inarticulate grunt. After retrieving his original book, he settled back into his reading nook, though his brow remained furrowed.

Aria smiled slightly. When she stood, the wobble in her knees was at least partly from relief rather than weariness. "I'll leave you to it, then."

"Gilly's party is tomorrow," he said without looking up. "I've been told you're the guest of honor. I've also been told you're under house arrest."

"My intention was to leave the castle tonight. Should you wish to accompany me, you'll want to be in Sutton before night falls. I'll meet you there, outside the inn."

After speaking, she realized the sleeping Cast wouldn't affect him, so the time did not matter, but she couldn't explain details of her curse, so she let it be.

"We'll see," he said.

She rolled her eyes and let him read.

That night, Aria dressed in traveling attire and a thick woolen cloak, gathered what she needed into a satchel, and scribbled a note for the servants to find, where she claimed to have gone in search of Eliza.

I'll return tonight with my sister in tow.

A bald-faced lie in every regard. Her father's soldiers had actively scoured the ports and countryside, and she carried no delusions about discovering what they could not. Especially when she knew Eliza best. The girl could disappear if she wanted—she'd had plenty of training living as the spare princess, invisible to most. Aria's longing pulled in two directions. She wanted Eliza to come home, but she also wanted her to be happy. Home could not provide that at the moment.

"Come with me," she urged Jenny. "We could stop by Harper's Glade before returning."

Jenny licked her lips. "Will the . . . will the crow . . ."

The poor girl was still terrified from witnessing a shapeshifter, though Aria had assured her Corvin was not a threat. At least she'd agreed to keep the boy's secret, which was more mercy than many people would have shown for a stranger.

"Someone should stay here." Jenny looked down. "So the castle isn't empty. In case."

As if the girl could stand alone against Casters if Widow Morton decided to make another ploy in her game of torment. The thought added to Aria's worry, but she was not going to force Jenny to travel against her will.

"If anything happens," she said, "stay hidden."

Aria left the castle and saddled her horse. A crystal night greeted her as she rode, sparkling with a full array of stars and not a cloud to conceal them. The moon offered the mischievous curve of its smile. Not a single guard stopped her on her way or shouted an alarm—they were all asleep beside their watch fires.

After exiting the gate, she looked back at the palace, slumbering beneath its curse. The descent of night always left her feeling trapped and hopeless, but tonight tasted like the crisp air of choice.

She leaned forward on her horse, rubbing the mare's neck and whispering about an adventure. The beast's ears pricked, and she danced a few steps on the road. Aria smiled.

"*Hyah!*" she said.

Together, they cantered into Sutton Town, each clap of hooves echoing in the empty streets. Approaching the inn, Aria saw a dappled gray stallion waiting patiently outside. It stepped forward at her approach, already bearing a rider.

But it wasn't Silas.

It was a more familiar figure.

"Baron!" Aria couldn't hide her smile, her heart galloping in her chest. "What are you doing here?"

As his mount pulled beside hers, she got a better look at him, at the soft shadows outlining his smile.

"Silas sent word you needed an escort. I thought the matter must be urgent, since he would never touch a messenger bird otherwise."

She was glad the darkness concealed the blush in her cheeks. He'd read her letter; he must have. He'd come to escort her personally. Did that mean . . . ?

You told him not to answer yet, she scolded herself. *And he's a gentleman, regardless of feelings.*

"Though I don't expect to meet other travelers in the darkest part of night," Baron went on, "if we do happen upon any, and I'm called into question for breaking house arrest, I hope you might offer me a royal pardon."

"Ensuring the safety of a princess pardons any lesser infraction," she said. "So I'll thank you for being my guard tonight. I can imagine no safer company."

"This way, then." He turned toward the southeastern road.

She blew out a breath, shoulders sagging. Then she shook herself back to reason and urged her horse forward to match his. Even without a direct answer to her confession, it was enough that he had come.

They rode in companionable silence, exiting the town.

"Now that I've met Silas," she said, "I believe I have the full measure of your social circle. Family and friends both."

"And how do you find it?"

"Half charming, half baffling. Fully an adventure."

His quiet chuckle was nearly lost in the clop of hooves. "Silas enjoys catching people off guard. He's good conversation, if you can appreciate that he always speaks his true opinion."

"He mentioned you talked about me."

"I . . ."

She gave a mischievous smile, hoping she made him blush. "It's only fair, since we've spoken of him as well."

"Not in the same manner, I assure you."

She bit her lip. While she considered another way to tease him, he spoke first, with more solemnity than before.

"I wish you could have met my father. That would have been the full measure of my social circle."

Me too. She stopped herself before speaking; Marcus Reeves had been a part of court. She'd surely interacted with him at some point, if she could only remember it.

Aria cast her mind back, searching for any memory.

They left Sutton behind and entered open country, where the nighttime air rustled with the sounds of hidden animals and an occasional light gust of air through the grass. A memory stirred with the breeze.

"You said your father never wore gloves."

Baron turned toward her, his expression outlined by the dim light of hope.

She nodded, certain now. "I remember the lord without gloves. He attended my twelfth birthday. There was a receiving line, where I was supposed to talk to every lord and lady, since it was my official entrance to society. He shook my hand, and his was the warmest handshake in all of court."

37

I t was a simple thing—knowing Aria really had met his father, that she *remembered* him—and it should not have truly mattered.

But it did.

Baron cleared his throat, trying to remove the emotion, but it remained lodged.

"You would have been with him, right?" Aria gave a quiet puff of air that sounded embarrassed. "I'm sorry I don't remember you."

"That would have been the year I first went to Fairfax, so no. And I'm sorry to have missed your birthday."

"Oh, all you missed was a scandal. My most public and humiliating."

Baron's eyebrows shot up. "Do tell."

She groaned. "Your father shook my hand, and he said my name was 'a wonderful break from tradition.' I see now he must have meant it earnestly, considering your name, but I'd had a bad morning. My parents had been . . . fighting." She shook her head. "Anyway, the lady behind your father in line leaned forward to add, 'The princess is as lovely to the eyes as her namesake is to the ears.' All wonderful things. Truly, everyone treated me wonderfully."

After an extended pause, Baron prompted, "And then?"

"My mother loves music, you understand, and her talent crosses two countries. The arias she composes are sung both here and in Patriamere."

Her voice had grown strangled, so even though Baron burned with curiosity, he did the respectable thing and said, "You don't have to speak of it if—"

"Out loud, *very* loudly, I told the entire court, 'Mother named me after the only thing she's ever loved.'"

"Ah," Baron said, wincing on her behalf.

"I never even apologized. We all just stood there awkwardly, and then the line continued, everyone pretending it hadn't happened. But I heard everyone whispering the rest of the evening."

Baron gave a sympathetic smile. "If I attempted to count the number of times I've regretted words to my father, it would be a quick path to unhappiness. We all have bad days. We all say things we don't mean, or mean only for the moment it takes to say them." He waved his hand. "Look at the twins. They would die for each other, but you wouldn't know it by the insults."

"That's understandable," Aria said. "They're . . ."

Baron watched her silhouette against the stars. She'd curled in on herself.

"Not you?" he prompted.

She looked away.

After another moment, Baron tugged at the reins, pulling Einar to a stop. He dismounted, then reached up to offer Aria a hand.

"Walk with me?"

Once she was on the ground, he gathered the reins for both horses in one hand. The other he kept wrapped around hers. They both wore gloves against the cold, but his heart raced all the same. She was near enough he could make out her features, the soft curve of her neck, the opposing curve of her cheek, the vulnerable prick of stars in her eyes when she looked up at him.

Softly, he said, "You very often criticize yourself. I noticed it early in your letters—apologies for questions, calling it unfortunate I had to *suffer* your conversation. You seem to think every normal behavior a misstep, but only for your own feet."

She'd urged him not to respond to her letter, and Baron had told himself to view the situation with logic, with a lifelong perspective rather than the rush of the moment. But stepping closer to her, all he felt was a rush. He released her hand and gently cupped her face.

"Aria, I have never seen you hold anyone else to this rigid standard. Why should the rest of us be exempt while you are condemned?"

She pressed her fingers to his, leaning into his hand like it was the only steady shore in a growing tide.

"I'm the future queen," she said. Her voice was so quiet, he strained to hear it. "I must be *perfect*, because any mistake I make could doom the entire kingdom."

Baron recognized a little of that same burden. He'd seen it in the worried lines of his father's face as the man cared for a hamlet. He'd felt it himself while fretting that he only caused danger for his brothers.

And Corvin had pecked him on the head for it.

Since her eyes had fallen, Baron tilted her head gently upward, lifting her gaze.

"If perfection is measured in caring," he said, "then you are perfect already. If it's measured by any other standard, then it has no purpose. If it damages *you*, then it is something to be avoided as far as I'm concerned."

She stared up at him, a swirl of starlight in her dark eyes. He found himself wishing he could trace every line of her face—smooth the worried furrow of her brow, feel the softness of her cheek. Before the joust, he'd held her bare fingers in his for the briefest moment, and the memory of it lingered with him still. His hands felt too warm within his gloves.

Unable to resist, he stroked his thumb across her cheek, and he thought he saw her shiver. She'd said she loved him. Could that really be true?

If he removed his gloves, would she shy away from the danger, or would she lean further into his hand?

"For years," Aria admitted, "I've kept track of every mistake. I write a mark for it in my mind. I know it's foolish. I know I'm not even marking the right mistakes sometimes. Exaggerating some, blind to others. I want to stop . . . but I don't know how."

The corner of Baron's lips twisted wryly. "It seems there are marks on both of us, of a different kind, but damaging all the same."

"How do you . . ." She drew in a shaky breath. "How do you walk forward *knowing* you'll get it wrong? How do you forgive your-self for that?"

"Me personally? I watch the twins, and I remind myself I'm at least not shoving family into walls."

As he'd hoped, she gave a tiny burst of laughter. Her lips re-mained parted, and with effort, he kept his focus on her eyes.

"We *all* get it wrong," he said, voice softening, "so perhaps the answer is simply mercy. Mercy for others, and mercy for ourselves. Besides that, walking forward is an ongoing path that doesn't end at a mistake. There's time to mend what can be mended, to improve at the next opportunity. You're strong enough for that; I've witnessed it.

"Tell me this—if I presented to the king tomorrow, if I stood again in the throne room and did everything the same, would you say anything differently?"

"Yes," she whispered without hesitation. "I'd argue for your place in court."

His heart lifted in his chest, drawing him forward, and he leaned in ever so slightly, captured by her warmth in the dark.

"But I *know* you now," she protested. "It isn't an improvement in myself, it's simply—"

"It feels like mercy to me."

She gripped his hand. Lashes fluttering, her gaze dropped to his lips, then rose again, the question as easy to read as any penned in a letter. Everything within him begged to answer.

Except one hesitation.

And what of her curse? his traitorous mind demanded. *Can you save her?*

With the wintry dark pressing all around him, bringing the even darker whisper of memories, Baron found his magic shrinking within himself, paralyzed.

For all his talk of mercy and moving forward, there was still one mistake he couldn't forgive himself for.

Slowly, he stepped back, lowering his hand. Aria gave a disappointed sigh that he pretended not to hear. For a while, they walked in silence, and then they remounted, continuing on the path ahead.

Just before dawn, they reached the northern side of Stonewall. Baron would have loved to show Aria his favorite parts of the city, to share breakfast at the bakery, but as it was, they took a small path around the city, curving to follow the thick wall until they reached the southern end and rejoined the main road.

The breaking day spread yellow across the sky, staining the clouds like ripening lemons. Herdsmen and their flocks spilled across the hills, one man drawing close enough to the road to gape at Aria's golden tiara. She gave a regal wave. Baron nudged his horse closer to hers.

It was only an hour's ride from Stonewall to the Reeves estate, but the more the sun rose, the lower Aria drooped in her saddle. When she slipped to the side, threatening to fall, Baron halted them both. He climbed down and fastened his horse's reins to her back saddle strap.

"I'm fine," Aria assured him, embarrassment clear in the color of her face.

"And here I thought you were cursed," he said gently. "May I?"

She scooted forward, and he hoisted himself up behind her.

"Besides," he added. "Einar has made the journey twice, so he deserves the reprieve."

After he settled, she leaned back, nestling against his chest and filling his senses with her lilac perfume, like the first breath of spring. He had to crane his neck to see around her, but he would have gladly ridden blind just for the comfort of her in his arms, a selfish impulse. Spending an entire day near her while warring within himself was going to undo him.

She'd pulled her cloak free so he wouldn't sit on it, draping it as a blanket instead, and her breathing quickly deepened beneath the rhythm of riding.

"You named your stallion Einar," she murmured.

"I'm rather predictable."

"It's clever. He's dappled gray, like the cloak . . ."

As her head relaxed against his shoulder, her voice trailed into sleep. Baron smiled. *Dappled like the cloak Einar wore to fool the first herald of heaven.* No one had made that connection before—even Silas assumed it was a token name.

Baron held her a little tighter.

CHAPTER

38

16 DAYS LEFT

Aria woke with a small gasp, disoriented to find herself moving. "I've got you," Baron murmured from behind her.

After a moment of paranoia, of quick breathing, she forced herself to relax again, tucking her head against his shoulder. His strong arms encircled hers, and against her back, she felt the steady, calming rhythm of his heartbeat. Her mind drifted back to their journey in the dark, to the moment she'd been so certain he was going to kiss her. He hadn't, yet he still held her like this. Aria had once joked with him in a letter about reading minds; she would have handed over the entire contents of the royal treasury to hold that power now, just to know why he'd pulled away.

They entered the Reeves estate. The path ahead led to the manor house, a simple, rectangular structure with warm shades of yellow and lattices of ivy. Flowerbeds and hedges lined both path and manor, everything bright and singing with life, a stark contrast to the winter left behind.

She smiled as she remembered his first letter. *No, I don't favor yellow.* How far they'd come since then.

To her left stretched Baron's personal orchard of lemon trees, lined in orderly rows stretching out of sight. Though the fruit had been harvested, the bright citrus still carried in the air, making Aria more alert through scent alone.

"It's still just as beautiful," she whispered. Perhaps more so, because this time she did not feel like a stranger visiting. Baron's letters had made his home as familiar to her as her own.

As soon as Baron dismounted, she missed his heat, her skin tingling at the loss. Even though the air itself carried an unseasonal warmth, it paled next to his. But he'd shifted into the role of estate lord, calling for a stablehand, ordering a guest room prepared, checking final preparations for the day's event. Aria contented herself to watch his staff. He'd mentioned how servants had feared him as a child, but things had clearly changed; every servant she watched spoke to him with affectionate respect and even love.

Upon entering the house, Aria was greeted by Auden Huxley, who protested that surely she was too busy to spend an entire day here, surely a royal heir had *better* things to do.

"Your concern is touching," she said, "but there is literally nowhere I'd rather be in the world than right here."

Over the man's shoulder, she smiled at Baron, who returned the expression.

Corvin dashed out to greet her, though she saw no sign of Leon. Rather than offering a bow, the boy grabbed her in a hug, chattering something about his falcons that she didn't entirely catch. She gave him a squeeze before releasing.

Mr. Huxley looked away from the display, perhaps searching the ground for an open grave, either to bury himself or Corvin.

"Yes, Corvin." Aria laughed. "I'd love to see the falcons."

"Let Her Highness get settled first," Baron said sternly.

She did so at once, following a servant to her guest room and thanking the woman for bringing in her satchel. Aria had shed her riding cloak and gloves—tossing them across the back of a chair—when a knock came at the door. She opened it, expecting to find an impatient crow-boy, but she found Baron holding a silver tea tray.

"Corvin will drain your energy the moment you give him the

chance," he said, "if the journey didn't do so already. I thought, perhaps . . ."

She practically melted against the doorframe. "Yes, *please.*"

With a smile, he entered, setting the tray on a small table between two chairs. The tea he poured for her looked normal—the
rich pink of raspberry—but when he slid one finger along the cup's
rim, the liquid glowed with a sheen of captured sunlight. Once the
light departed, the raspberry tea remained but the steam carried a
stronger scent, like fresh-cut cedar, heady and thrilling.

Baron turned, half-smiling as he caught her hanging over his
arm to view the magic. His gloved fingers brushed her arm as he
pulled back from the tray, shooting awareness through her. Perhaps
Aria should have stepped back to give him space, but she found herself rooted, unwilling to widen the distance between them. Instead,
she yearned to reach for him, to rest a hand on his chest simply to
feel his heartbeat.

So she did. He didn't move away.

"It's incredible," she breathed, glancing from the pink tea to his
green eyes.

"Not frightening?" He reached up and tucked a strand of her
hair behind her ear. She'd not had time to freshen up from traveling,
but she was not about to walk away from him now.

In daylight, she studied all the wonders of him that night had
concealed. His half smile brought out the dimple in his right cheek,
and faint signs of stubble contoured his jawline. Curiosity, rather
than severity, defined the curve of his eyebrows, as if he were always
pondering a question but hesitant to ask it.

Aria lifted her hand from his chest to trace her finger along
the edge of his jaw, then down onto his witch's mark, following the
gentle curves all the way to his collarbone. She hooked her finger
slightly under his collar. "No. Not frightening. Incredible."

His eyes held steady on hers, and when he spoke, his voice had
grown husky. "Dangerous though, by nature. I can't escape that.

Someone pointed out to me that every sword ever forged is dangerous."

"Yet have you ever been shunned for carrying your sword? Danger
is an intent, not a capacity. You're not dangerous, Baron. You're *incredible*."

Then Aria did something reckless—she leaned forward and
kissed his cheek.

It was a mistake. All night, she had managed to keep her emotions in check, but now that she had felt his skin beneath her lips,
she knew she wanted more of him, not less.

The scent of him was even more intoxicating than that of the
tea. He smelled like lemons and fresh air, like the soul of his beautiful estate captured in a person. And up close, his green eyes were
more enchanting than any magic. She hesitated, her face a breath
from his, wondering if she dared move closer.

She shouldn't. She'd given him the truth of her feelings but also
the freedom of choice. The next move, if it came, should be his.

With an inward whimper and as much willpower as it took to
resist sleep, she forced herself to pull back. Her trembling legs threatened to collapse beneath her, and though Baron would certainly
catch her, it would be undignified, so she reached for the teacup and
took a confident sip. The tea's rich spices excited her mind as much
as her tongue, easing the burden of weariness from every limb and
leaving her tingling with a renewal of self. She felt the warmth of
energy pulsing through her center, carried in every beat of her heart.

Or perhaps that was the man behind it, watching her every
movement with an unreadable mind.

"I see I've done it again." Baron's lips twitched, and he reached
out to brush one gloved thumb across her cheek, wiping away the
tear that had leaked at her sudden relief.

Aria blinked. "Perhaps I simply appreciate the deep notes of a
tea the way my mother appreciates the deep notes of a symphony."

"I'll leave the pot, then."

To her dismay, he headed for the door.

"Aren't we seeing the falcons?" she asked.

"I trust Corvin to keep you safe between here and the hamlet, and I promise to meet you there, but I would be remiss to leave one particular project unfinished."

"Project?" Aria's brow furrowed.

He cast a mysterious smile over his shoulder, then turned the corner out of sight.

Aria cradled her teacup, drinking deep of its scent and flavor, replaying every sensation of her lips against his cheek.

Then Corvin popped up in the doorway, breaking her reverie and asking if she was ready to go. Before leaving the room, she thought to check her reflection in the mirror.

And paused.

She looked like *herself*. Down a few pounds, perhaps, but the pale sickliness and the sallow cast to her face that she feared had become permanent had lifted. No longer a waning skeleton but a princess, one who seemed to have never met a curse. If only that could be true.

Aria tucked away the ever-present countdown in her mind. No doubt the cold of Northglen would reclaim her tomorrow, but she would take today, every blessed moment. For today, she set aside the worries about her curse, her kingdom, her sister, her future.

She turned to Corvin with a grin. "Show me *everything*."

Time passed too quickly, and after the tour of the hamlet, Aria had to rush to be ready for the party on time. Mourning the absence of Jenny, she borrowed one of the maids, Amelia, to help with her hair and gown. Aria had commissioned a winter gown of blue silk overlaid with shimmering silver. White embroidery crossed her left shoulder, spilling onto the bodice in a flurry of delicate snowflakes.

She realized now the gown was quite out of place in this pocket of the kingdom, where snow did not cull the lemons.

After fussing over details she couldn't change, Aria descended the stairs at last.

Baron had said the party would be spread over three rooms, which was apparently common for country estates. In one, guests could socialize at tables, even play cards if they desired. Another held food, and the ballroom, of course, provided for dancing.

But for now, a modest crowd had packed into the small entry room, awaiting a word from their host.

Huxley gave the welcome on behalf of the future lord baron, as was socially proper. Aria tried not to clench her teeth at the thought of Baron being silenced within his own home.

With a flourish, Huxley indicated her as the guest of honor, and then Martin gave her formal announcement, including every word of her very long title. Everyone stared at her, waiting.

They were waiting, she realized, for her to speak.

The quill in Aria's mind engaged itself with a flourish that put Huxley's to shame, reminding her of how dismally she'd performed when her father had allowed her to host Eliza's ball.

Her eyes found Baron's in the crowd, and she heard the memory of his voice. *If it damages you, then it is something to be avoided as far as I'm concerned.*

She locked the quill in a box.

"Friends." Aria smiled. "That's who I see here. Some I have yet to meet and some I am already familiar with. If you don't yet know me, you at least know Baron—Lord Guillaume. I thank him for opening his home to all of us."

She gestured in his direction, and he bowed in acknowledgment. He'd changed into a dark suit, and while he lacked his cane, he still wore his dress sword and his ever-present gloves.

"But I would personally like to thank him for something far greater."

She saw lords and ladies exchange glances. No doubt there were all kinds of rumors about why a Caster would hold the favor of a princess—Henry had confirmed it. Best to give them the truth, then.

"I have seen no greater example of loyalty to Loegria and the Crown than Lord Guillaume Reeves. For that, I hold the utmost gratitude."

She saw confusion on nearby faces, including Baron's. Funny that a man could be so insightful regarding others and so blind concerning himself.

"How many of us," Aria said, "could willingly be wounded and scarred as a child for no other reason than the demand of the Crown? Perhaps you've never thought of a witch's mark in those terms. It's not a punishment for a crime; there was no law broken. It is, instead, a requirement simply for existing, one no other free citizen of Loegria is required to bear. If enduring such a thing peaceably is not loyalty, I have never met loyalty.

"You are aware of my . . . encounter with Widow Morton, but I am not the only one to have suffered because of it. Thanks to the actions of these few Casters in rebellion, His Majesty has ordered house arrest for *all*, and once again, Lord Guillaume abides the law despite his own innocence. Despite the unfairness. If such a thing is not loyalty, I have never met loyalty.

"Finally, in addition to the laws forged by royal authority, there are lesser laws in society—the laws of how we interact, how we treat each other. Although these laws favor the Caster as little as official ones, Lord Guillaume stands tall when disparaged, controls his temper when slighted."

Her eyes returned to Baron's, forgetting the rest of the crowd. "My father told me the late Baron Marcus Reeves was well-mannered, a noble example in how he managed his estate, and a man who could be trusted to work for the good of court rather than his own ambitions. I can say with certainty that Lord Guillaume exemplifies every attribute of his father, even after being unjustly denied his rightful seat as his father's heir. If such a thing is not loyalty, I have never met loyalty."

Baron ducked his head, and Aria became aware of the crowd again, of the silence in the room focused directly onto her. Perhaps she'd gone overboard. It was difficult to read some of the expressions or what thoughts she might have stirred.

The box holding her mental quill rattled, begging release.

"All of this to say"—Aria gave a quick wave—"if you haven't yet had the pleasure of a conversation with Lord Guillaume, I invite you to take the opportunity before this event is out. I can think of no one in the kingdom more worth learning from. Now, let's enjoy the celebration."

Applause rippled through the room, and Aria turned away to hide her flaming cheeks.

Overbearing speech. Mark.

She sighed at the quill's return, sly as a falcon tricking prey to run in the open.

She sought the food room first, hoping to find a tray of the lemon tarts Baron claimed as the ultimate comfort food.

Her mouth watered at the first bite, and she gave a silent compliment to Leon, which would no doubt be joined by a dozen more by the time she made her way down the table.

A few members of court sidled up to her, complimenting her gown, her speech, her glowing health, and a collection of other attributes. Aria gave a practiced smile and let her enjoyment rest in sampling the food while others talked; for some people, holding conversation in the presence of royalty was a matter of great importance, and if it made them happy, so be it. She wanted Baron's guests to remember the party as a pleasant one.

Just then, she spotted Baron entering the room, immediately drawn aside by a small crowd of his own. His hand brushed his dress sword once before slowly relaxing to his side. The tenseness of his shoulders eased, and he leaned in slightly to engage in the conversation.

A warm glow spread through Aria at the sight—though it may also have had something to do with the combination of lemon and *chili* in her iced cookie.

"Excuse me a moment, everyone." She stepped away, looking for a servant with drinks.

She saw, instead, Silas.

He'd entered the room with a girl on his arm who looked to be Eliza's age. She wore a bright pink gown and brighter smile while he carried an air of boredom, perhaps because there were neither bookshelves at hand nor people to accuse of rebellions.

"Lord Silas," Aria said as he approached. "I thought you remained at the castle."

The girl beside him gave a small gasp, whispering, "It really is the princess!"

Silas raised an eyebrow. "I remained long enough to quell any rumors I'd run away with you in the night. Then, after your absence was discovered, I volunteered my noble services to return you safely."

Aria winced. "The thought of rumors hadn't occurred to me when I invited you. I'm sorry."

"You are a reckless sort, it seems."

"I am trying to improve, but it remains . . . difficult."

He nodded, then gestured to the girl. "May I present my sister, Margaret Bennett."

"Your gown is lovely!" Margaret burst out. "I so wish we had snow in this area."

"Come enjoy snow at the palace sometime. We have a wonderful hill for sledding. It's not dignified enough for a court event, but it's great fun with friends."

Usually, Aria went with Eliza. Her chest tightened at the thought, though she tried not to show it.

Margaret agreed, then turned as a trio of musicians began to play from the adjoining room. Without another word, she dragged Silas off to dance. Aria trailed, enjoying the music, drifting at the edge of the ballroom. The music was more upbeat than she was accustomed to, and as couples began to kick and spin, she realized it was *not* a dance she knew.

A short, stocky man stepped up next to her, and halfway through his bow, Aria felt a rush of panic. Then a voice spoke from behind him.

"Pardon me, Lord Roderick, but I have owed Princess Aria a dance for months now."

The unfamiliar lord stepped aside to reveal Baron, and whatever calm she initially felt at seeing him vanished as he took her hand and led her toward the quick-stepping chaos, where she would no doubt make a fool of herself.

"Baron," she whispered, "I've never seen this dance."

He squeezed her hand. "Things are often livelier outside the palace. It's three steps and a kick; all flash and no difficulty, I promise."

Then they were in the thick of it. Baron gripped both her hands, set her in an unfamiliar dance pose, and tugged her gently whichever direction she needed to go. Aria stumbled over her feet, then began to see the rhythm, with men and women facing each other for the steps and then angling away for each kick to avoid each other's shinbones. Her smile grew as she managed a few rotations correctly.

"You've mastered it," said Baron, his posture more relaxed than hers. Just as she finished a kick, he released one of her hands and spun her into a dip, then back up. She laughed.

"Thank you for the tea," she said. Without the gift of his magic, a lively dance would have been an impossibility. Instead, she felt energized, her steps high.

"Whatever you need, Aria."

He said it with such intensity, her heart kicked right along with her leg.

The music ended too soon, but when Baron moved to exit the dance floor, Aria held him back.

"What I need," she said quietly, "is to dance with you."

The intensity which had filled his voice now filled his eyes. Though the modest-sized ballroom was packed with people, it felt vast, filled with just the two of them and a sea of uncertainty. Up close, Aria could see that Baron's suit was not mourning-black, as it had been the first time they'd met, but rather a deep green, complementing his eyes. Perhaps that meant he was looking forward.

Perhaps he simply favored green. Aria bit her lip, holding back a smile.

"There's something else I need," she whispered, though she found herself blushing too deeply to say the single, final word caught in her throat: *you.*

She still held one of his hands. With far too much boldness, she pulled gently on the white glove, sliding it free of his fingers. He tensed, and she paused. When he didn't protest or move away, she claimed the second glove, sliding both into a pocket of her dress. His hands were beautiful—strong, smooth, and defined in the joints. His magic, his hands. Baron hid the most beautiful parts of himself from the world because that was what it demanded.

But there wasn't any part of him Aria feared.

She laced her bare fingers through his, sliding her thumbs across the smooth curves of his palms. She wondered if he could feel her heartbeat. From the way his breathing grew unsteady, he felt *something.*

As the music began anew, this time with a slower tempo, Baron kept one hand in hers and used the other to gently pull her closer. They glided across the floor, and she couldn't imagine how he safely navigated the other dancers when he never seemed to take his eyes off hers. That unruly lock of hair had fallen onto his forehead again, and this time, Aria reached up without hesitation to tuck it back, trailing her fingertips down the side of his face.

"Baron, I made a mistake," she confided. There was no quill for this, only a deep aching in her soul. "I told you not to answer my letter yet, but I'm losing my mind to the waiting."

The curse breathed down her neck with winter's chill, and while she held uncertainty about defeating it, she found she could not endure another unknown. If she was to die in a matter of days, she did not want to do so without tasting Baron's lips. Not if there was any chance he would let her. If there was any chance he felt the same yearning she did.

The music crested as Baron led her into an underarm turn. They'd drawn close to a wall, and Aria's outstretched fingers brushed the curtain as she turned; she saw a quick spin of the ballroom and everyone in it, lively, warm, engaged, the whole room glowing with the comfort of a world without cold. When she completed the spin, Baron stepped closer than before, bringing his lips right to the edge of her ear with a whisper.

"Come with me."

He grasped her hand and pulled her through a narrow doorway she'd not even noticed. It led to a cramped hallway, likely for servants to navigate between the kitchen and the entertaining rooms. It was empty except for the two of them. Afternoon sunlight spilled from a window slit in the outer wall.

With his free hand, Baron reached into his vest and pulled out a letter, folded and stamped with his seal. "My project from earlier. I thought I should deliver this one in person."

39

B aron hardly breathed as he watched Aria read. All night, he'd dueled his feelings, resisting something that could either re-make him or destroy what was left. Then she'd kissed his cheek in the guest room, called him incredible rather than dangerous, and he'd realized the match was already decided. It had been since her letter.

His reply was the shortest of any they'd exchanged, but he'd re-written it three times and then reread it enough to have every word memorized.

> *My Dearest Aria,*
>
> *So that you may have the words from my own hand: I love you. I thought to pinpoint the moment it happened, but the moment doesn't matter, because looking back on our encounters, I can only think it obvious I should have loved you from the start. If the choice is mine, I ask for a place at your side for the rest of our lives and forever.*
>
> *I would sign with all my heart, but it is yours already.*
>
> *Baron*

After keeping her eyes down long enough she must have read it twice, Aria refolded the letter and hugged it. She looked up with tearful eyes, her lips slightly parted, such raw emotion in her expression that he instinctively stepped toward her, cradling her face in his hands, his bare fingers chill with nerves against her warm skin.

"You've done it again," she whispered as a tear dripped down her cheek.

"Would you like me to stop?"

In answer, she laced her arms around his back, pulling him closer, removing any distance left between them. Baron's heart thundered, and he found himself shy. Not because he didn't want what she wanted, but because he wanted it so deeply he feared getting it all wrong.

"I've never kissed anyone," he blurted.

She was close enough that he felt her breath across his cheek, and the warmth of it melted his spine, leaving him wobbly on his feet. Clearly he wasn't thinking straight, ruining the moment with words, yet he couldn't stop.

"There was a girl at Fairfax who nearly . . . Well, as it turns out, it was only by dare that she came close to me to begin with, and, in the end, the fear of being touched by a Caster proved too much for her to follow through. Most people would not regard it as safe."

Aria was smiling. Not in a mocking way but in an adoring way, her eyes focused on his with such purpose he felt she saw straight through to his soul.

"Baron," she whispered. "Kiss me."

He wasn't fool enough to be told twice.

He sank his fingers into her carefully woven hair and pressed his lips to hers.

His magic—alert since she'd removed his gloves—now woke fully. For the moment, he held it at bay, wanting nothing to distract him from the feel of her lips softening against his, meeting him without fear. The feel of her arms clasping against his back, trying to draw him closer even though there was no space left between them. He smiled, breaking the kiss for a moment to catch a glimpse of her dark eyes, filled with the same wonder that surely must have reflected in his.

A Caster and a princess. It defied logic. But defiance had always been something of a specialty for Baron, and it had never been more delicious.

Leaning into the kiss again, he wrapped one arm around her waist, his other hand too enticed by her bare skin to stay away. His fingertips explored the shape of her jaw, the lobe of her ear, the wisps of hair at the nape of her neck. She gave a little sigh at his touch.

Overcoming restraint at last, his magic sang its own praises of Aria. The awareness of his own heartbeat faded as the song of her filled his every sense, tangling magic and truth, pounding like a rhythm he wanted to march to the rest of his life. She smelled like lilacs in summer and like ink in a letter; she tasted like lemon icing and mercy in the dark. He felt the silk of her gown and the urgency of her lips, asking more of him than he'd ever given and, miraculously, treasuring each surrender.

Then her curse reared, a hand silencing a reverberating drum, spilling like a dark stain over what had been a bright awareness.

Baron's magic screamed warning, and despite himself, he broke the kiss, stepping back in a retreat from the monster inside Aria.

"What's wrong?" Aria asked, a slight touch of panic in her voice.

Baron swallowed. "The curse. It's louder than before."

He hated the despair that shadowed her expression. He could spare her from this, if only he could be strong enough to use his power.

He *had* to use it.

"Close your eyes," he whispered.

Without hesitation, her lashes fluttered closed.

She trusted him.

She *trusted* him.

Baron gently brought his hands to the curve of her jawline once more, brushing one thumb along her cheek. He pressed his forehead to hers, closing his eyes and listening with magic to the song only he could hear. Her blood was like wine laced with poison, tainted in every drop, so thoroughly mixed he could not hope to find where poison began and Aria ended.

You have to.

He tried to sort the confusion, tried to guide his magic in a way that would isolate the curse, allow him to catch hold of it. But it slipped like a shadow through his fingers. His head began to ache with the effort of it.

They stood in silence, Baron's back pressed to the wall of the narrow enclosure as surely as it was pressed to the wall in the currently raging battle. The beast inside the girl he loved swallowed his every attack without flinching, and Baron's mind kept flickering back to his father's bedside, back to a day of darkness, back to—

Without meaning to, Baron gasped, sweat breaking out across his brow.

"Baron," Aria said gently. "It's all right."

His eyes shot open. "Am I hurting you?"

He was affecting her blood, after all. He'd not considered how it would feel from her side of things. Yet when he tried to step away, she caught his hands tightly in hers.

"It doesn't hurt. All I feel is tingling. Like kneeling too long and then standing. But you have to know, if you can't help me, it's all right."

He looked away. "How could that ever be all right?"

"Because I know—"

"Hey, lovebirds," drawled a new voice. "Get out of my passageway."

Aria gasped in surprise. Baron closed his eyes in a grimace. Had he been in possession of his cane, he would have used it to shove Leon back down the hallway into the kitchen.

"Leon," Baron warned. "Scat."

"It's *my* passageway, I said."

"I thought you didn't need it, since everything is already in the serving room."

"It was, but then I got bored and made these new meltaways. Pecan and sweet potato—learned that from the top-cut castle cook. Besides, you were supposed to bring Lady Highness to the kitchen already, so I thought you'd given up on the surprise."

Baron pressed his fist to his mouth, an attempt to hold back anything he'd regret.

Aria, ever graceful, asked if she could try one of the coin-sized cookies.

Leon lifted the tray proudly, then waited to hear her verdict.

"These are delicious!"

"Of course they are. I made them."

"And those lemon-chili cookies! I've never tasted anything like them before, where the spice seemed to enhance the sweetness. You're so inventive."

Leon started purring quite audibly. Aria's eyes widened, but to her credit, it was the only reaction she gave.

"Yes, I'm a cat," Leon said. "It's not fair if only the crow gets to be himself."

"Well, it won't be much of a *surprise*"—Baron shot Leon a look—"but there's something waiting for you in the kitchen."

"Gifts?" Aria blinked, staring at the small kitchen table. "Plural?"

Baron smiled, settling with his back against the pantry cupboards, arms folded across his chest. "I'm aware your birthday was several months ago, but seeing as we missed it, today seemed a good occasion for reparations."

"There's no need to make a fuss!"

"A fuss we have made," said Corvin.

"Open mine first," said Leon.

Despite her protests, Aria set into things with a smile. Leon's gift was a cake of his own invention, light and airy, topped with fresh lemons and sprinkled sugar.

"She's probably already full from the stuff in the serving room," Corvin said.

Leon shrugged. "You don't have to eat it, I guess—although you'll be missing out—but it's the name that's the gift. I call it 'Highness Cake,' because it's the kind of highness you are. High enough to make a real impact, but no so high it's left everybody behind."

Aria gave him a hug, which he wriggled out of immediately.

Corvin handed her a small bundle of cloth next.

"The best crown princess," Aria read from the attached note, "should have the best crown. May it keep you light as a feather. Happy Birthday."

She unfolded the cloth to reveal a delicate navy hair comb decorated with a bit of black lace and crow feathers.

"Not mine," Corvin said quickly. "That would be like giving you my hair."

Leon said, "So you gave her some other bird's hair. Classy."

"I love it." Aria pulled Corvin into a hug that he readily returned.

She unpinned her sapphire hairnet, shaking her dark locks loose with her fingers and doing terrible things to Baron's heart. Then, after two failed attempts, she managed a tight twist of her hair, using the comb to hold it in place.

"I don't often do this myself," she admitted with a touch of red in her cheeks, tilting her head back and forth. "How does it look?"

Since his brothers were present, Baron resisted the urge to pull the comb right back out and resume what he and Aria had started in the hallway. Instead, he simply said, "Beautiful."

"Now you can climb the palace easily!" Corvin grinned. "And you won't get hurt if you fall, at least not from a reasonable distance, like a rooftop."

"How . . . ?" Aria touched the comb again.

"It's an Artifact, Affiliate-style. Well, the feathers are." The boy danced one nervous step to the side. "Do you hate it now?"

"Certainly not. Although I can't promise to go leaping off roofs to test it out."

"If you wanted, I could actually let you fly. It's really—"

Baron cleared his throat sternly. "There will be no transforming the princess into a crow, thank you. She has enough magic to deal with as is."

Still, he couldn't fault the twins for a bit of excitement. Having someone other than Baron and Silas to be themselves around was a rare treasure.

Aria was a rare treasure.

She opened the final gift on the table, a bottle of wine from Baron; he'd always been more practical than creative in gift giving. All the same, she kissed his cheek in thanks, and that made any effort worth it.

"We'd best head back," he said. "I've robbed the party of both its host and guest of honor. Even with a three-room maze to lose us in, the absence won't go unnoticed forever."

Aria nodded, though she seemed distracted. She touched the back of her hair again. "I never thought to wonder what sort of magic Affiliates could perform. *Shapeshift*—it seemed self-evident. When I went to Northglen, I thought I was safe so long as I didn't drink anything Widow Morton had touched. That mistake cost me dearly, and there's still so much I don't know."

"To be fair," Corvin said, "you've only asked *Baron* about it. He's only one half of Casters, and Casters are only one half of magic. We're here too."

"What would it take for you to turn me into a crow, like you said?"

Baron tensed.

"Just some blood, like if I scratched you with a talon."

"At least that's a common theme I can follow."

She seemed so *relaxed*, standing next to two Affiliates and a Caster. If Baron had carried any doubt about the truth of her feelings from her letter, he couldn't doubt it now, not while she asked Corvin questions about transforming into a crow as if they were simply discussing the way he trained falcons.

Then Corvin surprised him by saying, "Fluid and Stone Casters used to be called something different, you know. They used to be Blood and Bone Casters."

Baron frowned. "How do you know that?"

"I read it in one of those books you used to have stashed under your floorboards."

"I found them first," Leon said proudly. "Baron thought we didn't know, but you can't hide something in a house from a cat."

In answer to Aria's questioning expression, Baron gave a sigh. "Family heirlooms, from my birth mother's side in Patriamere. They contained information about magic that's been lost in Loegria."

"May I read them?" Aria asked eagerly.

"I'm afraid they've been destroyed. My stepmother burned them when she left, though I still don't understand why."

Leon paled at the mention of his mother, and Corvin retook the conversation as if determined to bury any reminder of her.

"Anyway," he said firmly, "all magic ties to blood and bone, whether you're changing your own or someone else's. That's how Leon and I transform. That's how Baron makes tea or a Stone Caster makes a statue. When you think about it, rock and water are just the blood and bone of the earth."

"It's fascinating." Aria sighed. "But I'm afraid it doesn't help me stop Widow Morton. Unless you're willing to turn *her* into a crow for me."

"Oh, I'd do it! I'd peck her eyes out. But it wouldn't stop anything she'd already Cast. I'm sorry."

Aria smiled anyway. She caught Baron's gaze and nodded toward the door. But then Leon spoke up. The boy stood against the wall with his arms crossed over his brown apron. He kept his eyes on the other side of the kitchen.

"It's not what you don't know about magic," he said quietly. "It's what you don't know about Charlie."

Corvin frowned. "Since when did you know Charlie Morton?"

"Since Baron's eighteenth birthday party when Dad got too excited about his grown-up firstborn and invited half the court to overrun the house. I wasn't even allowed in the kitchen. Dad thought I'd get too worked up and transform in front of everybody."

Baron clenched his jaw. His father's worry over his two youngest sons had often kept them prisoners in their own house.

Then again, Baron had let Corvin fly to the palace, and he'd been discovered. If it had been anyone but Aria, it would have been a fatal mistake. He wondered what his father would think of him now, when he'd managed to fail every duty entrusted to him, from care of his title to care of his brothers.

Then he thought of Aria's words. *I can say with certainty that Lord Guillaume exemplifies every attribute of his father.*

Dared he imagine his father would feel the same? That he'd be proud of Baron's efforts even considering the results?

"I know birdbrain flew away when Dad wasn't looking," Leon went on, "but I couldn't. Then Charlie Morton came sneaking into my room. He'd been prowling all over the house, even lifted something from Dad's study. Sticky hands. He couldn't resist sneaking anywhere, he said."

"It's what got him killed," Aria whispered.

"That's not what got him killed." Leon's expression hardened. "Not really."

"Leon, what are you saying?" Though Baron had a sinking feeling he already knew.

"I promised him I'd never tell anyone, not even beak-face, and I don't know if it will even help to tell. It's not like it will bring him back." Leon glanced at Aria, a deep pain in his brown eyes. "But you didn't turn Corvin in when he was an idiot, so . . . if there's any chance it does help, I'll tell you. Charlie was a cat like me."

CHAPTER

 40

Aria returned to the party in a daze. Her practiced etiquette allowed her to hold conversations, to smile, to dance.

Even as her heart was breaking.

The deadly spy in her father's private council was only a lost boy, unrestrained in his own curiosity. Having seen Corvin transform, she could picture a cornered gray cat, a burst of mist, then a trembling boy with hands desperately extended, trying to explain. Met with a sword.

Her father had killed Charlie, and it wasn't about protecting the kingdom. It was from a misguided fear of magic. Perhaps he'd thought it a mercy to conceal Charlie's nature as a shapeshifter, so that members of court wouldn't look at Clarissa Morton with additional fear. As if anything could be a mercy after slaughtering her son.

Or perhaps he couldn't face the truth. One shapeshifter per century—that was the belief. If her father admitted Charlie's nature, he would have to admit the understanding of shapeshifters was flawed, and if it was flawed in one regard, it could be flawed in all. A landslide of uncertainty. Aria knew well the feeling of being trapped beneath that.

When she'd gone to Northglen to negotiate peace, she hadn't even known the woman she was facing, had no understanding of her son or her daughter, of the depths of her power and her grief, of the things she fought to defend with the desperation of a woman who'd lost everything else.

Aria had been a fool, and the marks in her mind tallied without an end to the condemnation. After getting *everything* so very wrong, did she even deserve another chance?

"Your Highness."

Something about the tone pulled her back to the moment. She stood in the entry room, nodding at the departing guests. Just beyond her, Baron stood at the door with Corvin and Huxley, thanking guests, shaking hands. Far more people conversed with Baron than with Huxley, even as the man tried to draw attention.

Earl Wycliff had lingered beside Aria.

"Forgive me, Lord Wycliff. I was distracted."

The man nodded graciously. His graying hair usually gave him a distinguished look, but now, he seemed only aging, tired. Though he stood upright, his face sagged with sorrow.

Looking at him, Aria's heart took another blow.

"I'm sorry about Henry," she whispered.

Perhaps he'd come to accuse her. To demand an explanation of how she could smile and dance while his son was on a ship to Pravusat, never to see his family again.

Instead, the earl said, "You carried no hand in Henry's fate. His Majesty has always enforced strict justice, but in recent months, we have dropped the justice and enforced what remains."

Aria wished she could defend her father.

She could only think of Charlie.

"I wanted to thank you for your earlier remarks, Highness. You made an impassioned case." Lord Wycliff glanced toward Baron, then back. "Marcus was a dear friend, and I thought I always treated his son with fairness, yet I now realize how that very thought was my first mistake, as if my fairness was consolation. I'm ashamed to say I even told the boy his loss of title was inevitable rather than an injustice, and in the same breath I told him what a fine example he was. I have been a hypocrite."

Aria blinked. "I . . ."

"I'm grateful," Lord Wycliff said, smoothly covering her deficiency. "You've opened my eyes. I know I'm not the only one."

"I'm very glad to hear it," she managed at last.

He bowed before moving to speak with Baron. No doubt the conversation followed a similar track, judging by the way Baron stood straighter and Corvin grinned.

Aria thought Earl Wycliff would resent her. Blame her. Instead, he considered her words. He thanked her. And if Henry's father could somehow still see her beyond the shadow of her father . . .

Perhaps there was hope for someone else.

Inevitability had been building within Aria, a recognition that any path forward could only point one direction, lead to one destination. If she refused to resign herself to shame and die in silence, then she could only revisit her worst mistake and give one last try to make it right.

After every guest had gone except Silas, who waited for Aria, she told Baron her decision.

"I'm going back to Northglen."

Aria's return to the castle was nothing like the comfortable journey she had enjoyed with Baron through the night. Instead, it was full of the silence of two strangers lost in their own thoughts. She wasn't sure what Silas thought about while he stared grim-faced into the distance, but it didn't seem any more pleasant than the subjects occupying her own mind.

She wished she could lose herself in the memory of a sunlit, secret passage and Baron's spine-tingling kiss, but her curse kept interrupting that just as it had interrupted the real thing. Stealing her happiness. Counting the days.

Sixteen days left.

Roughly an hour before they reached Sutton, Silas stopped beside a thin branch in the road. Aria wheeled slowly to face him.

"I'm not going back," he said. "I'm leaving the country either way, so I'd rather it be on my own terms."

Aria's hand tightened on the reins. "If you abandon the challenge, my father will view it as cowardice. He may escalate banishment to execution."

"Can't execute what he can't find. Besides, what's my guarantee he won't execute me for failing? From what I hear, no one expected what happened to Wycliff, and when I had my audience with the king, he made it quite clear he expected more from me than both previous attempts."

A fair point. Aria hated the truth of it.

"When I'm queen," she said, "you'll be pardoned, so come home. Don't keep your sister waiting."

Silas smirked. He wheeled his horse, then stopped. With a clear debate raging in his expression, he turned back again.

"Look. There's nothing I can do about your curse, though I would if I could. For Gilly's sake, at least. I owe him my life, and I've never paid that back. Apparently I never will."

Aria raised an eyebrow, waiting.

"Obviously, I have no right to ask favors."

She gave a quiet laugh. "Ask, Silas."

"My father's arranging a marriage for my sister to Rupert Bright-wood, the duke's son."

"The widower?" Aria frowned. Margaret hadn't even seemed to be eighteen yet, and certainly not in desperate straits.

"The widower, the raging drunk, and so on. My father doesn't care. It's only the prestige of connection to a duke's family he cares about. Maggie doesn't know yet. I'd hoped to find some solution on my own, but I find myself . . . out of time."

Aria nodded slowly, considering.

"As it happens," she said, "I lack a lady-in-waiting. I could re-cruit Margaret."

She would have elevated Jenny to the position, but she didn't dare risk her father's ire. Still, between Jenny's help and Eliza's constant company, Aria had never found the need for a lady-in-waiting.

"It's an honor reserved for the upper ladies of court," she added, "which should satisfy your father's desire for prestige. And he certainly can't protest if I require my lady-in-waiting to remain unwed as long as she's in service. Besides, this way Margaret can see snow."

"Thank you," said Silas, with more gratitude than he likely would have shown for anything on his own behalf.

Aria shook her head. "It's not a favor. As it so happens, I need something as well."

"Shrewd." But he didn't seem to begrudge it, instead waving for her to continue.

"My own sister, Eliza. She ran away a week ago, chasing Henry Wycliff. She suffers the same . . . ailment I do, and I worry constantly that she's in danger, that she's . . ." Aria took a shaky breath, looking away. "That she'll never come home."

"I can't bring her home if I'm exiled."

"I just want to know she's safe, wherever she is. I want you to ensure my father's soldiers don't drag her back. She deserves to make her own choices."

"This is a taller order than my request, Highness."

Aria looked at him with pleading eyes. "If you could just try. I have to know someone *tried*. I would go myself, but I have to deal with Morton."

If Aria couldn't fix that problem, Eliza would die anyway. As would Jenny.

"Very well," said Silas. "It's a deal."

He set off down the trail in earnest, and Aria returned to the castle alone.

Standing in the throne room like a prisoner brought for judgment, Aria withstood her father's berating, his claims that she made a mockery of him by breaking house arrest, and when he demanded to know the location of Silas Bennett—who was meant to have brought her home—she lied.

"He is gathering resources to break the Artifact. He'll be here shortly."

Her father did not believe her. He did not even pause to confer with his advisers, who stood in the wings, before giving an order.

"Search the countryside!" the king barked. "A whole battalion of soldiers! Find him!"

Aria looked out the stained-glass windows at the fading sun, drowning in the horizon. She thought of soldiers collapsed in sleep across the hills, exposed to the freezing temperatures of night.

"I lied," she said. "There's no point searching for him. He's gone to Northglen."

Forgive me, Silas. She had to try something to protect *all* the lives the king would damage.

"He knew he couldn't break the Artifact, and he feared you would have him executed. 'Better to join with Morton,' he said, 'if I'm enemy to the king already.' He finds her mercy greater than yours. Perhaps rightly so."

Lord Philip paled. Aria heard the guards whisper beside the door. Her father gripped the arms of his throne with white-knuckled hands.

"A coward and a traitor!" The king's face flamed to match the red edging of his uniform. "No doubt sent by Morton from the start!"

Aria could clearly see the cracks in her father. He was a patchwork of red and white, divided like stained glass, and she could follow the divisions like a map, one leading her back days, weeks, months, along a clear path in the growing wildness of his words and actions, in the justifications she hadn't even realized were justifications, in regret disguised as strength.

At Eliza's ball, he'd told her there was only one right path. *It is your consistency as a ruler that forges right. Consistency is the only foundation stable enough to carry a kingdom.* He'd ordered her to do her duty without looking back, without reconsidering and second-guessing.

In killing Charlie, her father had committed to a path. He would not renounce it, would not retreat. He was charging forward on sand, as if he could manifest a road through sheer strength of will, and Aria knew he would sink until swallowed. How many others would he drag down with him?

She had to prove he was wrong, but Aria had never convinced her father of such a thing in all her life.

"Father, I know the truth about Charles Morton."

The king stood with the suddenness of a lightning strike. Aria wished she'd climbed the dais before speaking, wished she didn't feel him bearing down from such a height, as if she were the one sinking in the ground while he stood tall.

"I know—"

"You have betrayed me," her father said, speaking right over her words. "It was not enough to confine you to the castle, I see. To your room, then, with guards posted outside at every moment. You will not leave it until this business with Morton is concluded, once and for all."

"No, *listen* to me. Charlie—"

"You will not speak!" he thundered. "You have lost your voice in this court, Aria. I can no longer trust it."

"You never trusted it from the start! You have demanded perfection of me all my life, and I have tried to deliver but fallen short every time!"

Controlled temper, said Baron in her mind, but her words were already galloping, and she could not find the reins.

"Everything I've ever done has been a mistake to you, and I've never even figured out who I want to be as queen because I've been so busy chasing this *impossible* puzzle of trying to be what you want!

I can't be. I can't. Because what you want is law without mercy, and I don't."

She gasped in a breath, having gone too long without air, and it seemed not just to fill her lungs but her soul. Like breathing in truth.

Her hands caught the reins at last.

"This is a mistake," she said. "Losing my temper. I admit my mistakes, Father. It was a mistake for me to go to Northglen. I wanted peace, but my attempt at it was selfish. When the Upper Court dismissed my concerns, I determined to solve things myself, to *prove my rightness*, when I should have raised my concerns again—and *again*, if I had to—until I was sure they were heard. Until the council functioned properly in considering the best path for the kingdom. Because what's *right* isn't selfish."

She looked up, not at her father, but at his advisers. "I wish to petition Widow Morton again for peace. I still believe it can be reached. I still believe *she* can be reached, and I know with all my heart that *peace* is what's best for *everyone* in our kingdom."

Things were different this time. Aria knew her enemy, and she was not hoping to prove herself a worthy ruler; she was only hoping to save lives—her own and others. The details of Widow Morton's curse had mystified her from the start. Why put everyone in the castle to sleep but make only one strike at night, one that was more warning than true threat? Why sentence the king's line to death but draw it out for one hundred days?

Widow Morton wanted peace too. At least some part of her did, the part that delayed, even now.

Silence had fallen in the throne room. Aria's father had composed himself, though the hold on his rage seemed tenuous, and she could see in his clenched jaw how near the surface it still simmered.

"I have given my command," the king said, looking to the guards, to his advisers, to her, daring anyone to contradict. "Guards, take my daughter to her room. Ensure she remains there. There will be no petition to Northglen, only an attack I have put off far too long. No small force of soldiers this time. If it takes the whole army, so be it. I want them mobilized in three days."

The guards and advisers stood pale-faced and silent. Aria caught Philip's eyes, his expression troubled. After a moment, he spoke.

"Your Majesty, I wish to consider Her Highness's request. Considering the circumstances, I don't believe she would suggest another negotiation with Morton if such a thing held no hope."

Joy rose inside Aria, bursting out in a smile.

The king pointed at Lord Philip, a lance of condemnation. "*Her Highness* is compromised by her curse. She suggests negotiation only as Morton's puppet, because the widow wishes us to be weak, to continue vacillating while she gathers power."

Lord Emmett spoke hesitantly, "Highness, can you prove Morton has no ability to direct you?"

"I don't know how I would prove that, Lord Emmett. I can only ask for you to consider the best path forward." With another glance at the setting sun, Aria added, "And I can say that I have a better understanding of the situation than anyone here."

"Guards," said the king, gesturing sharply.

"You may want to find a comfortable position," said Aria. "And a pillow."

The guards took only a step forward before their expressions glazed. Everyone in the room staggered and slumped, gripped beneath the sleeping Cast.

As the entire room collapsed, Aria stood tall.

She could do this. But this time, she would start with a plan, and it was not just a plan against Widow Morton she needed; it was one against her father. In three days, he would start a war, which meant she had two to stop it. One night to prepare.

On the next, she would return to Northglen, and no matter the outcome, her fate would be decided, along with her entire kingdom's.

CHAPTER

41

'm going back to Northglen.

The words haunted Baron. His own response haunted him even more.

Because instead of saying, "I'm coming with you," he hadn't said anything at all. He'd let the moment pass in the rush of Aria readying her things and Silas saying goodbye.

The parting with his best friend still ached.

"Come visit me in Pravusat," Silas had said, hands in his pockets, attempting to be nonchalant. "I'll teach you the best insults in Pravish, show you the ocean cliffs in Izili. Cat-and-crow will love it."

"Have you told Margaret?" Baron asked.

"Meant to. But she kept going on about how good I look with the princess and how I could pass any challenge. She's pretending hard, Gill, so I let her have it. Let her pretend one more day." He sighed. "I should have stayed away. I knew that. I kept delaying coming home . . . Over there, I can be myself, every part. Whether I slither or stand, they don't care. Here, my only use is puffing Father's legacy. I'd bear *his* title and *his* grandchildren, and I'd never be free of him. Never." He nodded and finished quietly, "It was always going to end this way."

End. How Baron hated the word. He had an ending with his parents, an ending with his best friend. Now he faced one with the girl he loved.

He couldn't let Aria go to Northglen alone. At the same time, he couldn't pretend to be useful when he'd proven his use quite clearly—Aria was still cursed. She would die while he carried the power to save her.

Just like his mother. Just like his father.

Huxley shut himself in his room for the night, grumbling about the party. Corvin had already snuck off, presumably to fly after feeling caged at the event. Baron expected Leon to go feed the herd of stray cats congregating around the back door.

Instead, he settled into the couch next to Baron. Leon rarely sought company, but perhaps he'd sensed that Baron could use the comfort.

At least until he spoke.

"How many times have I told you," Leon drawled slowly, "not to be an idiot?"

Baron sighed and headed for the stairs. Undeterred, Leon stalked right along behind. When Baron reached his room and tried to close the door, the boy shouldered in all the same.

"Leon," he warned.

"Don't 'Leon' me, *Guillaume*. Just because you don't like to hear it straight."

"What I'd like is a moment's peace. It's been a long day, one without sleep."

"You don't need *sleep*. You made Lady Highness a bottle of wake-up wine with a snap, and that's the least of what you can do. So why haven't you broken her curse yet? I saw you in that hallway, floundering."

"Let me assure you I am incapable in every way. I am under-experienced, under-skilled, and, if that weren't enough, under siege." He gave Leon a pointed look.

Leon scowled. "Don't you care about her?"

Baron braced his palms flat on the dresser top, shoulders hunched. He could still see Leon in the mirror, and he looked away.

"I'd expect this more from Corvin than you," he said at last.

"For once, he and I agree."

"What perfect timing."

Rubbing one hand over his face, Baron closed his eyes against a growing headache. His own mind echoed Leon's accusation. *Don't you care about her?*

He did.

Which made it hurt all the more, like lemon squeezed over a wound already bleeding.

"She's going to Northglen," Leon said. "Maybe she never comes back, or she comes back *doubly* cursed, or Morton just cuts to the chase and stabs her with a kitchen knife. You have to do something!"

Baron turned. "And maybe I get us both killed, don't you understand? If Widow Morton doesn't kill me, the king will, either for breaking house arrest or failing his challenge. And I can't *do* anything to save Aria. That's the problem."

Leon growled low in his throat.

Baron sighed again. He filled his washbasin from the pitcher beside it, though splashing his face did nothing to calm the storm inside. Not even the song of magic could reach him through the thunder.

"I didn't realize Dad's death made you a coward."

Baron's knuckles whitened around the basin's edge.

"People die, Baron. If Casters could save everyone, they'd save themselves, and they'd be immortal. Missing him is one thing. Even I miss him. Even though he was the worst dad sometimes. But blaming yourself is stupid."

"I *could* have saved him," Baron whispered. "If I hadn't frozen up."

Like he was freezing now.

"No, you couldn't have. I think you tell yourself that because you'd rather think it's your fault and have this weird, twisted hope it could have gone differently instead of admitting it was always hopeless. I heard the doctor, Baron. He said there was nothing anyone could do."

"Nothing *he* could do."

"Nothing *anyone* could do! He said it! You were standing right next to him, branded plain as day. Don't you think if a Caster could've helped, he would've told you to leap on in there? It's not like he wanted Dad to die. None of us wanted Dad to die! How come *you* get to carry all the grief like the rest of us don't *matter*?"

Too late, Baron heard the hiss in his brother's voice, looked up to see his pupils sharp in the mirror. Leon gave a loud, drawn-out yowl, canines sharp around his tongue, and in a burst of white mist, the boy was a cat.

Baron leapt forward, slamming the door closed. He hadn't seen anyone in the hallway, and he prayed that was accurate. Then Leon was on him in a hissing, spitting fit, a fluffy white monstrosity of claws and teeth twisted around his leg.

"Leon." Baron grunted. He shook his leg. "*Leon!*"

Leon clung more firmly, kicking with his hind feet. Even through thick woolen pants, Baron felt the gouges in his skin, and he finally reached down to wrench his brother free. Held suspended, Leon flung himself wildly from side to side until Baron lost his grip.

After dropping with a thump, Leon streaked into the corner and pressed against the wall, back arched and white fur spiked in every direction.

"We never should have written that first letter!" he spat, voice edged in a feline growl.

Baron grimaced as he rubbed his leg, spots of blood already seeping through the fabric of his pants. "What letter?"

"After the stupid ball! Beak-face wouldn't stop harping, and you wouldn't stop moping, so we wrote a letter to Lady Highness. Told her we had a pretty great brother and that life shouldn't be so complicated. Clearly she believed us." Leon's ears flattened against his skull. "Realms forbid I wanted to see you happy again. If I'd known it would make everything worse, I wouldn't have bothered!"

He scrabbled forward, disappearing under the bed.

Slowly, Baron turned back to his washbasin. He pressed his left hand to his throat, felt the brand against his palm, curled his fingers into his neck. He breathed. His other hand rested against the basin, fingers trailing in the water as he closed his eyes.

For a moment, the water sang, clear and pure with crystal notes. Then it wavered. Splintered.

He heard the voices of the past, swirling around him in the dark.

My lord, your father's collapsed! Come quickly!

What happened? He's—

They've carried him to bed, my lord.

The physician's on his way, my lord.

Baron, what do we do?

Father . . .

Lord Reeves, can you hear me? He's taken on fever. Hurry, Amelia, move these blankets.

The physician's here! Martin, bring him up quickly.

Lord Reeves? Unresponsive, stiff muscles, locked jaw . . . This is an advanced infection. My lord, I fear—

He's convulsing! Amelia, move the pillow.

Baron, what do we do?

Baron, do something!

Baron gasped in a quick breath, jaw trembling, throat tight. The final echo of the physician's voice lingered, quieting everything else in its morbid hush.

There's nothing I can do, my lord, I'm sorry. There's nothing anyone can do.

"Leon." Baron's voice cracked.

There's nothing anyone can do.

Leon was right.

Baron walked to his bedside and crouched. When he couldn't see Leon, he lowered himself to his stomach, peering underneath the bed slats at the shivering white cat pressed between them and the floorboards.

Extending one hand, Baron crooked his fingers. "Come here."

"No," Leon growled. "I'm not talking to you. I should have turned you into a cat and ordered you to go hunt mice in the filthy cellar. I still could."

"I understand. Come here."

Still bristling, his brother wiggled forward until Baron could reach to pull him free. It took both arms. Leon was more like a miniature lion than a stray cat; his long white fur bunched with extra volume around his neck like a mane, and he carried regal tufts of peach-colored fur along his nose and on the tips of his ears. He was also *hefty*.

The moment he was free, Leon flopped against the floor in front of Baron, tail twitching. He stared up with brown eyes of condemnation.

"I'm sorry," said Baron.

Leon rolled over, ears twitching to match his tail.

Baron pulled his pant leg back, winced at the gashes, and lowered it. When he stood, he limped.

"I'm sorry too," Leon mumbled. Then he said, "Aria's not like Dad. Someone *can* help her."

If Baron tried to help and failed, if he got himself killed and left the twins completely alone, how could he justify that?

The answer came with surprising clarity, an echo of Leon's earlier accusation: *coward*.

He'd meant to change a kingdom, for his own sake along with that of the twins, yet he'd retreated from every danger on the path. Hiding would not save anyone. Aria trusted him. Corvin and Leon trusted him. His father had trusted him.

Perhaps there was no hope for Baron, just an endless cycle of failed attempts to save the people he loved. He did not know how he could face that. He only knew that he could not save anyone without *trying*.

"I'm going to the castle," he said.

"About time," said Leon.

CHAPTER

42

15 DAYS LEFT

As dawn brightened the sky, Aria paced in her room, stepping over a collection of reading materials spread across her floor and occasionally stopping to jot notes in the journal on her desk. These were not the books on Casting she'd sought in the past; they were records of royalty. Family journals, a history of laws passed within the kingdom, records of trials and executions, peace treaties, trade negotiations, coronation transcripts. She circled at the heart of her family's legacy.

Weariness set into her bones along with the advent of day, and she paused only long enough to drink a cup of Baron's birthday wine before resuming her study.

Jenny entered with a quiet knock, and Aria shot the girl a quick smile before bending over her desk to record a line of thought. During the night, Jenny had helped her find the records she needed and carry everything to her room, but as dawn approached, she'd left to be ready for her duties.

"Welcome back, Jenny."

Rather than replying, the girl sniffled.

Aria straightened, bumping her desk and scattering a collection of loose parchment. She hopped over the mess. "What's wrong? What's happened?"

Jenny's face was drawn and pale. She wore her hair in the same two wispy, fraying braids as she had all night, though she usually replaited them each morning. Unshed tears shimmered in her brown eyes. Her voice emerged as a quiet rasp. "Some of the other servants . . . have noticed me falling asleep during duties. There's been rumors . . . daughters of the king and then a servant . . ." She swallowed hard, and a tear slipped free, followed by another. "His Majesty ordered I leave. So I wanted . . . to say goodbye."

Aria clenched her jaw at her father's continued rampage. "Tell him you can't leave yet, that you need time to find a new arrangement. One day. I need one more day."

"Highness, I—"

Aria grabbed her hands, squeezing tightly. "*Aria.* Just Aria. And I will not accept your goodbye. I will not lose another sister."

Jenny's eyes widened. She glanced at the door, as if guards would burst in at the very mention of her illegitimate heritage. Then she looked down at their joined hands. When she gave a small sob, Aria pulled her into a hug, and they held each other as the morning light grew brighter through the window slats.

When Jenny pulled free, she wiped her eyes and looked down at the carpet of disheveled parchment. "Do you need more help?"

Aria's laugh held a touch of panic. "Desperately. Here, this wine is from Baron. It'll keep you awake."

She thought Jenny might protest the magic, but she didn't, and they got to work. Jenny obediently moved books and stacks of parchment wherever Aria asked, and she listened as Aria read sections from her in-progress peace agreement. The girl's solemn, observant insights saved Aria a good deal of embarrassment.

A servant from the kitchen brought a breakfast tray, relayed by a guard through the door. Cook had made Aria's favorite breakfast rolls, baked with apples and maple. Aria ate two, insisted Jenny have the rest, and returned to work renewed.

"I'm missing something," she murmured, snatching up her grandmother's journal again. Queen Theresa's handwriting, cramped and shaky, made it difficult to read. More difficult still were her wandering thoughts, weighing down the page with random and inconsequential things.

"Dorothy Ames." Aria tapped the page, looking up. "The Affiliate."

Jenny paused, maple roll halfway to her mouth. "She was . . . executed."

"Almost forty years ago, when my father was a child. My grandmother sentenced her according to the law against shapeshifters, then made restitution to her family. But this entry is from the day my parents got married. Right in the middle of talking about marriage and alliances, my grandmother starts talking about Dorothy."

"Perhaps she felt bad? Dorothy was young. I never thought about that, since she was . . . a shapeshifter."

Aria's eyes widened. "Jenny, you're brilliant."

She searched through laws to find the ones concerning shapeshifters, then returned to her grandmother's journal, then to her own notes. The morning dwindled quickly, much too quickly for all Aria had to accomplish in a single day.

When lunch arrived, she'd returned to drafting the new peace agreement. Rather than setting her quill aside, she ate pear slices and dates while continuing to write. After her fifth draft went in the fire, she stood up to pace, drinking another cup of Baron's wine to stay alert during the day.

"It's getting better," said Jenny, turning the logs over to cover the ashes of Aria's failed attempts.

Aria smiled. She twisted her loose hair up, pinned it with Corvin's comb, and sat down to draft a sixth.

When a servant came to retrieve the lunch tray halfway through the afternoon, it was not anyone Aria had expected—it was Cook herself. Apparently the guards couldn't hold back the fierce woman, who no doubt threatened them with a wooden spoon until they allowed her to stand at the door.

"New challenger at the castle," Cook said. "Familiar sort, missing two brothers. Seems very determined. King won't be able to meet with him for another half hour."

"He'll be killed," Aria whispered in horror. With the way her father had responded to Silas's disappearance the previous day . . .

"Daft lad needs some help." Cook gave a pointed look.

Aria couldn't leave her room, and even if she could, her presence would not help her father's mood. In fact, if he saw her with Baron, he would no doubt think the entire thing somehow a trap.

The pit within her stomach grew, and she clutched the door. She wished he would have written, wished she could have spoken to him before he'd announced his intentions at the gate. When she'd told him she was going to Northglen, she'd not intended to endanger him by dragging him along, not when his first priority should be caring for his brothers. If she got him killed—

Cook grunted. "I've got dough proofing. It can't wait all day."

Whether the comment was meant to be veiled instruction or not, Aria took it as such. Baron would soon meet with the king whether she did anything or not.

"Of course. Just a moment, though—I've remembered I kept a plate from breakfast."

"Hurry it up, then."

Aria closed the door, then rushed to her writing materials. Her note to Baron was hasty and smudged, and she hoped it would be enough. She slid it beneath her plate on the tray.

Then she handed the tray to Cook and watched the woman disappear down the hallway.

Aria continued her work, but dark undercurrents swirled in her mind, rethinking every word of her instruction to Baron, imagining all the unpleasant ways her father might surprise her. Jenny had fallen silent, tending the fireplace to keep the room warm and comfortable.

A sharp *caw* came from outside the window, followed by another. Aria glanced at Jenny; the girl had gone white, but then she nodded, and Aria opened the shutters, spilling in a cloud of winter air along with a black-feathered crow.

Corvin perched on her bedpost, but then he spotted Jenny and froze.

Aria latched the window and gave him an encouraging smile. Even so, it was a minute before black mist began wafting from his feathers.

Jenny turned her eyes to the fireplace, stoking the logs with renewed vigor.

In a burst, Corvin was himself, standing behind the bedpost as if it could shield him. He eyed the poker in Jenny's hands. "I'm sorry I scared you," he said unsteadily. "Last time and . . . now."

For her part, Jenny seemed to be fighting a heart attack, clutching her free hand to her chest, knotting the fabric of her white shirt as she stole glances at the boy who'd moments before been a bird.

"He's harmless," Aria said. "Unless you're his twin."

"Hey!" Corvin squawked, lifting his shoulders like ruffling feathers. "Leon always starts it."

Aria smiled.

Jenny opened her mouth and closed it, apparently choking on air. After a few more struggles, she whispered, "I'm sorry. For the guards."

"*Oh*, that." He gave a half smile. "Thanks. Anyone else would still be calling them, so that makes you braver than most."

The girl's face colored, and she returned to stabbing logs.

"Baron?" Aria prodded at last.

Corvin grimaced. "I saw him get through the gate, but obviously I couldn't fly into the palace, except here. I know he wants me to go home, but I thought maybe I could wait here, and after you meet with the king, you could just . . . tell me it worked out. Feels silly now to say it."

"Unfortunately, the king has confined me to my room. Baron must meet with him alone."

A very dark part of her wanted to ask Corvin to turn His Majesty into a bird and make the problem fly away. If it wouldn't have risked the boy's life, she would have.

Corvin's eyes widened. "*My* father sent me to my room all the time, but I never thought anyone could do that to a princess."

Aria gave a short, breathy laugh. "In this, we're no different. Except my father has royal guards to enforce it."

"Then what about Baron—"

"I've sent him a note with strategies. I have full confidence in his abilities after that."

She did, but it didn't quash the fear that her father would find some new way to be irrational.

"The throne room has windows, doesn't it? I could go see what's happening."

"I know it's tempting"—Aria had considered sneaking out to eavesdrop as well—"but the best thing we can do for Baron is not distract him or do anything that risks my father's ire."

When the boy glanced at the window, Aria reached forward to grip his arm.

"If anyone in the kingdom can manage this," she said, "it's Baron."

Corvin nodded, though he still looked restless, ready to fly. Normally, she would have urged him to go home, but she did not harbor any delusions that he could fly in a straight line that didn't include following Baron. Safer, then, to keep him occupied.

She steered him into a chair, where he perched on the cushioned arm rather than the seat. He tilted his head, peering around her, then quirked a smile. "You like the comb."

Aria touched her hair. "I told you I did."

"Anyone could say it and not mean it. I gave my mom an Artifact once, but I never saw it again. I think she was embarrassed by me."

"I hope that wasn't the case." Aria thought of her own father and looked away. "But no matter the reasons, sometimes people we love do things that hurt."

"Baron says she's in Northglen."

Aria looked back with wide eyes. "Your mother?"

"She sent a letter. Baron can tell you. I don't really want to talk about it." He focused on Jenny. "When you visited the estate, you said you were from Harper's Glade, but I never got to ask about the Halloways. Did they really tear down that massive barn?"

Aria raised an eyebrow in Jenny's direction, expecting the girl to shrink away.

Instead, she took up conversation with Corvin. Though timid at first, Jenny began telling stories Aria had never heard, stories of her hometown, her childhood, her mother. She and Corvin both spoke animatedly about a lake which apparently grew overrun with frogs each summer.

Pulling a second chair beside Corvin's, Aria shepherded her half sister into it. Jenny barely seemed to notice, busy answering questions with more words than Aria had known she possessed, and Aria recognized something in the flush of Jenny's cheeks, perhaps even in Corvin's smile.

She grinned to herself, and without thinking, she turned, expecting to find someone at her shoulder, someone who would giggle with her and gladly tease Jenny every morning after.

But Eliza was still gone.

Aria closed her eyes, breathing until her heart remembered how to beat in proper rhythm. Then her gaze fixed on the door.

All her life, she'd felt isolated—that was the nature of royalty. She did not have friends in court the way others did. She did not attend a school or share tutors with other students her age. But she'd never felt *alone*. She'd had Eliza. She'd had her father.

Until Eliza abandoned her. It was the unkindest way to think of it, and Aria felt guilty for entertaining it, but the feeling remained, like a snake curled beneath a bush, hissing to make itself known each time wind disturbed the leaves.

Her father had abandoned her more directly, cut her off in everything except an official disownment, and even then, Aria felt bitterly certain he only maintained her inheritance because he still planned to marry her to some suitor of his choosing.

The venom of that pulsed deeply in her veins, stinging with every single heartbeat.

Yet in a time when everyone had turned away from her—

Baron came marching in the castle door.

She hated the danger he faced, hated that she couldn't face it with him, but even so, he would never know how much it meant to her that he faced it for her sake, that he stood by her instead of turning away.

She closed her eyes, wishing she could send another message to him along with her note, but she couldn't even manage the proper words. *Thank you* didn't cover it, and neither did *don't you dare lose*.

In the end, the best she could manage was, *Whatever happens, I'll meet you at nightfall. Just be there.*

CHAPTER

 43

Despite Baron's direct order, a crow followed him all the way to the castle, circling as he presented himself at the palace gate.

"All Casters are ordered to remain at home," the guard captain said.

"I understand. However, I'm also an eligible man of court, here for the Crown's challenge. I assume that takes precedence."

The four men currently on duty exchanged looks. In the end, they sent a runner to the castle, and they waited.

Baron allowed himself one glance up and saw Corvin sailing away—but not toward home. Around the other side of the castle.

He clenched his jaw and hoped Aria would send his brother home. These days, Corvin seemed to listen to her more than to anyone else.

At last, the runner returned: the Caster would be permitted entry, and the king would meet with him in half an hour. Baron wished the news came with a surge of hope, but he'd known from the start there was little chance he'd be turned away at the gate. Baron would either be permitted to challenge, or he'd be sentenced for breaking house arrest. There was no option between.

One of the guards offered to escort him, though it was hardly an *offer*. Baron gave Einar's reins to a stablehand, and he walked with confidence into the castle, head up, shoulders back, as if he belonged.

Every pair of eyes followed him as he passed, and so did the whispers.

The guard led him to an anteroom. Though there were cushioned chairs along one wall, Baron stood, his gaze fixed on the double doors leading to the throne room. He rehearsed words in his mind, though it seemed pointless. He'd not convinced the king concerning his title, and the odds there had been far higher in his favor. Still, he had to try.

Someone cleared their throat behind him, and Baron turned to find Cook.

She handed him a scrap of parchment. "Recipe for that kid cook you tend to."

Of course. "He'll be thrilled. Thank you for . . ."

When he looked down, the handwriting seemed to leap from the page, familiar in every loop and curl. Aria's.

He met Cook's eyes and said again, "Thank you."

"Tell him good luck." She seemed to mean it, her eyebrows furrowed, her spoon lowered rather than threatening. She glanced at the guard as if she might say more, then left.

The note was short; Baron read it at a glance. Then he tucked it into his inner vest pocket and waited.

In what seemed too short a time, the doors opened to admit him.

The last time Baron had faced the king, it had been in a ballroom, with the king on a single-step dais and a temporary throne. Now he faced the man in the throne room, where his seat seemed as permanent and ancient as Loegria itself, where Baron had to look up just to see it.

He'd followed a bear right into its den. For the moment, it hibernated behind a neutral expression, but Baron did not doubt the teeth that could emerge.

He bowed low, and then he waited.

"Give me one reason," the king said at last, "I should not have you sentenced for roaming free, Caster."

Baron's voice rang out with more strength than he'd expected. "Because, Your Majesty, I can break the curse."

"Better men have tried and failed."

"They did not possess my abilities."

"So . . . openly." The king shook his head, looking to the ceiling as if he wished to erase Baron from view. "So *openly* you speak of magic within my very palace. I remember you, Guillaume Reeves. We have had this conversation before. If I would not allow a Caster a seat in my court, what audacity goads you to think I will allow one a seat on my *throne*?"

During all Baron's preparation, that question had haunted him, and he'd been unable to offer an answer.

But Aria had.

With the same strength as before, Baron said simply, "The law."

The words echoed in a silent room. The king's advisers exchanged furtive glances, and the guards stood at straighter attention.

"Three laws," Baron said clearly, "to be precise. First, I bear a witch's mark, which leaves me free to practice benevolent magic under the branding law. I am no more an enemy of the State than anyone in this room, and I am guilty of no crime in either referencing or using my Casting. Second, any order of house arrest includes a right to petition the king under pressing circumstance. Third, and most importantly, by His Majesty's own words, the Crown's challenge is open to *any* eligible man within court. Even as a Caster, I am within the law to accept the challenge, and since it was for this purpose that I left home, I am protected under a right to petition the king."

One adviser seemed impressed, jaw hanging open. The other showed more restraint, though Baron certainly had his attention.

Had Aria been present, Baron would have kissed her senseless.

"You've grown more eloquent in quoting law, but I *make* the law," the king sneered, a threat in his eyes.

Baron felt a warmth right next to his heart, where Aria's note rested. She knew her father well. *Inevitably,* she'd written, *he'll reference his power.*

"Of a truth," Baron agreed, "and the law Your Majesty made was the Crown's challenge. Is it now void?"

Corner him, Aria said. *He won't repeal the challenge. It would show weakness.*

When the king didn't respond, Baron dared to push forward. "Your Majesty extended a call for those with the power and determination to protect this kingdom now and forever. Loegria branded me when I was a child, yet even given opportunity and motive, I have not abandoned it. I stand ready to protect this country, now and forever."

More specifically, the princess at its head. Baron had always hoped to change the country, but the desire to *protect* it had only come about since knowing her.

The bear rose from its throne, towering above the entire room.

"Execution," said the king.

Baron's heart stopped.

"That is the price for failure of the Crown's challenge."

With a low gasp, Baron managed to breathe again, but only just.

"You will take the challenge, *Lord Guillaume,* just as you wish, and when you fail, the punishment will be execution. In addition, you will not interact with the princess, and you will not be permitted to touch liquid within the walls of my palace. The only rooms you will set foot in are this one, the anteroom, and the Artifact room itself. Two members of my personal guard will accompany you at all times."

Baron thought he should say something heroic, but any echo of Einar he'd managed to summon for himself had vanished under the mention of death. He barely managed, "Yes, Your Majesty."

"If this is the pyre you choose to burn upon," said the king, "so be it."

CHAPTER

44

Though it was hard to pry Corvin away from Jenny, Aria made sure he headed home before nightfall. Jenny offered to accompany her to Northglen, but the girl trembled as she said it, and Aria wouldn't put her in danger.

"I need a different kind of help." Gesturing to a stack of parchment on her desk, she said, "I've written summons for the Upper Court but not managed to send them. Half go by falcon to nearby estates. The others are scattered within the palace. I *have* to have at least ten members in attendance to hold an official meeting."

Jenny nodded, realizing the need. "I'll deliver them, Highness."

Aria thanked her with another hug. Then she forced her door open—*forced* because there was a guard slumped in the way, and she had to drive her shoulder in to dump him on the floor. She whispered an apology.

Then she ran down the hall toward the Artifact room. She'd already heard Baron's verdict from the guards.

He met her on the main landing, outside the Artifact room, and his smile set her heart pounding more than the run down the stairs. She crashed into his arms, sending him stumbling back a pace, laughing as he caught them with one hand on the wall.

"At least there's no wall of knives this ti—"

She stole his words with a kiss, delivered with all the fervor she felt knowing he'd come to the palace for her sake, knowing the danger he'd braved. After a day of drafting the same agreement a dozen times, she'd spent all her words, so she wrapped her arms around his neck and breathed deep the scent of lemons and kissed him with all the passion words could never say.

Though Baron held frozen at first, he quickly melted, and he returned softness for her urgency, kissing her in a way that calmed her heart, that made each solitary beat heavier and more meaningful, reverberating through her entire body. He wrapped his arms around her waist and held her with a solid strength that promised to catch her whenever needed.

Then he pulled back, kissing her temple before whispering, "Thank you for your message."

"I can't believe you came," she whispered back, her cheek pressed to his.

"I only hope you can forgive the delay. There was a bit of cowardice involved."

Aria scoffed. She pulled back to look in his shadowed green eyes. "I can think of no one braver."

"A princess comes to mind. One who repeatedly meets alone with Casters."

"Most people would call that foolishness."

He brushed his bare fingers across her temple and around her ear before cradling her cheek. "It's trusting. Why should that be a bad thing just because Widow Morton took advantage? I can say with certainty it changed my life for the better. And from this moment on, whatever foolish or dangerous thing you find yourself required to do, you don't have to do it alone."

Aria kissed him again. The two of them alone in a dark castle made for its own kind of oasis, one she wished to stay in forever, to hold as a refuge while the storm raged outside, waiting for her.

Unfortunately, there was only so much time in the night, and some things could not be delayed. She broke for air, resting her forehead against Baron's.

"To Northglen?" she managed, dreading the journey.

Baron kissed her once more, tender and lingering, the light brush of his fingers sending shivers along her neck.

"To Northglen," he agreed.

The sky Aria had enjoyed only two nights previous now seemed ominous, oppressively dark beneath the empty new moon and scattered gray clouds. Even the lanterns she and Baron carried seemed to shrink against the cold night, lighting the path only a few feet ahead and sputtering fearfully in the wind as they reached the mountain.

Already dressed in a thick wool riding coat, Aria still pulled on a heavy cloak once they began the climb up the mountainside. Before leaving the palace, she'd gathered her new peace agreement, along with the false Artifact, and then raided her father's closet for something Baron could wear, only to find everything made of pristine white fur and emblazoned with the royal crest. In the end, she took her mother's riding cloak, which was black wool with a black fur lining, practical for travel.

She'd told Baron the truth, and as he fastened the cloak and pulled the hood up, he didn't miss the opportunity to tease her—dipping a curtsy and asking if he looked like a queen.

"Oh, hush." Aria laughed.

"Don't tell the twins I wore the queen's attire for an evening. Leon would never let me live it down."

"I'll tell him you made a stunning queen, and I'll enjoy it every time he calls you 'Her Majesty.'" She sobered. "Are they all right, do you think?"

"Safer than we are. I worried Corvin would try to follow us, but I've not seen a crow, and I take that as a good sign."

"It wouldn't be hard for a black crow to disappear in this dark."

"Harder for him than most. Don't tell him I said this, because it's my main method of keeping track of him, but he's very fond of that *caw*. He makes for a louder-than-usual crow when transformed."

She had thought Baron's crow quite vocal from the start. She smiled fondly.

A gust of harsh wind caught her hood, and Aria pulled it snug, angling away from the wind. As she moved to remount, Baron stepped closer in the lantern light.

"There's something you should know. The woman with blonde hair you mentioned is my stepmother. I had my suspicions when you first told me of her, but it was confirmed when I sent a letter to Northglen. Her only response was to invite me to join the movement."

He scowled into the wind, face set in hard lines, and for a moment, Aria was stunned, both at the bitter fate and at seeing Baron truly angry for the first time.

"I'm sorry," he said, "for my family's involvement in what's happened to you."

She shook her head. "Family or not, you're not responsible for her actions."

"No, but when I see her, I'll demand an honest answer."

They remounted and continued up the steep path.

No matter how Aria had rehearsed, preparing her words and steeling her nerves, the moment she stopped before Morton Manor, she found herself shrinking within her cloak. A particularly strong blast of wind extinguished her lantern, and it seemed to her an omen of everything about to come.

Despite the late hour, the mansion was lit, cold rays of light flaring from the windows into the night. The main door opened, and a broad-shouldered man stepped onto the covered porch. Aria recognized him by description only—Richard Langley. Stone Caster.

"I've come to speak to Widow Morton," Aria announced loudly. The wind still snatched half her words. Her fingers felt like icicles around the reins.

Mr. Langley eyed them both, then stepped aside without protest, holding the door.

Though it felt very much like walking straight into a trap, she and Baron entered the mansion.

CHAPTER 45

Baron had never visited Morton Manor before. The square building was all hard edges and imposing pillars, pale as exposed bone, without any of the greenery marking his own estate. The front entry led to a long hallway with branching doors, and it might have been a maze for how identical each door looked. Widow Morton had posted her supporters like sentinels.

Walking with one hand on his sword, Baron scanned the grim faces lining the hall. Richard Langley escorted them past four branded Casters, including Weston Knowles, who looked away under Baron's gaze. There was no sign of Sarah.

Langley led them to a ballroom where Widow Morton stood, dressed in full black, with a slanted veil that shadowed her eyes.

Baron felt a momentary pang of sympathy. Though he'd abandoned his own mourning attire, it did nothing to erase the loss of his father. He could not excuse the woman's actions, but he understood the quiet madness of grief.

Widow Morton spoke with a flat, emotionless tone. "You've roused my entire household, Highness, so I assume it's for good reason. A special event, perhaps? I believe we could all be persuaded to attend a royal funeral."

Pushing his thumb against the guard, Baron lifted his sword an inch from its oiled scabbard.

"Stand down, Reeves," Morton snapped. "I have no desire to fight my own, no matter how questionable their choice of company."

"You've fought me from the start. Every action you've taken these last months has only harmed Casters."

"And the actions of our country's leadership has done you greater favors?"

"Yes, actually." Baron glanced at Aria, who looked pale but determined. "At least one of them. I suggest you hear her out."

"We've spoken before. I've never been impressed."

Aria drew in a deep breath and stood with head high. "In our first negotiation, I made a mistake. I was speaking for my father, even after you asked for my voice. I'm ready to give it now."

The widow smiled, an empty expression. "Too late."

She gestured toward a pillar, and a young girl as thin as Corvin and surely near his age inched into view. After glancing at Baron and Aria, the girl hurried to the widow's side.

"You've not met my daughter, Leticia." Widow Morton braced her hands on the girl's shoulders. "Be proper now, Lettie, that's a good girl."

Lettie swept a curtsy, though her wide eyes appeared terrified.

Baron hadn't been expecting the girl, but Aria didn't seem surprised.

"Lettie is the reason you've done all this, isn't she?" she said. "She's twelve now, and you didn't want her branded as you had to be. You didn't want her to suffer for magic the way Charlie did."

The widow's eyes hardened. "You've been studying my family, I see, but I have no interest in your grasping conclusions. Lettie, please show Her Highness the proof she knows nothing at all."

Lettie stepped forward, raising both hands. A Caster, Aria had implied, but the girl was too far away to touch either of them—unless she was a Stone Caster and intended simply to bring the house down around them all.

A hazy blue glow wafted from the girl's fingertips, like the mist of transformation. But she did not change shape.

Instead, a blue circle of light appeared around Baron, and before he could do more than gasp, it swallowed him whole.

The third Casting type. A Portal Caster.

No matter how many times Leon called him an idiot, Baron had never truly felt like one until the blue light transported him to a windowless basement room. He could blame it on the fact that he'd never gone head-to-head with another magic user, never needed to anticipate what attacks could come; he could even blame it on the fact that Portal Casting was meant to be a *myth*. But the reason wasn't terribly important.

What mattered was that he'd left Aria alone.

A lamp affixed to the wall illuminated the cold gray stone of the floor and walls. The wooden beams above echoed with the sound of footsteps.

Between Baron and the single staircase leading upward stood a woman with pale blonde hair, like Leon's.

Sarah looked older, and Baron's mind had to adjust to the fact that they'd spent *four years* apart. Four years that seemed to contain every major event of his life—accepting the mantle of adulthood, losing his father, falling for Aria. He'd been foolish to expect his stepmother to look exactly as he remembered; they were both different people.

She caught his gaze, her brown eyes a perfect mirror of the twins', and she sighed.

"When you sent your letter," she said, "I had a feeling we'd end up like this. You're so much like Marcus."

"Hello to you, too, Mother."

That stopped her short, and he took a grim satisfaction from her wince. Though he'd usually called her Sarah, there had been times—times of vulnerability, illness, joy—when he'd slipped. She was the only mother he'd ever known.

"You invited me here," Baron said tightly. "I came."

"I invited you as part of what we're doing. Instead, you marched in with the enemy."

"The girl you call an enemy is the girl I love. I'm going back to her. Don't make me go through you."

"*Love?*" Sarah's eyes widened, and she gaped for a moment before recovering. "She's taken you in with promises, no doubt, but they aren't real."

"Unlike your promises. 'Freedom for Casters' was, I believe, what Widow Morton promised Edith and others. So far, as a direct result of the actions taken by those here, I have experienced increased prejudice and even house arrest. I fail to see the freedom."

"That isn't fair, Baron. We are in the middle of change, not at the end of it."

His breath caught; he hadn't expected her to still call him Baron.

He remembered the first time Sarah had visited the Reeves estate. He'd been six, and his father had awkwardly explained something about women and courtship before simply calling Sarah Hatcher a "special friend."

When she arrived, she smiled at Baron in a way that seemed both reserved and thoughtful. Trustworthy. When he told her his father called him "Baron," she didn't laugh. She didn't even hesitate.

"You will be in the future," she said, as if it were the most logical thing in the world. "May as well try the title on early."

By the same logic, Baron asked if she'd tried on the Reeves title. Though Father had choked at the question, Sarah had shared the mischievous joke for what it was and responded, "'Baroness Sarah Reeves.' That does have a certain majesty, doesn't it? Perhaps one day."

"One day" had come in a matter of months, and the twins soon after that. Baron had thought he might hate sharing his father with anyone; instead, he loved his new family with the same fierceness—the same rightness—he felt inside when magic called. Sarah wasn't afraid of him, and she wasn't afraid to let him hold one of the new babies while her arms were full with the other. Sometimes she would reach out and ruffle his hair the way he thought a real mother would.

And after all that . . .

"I'm sorry," Sarah said, "about your attachment to the princess. Truly. We all wish there was a different way, but there isn't. Think of the twins."

Baron's fingers tightened on his sword. "The way you thought of them when you abandoned us all? When you declared us *damned*? How does that reflect on you—the hidden Caster?" He scoffed, shaking his head. "Do you know how many times I wished someone *understood* me? Father tried. He did his best. Now I find that you were right there for years as I struggled with magic, as Corvin and Leon struggled with magic, and you never said a word."

She flinched. Slowly, she folded her arms in, cradling her elbows as if bracing herself. "I did not declare damnation as a curse against my family. I simply had my eyes opened, at last, to the horror of our reality."

"I don't know what reality you were seeing, because I always thought we were happy until you tore the cornerstone from the foundation."

Baron glanced toward the stairs, feeling his heart crack, one part pulling him toward the girl in danger, one part begging for an answer from the woman before him.

Clenching his jaw, Baron focused on Sarah. "Father was different after you left. Harder on the twins. Worse in his temper. He *grieved* you, and where before he'd always been optimistic about our place in the kingdom, he started to carry a shadow of your damnation. He feared he'd lose all of us the way he lost you."

Sarah opened her mouth, but Baron wasn't finished.

"Grieving—are you familiar? Six months ago, when Father died, you didn't come to the funeral. You didn't send word, didn't check on us at all. If you want *any* hope of me trusting you after that, you'll stand aside, and you'll let me get to Aria before I lose her too."

When Baron had hired an investigator to find Sarah, he'd told himself it was for the twins—the twins needed a parent, the twins needed support in their grief. That had only been half the reason.

Because Baron had needed her too.

They locked eyes, and he waited.

But Sarah did not move.

CHAPTER

46

Aria lurched for Baron as he disappeared, but her fingers only closed over a wisp of blue mist before even that vanished.

Rounding on the widow, she cried, "What have you done to him?"

"Oh, do calm down, Highness. I said I wouldn't harm another Caster."

"Considering the lies you told me about peace, how can I believe anything you say?"

"You tell me—you're the one who came to *talk*."

Aria flinched beneath a wave of helplessness. Why had she ever thought she could do this, that any visit to Northglen could end happily? In her planning, things seemed rosy and hopeful, but now that she stood in Morton Manor once again, all she felt was the cold of the looming mountain.

Though large pillars crowded the space, awkwardly dividing up a room that ought to have been open, the ballroom contained one stunning feature—three massive floor-to-ceiling windows that took up an entire wall. The view looked down on the leeward side of the mountain, protected from the wind but still seeping cold like the beating heart of winter. She could see such a canopy of stars it felt like looking out into a realm of heaven, and below that, the shadow of the castle itself, far down in the valley. Her distant home. Unreachable.

With all the other writing Aria had done that day, she'd forgotten to pen her parents a letter. If she never came home, there would be no message, nothing left except an ongoing curse and her father's fury.

Widow Morton patted her daughter's shoulder. The girl flexed her hands with a wince, as if they ached, but she leaned into her mother's touch.

"You've discovered my son was special," Widow Morton said. "Lettie, here, is even more so—a type of Caster not seen in centuries. If we stick to the categorization of fluid and stone, I suppose she could be called a Portal Caster."

Aria swallowed. "And if we used categories of blood and bone?"

"You *have* been studying, Highness. In that case, amid blood and bone, she would be *soul*. She can transport a person or object somewhere new without even touching them; they need only be within sight. By combining my power with hers, we can achieve communication across a kingdom and who knows what other wonders." Widow Morton's grip tightened protectively. "Can you imagine the fear such a power would cause?"

Aria could. And she knew exactly how her father dealt with fear.

"I am not my father," she said. With effort, she turned away from the view of the windows, putting the castle's shadow out of sight. From her vest, she drew out the document Jenny had helped her shape. "I wrote a new peace agreement, one with true freedom for magic, one without brands or registration of any kind."

Widow Morton took the parchment, but rather than reading it, she cast it aside. It fluttered to the ballroom floor.

"I told you." The widow's expression hardened. "It's too late."

For the first time, Aria noticed something in the woman's expression, something beyond the anger. There was a familiar sallowness to her cheeks, a deep color beneath her eyes.

In horror, Aria whispered, "Is the curse . . . affecting you too?"

She remembered Widow Morton's last visitation in her water

mirror, the night of Eliza's awakening. Something had seemed off about the widow's appearance. Tiredness, she now realized. The widow had demanded to know how Aria resisted the effects of the curse, perhaps because the Cast was not behaving the way its Caster had anticipated. Perhaps because it had turned on its master.

"Is it *killing* you?"

"Lettie," said the widow. "Leave us."

"End it!" Aria said. "This is madness. Please, listen to me—we can resolve this peaceably. End the Cast, and let's *talk*."

The widow's expression darkened in response. It was like talking to the king.

"I will end it," the woman said. "Lettie, *out*."

When her daughter didn't move, Widow Morton gave her a firm push toward the door. The girl stumbled. She looked at Aria with haunted eyes, and Aria recognized the expression—that of a child without a voice.

"You don't have to do what she wants," Aria told the girl fiercely. "You don't have to *be* what she wants."

Lettie looked away. She hurried to the door with her head down, ducking into the hallway.

Leaving Aria alone with a woman intent upon killing her.

CHAPTER

47

"Move," Baron repeated. "Please."

Sarah stood firm. "I can't. Listen to me, son, your father had—"

"You don't get to call me *son*. Ever."

"Your father had a beautiful vision and a silver tongue. When Marcus and I first met, and for years after, he convinced me to see that future world he imagined, where you brought a voice of reason to court, where magic slowly became accepted. I was willing to wait, to work. Until I realized there wasn't time.

"Haven't you seen what's happening in the kingdom? First Corvin with his transformation, then Leon with his. Your friend Silas. Charlie Morton. Others, many others. Affiliates aren't this common; they never have been. Lettie was the tipping point—a forgotten type of *Caster*, Baron, think of it. In a single generation, something happened to magic within our kingdom. It runs rampant in secret, and every day it does, that secret threatens to be exposed. Lives are in danger *every day*. Charlie was only the first, and Clarissa saw that, so she accepted what had to be done."

"You've planned this for years," Baron realized. "*You*, not Widow Morton."

"I tried to convince Marcus first"—her expression hardened—"but he cared more for loyalty to his *king* than to his *children*."

"Don't you *dare* speak of loyalty when you left us," Baron snapped.

"Everything I've done I did for your sakes. Marcus wanted to abide the law, no matter how horrific that law was. He let them brand his own son!"

"Not without my permission."

"*Permission*? You were *six*!"

"And I already knew something of sacrifice. Perhaps I didn't understand the details, but Father explained his reasons to me, and he gave me a choice." Baron gestured to the cramped basement room. "Tell me—what choice did you offer me in this?"

Sarah's mouth set in a hard line.

"You say you tried to convince Father of your plan, but I doubt you gave him the full picture. Did he know the truth about you?"

"My parents sacrificed greatly to spare me a witch's mark. If I'd told anyone, even my own husband, it would have negated that sacrifice. Sometimes we must put on appearances, even when it hurts us to do so."

Baron had never before pitied his father.

Then he had another realization. *Appearances*. "You never burned my mother's books, did you? When you left, you took them. You *used* them. You're using them still."

Widow Morton's curse was a feat Baron couldn't explain because she had a resource Baron had never been able to fully study.

"Yes," Sarah admitted quietly. "Leon couldn't help bragging he'd found a secret, and once I saw the books, I realized what was possible. I had never imagined a curse could be spread not just through blood but through *bloodline*. I never would have thought myself capable of holding a sleeping Cast over an entire castle. Thank the realms that Patriamere held to knowledge we erased."

"I should have burned them myself." Baron trembled as he spoke. "You involved *me* in a plot against the king, a plot to bring down the country I love."

And he did love it, flaws and all. He could not separate the most terrible parts of his homeland from its most wonderful. He could only fight to improve it all together.

He'd learned that from his father.

"You took the one inheritance I had from my mother," Baron whispered, "and you used it against me."

"No, Baron." Sarah's voice cracked, and she clenched her jaw, resuming her firm posture. "*Not* against you. I've been begging you to understand. This has all been to protect you, to protect Corvin and Leon. I never . . . I *never* would have left if not forced. But I had to act. I knew a reckless revolt would only make things worse, so I had to find allies. I had to establish protections."

"And what good have your protections done you?"

"We are ready for the day the king marches his army. With that act of aggression, no one can argue our response, and when his soldiers fall helplessly asleep in their camp, even a large force becomes easy to manage."

"This isn't right," Baron whispered.

"That's Marcus talking."

"It's *me*, Sarah. I see you're unable to hear anything beyond your own fears, so I will say this clearly." He drew in a breath and looked at her with steel in his eyes. "Step aside, or I will force you to."

Sarah only stood with more firmness, lifting her hands in readiness for Casting. "The princess is gone. You have to accept that. But you can protect Corvin and Leon. Your help would make all the difference in our efforts. You could help us build a kingdom where we'd all be safe."

"I don't want a kingdom without Aria."

"Then we are at an impasse. If you take a step, I'll lock you in place. Your Casting options are not nearly so harmless. Will you boil my blood?"

Baron hesitated.

Sarah softened her voice. "I know you, Baron. You have the kindest heart in the kingdom. I know you're not dangerous."

When Aria said it, he felt lifted. When Sarah said it, he felt patronized. Baron was not dangerous, not inherently; he preferred tempered reactions, diplomatic solutions.

But he could be.

"Step. Aside," he repeated.

Sound from above stopped her response—first a scream from Aria, then the loud shattering of windows.

And Baron became dangerous.

ria tried to plead her case, but every argument fell on deaf ears. She'd been wrong to think Widow Morton could still be reached. Rather than entertaining a conversation, the woman pulled a small white towel from her pocket, still bearing the rusted-brown streaks of Aria's dried blood.

"I know you think my curse cruel," she said, "but I was as kind in it as I could be. You've had time to make peace with your family, to prepare for the end, to even attend a few dances. I gave you the opportunity for the goodbye my son never had. Now that the Cast has taken root in your sisters, it's time to be finished with the source."

Wind howled against the windows, a beast calling to be fed.

"You think to destroy the king"—Aria's eyes burned with tears—"but you are just like him."

The widow nodded, lips pressed to a line. "Perhaps I am."

She crumpled the cloth in one fist, and at her touch upon the dried blood, fire burst to life in Aria's veins.

She screamed. Her knees buckled, bringing her to the hard ballroom floor with a *crack*. She twisted onto her side, writhing, pain clawing in every limb.

Aria's eyes fell on the large glass windows as she sought the final comfort of at least seeing home. But all the stars had vanished, and the darkness outside was moving, swirling like a river. She thought it a result of dizziness until she realized nothing was moving except that giant shadow in the sky.

Distantly, she heard a *caw*. Then another. Then a hundred cackling voices took up the call, pressing closer, closer—

Until the windows exploded inward.

Widow Morton shrieked, turning aside from a waterfall of piercing shards. She dropped the towel, and Aria's pain vanished, allowing her to gasp in a sweet rush of cold air. Amid the falling glass, a collection of rocks bounced across the polished hardwood floor. Rocks about the size a bird could carry.

Aria pushed herself to her knees as a murder of crows swooped into the room, assaulting her ears with a cacophony of ca-*caw*s. They swarmed Widow Morton, tearing at her hair and clothes, shrieking their battle cries. The woman screamed her fury right back, grabbing wildly, dropping each bird she touched to the ballroom floor. But for every dead crow that hit the ground, another swooped in with talons extended.

One crow flew on a wobbling course toward Aria, crashing beak-first into the floor.

"Corvin!" It was half laugh, half sob. Though he'd put himself in danger, she could not have been more grateful for the rescue.

Then black mist puffed, and Leon sprawled on the floor, moaning. A second crow glided in to perch on his back, one mischievous brown eye focused on Aria.

"You thought *I* fly like that?" He gave his little rattling crow laugh.

"Get off me." Leon hissed, swiping at the bird.

In another puff of mist, Corvin stood beside Aria, one hand extended to help her to her feet. She took it gratefully.

"Where's Mom?" Leon demanded.

"I haven't—"

A thunderous roar shook the ballroom.

Aria staggered, turning to see a lion at the entrance. Richard Langley stood behind the beast, one arm raised to hold back the other Casters while the Affiliate loped into the room. From somewhere down the hall came the sound of crashing swords.

"He's bigger than me!" Leon shouted, scrambling backward across the floor. "He's a lot bigger! Bad cat!"

Corvin's face had gone pale. "A *lion* Affiliate? That's not fai—"

The golden monster pounced on the boy, cutting him short and knocking Aria aside. Corvin screamed in such pain it nearly brought Aria to her knees again. The lion's claws tore through the flesh of his thigh, dripping blood to the floor as the monster held him pinned.

"Call off the crows, boy!" the lion roared.

"Stop it!" Aria threw her weight against the beast, achieving nothing. "Stop! You're killing him!"

The crows fell silent, retreating through the broken windows.

Widow Morton stood alone in a lake of black feathers and glass, her veil gone, her brown hair hanging limply around her face. A cross-hatching of bloody gashes marred her skin, and the end of one of her black sleeves hung in scraps by a thread. She snapped the thread.

"A less elegant death, then," she snarled.

While Aria struggled to move the lion, Widow Morton caught her by the arm and hauled her forward. Aria tried to twist away but slipped on the glass-covered floor.

"Goodbye, Highness."

Then Widow Morton shoved her through an empty window, off a cliff, and into the night air.

CHAPTER

49

Baron acted on instinct. When Sarah looked upward at the sound of shattering glass, he drew his sword. Too late, she saw the movement and grabbed for him, but he had the longer reach of a weapon. He flicked his wrist, a quick, deceptively easy movement that had won him a hundred duels, slashing across her arm.

The point of his sword came away marked by a streak of blood that he brought to his fingers, his ears already ringing with magic.

He halted her blood flow, and Sarah collapsed to the floor. It twisted everything inside him to hurt her, and he held the Cast for only the precious few moments it took to leap over her fallen body and onto the stairs. Then he allowed the blood flow to resume. If she quickly recovered and gave chase, so be it.

He ran for the ballroom, following a flood of noise—the shrieking of crows and people alike. The Casters haunting the wide doorway were not prepared for someone attacking from behind, but Weston, who had hung at the back of the group, caught a glimpse of Baron's approach. Turning with a shout, he drew his own sword.

Baron used the force of his charge to knock the weapon aside, but Weston had enough skill to keep ahold of his weapon and grab with his other hand, forcing Baron to shy back from his Casting.

"Stand down, Weston," Baron panted. "We're friends."

Though Weston was five years older than Baron, he'd not

activated his Fluid Casting until after his first Casting test. Baron had taught him how to make wine.

Weston fell into a defensive stance, jaw clenched.

Then a *lion* roared, shaking the very walls.

Though they both staggered, Baron recovered first, darting forward. Weston parried his slash but reacted too slowly to the follow-up lunge, and Baron's blade slid right past his to pierce the man's shoulder. Weston cried out, and Baron shoved his forearm into his friend's chest, pushing hard until he pinned Weston against the wall and opened a path. Then he spun out of reach, drawing his sword free, throwing himself past the other stunned Casters and into the ballroom.

Just in time to see Widow Morton shove Aria through an open window.

"*No!*" Baron screamed. If he'd dealt with Sarah faster, if he'd—

His shout drew the lion Affiliate's attention, and in a flash of white, Leon transformed, already flying in a leap. His fierce yowl was nothing like the heart-stopping roar of his counterpart, but it was enough. He slashed his own claws through the lion's fleshy nose, drawing blood, and the giant lion poofed into a scrawny yellow housecat.

"Start running, whiskers," Leon snarled.

Once transformed by Leon's magic, the lion Affiliate fell subject to his commands like any other housecat. A battle of Affiliates was all about who landed the first strike.

Under Leon's command, the yellow cat skittered around before darting out of the ballroom. It would be a race to see which would happen first, Leon's magic wearing off or the cat dropping of exhaustion.

Corvin moaned, curling around his injured leg. He was already pale and shivering. Even with both hands pressed to his thigh, blood continued to flow past his already-slick fingers, pooling on the floor beneath him.

Baron had been frozen—staring at the broken window where Aria had disappeared, his heart pounding out that repeated denial *no, no, no*—but seeing Corvin's pain, he lurched forward at last.

From behind, he heard Sarah's anguished voice. "What have you *done*? Those are my sons!"

While she held the other Casters at bay, Baron used his blade to shred his vest, then, nudging the boy's hands aside, he wrapped Corvin's leg as tightly as he could. In the back of his mind, he saw his father. Heard the swirling echoes.

Now he could see Aria as well. One more person he'd failed. One more love he'd lost.

Not Corvin too.

"It hurts," Corvin whimpered.

"I know." Baron touched the boy's cheek, leaving a red thumbprint. "Deep breaths, Corvin. You'll be fine."

He tried to believe it, but he felt the danger in the keening song of Corvin's blood on his hands. Even with the gashes bound, blood soaked the wrapping. Something was wrong. The injury was too deep, or in a bad place.

"Baron, do something!" Leon begged, his voice high and frightened.

He'd said the same thing while Father had been dying.

What had Baron done then?

There's nothing I can do, my lord, I'm sorry. There's nothing anyone can do.

Baron's magic shied back from the blood, curling within him like a child huddled after a nightmare. It was happening again. It was happening *again*.

Nothing anyone can do.

"Am I dying?" The thought seemed to have just occurred to Corvin as tears spilled down his cheeks.

Sarah rushed over, falling to her knees beside the boy, her blonde hair frazzled. She glanced at the wound, then clutched Corvin's face with both hands. "Baby, it will be all right. Shh. It will be all right."

Her voice cracked with panic. Baron could see the strain in her expression, but there was no glow to meet it. Nothing her magic could do to fix her son.

Watching her effort transported him directly back to his father's room. He could picture himself seated beside his father on the bed, clutching his hand with that same desperate strain as his father thrashed, keeping hold long after it fell limp. He'd *tried*.

He hadn't failed his father. He couldn't control the outcome; he could only control the effort, and he'd given everything he had.

If nothing could be done, Baron would fight a battle across the three realms of heaven to be sure. And after that much struggle, after knowing he'd given everything he could, he would grant himself enough mercy to accept the result.

"Hold still, Corvin," he whispered. He pressed one hand to the bandaged wound and gripped Corvin's in the other. He closed his eyes.

Everything vanished but the rhythm of his brother's heart, panicked and erratic. Baron eased it, like a conductor slowing the tempo of an orchestra to let each note sing with greater distinction. The song of blood took on color in the dark, a faint glimmer of red outlining the network of branching rivers that made up Corvin's life. Baron sensed the one veering off course, torn by violence, and he reached in the darkness to soothe it, guiding it back into place. It reared at his touch like an abused animal, rejecting his influence.

The rivers grew thinner, the red color fading. The song skipped notes. He was running out of time.

Baron clenched his teeth, then injected more force to his Casting, abandoning requests in favor of commands. A sharp ache pounded at the back of his skull, but he pushed it away, returning to the red song.

Finding the path again in the dark, he caught and held.

The song screeched, fighting the rhythm, fighting *him*, but he held.

Slowly, slowly, the pressure against his mind eased.

The rivers ran straight in the darkness.

The song calmed.

For one horrifying, *terror-filled* moment, Baron thought he'd lost Corvin. That the effort hadn't been enough. But then he felt the boy squeeze his hand, and he opened his eyes to find his brother blinking lethargically, cradled in Sarah's arms. A faint golden glow faded from Corvin's leg.

Corvin looked down at his wound. "It still hurts," he said nervously, "but . . ."

"But not like before?"

He shook his head.

With a great sigh of relief, Baron sat back, releasing his hand. The weight of the almost-loss mixed with the triumph of success left a strange, bittersweet taste in his mouth.

"It isn't healed," he said. "I've just dammed the bleeding, but it will last a few hours, long enough to get a surgeon for the rest."

Corvin gave a shaky smile. At least until Leon whacked him on the shoulder.

"Next time, don't get skewered, you skinny chicken. Don't you know cats eat birds?"

"I'll peck your eyes out, *cat*."

For once, Baron was relieved to hear the bickering. Then Widow Morton approached, and he tensed.

The widow had taken a beating in the form of sharp talons, and trails of blood marked her bare arm where she'd lost a sleeve. A gust of winter air blew in from the gaping windows behind her, swirling with a trail of snowflakes.

Sarah gave Corvin a squeeze, then stood to meet Widow Morton. She drew the other woman off a few paces, and their hushed argument couldn't be heard until Sarah's voice rose.

"—to keep my sons *safe*! That was the point of *everything*, Clarissa!"

Widow Morton shot back, "Then you should have warned them not to align with the princess!"

Baron looked at the broken windows leading to a black night. Aria hadn't even screamed as she fell, her face reflecting only sudden shock. He felt that same shock within, still frozen in the loss, not yet processing the deep pain that was to come.

"Don't worry, Baron." Corvin poked his knee, drawing his focus. Though still horribly pale, the boy managed a mischievous smile. "She's wearing my comb."

CHAPTER

 50

Aria plummeted only a moment before the world slowed, the air softening against her skin, her body growing light as a feather. Snowflakes drifted past her in the air, and she drifted in the same way, still falling but gently, slowly. Her skin prickled with goose bumps. She looked down at a sheer black drop.

Trying to breathe calmly, she pressed one hand to her hair, clutching the comb that had saved her life. With the other, she reached out, grasping at snowy boulders in the cliffside and fumbling with scraggly bushes until she caught purchase at last. Once she was no longer falling, the feeling of regular weight returned, thumping her against the cliff, and then she hung in place, dangling from the side of a mountain she otherwise would have been dashed against.

Frigid wind howled in the dark. Even guarded from the direct blasts, Aria felt the swirling eddies of it, and her bare fingers soaked in the cold of the rock. She shivered. Looking up, she saw the light of the mansion spilling into the night, and her insides shriveled. Had she fallen so far in a matter of seconds?

She looked down.

Mark. You already looked down and regretted it. Repeating the same mistakes. Never learning.

Aria closed her eyes, tucking her head against her extended arm, the other clinging to a prickly bush beside her shoulder. She shivered in the night. She'd locked the quill away, yet it returned. She'd *burned* it, yet it returned. It always returned.

Repeating the same mistakes. Never learning.

She'd disobeyed her father again. Returned to Northglen again. Chased the same circles of conversation with the widow and emerged from the encounter even worse.

Repeating the same mistakes.

She was eight years old again, making strokes on a paper, watching with dread as the marks kept coming and coming and coming. A hundred. More.

Never learning.

"Fine," she whispered to the quill. "Now what?"

It hovered without answer. It didn't *have* answers; it didn't have solutions. Only condemnations. If Aria held to the mountain forever without moving—if she didn't think, didn't *breathe*—it would have nothing to criticize. Without her efforts, it would be useless.

It was already useless.

When Aria wanted to learn to swim as a child, her father took her to the lake a few times a week for the entire summer. The first time in the water, she clung to him and cried, never trying to paddle her arms or move from his embrace. She told him she never wanted to go back, but as usual, he didn't listen, and after finding herself back at the lake a second and third time, she accepted she would have to *do* something about her fears. For a while, she paddled weakly. She hated water in her face. She thought of drowning and couldn't breathe. But her father continued bringing her back. After weeks, she could swim on her own. By the end of summer, she was sneaking out to the lake without him.

Yes, Aria kept repeating mistakes. Because she was going back to the lake. She was paddling weakly and gulping muddy water and failing to float. But she kept coming back.

Maybe she hadn't learned yet.

But she would.

Success would not come by hiding, by fleeing. It would come by returning to the lake.

Aria set her jaw, and she started climbing. Her fingers slipped in powdery snow as she reached for handholds, and she hissed as she grasped sharp rock edges and prickly brush. The skin of her hands reddened and ached. A cut along her palm stung with every movement, then grew numb.

Corvin's comb proved to be a lifesaver once more. As she climbed, she felt lighter and lighter. Each push lifted her higher, until she began lurching up the mountainside, catching new holds with more ease. For a moment, she almost felt like she was flying, racing toward a starlit sky almost within reach.

At last, she wedged her boot against a rock, heaved herself upward—

And her fingers caught the mansion's foundation.

Above and to her left rose the gaping windows of the ballroom. Aria eyed a narrow window to her right, where a stone ledge extended at its base. She leapt toward it and caught hold. Though her teeth chattered, the cold couldn't prevent her triumphant grin.

Then she nearly lost her grip as the window opened and Lettie's timid face peeked out.

Aria found herself swallowed by a circle of blue light. This magic was nothing like the exhilaration she'd experienced while climbing the mountain; this was a split second of feeling like a mind without a body, falling into a pit without a bottom.

Then came a moment of *actual* falling, ending abruptly by a lurch into new surroundings as Aria stumbled on a rug and landed hard on one knee. Her stomach flipped, nearly losing its contents. Her numb hands needled painfully in the sudden warmth, her eyes watered, and she couldn't hear until her ears popped.

"Sorry," said Lettie. "I think I pulled too hard. It's more difficult when I move myself along with someone else."

They were in a bedroom. Aria thought at first it was Lettie's, but the pristine arrangement of every item was not the work of a child. The bedcovers and pillows had been settled with perfect symmetry, and though the furniture was clear of dust, the room smelled musty and unused all the same. It felt like stepping into a preserved tomb. Even the fresh flowers on the mantel felt more like a graveside offering than an addition of life.

Charlie's room.

Lettie rubbed her hands. Her fingers shook.

"Does it hurt?" Aria asked. She paused to swallow down the remaining nausea. "Using magic."

After hesitating, Lettie nodded. "No one else says so, but mine does. Mine has always been different."

"It's hard to be different."

Lettie nodded again.

Aria meant to stand, meant to be strong, but she sank to the floor instead, crossing her legs beneath her, grateful for trousers. She couldn't tell if the dizziness was from the climb or Lettie's magic or both, but either way, the room wavered, and she breathed shallowly.

Lettie took a few quiet steps on the rug. She brushed her fingers over a cushioned chair beside the bed and smiled faintly.

"Charlie was different too. He always slept here, and Mama got so mad that he wouldn't use his bed, that he wouldn't be human. He just loved being a cat."

"I wish I could have met him," Aria said honestly.

"You would have liked him. Everyone liked Charlie."

"Why did you bring me here, Lettie?"

The girl tensed. She knotted her hands in her skirt. Then she pulled a folded sheet of parchment from her pocket.

"I took it earlier," she said, hanging her head. "I'm sorry. I just wanted to know what it said."

Aria hadn't even noticed the moment the peace agreement had vanished; her attention had been rather captured by other things.

Lettie unfolded it. "You wrote about Charlie."

"I want to prevent what happened to him from ever happening again."

"It's my fault," Lettie whispered. "He wanted to sneak around the castle, and Mama locked him in our rooms so he wouldn't. He was so sad. I . . . I wasn't supposed to, but I . . ."

At once, Lettie's whole body shook, a trembling autumn leaf moments from falling.

Aria climbed to her feet and stumbled forward. She took the girl's hands gently in her own. "Lettie, listen to me. It isn't your fault."

But the girl rambled on, telling the story that probably played on repeat through her mind every night. "Anytime we went somewhere new, he always explored, and he never got caught. He never got caught—until I helped him. I wish I could take it back. I wish I never had magic!"

"Shh," Aria murmured, rubbing soothing circles on the girl's hands.

"When Charlie died, Mama was so angry. She's never been so angry. She broke the dishes one by one because Charlie would never eat again." Lettie's voice shrank as tears leaked from her eyes. "If she knew I was the one who helped him, she would have cursed me, not you."

Aria steered Lettie into Charlie's chair, giving her a gentle push so she sat. Lettie burrowed into the cushions, rubbing her cheek against the soft velvet of the curving back. She hugged a pillow to her chest, her breath coming in hiccups.

"Did you know I have a sister?" Aria took a shaky breath of her own. "Two, actually, but my sister Eliza and I did everything together. We used to go riding and have picnics. She made me laugh."

Lettie slowly calmed, watching her with tearful blue eyes.

"Something bad happened, and I promised Eliza I would fix it, but I couldn't. She ran away from home, and I thought it was because of me. But she left me a letter that said it wasn't, that said she loves me. Lettie, if Charlie could send you a letter right now, I think he would say it wasn't your fault. He would say he knew you just wanted to make him happy. He knew you loved him. And he loved you too."

Lettie sniffled, wiping her nose. She opened her mouth to speak, and then her eyes moved to the doorway, and she froze, trembling again.

Aria's stomach fell. She turned to see Widow Morton haunting the hall like a dark shadow.

"I thought I rid myself of you, Highness." She stepped into the room. Her gaze roamed from the untouched bed to the vase of grave-side flowers, and as the line of her mouth tightened, Aria saw the cracks in the woman's anger, trails leading to a bottomless pain Aria could never hope to understand.

All the determination she'd felt while climbing a mountainside vanished, stolen like breath from her lungs in a blast of wind. Twice, this woman had tried to kill her, and the odds of Widow Morton's success still felt inevitable. Aria had no weapons, no magic, no armies, no true power at all. If she were a Caster, if she were a queen, perhaps she would have a chance. But she was just a helpless girl.

"Mama . . ." Lettie shrank in the chair.

Widow Morton didn't look at her daughter but at Aria. "I can never forget the last time one of my children was alone with royalty."

"She didn't hurt me," Lettie whispered.

"So I see."

Aria caught her breath once more, daring to feel a thin spark of hope. One thing was certain: If she surrendered now, Widow Morton and the king would both continue their forward rampages. The kingdom would go to war. Even without weapons, without magic or means, Aria would fight to her final breath to prevent that. She was the only one who could.

She thought of her own mother, remembered her words in the music room, urging Aria to do what was right. She still didn't know what was right.

But she agreed with Baron.

We all get it wrong, so perhaps the answer is simply mercy. Mercy for others, and mercy for ourselves.

"I was Lettie's age," Aria said. "My twelfth birthday—Were you there? Most of court was—when I announced my mother had named me after the only thing she ever loved."

Widow Morton raised an eyebrow but attempted no murder. For the moment.

"I believed that for years—until I realized my mother's name is Marian. 'Aria' is the heart of it." She gestured around the room. "'Clarissa' and 'Charles' don't quite line up the same, but Charlie was your heart, wasn't he?"

The widow snorted quietly. "What a foolish question."

She stepped to the dresser, lifting a small, decorative box that had been perfectly centered upon it. After feeling at the neckline of her dress, she pulled out a key on a thin chain and used it to wind the music box, which echoed with a tinkling lullaby. The box was painted in soft pastels, with the silhouette of a dancer across the lid.

Lettie smiled, wiping her nose. "Charlie's music box."

"I had this made before his birth," Widow Morton said, "when I was certain I was having a girl. But Charlie loved it all the same. He wouldn't sleep without it, even as a teenager. I think he did it half to tease me. He was always . . ."

Her free hand curled into a fist, pressing white-knuckled against the dresser. Whether she trembled with grief or rage, Aria couldn't tell. Perhaps both. Surely both.

She didn't know what conversations Widow Morton might have had with her father between Charlie's death and her hostile letter, but she knew what would have been absent from all of them—an apology. That was something her father could never give. He had to be right.

In the face of that, Aria couldn't blame the woman before her for wanting to crack foundations and watch things fall.

"I'm sorry," Aria whispered. "I'm so sorry for what my family did to yours."

Widow Morton whirled, music box clutched in one hand, poised to smash it to the ground, but Aria leapt forward and caught her hand, their bare fingers overlapping around the fragile box. A shiver ran down her arm at the thought of what the Caster could do with a touch, but she did not retreat.

Widow Morton stared into her soul with wild eyes, a deep gash across her cheek scabbed with fresh blood. "*Twice* you have come into my home with empty words! I tried to listen, but in that hollow, I heard only the screams of my son."

"I can't fix it," Aria said, voice breaking. "I wish I could. Nothing can."

"*Excuses*! When Peregrine murdered Charlie, he offered excuses, and now—"

"I *can't* fix it," Aria repeated. "Not if I write a thousand peace treaties, not if I die a hundred deaths. You *can't* fix it. Not if you kill every member of my family, not if you collapse the entire kingdom. Your son is gone. We can't fix that. *Nothing can.*"

Widow Morton recoiled, leaving Aria holding the music box. The woman stared at it.

"But if you let me," Aria pleaded, cradling the box, shielding it in both hands, "I will protect your daughter. I'm sure I'll make mistakes—more than I want to; worse than I want to—but I will fix them. I'll learn. I'll negotiate and study and *listen* until I find the path forward.

"When I sat with you the first time, you asked what reparations *I* could make, what *I* could offer. This is what I want. Please just let me, and I'll protect instead of destroy."

Lettie darted from the chair, wrapping her arms around her mother.

Slowly, the anger drained from Widow Morton's expression, leaving behind a pale emptiness. The widow held to her daughter.

"I believe you, Highness," she said softly. "But it's too late. I can no longer break the Cast. I felt it when we touched just now. The curse has grown beyond my reach, and I have doomed us both."

Just as quickly as Aria's heart had swelled, it shattered.

Widow Morton had stormed off into the manor after her heated argument with Sarah. Baron took heart that the remaining Casters seemed more nervous than hostile, and they were quick to respond to Sarah's instructions. Because Corvin was not fit to travel, Sarah ordered one of the Casters to ride for the small town where the nearest surgeon resided. Richard Langley personally bandaged Weston, who would also need to be seen by the surgeon.

"You have to go," Corvin whispered to Baron. "You have to help Aria escape."

Baron knew Aria well enough to know escape would not be her intention. In fact, odds were high she'd already snuck her way back into the mansion. He glanced at the doorway, but it held a congregation of Casters, and he was hesitant to leave Corvin.

"I'll do it," Leon grumbled. "Nose around and see what I can find."

Barely a moment later, a white puffball slunk off into the manor. If Sarah noticed the large cat brush against her leg, she said nothing.

"Are you mad we came?" Corvin asked.

Baron said, "Right now, I'm focused on relief. We can discuss 'mad' later."

"You should have seen Leon try to fly. He hit a tree."

Despite himself, Baron snorted.

Corvin grinned. Then his eyes drifted to his mother at the door. "Do you think . . . I should talk to her?"

"If you want to."

"You wouldn't be mad?"

"Corvin, you worry far too much what I think. Whether you're breaking heirloom vases or ballroom windows, you're my brother, and I love you. Anything else is secondary. So what matters regarding Sarah is what *you* think."

"I think . . . maybe I break too many things."

They shared a smile. When Sarah returned, Baron waited for a nod from Corvin, then stepped away to give them a private moment.

Leon returned at last, padding softly into the ballroom. Judging by the layers of dust darkening his thick fur, he'd snuck through all kinds of uncharted manor areas. Though he shook himself, most of the grime stuck.

Baron crouched in front of him.

"Found her." Leon's whiskers twitched. He sneezed. "Good and bad news."

"How bad?"

"Let me tell my thing, Baron. Good news, looks like she melted the winter witch's heart. Bad news, Widow Curseface is the worst Caster alive and can't fix her own curse. Good news, you can, since you fixed birdbrain."

"Bad news?"

"Can you not see my fur?" Leon licked one paw, then gagged. He shook his head. "They're heading back here, along with some girl. Charlie's sister, I guess."

Baron glanced at Corvin. Sarah had helped him stand, all his weight carefully leaning on his uninjured leg. For the moment, Baron needed to tend to his family.

As he approached, Sarah glanced at him, then down at the floor, streaked with thick blood. "I wanted to get him cleaned up and settled before the surgeon arrives. There's a guest room just down the hall."

Corvin cocked his head rebelliously. "I told Mom I can walk, but—"

Baron picked the boy up. Sarah shot him a grateful smile.

"I'm sorry," she said. "I wanted . . . I'd hoped . . ."

She trailed off, and Baron didn't have the words to continue that conversation.

"Which room?" he asked.

By the time Corvin was settled in bed and Baron had cleaned himself up as much as possible—washing his hands, discarding what remained of his vest—Widow Morton found him. When she nodded toward the hall, he followed, and they stood beneath a glowing sconce.

"I heard you can't stop the curse," he said, speaking first.

She'd changed into a new dress and refastened her hair but hadn't replaced her veil. Her face bore a deep gash that would likely scar.

"I made a mistake with the Artifact," she said.

"Sarah brought me the bloodied towel, but I can't sense—"

"That's because I lied to Sarah." Widow Morton kept her gaze on the wall, arms folded, shoulders sagging. "I thought myself terribly clever. A common Artifact could be discovered, captured, tampered with, so I anchored to something no one would suspect. I anchored to the person I cursed."

Baron's eyes widened. "*Aria* is the Artifact?"

"I kept a decoy Artifact and told no one the truth. Mere weeks in, I realized my mistake. The curse was meant to deteriorate, but as it eroded its subject, it also eroded the Artifact, creating the very danger I'd meant to defend against."

"That's why it rebounded on you."

"Among other things. It gave Her Highness increased resistance—aided, I suspect, by your own efforts—and delayed spreading. When I felt it tonight . . ." She sighed. "I thought I'd employed a monster on a leash, but I have tried to leash lightning."

Baron studied his hands, tracing his thumb along the lines of his palm. Though he'd scrubbed off every drop of Corvin's blood, his ears still rang with the faint echo of a red song, calling like a far-off trumpet on the wind. It was not haunting; rather, it was invigorating. He felt the way he did after mastering a sword form. He felt the drive to repeat the success, the confidence that he *could*.

"I will break it," he said.

Widow Morton met his eyes at last. "Your success with your brother is impressive, I'll admit. A wound of that severity would have been beyond my abilities."

Baron heard a note of hope in her voice.

Then she said, "But the curse has almost run its course. Its hold on the princess is deep, and I fear in anchoring it as I did, I have blurred the lines irreparably. I could not feel the separation between the girl and the magic."

"Luckily," Baron said, "I know the girl far better than you do."

"It may overtake you. At the very least, even if you succeed, I fear there will be effects on you both."

"Then I will suffer the effects," said Baron. "But I will not surrender without trying."

He found Aria alone in a sitting room, her journal on her lap, a quill on the small table beside her. She brushed one finger absently down its frills while her eyes scanned the page, brow furrowed in thought.

Baron smiled. Then he sat beside her, drawing her attention.

With a snap, she closed her journal, sitting up too rigidly, a posture born of nervous tension. "I was just revising notes for tomorrow. I've summoned the Upper Court, and I have only one chance to . . . Well, anyway. Corvin's all right? Leon still seemed shaken when I spoke to him, but he said there's a surgeon on the way, said you have things in hand, and . . . uh . . ."

He was staring, he realized. Not intensely, but focused. Just soaking in the image of her and what he loved so much about her. Though she was obviously frightened, she was still trying so hard to be brave, still caring for others.

Baron folded one leg onto the couch, his knee pressed against her hip, his body angled to face her. He rested his elbow on the back of the couch, his arm curling loosely behind her, fingertips brushing her far shoulder just to be certain she was solid. That she hadn't been lost.

Aria shifted closer to him, resting her head against his arm.

"I spoke to Widow Morton," he said softly.

"Right, so she told you . . ." Her fingers tightened around her journal, creaking the leather. "That's why I have to figure this out. I may have a way to deal with my father, but I have to figure out how to make peace last if I'm . . . I'm . . ."

"I saw you fall." The words scraped his throat even now, remembering the moment his heart had stopped.

Aria winced, as if remembering along with him.

"I thought I'd lost you forever."

She kept her eyes on her journal and spoke with forced cheer. "Thankfully, Corvin bought me a few more days. I'll have to make the most of them."

A few more days. As if that could ever be good enough.

Baron would not be satisfied without an entire lifetime of Aria.

"Aria." His voice had gone hoarse, and he felt her shiver. "The curse can't take you. I won't let it."

She looked up at him, her hair catching a glow from the lamp behind her, peeking like a ray of hope.

Baron slipped the journal from her hands, dropping it to the floor. He intertwined his fingers with hers, leaning in until their faces nearly touched.

"Do you trust me?"

To his surprise, she gave a thin, heartbreaking laugh. "All these years, I knew I had to accomplish everything myself. I had to be capable of it all. Now I realize how wrong I was—I *can't* do it all. But I can choose who I trust to help." Holding his gaze, she nodded, and her voice grew tender. "Yes, Baron, I trust you. More than I've ever trusted anyone."

He felt the weight of that trust settle into every bone, a sacred burden he would never betray. With reverence, he said, "I'm about to kiss you like your life depends on it."

He heard her breath catch, and then she tilted her head to meet his lips. He curled his fingers around her shoulder, drawing her to him, and in return, she released his other hand to fist both of hers in his shirt, clinging like he was the anchor to life itself. He gently stroked his fingertips down her arm, tracing a line from her elbow up to her wrist and back down. As she trembled in his arms, he wondered if she felt the same fear of loss he did, the same desperation to make a brighter future they could share together.

Aria reached up, tangling one hand in his hair, her lips moving against his with more force. Baron held steady for her, letting her take whatever strength she needed, until her trembling eased, until he felt her soften.

When he reached for her hair, his fingers hit the feathered comb, and he tugged it free. Her hair tumbled over her shoulders—and his arm—with a wave of lilac scent, tightening Baron's chest with a surge of longing. He shifted, catching her waist and pulling her into his lap, feeling the warmth of her all along his chest. They fit together like lemon and leaf, like sword and sheath, like two halves always meant to be whole.

And with that sense of *wholeness* suffusing him in every bone, he opened his mind to magic.

At once, his world fell into night. A storm raged in the darkness, and he could not make out shapes in the pitch. When he strained for light, the darkness swallowed it, a flash of jagged blue lightning vanishing into black. The song of Aria's blood was thunder in his ears. Though his head began to pound, he forced more flashes of light. Each one highlighted a silhouette, blurred at the edges, two things masquerading as one. The curse lurked as a shadow behind Aria, revealed only in light, copying the contours of her edges perfectly. It had become her, and in all the duels Baron had ever fought, he'd never been so outclassed by an opponent.

His breathing grew ragged, but he did not surrender. He held Aria more tightly, shifting them both on the couch, his palms steady against her back as he struggled to save her from the storm.

Aria's lips slid to his jaw, then to the side of his throat, trailing kisses down his witch's mark and rendering him quite unable to breathe. For a moment, Baron lost his hold on magic.

Then he grinned. From the moment they'd first met, she'd been catching him off guard, reorienting his world to face an entirely new sun, the light of it brighter than he'd ever imagined.

He seized that light, and he turned it on her curse.

"Baron—" she whispered.

"Concentrating," he murmured back, smiling as he recaptured her lips.

She relaxed into him, resting her hands against his chest.

He allowed himself to exist fully in the moment, in the feeling of her weight against him, of her skin on his. Instinct, not thought.

The curse had made itself Aria's image, but Baron knew the difference. He knew her *details*—had felt her kindness, her embarrassment, her fear, her joy. He'd inspired her laughter and wiped her tears. Every moment they'd shared, every touch, every word in every letter, filled his awareness of Aria with color and betrayed the shadow's hollow dark. With magic, he focused every memory into light until it was no longer brief flashes but a blazing sun, until it cut the storm and began stretching the shadow, driving it back.

Finally, only a pinprick of contact remained, a thin slip of darkness clinging to Aria's heels.

In the kiss, Baron playfully nipped her lip.

In his mind, he cut the tether.

With a gasp, Aria drew back, holding Baron's gaze with wide brown eyes.

He tucked her hair behind her ear, winding his fingers in the silk of it. "I didn't hurt you, did I?"

"Just a tingle," she whispered. "Is it really . . . ?"

With a smile, he kissed her again.

CHAPTER

 52

Aria insisted on returning to the castle alone. Corvin needed his family with him, and Baron wouldn't have been permitted in a meeting of the Upper Court. Besides, she was about to kick the court as if it were a beehive, and it would be easier to contain the damage with fewer people around to get stung.

"This is my duty," she told him, "and I'm ready to face it."

Though she would have preferred to spend a few more hours kissing him, even if her knees had not yet recovered from the last one. It was a miracle she didn't wobble as she walked, as dizzy and euphoric as she felt inside. Her skin still held the warmth of his touch. Her soul would never be the same, and not just because he'd rescued her from the open grave of a curse.

Aria was quite convinced that no damsel in any of Eliza's sonnets and swooning tales had ever been kissed as thoroughly or as perfectly as Aria had been kissed by Baron.

With her curse broken, she felt renewed. *Unstoppable*, even. Like she was galloping on horseback toward a dawn just breaking the horizon. The cold she'd carried inside for months had melted, leaving behind a crystal-clear hope for the future. A future with Baron. A future of freedom for everyone in her kingdom.

She requested only two things of Widow Morton before she left:

a ratified signature on the peace treaty, and a breaking of the false Artifact. Widow Morton provided the first, Sarah the second.

Aria didn't have an opportunity to speak with Sarah Reeves directly, but the twins made a more convincing case than she ever could, and with great hesitation, the woman also released the sleeping Cast over the castle. Though she made no outward threats, her eyes tracked Aria, promising a far worse curse if promises weren't kept.

Baron's stepmother was not the only one feeling anxious; the other Casters eyed Aria nervously, even after her peace agreement was read out loud and endorsed by Widow Morton. Baron promised to speak with them further, apparently confident he could break through their fear and connect with at least one of them. Aria knew it would be a long road ahead, but at least the journey had started.

It was up to her to see it through.

As she retrieved her riding cloak, Lettie caught her in the hallway.

"I can transport you," Lettie offered. "It's almost dawn already, and Mama said it's important you get back quickly."

Aria protested, "I don't want to hurt you. Besides, all the way to the palace—"

"I can do it. I helped make the water mirrors—they were at the palace—and it's only one person. I can do it."

"Thank you," Aria said, gripping her bag. "If it truly isn't a bother, I could use the help."

Lettie smiled, blue mist already swirling around her fingers. Just before the light enveloped Aria, she heard the girl's final whisper.

"Charlie would have liked you."

In a flash of blue light, Aria's senses vanished, then reformed. Her second experience with portal magic went more smoothly, though it was certainly disorienting to suddenly be in her bedroom with no more than a flash of light and a few blinks. It was like a dream, and she stood still, waiting for something to jar her awake.

"Aria!"

That did it.

Aria turned, finding Jenny in her room. The girl had apparently been pacing, judging by the groove in the rug, though she now rushed forward with relief in her expression.

Aria hugged her sister.

"I felt it," Jenny said. "The difference, the . . . lifting. I almost slept, but I wanted to be here when you returned."

That meant wherever Eliza was, she was now safe as well. Aria breathed deep the relief. Then, with a final squeeze, she stepped back. "Get some rest. You deserve it."

"I delivered the summons."

Aria nodded her thanks. From her desk, she took her grand-mother's journal, adding it to her bag along with her own and the broken Artifact.

Everything was ready, and it was time.

Aria arrived first for the meeting. Her steps echoed quietly in the throne room, and she savored the morning light through stained glass, grateful that the warmth filled her with strength instead of stealing it. With confidence, she climbed the dais and sat in a throne.

One by one, other members of the Upper Court trickled in. Aria counted each arrival. She would need ten to hold a trial.

Lord Philip and Lord Emmett arrived together. Philip studied her intensely as he took his seat, as if knowing she chased something more dangerous now than what she had sought in the records room.

Earl Wycliff gave her a deep nod as he passed.

Duke Crampton was noticeably absent. Aria had hoped he would attend, even included specific pleading in her summons, but she hadn't seen the man since Kendall's banishment. Instead, Marchioness Elsworth was next to arrive, and she gave Aria a suspicion-filled glance before curtsying.

Five seats filled, including Aria's.

Five to go.

Her heartbeats counted silently, caught in a loop that began again and again until the next arrival.

Five, four, three, two, one. Five—

Duke Brightwood, the most cheerful of the congregants, who made a joke no one laughed at.

Four—

Marquess Haskett, more reserved than usual.

Three—

Countess Redford, complaining of the late notice.

Two—

The king.

Aria's father climbed the dais and stood before her. He wore his white uniform, his tired eyes showing red. "What is this?" he demanded, brandishing his own summons. "I've not given permission for you to leave your room."

Slowly, Aria stood. She resisted the urge to look at the door, her heartbeat pounding in the frozen count of awaiting a final person. *One, one, one.*

"Your Majesty," Aria said. "I have called for a Trial by Upper Court. As heir to the throne, I am still a member of Upper Court, authorized to provide summons and attend meetings."

A small part of her feared he might disown her on the spot, out of spite if nothing else, but he did not.

"Indeed," he said, tucking the summons into his uniform jacket. "And who do you wish to put on trial, Aria? Our newest challenger, perhaps? He is nowhere to be found and therefore subject to execution."

A new figure slipped through the door, drawing Aria's gaze, and her heart beat once more.

One.

The queen wore trousers and a shirt without a vest, as if she'd come straight from the music room, as if she'd debated attending until the last moment. Aria couldn't remember the last time her mother had come to a meeting of the Upper Court, and truthfully, it had felt foolish writing the queen a summons at all. Yet here she was, the final needed member, making the entire trial possible.

Queen Marian took her seat without a word, ignoring the sharp look from her husband.

That's ten, Aria thought. When she addressed her father again, her voice had grown stronger.

"Lord Guillaume has three days to report on the Crown's challenge, and you did not forbid him from leaving the palace. Though we *should* speak to the matter of my curse. I owe you the truth, Father."

What a relief to speak the word *curse* with no restraint. Though she felt weariness, it was only an ordinary weariness from exertion, from a night facing dangers and climbing cliffs. The current trial was her final cliff to conquer.

Aria gestured for her father to take his seat, and he did so stiffly. Then she called the meeting to order.

"First," she said, "proof I am not under Widow Morton's thrall."

She pulled the Artifact from her satchel, holding the bronze cube tightly in her hand. Then she untied the thin string that secured it and opened her hand, allowing the pieces to fall with the ringing sound of bells against the marble floor.

Along with Henry, she'd taken a hammer to that Artifact. Tested it with blades, with bluntness, with heat. It had never wavered. One touch from Sarah, and it fell apart; the woman said it would have done the same if submerged in salty water, which somehow acted as a neutralizer for the strengthening Cast she'd applied. Aria smiled wryly—she still had so much to learn about magic.

"The curse is broken!" Duke Brightwood shouted. Murmurs passed between the others in attendance.

"How is this proof?" Marchioness Elsworth asked suspiciously.

"This is the Artifact my father's soldiers captured from Widow Morton, the one my father based the Crown's challenge upon. Did you question its anchoring to my curse when it was first presented?"

The woman fell silent, and no one else offered protest.

"Does this mean the latest challenger succeeded?" Lord Emmett asked.

"I'll let him make his own report," Aria said. "I wish to speak of my interactions with Widow Morton, beginning months ago, when I traveled alone to Northglen. While I was in the curse's grip, I was restrained from speaking of these things, but I am now free."

Aria recounted the events truthfully, as promised, not shying from her own mistakes, from Widow Morton's raw grief, from the actuality of the woman's curse. She spoke of her sleepless nights in a silent castle, of her search for a way to counter the effects by interrogating the only Caster within court.

As she spoke, her father sat with his elbow propped on the arm of his throne, his chin resting on his fist. His dark eyes and thinned lips didn't give much hope regarding the way he received her story, but Aria pushed on nonetheless.

"My attitude toward magic began to change," she said, "the more I witnessed the uprightness of a Caster in possession of it."

The only truth she held back was her discovery of Corvin. She was not about to expose the twins or Lettie to mortal danger when the laws were still uncertain. Instead, she said only that Baron had gone with her to Northglen, they'd faced Widow Morton together, negotiated a new peace, and he had broken her curse.

Aria unfolded a sheet of parchment to display Widow Morton's signature and seal. To her relief, the ink didn't run. "I hold here the ratified document, in which the widow has agreed to cease all hostilities, provided we do the same. Widow Morton and her Casters do not want war. They want justice, protection, and equality."

Her father snorted, causing Aria to blush. By reflex, she found herself mentally reaching for a quill, but she pulled her shoulders back, stood tall, and breathed in the moment without judgment.

Lord Philip rose from his seat in the right wing, approaching the royal thrones with hand extended. "Highness, may I?"

He studied the agreement with furrowed brows, returning to his seat. The document passed next to Lord Emmett, then to Marquess Haskett, who gave a low grunt, his eyes wide. Duke Brightwood leaned in to see.

The document made its way to the other wing, and quiet, concerned discussions whispered in its wake.

"Someone say it," Marquess Haskett snapped.

"Highness . . ." Philip looked aghast. "This agreement includes protections for *shapeshifters* as well."

The king's eyes narrowed as he read the agreement at last. Aria thought perhaps she should have read it out loud to begin with. She'd never conducted a meeting like this before, but now that she thought about it, her father always had an adviser read important documents aloud.

She swallowed the mistake and pressed on. "*Affiliates*, Lord Philip—a type of magic user similar to Casters. They are members of our kingdom like any other, and it is unthinkable to execute any person simply for existing. Such a thing makes us a tyranny."

She paused, then reached for her grandmother's journal, tucked into her satchel. "During my grandmother's reign—"

The doors to the throne room swung open, admitting a guard with hurried steps. He bowed at the base of the stairs.

"Your Majesty, Mr. Auden Huxley requests to be seen immediately. He claims knowledge of a dire threat against the kingdom."

Aria could have strangled the steward. Especially when her father ordered for him to be admitted.

She protested, "There is a trial in session—"

"I'm not convinced there *is* a trial in session," the king retorted.

Leaning on his cane, Mr. Huxley limped into the room and

made his bows. With more melodramatic paleness and shaking than necessary, he gave the accusation Aria dreaded.

"The Reeves twins are shapeshifters, Your Majesty! I watched them—both of them—turn into crows and fly off into the night!"

Panic erupted in a rush of voices.

Aria felt that same panic grip her, but if she faltered now, she would fail all of them. So she thought of Baron—*controlled calm*—and spoke over the din.

"Thank you, Mr. Huxley, for bringing this to the court's attention. I have my own witness to add to yours."

Curiosity captured the crowd, drawing everyone's eyes back to her, as she had hoped.

"First, a correction. The Reeves twins are Affiliates, which is the proper term. Terms matter—we would not refer to a tailor as a butcher even though they both do a great deal of cutting things apart."

Perhaps she should have refrained from gruesome images while presenting a defense of "dangerous magic users." Once again, she swallowed the mistake and continued forward.

"Second, they're not both crows. One is Crow-Affiliate and the other a cat. By this inaccuracy, we see the danger of presenting a hurried report, of acting before we possess all the facts. Most important of those facts would be that neither of the Reeves boys presents a threat to the kingdom. Corvin Reeves, the future lord baron, even saved my life using his magic."

"They're wild beasts!" interjected Marquess Haskett. "Animals presenting human faces to lure in prey."

"They are no such thing," Aria said sharply. "Have you met them, Lord Haskett?"

"I have." Earl Wycliff's deep voice cut in with inarguable certainty. "Marcus was a good man who raised good sons, and those twins are both friends with my youngest. They've spent time at my estate. They're not exactly the picture of manners, and perhaps that wildness can be attributed to magic, but I refuse to consider them a danger."

Aria could have hugged him.

Her father glared daggers at Earl Wycliff. "You speak in defense of dark magic in my court, Wycliff?"

"I speak in defense of the innocent, Your Majesty." He hesitated. "Someone has to."

And Aria saw it—

She saw her father's flinch.

Her palms grew sweaty. The moment had come.

"This is nonsense," her father growled. "There is only one course of action regarding shapeshifters—"

Aria interrupted. "The Reeves boys aren't the ones on trial here, Father."

"No one is on trial," he shot back. "You have called a council but presented no accused."

"I present one now." She took a deep breath and spoke the words. "I accuse you, Father, of the unlawful murder of Charles Morton."

There was no going back.

CHAPTER

53

Stunned silence fell in the throne room as ten people attempted to process the unthinkable—a king accused of murder.

During Loegria's founding, its first king had established a power balance within court. As Aria's father so liked to remind everyone, a king's word was law. Except in one area.

A king could not pardon himself.

"During my grandmother's reign," Aria said, speaking to them all, "a law existed to execute Affiliates upon discovery. There were no qualifications to the law, not for age, not for innocent intentions. Dorothy Ames, a ten-year-old girl, was discovered to be Fox-Affiliate. Tried and found guilty of nothing beyond existing, she was executed. The event haunted Queen Theresa to her deathbed, and, consumed by guilt, she finally revoked the law in perhaps the final action of her life."

"There has been no such change to the law!" Lord Emmett sputtered.

"There was," Aria said forcefully. "My father just didn't tell you. He didn't tell anyone."

She snatched her grandmother's journal, flipped it open to a marked page, and read: "Though I feel myself fading, I have spoken to Perry, and I can rest knowing my son will enact the change I have made. I leave behind a true reparation for my mistake. No longer will her little voice demand justice from the grave."

Though the writing was too small for them to read at a distance, she turned the journal, showed the proof. Shocked expressions echoed back at her.

Except from her father.

Who sat as a statue on his throne.

"This is speculation!" protested Lord Emmett. When he looked for support, he received nods from a few of the others. "Queen Theresa, may she rest, grew unstable near the end, and that entry doesn't even mention Dorothy by name much less state a change to the law."

"Her name may not be in this specific entry, Lord Emmett, but it's scattered throughout my grandmother's journal, beginning with the day of Dorothy's execution. I believe there was not a day that passed she didn't think of her. Even on the day of my parents' wedding, when she claims to be filled with hope for her son"—Aria flipped to the page quickly—"she writes about 'little Dorothy, from whom has been stolen the opportunity for hope or happiness, from whom I have taken all but a voice in the grave.'"

"What does this have to do with Charles Morton?" Countess Redford asked.

Lord Philip answered, his voice haunted, "Charles Morton was an Affiliate."

At the base of the stairs, Auden Huxley mopped his forehead with a handkerchief, looking like he regretted ever coming to the palace. The guards stood at rigid attention. No one seemed able to look at the king.

No one except Aria.

"You had no idea, did you? That Grandmother recorded it." Aria's voice took on a hard edge. "I had a lot of solitary nights for reading, Father. You didn't tell anyone because you couldn't live with your mother's regret—it meant she made a *mistake*. It meant she was not a flawless monarch, as you believe we all must be, and in your eyes, revoking a law would have displayed weakness in the Crown.

What did you care about little Dorothy? You were too young to attend her execution. You didn't have to hear her screams in memory as your mother did; you only knew that when she spoke of Dorothy, it made you uncomfortable. Her regret made you uncomfortable.

"So you ignored the new law. You buried it. And when Charlie Morton was discovered to be an Affiliate, you broke that law, taking the very path your mother tried to protect you from, repeating her mistakes but far, far worse, because at least she had the strength to admit them."

She snapped the journal closed.

Court members and guards alike maintained a funeral hush, all of them staring at the king and his daughter, opposing forces on the dais. Aria's father met her eyes, but he remained stone-faced. He didn't speak.

Say something, she willed. Inside, her anger boiled together with grief, mixing in a steam that misted her eyes. Her fingers trembled on her grandmother's journal.

Though she'd thought it frozen and abandoned on a mountainside, a quill reared in her mind, too quickly to halt, this time with only one accusation.

Who brought you to the lake?

She remembered swimming with her father, clinging to his neck as she cried in fear of drowning. She remembered his strong arms holding her close, his deep voice rumbling softly in her ear. "I won't let go until you're ready, Aria."

The unshed tears burned her eyes. She clenched her teeth.

I'm not ready, Father.

I'm not ready.

But she had to let go.

She released her quill, the one that had tried so hard to shape her in her father's image, and she released the words clenched behind her teeth:

"For this crime of lawbreaking and treason—betrayal of the

previous monarch—it is the duty of the Upper Court to decide if King Peregrine may be pardoned. I submit nay."

Then she waited, and her heartbeat began the count. It would take a majority vote to convict her father and remove him from the throne.

For a long moment, no one moved.

"Your Majesty?" prodded Lord Philip, his voice hoarse. "Have you no defense?"

The king said nothing.

The queen stood. "You may think this is pettiness, a vendetta for other reasons, but my mother-in-law spoke to me about Dorothy. I remember her regret. As for the rest of it—I believe what has been presented. I submit nay."

Marquess Haskett scoffed. "Her Majesty hasn't attended a meeting in a year, and she comes to dethrone her husband? This is nonsense. I submit pardon."

"I submit pardon," Countess Redford agreed.

Aria felt the shift in momentum threatening to grow, but Earl Wycliff stood as a rock to stop the river.

"I hope we might all consider the full circumstances of recent events in this court," he said gruffly. "In truth, something fractured the day Charles Morton died, and we have felt the growing effects ever since. Now we have found the truth of it. I submit nay."

Three against pardon. Two in favor.

Aria looked at Lord Philip. The man stared helplessly back. She knew there was a lifetime of duty warring inside him—the debate of loyalty to country against loyalty to monarch, with the division between them nearly impossible to find.

The man's lips moved, and it took Aria a moment to understand the silent question: *A featherstitch?*

In response, she moved her eyes to the peace treaty, resting on the bench before him. Her father had intended to march against Northglen in war; Aria had sacrificed for peace. It was the best argument she could give in her defense—the proof of her own loyalty to Loegria.

Philip stood. His first attempt at speech made no sound, and then, in agony, his voice emerged. "I submit nay."

Four against.

But it was not yet a majority, and Marchioness Elsworth submitted pardon.

Only Duke Brightwood and Lord Emmett remained.

Duke Brightwood stood. He rarely spoke on the topic being discussed in meetings, instead offering quips and droll comments, but today, his smile had vanished.

"I will not dethrone my king," he said. "I submit pardon."

Four against pardon. Four in favor.

All eyes turned to Lord Emmett, the final adviser.

He stood and quietly said, "The evidence is not enough for me. I submit pardon."

Pardon held the majority. Aria's heart slowed in her chest, each beat thudding dully against her rib cage, like a prisoner who'd beaten her fist so long against the door she'd lost all strength to continue.

Queen Theresa's journal slipped free from her fingers, and turning in surprise, she saw her father held the journal, opening it to the pages she'd marked, one after another. He stared down in silence at his mother's handwriting. After turning to the final entry, he lingered. Then he closed the cover.

He stood. "This trial is decided."

Aria looked away, so she did not see her father's face when he said—

"I abdicate."

She whirled back, gaping along with the rest of the Upper Court. Her father met her gaze, brows furrowed, dark eyes shining with a profound pain, and then he reached out to grip her shoulder. Not for comfort, but as a man who'd lost his steadiness on the ground.

"I made a mistake," he whispered, pressing the journal into her hands.

For a moment, his grip lingered, painful in its strength, then he walked down the steps of the dais, exiting the throne room.

Aria watched him go, adrift in the lake.

Until, with effort, she remembered how to swim.

"Respected advisers," she said, drawing in a deep breath. "It appears I'll need a coronation."

EPILOGUE

ONE MONTH LATER

The letter arrived by standard post rather than by falcon, and it seemed a waste not only of post but of good parchment—three scrawny lines isolated in a sea of blank space. All the same, Aria smiled when she read it.

> *Your sister's safe.*
> *I heard about your revolution and would just like to say:*
> *I knew it.*
>
> *Silas*

"Not one to gloat, is he?" She passed the letter to Baron, who sat beside her on the garden bench.

He gave a low whistle, his breath puffing in the winter air. "Over a dozen words. He truly couldn't resist."

Aria wished the news were stronger—that Eliza was on her way home, or that she was at least sending a full letter of her own—but she accepted the relief of *some* certainty. There had been precious little of it in recent days.

She tucked the letter away to protect it from the falling snowflakes. Baron wrapped an arm around her shoulders, and she snuggled into his woolen coat. From another part of the garden, she heard playful shouts and at least one instance of "you skinny chicken!"

The surgeon had finally declared Corvin's leg healed enough to endure light exercise—though the boy required a cane for support—and he hadn't wasted a moment.

"I see Corvin's studying hard," Aria said.

Baron nodded, his cheek rubbing against her hair. "This new steward is frightfully lax compared to the last; the boy may never receive a proper day of education."

"Oh, I imagine he'll learn by example. This steward is the best *baron* I know."

Her first choice would have been to restore Baron's title, but he'd suggested taking the stewardship instead. After all, it wouldn't be long before he married the queen, and then Corvin would bear the Reeves title anyway.

Queen. Aria still struggled beneath her own title. The girl who'd worked so hard to prove herself worthy of it seemed like a different person to her now, naïve and uncomprehending of the burden she asked for. But she'd been told by Lord Philip that a little humility did a ruler good. At the very least, everyone seemed willing to be gracious as she grew into the position.

"Your Majesty," said a quiet voice behind her.

Aria grimaced at the term of address, but by the time she turned, her expression was pleasant. Margaret Bennett stood on the stone path, her palm extended to catch snowflakes. She dropped it quickly.

"You asked me to fetch you ten minutes before the meeting with your advisers," Maggie said apologetically.

Your advisers. *Your* Majesty. Each time she heard herself given possession of things that had always been her father's, something inside her shrank.

"I fear I made a mistake," Aria confided to Baron, "thinking I could manage a kingdom."

Baron squeezed her shoulders and kissed the top of her head. "You didn't."

She'd once thought to find a suitor who balanced her reckless-ness, but she'd never imagined one who reaffirmed her choices, soothed her fears, and stood beside her through every imaginable danger. It was not her fault; how could anyone predict meeting someone as perfect as Baron?

He winced, pressing his fingers to his forehead.

"Headache again?" Aria asked, and when he nodded, she wrapped her arms around him in a comforting hug.

Between healing Corvin and saving Aria, Baron suffered frequent headaches as a side effect of overexerting his Casting. They'd grown *less* frequent as weeks passed, so Aria continued to hope the effect would vanish altogether, though Baron didn't seem as concerned about it as she was.

For her part, Aria had trouble falling asleep some nights or found herself waking well before dawn. Some days, she could not shake the echo of fatigue. But for those days and nights, she kept a bottle of Baron's wine nearby, and she counted herself lucky that whenever she was falling, he had the strength and willingness to catch her.

Baron stood, and Aria clung to his hand, unwilling to part so soon. He looped one arm through hers as he walked her down the path to the castle. Maggie trailed at a distance, offering them privacy, or perhaps only distracted by snowflakes. Though Maggie could never fill the gap left by Eliza, Aria found she liked the girl's quiet enthusiasm, and she was kind to Jenny.

Nearing the castle's side entrance, Aria glanced upward and caught a glimpse of her father on his balcony. She gave a tentative wave, which he answered with a nod. He always seemed to glower when seeing Baron, but he'd not said anything to discourage her courtship, and when Aria had announced her intention to marry a Caster, he'd said her choices were her own.

They no longer met in his study for evening games, and most days, her father hardly spoke at all. Aria saw him most often standing before a fireplace, the flames reflecting in his haunted eyes. She hoped his pain was like Baron's headaches and that time would bring a healing.

Perhaps that was unfair to Charlie's memory. Perhaps she should have hated her father. But she couldn't. Seeing his grief, knowing he'd made the choice to leave the barreling path, she couldn't help but extend mercy. He was her father.

After a moment, the former king disappeared, and Aria released a quiet sigh.

Baron pulled her back into an embrace, cradling her without speaking. She rested her cheek against his shoulder and breathed deeply the bright smell of lemons, like a burst of happiness.

"How are things with Sarah?" she asked, since his situation was not so different from hers.

"Difficult. Awkward." He rubbed her back, his chest rising and falling in a comforting way against hers. "These things take time."

"I know. I just . . . I know it will never be the same, but I worry it will never repair at all."

"I believe it will. But if not, you won't be alone."

She looked up at his green eyes, full of promise, and found herself unable to resist. Catching hold of his coat collar, she pulled him into a kiss, savoring his warmth in the winter.

"Your Majesty," Maggie whispered loudly. "It's much less than ten minutes now."

With a groan, Aria pulled away. "Yes, I understand. I'm on my way. Mostly. My legs are trying, but my heart resists."

Baron chuckled. "Before you go . . ." He pulled a letter from his pocket, handing it to her with a smile.

She grasped it tightly. "I'll see you soon."

Though it was never soon enough.

As Aria walked toward the council chambers, she unfolded the letter, not caring that it probably would have been wise to leave it for after her meeting. She needed to focus on matters of the kingdom—serious matters, like correcting old laws, hearing petitions of people insisting their life and livelihood were now in danger from magic users, and so on. It seemed everyone in Loegria needed Aria's attention at all times. Since she'd chosen this path, she tried to be optimistic in it.

Truthfully, the only thing that made a bright attitude possible was the very thing she held in her hand.

A simple piece of parchment that began with *My Dearest Aria*.

ACKNOWLEDGMENTS

This book has undergone a lot of growth and change through the years, and there are many fabulous people who helped it become what it is now.

My beta readers: Brooke Adams, Brianne Bird, Rachel Bird, Constance Dalrymple, Jami Diewald, Megan Dunn, McKenna Gillette, Alyssa Green, Melissa Hokanson, Lindsy Isackson, Brady Lowham, Karen Lowham, Ashley Nicolaysen, Ashlie Olson, Moriah Pond, and Jessica Shepherd. Thank you for all the warm encouragement, the kind words, and the gentle guidance.

My critique group: Allison Mathews, Bri Stephens, and Katie Stone. Thank you for making me feel like a powerhouse writer and like a humbled student, all at the right moments.

My publishing team: Bre Anderl, Garth Bruner, Heidi Gordon, Callie Hansen, Lisa Mangum, and Chris Schoebinger. Thank you for putting in the legwork and the late nights to make this dream come true. Shout-out to Jessica Guernsey for being the extra eyes on my project, and a heartfelt thank you to everyone else at Shadow Mountain for all your dedicated work.

Lastly, a special thank you to YarningChick, who was a good friend when I first started writing, who once told me I should write a Twelve Dancing Princesses story, which—through the general chaos of life and over the course of more than a decade—turned into *Casters and Crowns*. It's not what either of us meant back then, but if you get the chance to read it now, I bet you'll love it. Thank you, fellow CR fan.

ALSO BY
ELIZABETH LOWHAM

"Suspense-building flashbacks. Soul-searching, cautionary realism. Beauty herself is an intriguing, well-crafted original. . . . Readers who appreciate narrative risk-taking are well served."
—KIRKUS REVIEWS

"[This] sensitive and slow-burning retelling . . . stands out in its portrayal of themes surrounding trauma and recovery alongside familiar musings on perceived differences between humans and monsters."
—PUBLISHERS WEEKLY

"A darker and bittersweet retelling of the familiar fairy tale, laden with an equal dose of humor and tragedy. . . . The author writes with a lyricism that draws readers in."
—COMPASS BOOK RATINGS

SHADOW
MOUNTAIN
PUBLISHING